THE HORSEPOWER WHISPERER

BY

BOB BLACKMAN

PART ONE OF THE SOUL TRADER TRILOGY

HOW, OF ALL THE SOUL TRADERS, IT WAS HOB WHO
DISCOVERED THE PLOT TO DESTROY OUR VERY SOULS.

AND HOW THE GREAT STRUGGLE BEGAN BETWEEN
GOOD, EVIL AND THE FORCES OF BLAND

ANARCHADIA

www.anarchadia.co.uk

First published in Great Britain in December 2007 by

Anarchadia Publishing

Copyright © Bob Blackman 2007

ISBN   978 0 9555927 0 6

Anarchadia Publishing
PO Box 119
Liskeard
Cornwall
PL14 9AN

For H.M.G.

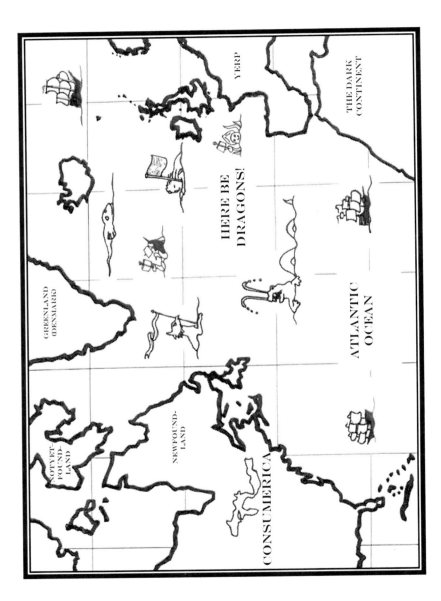

Map 1. Anarchadia remains unmapped and lies in uncharted waters

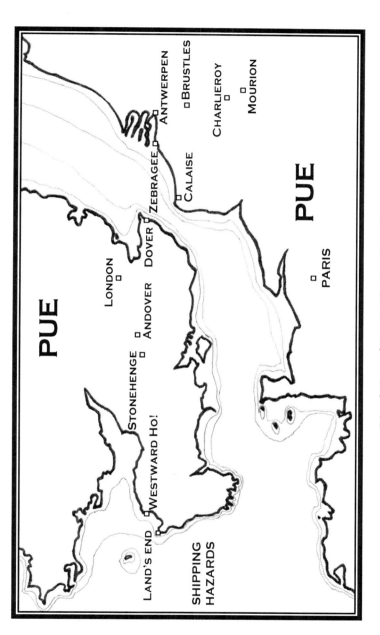

Map 2. Part of Post Unification Euphobia

ADDITIONAL WEB RESOURCES

You might read this book and find that afterwards you have
more questions than answers.

In that case, I cordially invite you to explore the Anarchadia website.

Its additional multi-media features include blogs, links, news, interviews,
glossaries, readers' questions and additional artwork.

It may reassure you, confirm a funny feeling, help you recollect a distant
memory, make new connections or allow something that has piqued your
interest to metaphorically emerge from the shadows of obscurity.

It may also serve as a warning to the curious.

www.anarchadia.co.uk

ANARCHADIA

BOOKS WITH GO FASTER STRIPES

CHAPTER 1

Once upon a temporal anomaly, a warning light blushed self-consciously in front of a beautiful young scientist. It had never warned anyone before, let alone someone so good-looking and clever. It found itself in earnest, prompted by sophisticated sensing instruments into raising the alarm.

Therese Darlmat had been using her temporal anomaly to take a little time out. Whenever she felt overcrowded by the less brainy, she liked to gaze at the stars through her gull-wing glasses, pondering on the frayed and patchy fabric of whatever universe she happened to be in and wondering if a stitch in time really could save nine. She had been admiring the Krill Nebula when she noticed a curious red glow about its nether regions and it took a little time for her to realise that she wasn't looking at a new gas cloud but the reflection of the warning light in the glass of her windscreen.

There were a number of what she called idiot lights on the dashboard of her car and most of them told her things she already knew. There was just one to which this rule did not apply and this was the mother and father of all idiot lights. Therese had considered etching "The End" into its lens. Now that it was illuminated she was glad she hadn't.

She took a closer look at it and it burned with shame. There was nothing wrong with her car, a pink six-wheeled Cadillac Rushmore convertible. Somewhere and somewhen beyond the safety of her temporal anomaly, a universe was collapsing.

Therese was endowed with timeliness as well as comeliness. She had a brain so huge that she could turn base dimensions into time. Her temporal lobes, which, in the female of her species were usually given over to remembering birthdays, were now so highly developed she disguised her high-rise forehead with an immense blonde beehive. Despite the size of her brain, she avoided the need for any unsightly cervical supports since women's brains are not as dense as men's. Her neck was so dainty it suggested that her head was filled with nothing but helium.

Apart from her towering intellect, the rest of her was in the most attractive proportions. Prior to devoting herself to science, Therese had made a fortune from a high-profile modelling career.

She tapped her elegant fingers on the ivory-coloured steering wheel and moved the column gear-change lever from N for Neutral to D for De-materialise. The Cadillac shifted. Its tail lights glowed red, then orange, then yellow and finally white as Therese flicked through the physical dimensions as if they were gears on a gearbox. A standard Cadillac Rushmore had a one thousand cubic inch V16 engine but Therese had souped it up by incorporating a fusion reactor in the glove compartment. This didn't make it any faster. It made it instant.

She liked to call her temporal anomalies "blonde moments" and, having perfected their creation, she found that stepping outside the dimensions of length, breadth and height was easy. Therese discovered that alongside her own universe were all sorts of other ones that stretched off into the distance in every direction. She came to appreciate their more varied spectra of light, their varied flora and fauna and the need for a whalebone corset in the very ticklish ninth dimension. She also came to spot little paraversal problems, like dimensional instabilities and lavatory seats that had been left up. True to the acceptance speeches she made whenever she won a Miss Universe contest, she did what she could to make the paraverses better places.

She had just saved yet another galaxy from getting a wet bottom on the pot when the warning light came on.

Without the universal tyranny of light years, her temporal anomaly gave her remarkable insights into the negotiable nature of the laws of physics and allowed her to laugh at any deadline, no matter how severe. Sometimes, Therese would restyle her hair a little differently during a fleeting visit to her temporal anomaly just to see if anyone noticed and if they did she would nip back and return it to the way it was, out of sheer mischief. She liked to think that sort of behaviour was behind her but the possibility of doing it again still appealed.

The Cadillac shifted through time and space and Therese caught the collapsing paraverse in her headlights. However, even within the safety of her temporal anomaly, she exercised caution. If her by now incandescent idiot light was correct, there was no telling how far the instability could spread. It might even jeopardise her own bubble out of time.

Therese saw flashes of unnatural physical phenomena rippling across the sky, making the stars twinkle brightly for a moment. She checked her position on her CadNav using Astroroute and dived down to a blue-green world mostly covered by water. Then she chose her future parking spot through her chronoscope and moved the column change lever from D to R – R for Rematerialise.

Her sudden appearance in the middle of an emergency summit meeting caused uproar. The Cadillac Rushmore convertible, with its tailfins and six headlights, had been styled by Harley Earl and his team at General Motors' design studios during the chrome-laden nineteen fifties. It subsequently proved too outrageous for the North American market and had been a commercial failure. Since modifying her Cadillac for pan-dimensional interstellar travel,

Therese drove it with the top down because headroom was always a problem in whatever dimension she inhabited. Fortunately, the force field in her handbag, which took care of rain and the odd meteorite shower, also protected her from the hail of bullets that the already jumpy security forces hurled at her.

The guards stopped shooting because of dangerous ricochets and it seemed wrong to shoot at someone so good-looking.

An elder statesman approached, signalling reassurance.

Therese selected P for Park and alighted from her car. Her exquisitely cut white lab coat, which fitted her as well as any little black dress, showed that she was unarmed but as the elder statesman stood before her he viewed her towering beehive with suspicion. This was nothing new for Therese.

"Your universe is dying before its time," she told the assembled delegates, "but I might be able to help."

"Madam," said the statesman, "I apologise for our inhospitable welcome."

"I quite understand," Therese replied. "If I'd announced my arrival you would never have believed me or let me in."

The conference hall was full of tables and at each one was a distinguished individual. Triangular-section nameplates indicated their country of origin. Therese became aware that all around the upper walls, in the press galleries and glass-fronted windows for the simultaneous translators, people wearing earphones were looking at her, then each other, then at her again.

She glanced at the triangular nameplate at a vacant desk. The elder statesman was called Mr Post-Unification Euphobia or Mr PUE for short.

"Our universe?" echoed a younger leader of a superpower.

From her experience of beauty pageants, Therese took him to be Mr United States of Consumerica, or Mr USC to his friends.

"We thought it was just our world," he said.

Therese sighed. "No; it's much more serious than you first thought."

"Just how much more serious can it get?" demanded an intimidating woman in a red silk robe. She sat at a desk triangularly labelled either *Federation of Gondwanaland* or *Toblerone*.

Therese didn't even begin to explain that their troubles were affecting neighbouring paraverses.

"Do you know what might have caused this?" she asked.

"Ah," said Mr USC.

"It wasn't us," replied Mr PUE.

"We've been trying to stop it for years," said Ms Federation of Gondwanaland or Toblerone.

"Stop what?" asked Therese.

"The Wild Hunt," said Mr USC.

"What's that?"

Mr USC paused before answering her. He took an infra-red button box and called up some poor-quality video images on the main screen.

"The Wild Hunt is the eternal chase," he explained.

And there it was, a speeding procession of the most disreputable vehicles Therese had ever seen.

"It's been going for thousands of years," he went on. "It used to be a survival ritual but now it's taken to wheels and become mechanised. We've been trying to control it, from a road safety aspect as much as anything, and we've encouraged alternatives and built motordromes for them to race in, but the Wild Hunt just carries on. It does things to time and space, you see – things we don't fully understand."

Mr USC glanced at some scientists, who all blushed deeply.

"The Wild Hunters," he went on, "lose themselves in the thrill of the chase and can find themselves in quite alien surroundings."

"That's a classic description of a fost," said Therese, "a leakage into an adjacent paraverse. Every time it happens, your universe is destabilised."

The screen was now showing pictures from some video game. Law enforcement officers pursued a poorly animated image of a sinister looking man on a supercharged motorcycle. They were closing in on him but whenever they had him cornered, he somehow slipped away.

"This is Hob," said Mr USC. "He has many other names. Some say he leads the Wild Hunt."

"That isn't actually him," admitted Ms Federation of Gondwanaland or Toblerone. "He's very difficult to capture, even on film. We've had to digitally animate him from survivors' descriptions."

Therese watched Hob riding his bike down stairs and bursting through apparently impregnable roadblocks.

"We would particularly like him to help us with our enquiries," said Mr USC, "but so far he has chosen not to."

"We had him cornered," added Ms Federation of Gondwanaland or Toblerone, "but he doesn't seem to exist by the normal rules of physics."

Therese, who didn't either, said nothing.

Mr USC froze the video on the best image they had of Hob. He wore a black leather jacket that looked like it had been down the road a few times, jeans, a plaid shirt, big boots and a black open-faced helmet with a peak. His eyes were covered by a black visor.

"He's made fools of us all," put in Mr PUE.

Hob's slightly crooked teeth caught the light as he grinned at them from the big screen.

"So where is Hob?" asked Therese.

CHAPTER 2

Hob was daydreaming happily about superchargers when he felt a tremor through the frame of the jumbo jet. They had been flying for hours, diverted from their course by extreme weather events. While the storm raged outside, weary stewardesses collided with each other and sprinkled passengers with sachets of salt and plastic cutlery.

Hob congratulated himself. He had got away with it again, and was now putting as many miles as he could between himself and his would-be oppressors.

He checked the darkness outside but merely saw his own reflection. He made an incongruous figure for air travel since he was still dressed for the Wild Hunt. The stewardesses had tried unsuccessfully to get him to remove his crash helmet. He'd laughed when they'd asked if he was a nervous passenger but, when they'd explained that he was making the other passengers uneasy, he'd laughed even more. Of course, he refused to take it off. He said it would be a character-building experience for the others. He enjoyed building people's characters.

Hob had a highly developed sense of mechanical sympathy. Although everything looked normal outside, the Song of the Machine, in which he was particularly well versed, was approaching a dirge.

"How much longer?" demanded someone a few rows ahead.

"Just a couple of hours, sir," the stewardess replied.

"Haven't we outrun the storm yet?"

"It's still keeping pace with us." She carried on scattering salt as if re-enacting a Biblical proverb – anything to distract the passengers from their suffering.

Hob couldn't understand what the fuss was all about. He could think of far worse places to be. He considered moving back to the aisle seat so that the thighs of the stewardesses could brush his shoulder again. He liked steward-esses a lot and, apart from the issue of his crash helmet, he was easily the most charming passenger on board.

Instead, he stayed put and tapped the window. After an interval, tiny, mischievous female faces appeared outside, long hair flapping around them. Hob glanced back at his fellow passengers, even though he felt sure none of them had the gift of the sight. From his battered leather jacket, he pulled out some weather-forecasting symbols. He held a black cloud with a lightning flash towards the window. The faces nodded. He showed them two wind symbols, stuck together for greater emphasis, which he pointed to the north-west. He also held up some numbers to indicate 150. The faces threw back their heads and laughed, white teeth flashing in the lightning. Hob held up a black cloud with drops of rain in each hand. He pulled off two drops from one and held it under the three drops of the other. The furies looked at each other and rolled their eyes. They gave Hob a thumbs-up and were gone.

Hob sat back. Into every life a little rain must fall. It was just his fellow passengers' bad luck to be chased half way around the world by a storm that registered at least thirteen on the Beaufort scale, when the Beaufort scale only went up to twelve. Severe bad weather was just Hob's way of coercing public transport into going where he wanted it. It was much more interesting than chartering a flight and the experience would touch the souls of his companions.

The Song of the Machine from the outer starboard engine had become funereal. Hob was interested to see how his fellow passengers would react when the engine failed and they began flying downwards.

The passenger ahead of him was still complaining.

"And where will we be landing?" he asked another stewardess who'd run out of ghizzits.

"Possibly Mourion. It's in the Euphobian trading block."

The passenger huffed and puffed and said he knew perfectly well where Mourion was and that it was half way round the world from where they should be.

Hob had never heard of Mourion, but he thought it could be a fun sort of place.

The bad vibrations were getting worse. Restless children ran around, their more elemental natures alerting them to the strange atmosphere around them. They played tag and I-spy and inevitably I-spied Hob's rucksack, securely belted into the middle of the three seats he had taken as his own. And the more they I-spied it, the more certain they became that it moved every time they glanced away. And somehow, when they looked at it, Hob's rucksack looked back at them. Hob bared his fangs at them and the children ran away.

Before angry parents could complain, there was a bang and a flash of flame from the ill-starred engine as it exploded.

There was an undignified scramble for life jackets and the inevitable sound of some of them being prematurely inflated. The captain appealed for calm, but even over all the shouting the co-pilot could be heard issuing a May-day message in the background, which rather spoilt the effect. As the call to "Save our souls" went out across the ether, Hob slumped down into his seat and sank out of sight. Then someone in a window seat shouted, and everyone rush-ed to starboard to look out at the engine that lit the night.

Hob was rising out of the wing, as if powered by the plane's hydraulic system. He stood for a few seconds, silhouetted against the flames as the sky twirled around the plane, and then he walked across the wing, in complete defiance of the slipstream and the furies' storm. His fellow passengers made out the motif of a wheeled cross on the back of his leather jacket. Above this wheeled cross was the legend *Terminal Murrain*.

Hob walked right up to the blazing engine and climbed down inside it. Within the inferno, he pinched shut severed fuel lines with his fingers. The flames went out and he pointed and said, "You!"

A terrified gremlin flattened himself against the inner cowling.

"So," said Hob, "who didn't know that Old Weird Wheels was on board?"

The gremlin stared at him in horror.

"I'll give you a clue," said Hob. "It's somebody in this ruined engine but not me."

The hapless gremlin began to emit a torrent of noises like the screech of worn bearings and the gnashing of mismatched gear teeth. He gesticulated wildly, rolled his eyes and leapt around the shattered engine like an amphetamised monkey.

Hob caught the gremlin in mid air. "Curiously strong mint?" he asked and, before the gremlin could refuse, he squeezed his neck to pop his mouth open and fed him something hard and white. A swift blow on top of his be-horned head, and the gremlin gulped and stiffened. Ice frosted his ugly features and his eyes glazed over. Hob clapped his hands together and the freeze-dried gremlin exploded like a meringue case.

"Next time, check the passengers," Hob growled.

The cloud of dust slunk into a crevice within the engine cowling.

Hob took a mint himself and set to work.

"As these revs have been revoked, I call them into being again! May these thrust winders and fan spinners be whole once more!"

He prised some missing fan blades out of the engine cowling.

"May these fan blades and combustion chambers develop thrust sufficient to stop the earth in its rotation if called upon to do so!"

In his fingers, the blades twisted and writhed until they were the right shape again.

"May the Song of the Machine be accompanied by the close-fitting, fine-tolerance turbine whistle of contentment!"

Hob counted up the turbofan blades and carefully fitted them all back together and when he wasn't whispering up horsepower, talking the torque or delivering the thrust of his doctrine, he hummed the Song of the Machine.

The gremlin, who had thawed out and reconstituted himself, watched closely from his crevice. As Hob's humming grew, he joined in.

"I am the metal guru," muttered Hob, "Master of the Engine Henge. I also dabble in carbon fibre."

The gremlin looked impressed at his dabbling.

Hob took the ends of the severed fuel line between his grubby hands and breathed on the pipes, mightily and mintily, before sticking the ends together.

"Of course," he added, in a more modest tone, "I prefer reciprocating piston engines."

The gremlin rubbed his little hands together.

Hob suddenly grabbed him. "You realise what this means, don't you?"

The gremlin gulped.

"No more mischief from you on this trip."

He put him down and traced powerful sigils into the alloy of the engine cowling, as if his black fingernails were made from industrial diamonds. "Your job is to make sure this plane gets us to Mourion."

The gremlin nodded, eager to help.

"Good," said Hob. He went back to work for a bit and then said, "I thought these things were supposed to fly all right with two engines gone."

The gremlin nodded and began to speak rapidly about such a litany of mechanical and electrical disaster that anyone with even the remotest degree of mechanical sympathy would have cringed and shuddered to hear him but Hob just kept on working on the jet engine, glancing at him from time to time. Occasionally, he said, "You didn't!" or, perhaps, "You did!" and once he said, "Ah, so both port engines are operating at barely half thrust!" and when the gremlin finished describing with gestures how he'd over-ridden all the safety systems, Hob laughed and said, "You little tinker! Of course, this is going to make me look absolutely brilliant when you put all this right!"

The gremlin nodded eagerly and, without Hob saying another word, disappeared. By the time he re-appeared, Hob was sitting on the edge of the turbofan's intake, dangling his legs over its lip.

"All done?" he asked, and the gremlin nodded and sat down beside him.

"I'm going home," said Hob, conversationally.

The gremlin wasn't used to Horsepower Whisperers opening up to him and didn't know what to say.

"To Anarchadia," Hob went on. "Of course, usually I would fost but sometimes I choose not to."

They sat companionably on the jet's cowling for a few moments, watching the approaching earth spinning in front of them, as if the planet were in a tumble dryer.

"I haven't been to Europe for years," said Hob.

The gremlin thought for a moment and became quite agitated, speaking rapidly in his strange language.

"What?" said Hob. "Euphobia?"

The gremlin nodded.

"Don't you mean Euphoria?"

The gremlin chuckled and shook his head emphatically before going on.

"Whaddya mean, 're-branded'? That's ridiculous! Why would they want to re-brand a continent?"

The gremlin explained as best he could.

"Socio-political entity?" Hob translated.

The gremlin gave a Gallic shrug.

The clouds were boiling into strange shapes as they plunged through them. Some looked like racing cars, coursing through rolling landscapes, snaking through mountain passes and weaving their way through forests. When the full moon came out, strange clouds gathered around it, turning it into the headlamp of an enormous motorbike.

"*Nosferatu!*" exclaimed Hob. "Look! That's me on *Nosferatu!*" and the two Hobs grinned at each other before the clouds broke up into another race, this time with endurance sports cars. "The furies are putting on a splendid show! They're advertising the next Wild Hunt for when we land in Mourion."

The gremlin was puzzled. If Hob was unaware of the re-branding of Europe, was he aware of any of the other changes?

"No," replied the Soul Trader, looking down onto the darkened land below them, "but it can't have changed that much."

The gremlin tried to reconcile this with his own knowledge of Post-Unification Euphobia, but failed.

"Mourion can't be far from Spa and Lee Age," said Hob peering into the gloom.

The gremlin wondered if he referred to the old road racing cities.

Hob nodded. "Mind you, they're having terrible weather down there at the moment. The Low Countries could flood. I might have to send you out for an olive branch."

The gremlin pulled a face.

"How high up would you say we were?"

The gremlin made a pessimistic estimate.

"Look at all those long faces," said Hob.

At every window down the fuselage, anxious passengers peered out.

"Do you think it might cheer them up if we re-started the engines?"

The gremlin thought it probably would.

"It might even make them grateful."

The gremlin suggested that this was not unlikely.

Hob grinned. He picked the gremlin up by his overalls and hurled him into the storm to land in the air intake for the inboard engine, which had also stopped but without catching fire. He waited for the gremlin to compose himself after a rather heavy landing and then shouted across, "After me."

Hob took the central spinner of the turbofan in his grubby hands and gently turned the engine over.

Somehow, despite the size difference, the gremlin managed to do the same.

Everything being in order, Hob began to wind the turbine up to operating speed and said, "I call these engines once more into power and glory, revs without end, ring ding a-ding!"

The gremlin chuckled ecstatically as the turbofan blades of his engine whizzed around.

"Sing the Song of the Machine, my well tuned wonder!" yelled Hob. "Trouble's going!" and he spat a ball of flame into the engine.

The gremlin muttered something similar and also spat with results that surprised even him.

First one, then the other, the engines, burst back into life and the Boeing 747 yawed to port under the sudden surge of power.

"Trouble's gone!" shouted Hob, above the roar of the engines. "Bloody hell! Is that the ground?"

CHAPTER 3

As the pilot hauled back on the control column in a vain attempt to pull the plane out of its dive, grubby hands covered his and pulled the lever further back than it normally went. Through the windscreen he saw the ground rushing up to him but no reflection of the figure behind him.

Wings sprouted from Hob's shoulders. He flapped them in the confined cockpit and he yelled with the pilot as they strained to bring the nose of the 747 up again.

Somewhere a line of rivets popped out with a sound not unlike that of a zip fastener undoing and together they added their voices to the scream of the engines.

The plane banked to climb and a wing tip twanged a telephone wire as the Boeing struggled valiantly back into the sky.

Hob flapped his wings a few more times and looked out of the starboard window. Then he relaxed, tucked his wings back into his leather jacket, grinned at the ashen-faced crew and stepped out of the cockpit.

"There he is!" exclaimed someone, and Hob found himself being mobbed. Men thumped him on the back and whooped, children cried and air hostesses sank into the arms that had saved them.

"Oh please," he said above their grateful cries, "please."

"What you did just now was incredible!" said the loveliest of the hostesses. She undid her hair and shook her shining tresses over her shoulders.

The captain appeared beside her and pumped Hob's hand. "Unbelievable!" he said. "How can we ever repay you?"

"It was nothing, honestly," said Hob, bashfully. He looked around for his rucksack. A few rows away, he could see something wriggling along the floor. "Excuse me," he said, squeezing through the crowd.

"You saved our lives!" insisted the air hostesses.

"We are forever in your debt!" cried the passengers and crew.

Hob held up his hands. "There's no need, really," he insisted.

The rucksack was furiously making for the emergency exit, like a baggy nylon caterpillar.

"You saved our lives!" said a little boy.

Hob paused and knelt down in front of him. "Did I?"

"Yes!" everyone said.

"Did I really?

"Yes!"

"It was only an engine on fire."

"We were all doomed!" pointed out the crowd. "How can we ever repay you?"

"Well, I don't know," said Hob thoughtfully, gazing at the ceiling, trying not to smile. "Hmm. Let me think."

He grabbed his rucksack from under a seat. It stiffened initially but then went limp like a kitten.

He stood up, slung it over his shoulder, and stroked his chin. "I wonder …" He clicked his fingers.

"Yes?"

"There is something you could do for me."

"Anything! It's yours!"

"That's incredibly generous of you."

"It'll be the least we could do!"

Hob laughed. "I understand what you mean."

"Tell us!"

"No, it's too ridiculous!"

"It's yours!" they cried.

Hob smiled fiendishly. "Well, seeing as you insist, how about a small token of your gratitude?" and he took off his rucksack and winked at the gremlin and the furies who were peering in through the cabin windows.

CHAPTER 4

"So you don't know where he is," surmised Therese.

"Not exactly," admitted Mr PUE. "We often know where he was but if we get too close to where he is, he fosts."

"And from what you've just told us that can only make matters worse," said Ms Federation of Gondwanaland or Toblerone.

Therese reached into her pocket and pulled out a time bar. "It can't make matters any worse," she told them gently. "I'm afraid you have no future."

She broke off five minutes from the time bar and let this sink in for a few moments.

There was silence as the unfutured wondered about it.

"So … is there any point in colonising the moon?" asked Mr PUE.

"Not really."

"Or reaching for the stars?" asked Mr USC.

Therese shook her head.

"No future," Mr PUE echoed sadly.

"Not at the moment," Therese replied, "but …"

"Strunts!" shouted Ms Federation of Gondwanaland or Toblerone. "I knew we should have invited someone from Anarchadia!"

She picked up her Toblerone name plate, ripped off its wrapper and began to eat it.

"We couldn't invite them!" insisted Mr USC.

"It's because of their lack of co-operation that we can't control the Wild Hunt," said Mr PUE.

"And who would we have invited?" demanded Mr USC. "All of them?"

"Wait a moment!" Ms Federation of Gondwanaland said to Therese, with her mouth full. "If we have no future, then you must be unfutured, too!"

"Thank you for your concern, Ms FOG," Therese, replied "but that's not true."

The delegates looked at each other and began murmuring.

"You're wasting time," said Therese. "Your universe has become unstable. Its dimensions are no longer in balance. All it needs," she said, looking around them, "is a little extra length here, a little more width there and a little less height in, well, quite a few places actually."

"Won't that take ages?" asked Ms FOG.

"Ages," agreed Therese. "Fortunately, I am an alphysicist."

"A what?"

"An alphysicist."

"Would that be like an alchemist?" asked Mr USC.

"In some ways. I can turn base dimensions into time. Every when I go, time sprouts and buds. It grows wild and so abundant that I collect it and experiment with it, sprinkling wild time here and then just to see what it does. I can lengthen holidays and delay the inevitable."

"Won't this cost an awful lot of money?" asked Mr PUE.

Therese smiled. "You can owe me."

"There has to be a catch somewhere," said Ms FOG.

"There is no catch," said Therese. "I have plenty of time."

"But we don't," said Ms FOG.

"No and we shouldn't waste it," said Therese, unwilling to use up another time bar on the unfutured.

She produced a powerful laser measure and, to the accompaniment of several intakes of breath from her onlookers, and pointed it in the three usual directions, as well as a couple of not so familiar ones.

"Hmm, that's three hundred light years off here, a hundred off here and a wedge under there, and equilibrium will be restored."

Therese climbed back into her car and selected D to re-stabilise the unfutured's paraverse.

CHAPTER 5

"That's not right," declared Hob as he waited for his luggage.

He exchanged a glance with his rucksack. He'd been counting out the souls that he'd just saved.

"Stocktaking never was my strong point but I was sure I had more souls than that!"

The rucksack began to shake with mirth.

"Not a word to anyone about this, Fortunato!" snapped Hob.

The rucksack slowly stopped giggling.

Hob counted out his new souls again, this time more carefully. The luggage carousel started, and people moved away from this strange looking man holding a conversation with his hand luggage.

"I was right! I've been short changed!"

Hob looked up at the people around him, his fellow travellers from the jumbo jet. Studying them closely, he divined that none of them had souls to call their own.

The note of the conveyer belt dropped an octave as a large wooden packing case emerged. Under its weight the belt nearly stopped moving. There was a faint smell of burning rubber and the crate crashed onto the carousel, making the floor shake and the waiting passengers step back.

Hob stood up, pulled his rucksack over his shoulder and walked over to the carousel. He picked up the crate, turned it the right way up and hoisted it onto his shoulders as if it were empty.

Moving through the crowd, Hob's hackles began to bristle. As a Soul Trader, he'd learnt to trust his most atavistic instincts and now he paused to make sense of what they were trying to tell him.

Everyone should have a soul but some of the terminal staff did not.

Hob came to a halt and looked around the crowd. From behind his darkened visor he could tell that they, too, were spiritually lacking. One or two good souls stood out but these had a desperate quality about them, and looked quite out of place in such a dearth of spirits.

Hob frowned. This was not the work of any Soul Trader.

Before the "Anything to declare" channel he said, "By the spanners of St Bendix! I haven't been short changed, Fortunato. They never had souls to volunteer!"

He exchanged a glance with his rucksack over his shoulder.

Standing in front of the customs area, with an enormous crate upon his shoulders, Hob caught the attention of a man in uniform. Usually, he ignored the attentions of authority, but as this evidently soulless customs official approached him, Hob returned his gaze with frank curiosity.

"Excuse me monsieur, would you just step this way?"

Hob nearly blurted out, "But you should be dead!" but this would have been incredibly rude. Instead, he did as he was told, for once.

"What do you have in your crate?" asked the customs officer.

"*Nosferatu*," Hob replied, staring at him intently.

"Would you mind opening it?"

"Yes," said Hob.

Hob was a Horsepower Whisperer and had a way with languages. But he was too fascinated and appalled by the customs officer to really pay attention.

"Thank you, sir." The customs official stood in front of him, barring his way.

Hob frowned but waited to see what the soulless one would do next.

The official gestured towards the crate. "Well?"

"Well what?"

"Are you going to open it up or not?"

"No," said the distracted Hob.

"Then we'll run it through the X-ray machine."

Again, quite out of character, Hob complied by putting his packing case on the conveyor belt that fed the X-ray machine.

As he unshouldered *Nosferatu*'s crate, he studied the fellow's state of being. He detected no joy in the man, just a grim satisfaction and no sign of a soul.

The X-ray machine was a particularly big one. At the other end, a large case containing a double bass was being caressed along its curvaceous flanks by lead-lined strips, as if the X-ray machine was loath to let it go now that it had yielded up its secrets.

"May I see your passport, monsieur?"

Nosferatu's crate began to enter the X-ray machine.

"Of course," said Hob "If I had one, of course you could see it."

Hob spoke to everyone in Anarcho-English, as if they were in the Wild Hunt. They replied in whatever language they liked and, supernaturally, Hob understood. It was just like talking to gremlins. Hob didn't actually speak gremulin himself. He spoke Anarcho-English to them and they replied in gremulin, each understanding the other perfectly. Hob treated those who spoke other languages just like bigger gremlins. Many citizens of the world chose to speak English anyway, for they had a quiet pride in their facility for languages and it was near enough to Anarcho-English for most purposes. But you couldn't whisper up horsepower without using Anarcho-English. It had a fantastic vocabulary and there was a word for everything. There was even an expression for these words for everything – they were called moats juiced. And you could tap into any zeitgeist you liked.

The customs official looked at Hob in a funny way. This could easily have led to a fight in other circumstances but the operator of the X-ray machine let out a stifled cry.

"What is that?" she muttered.

"*Nosferatu*," Hob told her.

"It's a motorbike," she said, frowning and shaking her head.

"Of course," said Hob, "a supercharged Vincent with a disc brake conversion and an Egli frame."

"That is not allowed!" exclaimed the machine operator.

"Motorcycles are contraband items under the Standard of Living Directive," added the customs official.

"Don't be ridiculous!" replied Hob.

Official figures coagulated around him. He felt restraining hands on the arms of his leather jacket.

"I'm afraid I'm going to have to ask you to remove your crash helmet and visor," the official told him.

Hob jutted his jaw out of his open face helmet. "You're starting to annoy me," he told them.

"I'm afraid I have to confiscate this item," the customs officer told Hob, as they watched the image of *Nosferatu* pass over the screen.

"Yes, be afraid," replied Hob, "be very afraid."

"What's in your rucksack?"

Behind Hob, hands loosened the straps of his rucksack and pulled it over his arms.

"You really don't want to look in that," said Hob, guaranteeing that they would.

They carried the smirking rucksack over to the conveyer belt.

"Is there something living inside this?" asked one of the women carrying it.

"Not exactly," replied Hob.

His rucksack glared at the lead strips, which recoiled from touching it as it slid into the X-ray machine, with a stiff upper zip.

The officials gathered around the screen and looked at each other, unable to believe their eyes, as the image of its insides came onto the screen.

The lead strips at the far end flipped themselves on top of the cabinet to get as far away as possible from Hob's rucksack, which emerged smirking. Two customs men picked up Hob's rucksack and carried it over to a table.

"Whatever you do, don't look inside," said Hob but it was too late.

The customs officials unzipped Hob's rucksack, looked inside and became very still. Slowly they looked up and stared at each other. Then they pulled out their guns and Hob went down in a hail of bullets.

CHAPTER 6

When Therese finished refuturing the unfutured, she used her chronoscope to check her parking spot in the conference hall. The instrument resembled a microscope and hinged out from under the dashboard of her Cadillac. It was just as well she had checked her parking spot. The hall was full of people. There was no longer room for her enormous car so she chose R and re-materialised in the corridor outside.

Before switching her Cadillac off, she checked her instruments. The idiot light slumbered in grateful obscurity.

"My dear lady!" exclaimed a delighted Mr USC, as she entered the hall. "My scientific colleagues tell me that the dimensional instability has been corrected!"

Many people, with foreheads only a little lower than her own, beamed at her.

"How can we ever thank you?"

"Don't thank me, sir, it's just my hobby."

"Well, for an enthusiastic amateur you have done marvellously," said Mr USC.

"I congratulate you, too," said Ms FOG.

"And so do I!" exclaimed Mr PUE. "Just think what you could have achieved if you had really tried!"

The other delegates looked Mr PUE, who also seemed ill at ease with this outburst.

"I have taken care of everything," Therese told them. "You are now the re-futured. I have restored your dimensional stability and endowed you with some of my spare time."

"Ma'am," said Mr USC, "you surely must have a great deal of time on your hands."

"More than you could possibly imagine. I have the Midas touch for the fourth dimension. I am always making time for people and, in their gratitude, they create vast chronological debts in their bids to repay me."

But Mr USC appeared troubled. "Do you mean to tell us that you are actively engaged in a re-distribution of time?" he asked.

"In a way, I suppose I am."

"You take from the time rich to help the time-impoverished?"

"No. They give their time freely. They are grateful, you see, and I get so much more in return. They pretend that they can make time for me. They even call it quality time."

"How can one make time?" asked Mr USC.

"It's a gift. Either you can or you can't. I'm lucky. I can. But others can't and fool themselves into believing they can. So I return it to those who need it most, by sowing it around them. It's not my fault they mistake wild time for dandelion clocks and devote their lives to weeding their lawns."

"So you accumulate time for yourself and on behalf of other people," said Mr USC carefully and with a significant glance at his colleagues. "You enjoy a vast time income."

"Yes," said Therese, who could see where this was going. "After the work of several lifetimes, I have succeeded in making time out of length, breadth and height. And, no, time is not money. It is far more valuable. Normally, it can only be spent once but I can roll a couple of centimetres into a five-minute pack of chewing gum. And by using these chocolate-covered time bars I have put off the inevitable until you can all be re-futured."

"I suppose you use wild time for a little extra seasoning," suggested Mr PUE.

Therese smiled. "Humour often fails in the face of apparently certain doom, so I have taken the opportunity to give Mr PUE, here, a funny five minutes."

Therese turned to the man whom she believed to be Mr PUE.

"That's how you've suddenly become so frightfully witty," she told him. "It's possible that your colleagues will find your remarks a little obscure until they're used to it.

"Of course," he said. "It's the secret of good timing."

"What's the secret of good ti …"

"Comedy!"

Mr PUE paused and frowned, suddenly unsure of himself.

"I think you'll agree that was a big mistake," muttered Ms FOG.

"Of course, it works better on some than others," admitted Therese.

"Did I ever tell you the one about the Euphobian, the Consumerican and the Gondwanalese who …"

"But now I really must be going," Therese interrupted, and she left before anyone could ask any details.

She walked out of the conference hall and into the corridor where her car was parked, thinking about Hob and the Wild Hunt. She thought that, even with its standard 1000 cubic inch V16 engine, her Cadillac should be able to keep up with him in the Wild Hunt.

As she came through the last set of fire doors, she stopped.

A row of grotesque figures sat along the Cadillac, insolently dangling their stubby legs over its wings.

"Who are you?" she asked them, from outside the parking force field that they had infiltrated.

"We are responsible for this paraverse," said one, who looked like a small cyclops.

"We are its grauniads," said another, who might have been a medusa.

"Don't you mean guardians?" asked Therese.

"Don't ever call us that!" snapped another grauniad, somebody's withered grandpa, who wore nothing apart from a flying helmet and socks.

"We can't allow you to meddle with this paraverse," said a many-armed Kali figure in a long sleeved sweatshirt.

"Meddle? I've just repaired it!"

The grauniads began to speak in turn.

"You must not repair it."

"Or save the unfutured."

"Especially not save the unfutured."

"Or turn them into the refutured."

"This paraverse has become unstable once."

"It will become unstable again."

"Only this time it will be much worse."

"You must have seen how it was beginning to affect the paraverses around it."

"This effect will be exacerbated if you refuture the unfutured."

"This paraverse will become progressively more unstable."

"Irrevocably unstable."

"Allowed to continue, it will affect its neighbours and they will all collapse."

"Is this because of Hob and the Wild Hunt?" asked Therese.

"Yes!" they all said.

"There's no knowing where it might all end."

"It has to stop."

"This paraverse cannot be allowed to continue."

"The refutured must be defutured."

"You will have to defuture them."

"Me?"

"Of course."

"You were the one who refutured them."

"It's only fair that you should now defuture them."

"Otherwise the fosts will get worse."

"And if I don't?" asked Therese.

The grauniads considered their options.

"We take you back to the unfutured paraverse."

"We keep you there in this force field."

"And we let your tyres down."

"Metaphorically speaking."

"I prefer alphysically speaking."

"And defuture the refutured."

"You included."

"But we'd much rather we don't have to."

"And that you undo what you've just done yourself."

"And live long and prosper."

"In another paraverse."

"Or another temporal anomaly."

"A long way from here."

"I see I don't have much of a choice," Therese told them.

"It's actually a very easy choice," said the little cyclops with a smile that reflected his single eyebrow.

The grauniads watched her in silence.

"All right," said Therese. "I'll do it."

She opened the force field and joined them.

The grauniads didn't move immediately but slowly they slid off the bonnet and gathered closer to Therese, barely coming up to her knees.

"What if I stopped the Wild Hunt?" she asked them.

"You can't."

"Believe us, we've tried."

"This paraverse must come to an end."

"That's the only way."

"Okay but let me use my car."

"Very well," said the little cyclops. "You may use all the resources at your disposal but please do your duty for the sake of paraversal stability."

Therese nodded. She sat behind the wheel, fired up the Cadillac and swiftly defutured the refutured in a controlled demolition that left all the other paraverses unscathed.

Afterwards, there was no paraverse to return to. There was no sign of the grauniads, either.

For a few minutes, Therese believed she had resolved the situation and that no loose ends remained. She was intrigued by the idea of the Wild Hunt, however. She wished that she had been able to witness it for herself but it had belonged to another era, an unstable era that was now closed to her, temporal anomalies notwithstanding. And she would have liked to have met this Hob character. It seemed they had much in common.

But as she mourned the passing of this strange paraverse, she began to notice something odd about the way the remaining paraverses lay together. Where she might have expected a slight depression, there was now a lump.

Therese was sure it hadn't been there earlier. She looked around for the grauniads but they were nowhere to be seen and as she studied the bulge from the driving seat of her Cadillac, the red idiot light came on again and there was the flare of a nascent fost.

CHAPTER 7

Necessity is supposed to be the mother of invention. The identity of the father, however, is often disputed.

On realising that that they had been defutured, the unfutured produced a time capsule sired by desperation out of necessity.

Kevin Mullins hadn't been their first choice of chrononaut. He'd just been visiting the physics lab at the time, along with many others from the university campus. He arrived just as Archprofessor Richard Head, who had masterminded the project, set off to rehistory his fellow defutured. Archprofessor Head's mission was to travel back in time and ensure that their ancestors took different choices at key stages of their development. However, in the last few minutes of the dying paraverse he became so overwhelmed by the occasion that he got left and right mixed up, something quite common amongst those with very high IQs, since nature has a mischievous way of compensating, and he pressed the wrong button and went forwards instead of backwards, earning himself even less of a future than before.

One minute Kevin was watching Dr Head setting off heroically in the wrong direction to face the doom that surely awaited them all; the next, hands were bundling him into another time capsule next to him and switching it on. As they closed the hatch, distorted faces appeared at the porthole and told him to check the instructions in the glove box.

"What?" was all Kevin could say but the defutured outside merely replied, "And hurry!" before they slowed, froze and then began to re-enact their last few moments in reverse, except that nobody opened the hatch and pulled him out. By the time the industrial revolution was shrinking in his rearview mirror, it had dawned on Kevin that he was the only survivor and that the task of rehistorying the rest of his kind was now his.

The time capsule flew through time fairly accurately thanks to a subtle rifling to its surface. It rotated about its axis at a hundred revolutions per millennium, which doesn't sound like much but at the speed Kevin was heading into the past, it made him feel quite sick.

Kevin realised he knew nothing about temporal anomalies or dimensional instabilities. He was a palaeontologist who believed time was linear. He had no idea it was some wriggly, curly thing like an out-of-control fire hose.

He wondered if it was his knowledge of the past that had singled him out for the task of rehistorying the defutured but by the dawn of the Roman Empire he realised that his selection had been dictated simply by his proximity to the spare time capsule. He had just been in the right place at the right time.

A little later – or perhaps earlier, seeing as the Jews were now marching backwards into Egypt – it occurred to him that someone from the physics department might have been a better choice but in the middle of a plague of locusts of, frankly, Biblical proportions, he realised that Archprofessor Head's fate might have put them off. If this was the case, he could hardly blame them.

From the outside, the time capsule resembled an egg, an egg with a hatch, a hatch Kevin was not going to open again until he'd safely parked up somewhere. Some of the junior physicists had spatter-painted Dr Head's capsule in brown. Kevin's spare one was a pale eggshell blue but the illusion was rather spoilt by a black go-faster stripe. It also had a domed porthole at the sharper end.

It was obviously a prototype. Loose wires swung around him with bits of duct tape clinging frantically to them, like inept trapeze artists. A plastic fork, still with evidence of tomato sauce on it, struggled to support the transcendental cones behind the sun lounger on which he sat, and old lavatory-roll inner tubes insulated the octo-lithium crystals that dangled on bits of string in the jam jars in which they'd been grown. If anything went wrong, he'd be stuck and the defutured would never be rehistoried.

After six thousand years, he managed to open the glove box where he found the operating manual. The first line read "Thank you for choosing this time capsule. We hope it gives you many years of reliable service."

Momentarily distracted by Atlantis rising out of the sea, Kevin flicked through the sheets and, fighting his time-travel sickness, gradually worked out how to stop, start and steer the time capsule. He'd never muddled left and right, so temporal shifting was easy for him. In fact, he was burying himself in the past quicker than any palaeontologist, before or since.

He couldn't say at what stage of the journey the idea came to him but by the start of the last Ice Age he'd decided not to rehistory the defutured just yet. Despite their parting words to him, there was no hurry. Kevin had all the time in the world. He even had over two weeks of his leave allowance owing. Of course, if it remained untaken by the end of the year he would lose it for ever and technically, the end of the year had been brought forward. But Kevin felt he deserved a holiday. And if he couldn't take some time out then who could? And there wasn't anyone to stop him.

Having taken that decision, Kevin realised with a thrill that he could make an impossible dream come true. He could take a short break in the Cretaceous period.

So he carried on until just before the dinosaurs had died out. He gently began to decelerate and the time capsule responded promptly to its makeshift controls. The world outside stopped spinning and he gazed out of the porthole onto a dream made real. In fact, Kevin wondered if the gaming-console joystick and the porthole were part of an elaborate hoax but when he cracked open the hatch of the egg, there were no smart-arsed physics students shouting "Surprise!"

He smelt the air of 65 million years ago. It was purer than anything he'd ever smelt before and his blood sang with some ancient recognition.

Savouring every moment, he climbed out and felt the ancient earth beneath his feet, except that it was actually newer than when he'd last stood on it. He grinned with delight and shielded his eyes from the glare of the sun, which was not the angry dying purple affair he'd known all his life but a healthy, brilliant orb that beamed back at him with youth. And all around him the young air was filled with the songs, hums, squawks and cries of creatures that had never been heard before by any human.

Kevin took a few steps on quaking legs and then lay down for a bit. He was entirely alone – more alone than anyone could ever have been before – yet he felt so serene. He'd never realised how intensely annoying being part of the human race had been. He was probably the only person who had realised this, would ever realise this. The need to save his race became less pressing.

As he lay there, gazing at the sky and marvelling at the occasional flying creature, he kicked off his shoes and wriggled his toes in the prehistoric air, briefly introducing athlete's foot to the last of the dinosaurs. He stroked the nodding ferns and buried his fingers in the dark rich soil and felt the earth turning about its axis beneath his back. He must have felt it before but never noticed it. It was movement through space over time, a gentle progress that he'd been without while he'd been travelling in the defutured's egg.

Kevin was in sensory overload. It was as if his genes were remembering more than he had ever learned. Every plant or insect was somehow familiar to him, although many were unknown to science. He had the same feeling about the flying creatures, too. It was as if he'd just come home, after many years away, and now that he was here he could see a lifetime's work, if he wanted one, naming and cataloguing everything.

A shadow fell over him. Disorientated by his time travelling, Kevin wondered if the sun was getting low. Perhaps he'd dozed off, because as he opened his eyes he found they were gazing into another pair, a pair that flashed again with that ancient sense of recognition.

"Oh my," he said. "I suppose it was only a matter of time."

They stared at each other for ages.

"Do you have a name?" Kevin asked at length but he received no reply. "If not, I shall name you. You will be the mullinsosaur."

Kevin saw a flicker of something in the reptilian eyes. It was the effect of being named. It was an acknowledgement of one being to another, a confirmation of existence, and it carried a certain power – a certain magic.

But the mullinsosaur didn't like this new sensation. It was unfamiliar and distracting. Being named made it look, made it stare, and, if it had had any, it could have lost its underwear. It didn't like being made to feel so uncomfortable by such a strange and impertinent creature as Kevin Mullins and decided to deal with him in what might be called the time-honoured fashion.

Kevin read the mullinsosaur's thought processes through its eyes. It wasn't difficult. He was more highly evolved, after all. The ancient flash of recognition, he now realised, was not one of welcome familiarity, at all, but one of predatory contempt. The mullinsosaur viewed Kevin simply as a very large, very strange, tree shrew. Kevin was neither defutured nor rehistoried. He was extinct.

CHAPTER 8

Therese hit the overtime button on the dashboard and the Cadillac began to travel, not in years but in aeons.

The paraversal bulge was at right angles to everything else and it was unlike anything she'd seen before. It seemed to be one big fost, which suggested to her a connection with Hob and the Wild Hunt, and yet, as she pursued it in her own temporal anomaly, she began to change her mind. The Wild Hunt fosts, which had alerted her to the plight of the unfutured in the first place, were transient flashes and not at all like this stark streak into prehistory.

She gripped the steering wheel between her knees and lifted her chronoscope to her eyes. The Cadillac was gaining in time, and soon she would be able to see who or what it was that she was chasing. Therese de-selected D on the column shift and then, still in overtime, she selected R to bring her car down a few minutes after Kevin had ended his journey. From within her force field she checked her surroundings and saw a dinosaur finishing its meal. Not far away was a giant egg.

Therese was no palaeontologist. She didn't know it wasn't a real egg. The go-faster stripe should have been a clue, but she was more interested in the fate of the time traveller.

Something about the meal of the dinosaur attracted her attention. She moved the Caddy closer, using its original propulsion system, an isolated use of fossil fuels for that era. She alighted gracefully and, taking her hand bag with her, stepped up to the dinosaur, which, naturally enough, tried to bite her, only to break a few teeth on her force field.

Therese grimaced at the sight of Kevin's remains.

"So," she said, "Nick Hob. I've caught up with you at last."

The dinosaur padded around her and tried to attack her from behind.

Safe within her force field, Therese looked around. She was rational and not really spiritual, but she had a feeling that the recently deceased could hear her.

"So where is your Wild Hunt now?"

She glanced at the gauges on the dashboard of her Cadillac.

"My goodness, you were a dangerous man," she told the mangled corpse. "You've led the Wild Hunt into oblivion. As your memorial, you now have the fost to end all fosts – one that was your undoing – a new paraverse that runs in a different direction to all the others."

She got back into her car and looked up at the dinosaur that was still trying to gnaw its way through to her. Teeth tinkled against her force field and gathered in a fairy ring about its base.

"Stick around for some more treats," she told it. She selected D, and the dinosaur fell flat on its face.

CHAPTER 9

"Hey!" shouted Kevin, waving translucent arms. "That's not Hob! That's me!"

He was floating up by the treetops, and the sensations of the world he was leaving were becoming fainter. He looked down on the mullinsosaur spitting out soil, and wondered what else he could have done to attract the attention of the beautiful young scientist who'd just been there. But she hadn't even noticed the time capsule. She had just teased the dinosaur before leaving instantly in her six-wheeled car.

Apart from the sky, which was growing brighter, everything was growing fainter. The sounds of the forest were barely reaching him, replaced by a gentle twinkling sound. It wasn't loud; it had a different sort of potency. It was vaguely musical and the sudden sunset pulsed gently in time.

Kevin continued to ascend slowly. He floated past a fallen tree and some dead flowers. He looked around and saw other creatures rising up with him. There were insects and molluscs, frogs and pteranodons, tree shrews and crocodiles, even a baby dyoplosaurus with doe eyes and undeveloped spikes and armour, waggling the little club at the end of its bony tail as it explored its new state.

Kevin saw more animals above him, funnelling up towards a white light that although intense was not painful to look at, and all the time the music, which seemed to be playing backwards, wafted over him with waves of colours that went beyond those of a normal sunset.

Any fears about getting too close to the predatory dinosaurs evaporated when he realised that he was already dead. They no longer looked hungry but strangely at peace.

He noticed that he was rising faster than any other creature. His progress was quite dignified, but he easily outstripped the magnificent dragonflies with diaphanous wings about a metre across. Strange snails glided past his feet as he outpaced them simply by standing still. There were earthworms and beetles pottering along in the slow lane, with dinosaurs hogging the middle lane like badly driven juggernauts. Small, early mammals zipped past the dinosaurs, overtaking and undertaking but quickest of all was Kevin Mullins.

Contemplating their abundant variety, Kevin marvelled, despite his unshakeable belief in evolution, at the fun that had been had by whoever had designed these creatures.

The newly dead were converging into a cone. The music had grown without becoming louder, and although its tune was still just beyond him it penetrated his soul. If it was indeed playing backwards, it was taking steadying steps for a great leap forward. With each pulse of sound and every twinkling note, the colours of the sky gently changed and swirled. And what colours they were, too!

Now the cone was turning into a spiral. It occurred to Kevin that this might be how DNA would look if it was made up of gently twirling prehistoric fauna and flora. Behind them, the sky winked at him in splashes of all the colours of the rainbow, plus a few new ones it had been saving for a special occasion. In time with the music, the colours changed, blooming and fading and none of them clashed.

Although his spirits were soaring and expanding, Kevin felt his soul would burst if he heard the music played properly. All his life he had been a stranger to this sort of intense sensation, and he wasn't sure he would be able to withstand it. The flow of music, colours and lights was easing him into a wider set of perceptions. He began to detect the subtlest and richest of smells, as if a palette of perfumes had been opened nearby and, now that he'd lost it, his skin communicated all sorts of subtle sensations.

There was a deep sense of welcome for everything. Something was resonating inside him, although what there was of him left to resonate was unclear. Yet it was happening. He could feel it, and so could the other sparks of life around him as they span gently around each other.

Kevin's spiritual hackles rose in some ancient reflex that was not unpleasant. There was another feeling of genetic recognition, this time one he could trust.

He caught the eyes of those closest to him in the spiral and saw they were sparkling with pleasure. He remembered the baby dyoplosaurus. Had it been chortling with joy?

Kevin realised he was grinning, too. Everything smiled back at him, and their sparkling eyes or blossoms were reflected in the sky around them, which bathed them, in more colours and more lights, with even greater intensity.

And Kevin's soul sang in answer to the music, and added its own tune to the harmonies.

Gently, the spiral unwound as they ascended. Kevin felt no need to wave farewell. His fellow travellers were part of him now, and where he began and ended was uncertain and irrelevant. As they parted company, those with eyes left little points of light that flowed around him in the colours, and those without eyes left songs made up of fragrances.

Kevin looked up and around. He was alone and part of the music now, beyond all sight of the earth, harmonising with the colourful sensations and perfumes. He couldn't see any other once-living thing.

Then he looked down. Some of the lights were congregating below him. He began to make out a stronger light at their centre. He couldn't decide whether it was bigger or brighter, but, as he tried to focus on it, the colours slowly stopped swirling and the music paused.

There was a bass throbbing and the colours began to pulse with a sudden impatience. The light began flashing in return, signalling its approach.

For several agonising moments Kevin didn't move. It was like the stomach-turning stillness when a roller coaster reaches its summit before falling back to earth.

The bright light approached rapidly.

Kevin had a vague feeling he ought to get out of the way.

He held his breath. Old habits really did die hard.

The music steadied, composing itself before changing up a gear, and the colours trembled with anticipation.

The light leapt at him and in its passing moments it became a strobe light. Kevin blinked rapidly, adding to the sensation. Everything was flickering. Colours swirled. Sounds throbbed through him, yet his soul sang out in answer to their passing. There was a whiff of hot, exotic oil that seemed strangely familiar, and a blast of heated wind.

The light soared upwards and onwards. The music changed up a gear again, then another and another, throbbing in ascending tones. There were new, highly spirited, notes to its tune, and Kevin felt an even greater kinship with them. And yet there was a kind of reckless danger about this new song.

For a moment, Kevin thought he was in another spiral but then he realised he was viewing the pulsing colours through the spokes of a giant wheel. The colours themselves seemed to be spinning palettes and soon he was seeing wheels within wheels. Some revolved slowly while others became points of pure white.

He looked up at the speeding light, which was not so bright now that it had passed him. It was turning in a broad arc. It grew brighter again as it curved down towards him. However, Kevin gradually became aware of something else approaching from below. The colours and the music were waiting again, but this time there other lights.

The music burst all around him. Kevin felt he was in the middle of a firework display of complementary colours. There were harmonious collisions of sound, and then the accelerated spiralling lights swept above him.

The first light had swooped back to him as the others soared overhead. Through the spokes of many wheels he watched it float down and realised that, beyond it, the other lights, after dimming and slowing, were also turning to face him again, spinning colour-wheels billowing in their wake.

Kevin was in the centre of his own wheel. He felt he was watching some old film, catching glimpses of action through the rotating reels of an ancient film projector, and the music revved in time with each passing of the spokes.

He could make out vague shapes among the lights that swirled around him. He strained to recognise them, and as music poured out of him there were answering songs from all the lights that swept by. He was sucked up by their wake and when they shot past he could feel puffs of heat.

As the stream of lights turned back towards him, Kevin focussed on the first light. It circled him, exuding an air of curiosity and came nearer. It took on an outline as it slowed. Kevin saw spinning wheels within its shape and, suddenly, he began to make sense of it, and the other lights became less abstract, too.

With a terrible thrill, he realised what this supernaturally quick thing was. It was leading him and all the other creatures in the ascent to heaven.

It was a dinosaur on a motorbike.

CHAPTER 10

Kevin found himself standing on a cloud. The music had gone, but somewhere close at hand he could hear what sounded like exceptionally beautiful wind chimes. He saw a splendid pair of gateposts shimmering among the clouds and on one of them hung one of a pair of brilliantly white gates, an unearthly example of wrought-iron work. The other gate was lying in front of it on a pair of trestles. A piece of cardboard was propped up beside it with the words "Wet Paint" written on it in unnecessarily beautiful writing.

Kevin took some steps closer.

A cheerful fellow with a big beard and overalls emerged from the gateway.

"Hello," He said. "I'm terribly sorry but We're not quite ready for you yet."

"Oh," replied Kevin. "I'm not expected, then?"

God, for it was He, put His pencil behind His ear. "Not exactly, no. In fact you're terribly early – by several thousands of millennia, in fact."

"Perhaps I could lend You a hand."

"That's very generous of you."

God was looking around.

"Er, have You lost anything?"

"Yes, I'm afraid I have. There should be a book here somewhere. Can't see it, can you?"

"No."

"Sophia? Sophia!" called God. He hardly raised his voice but it carried a long way.

"What?" came an answer from a nearby cloud.

"Have You seen that book? You know the one. I'm going to put everybody's name in it and whether they've lived a worthwhile life or not."

"No, I haven't. You probably put it down somewhere while You were creating something."

A pleasant-faced woman in an apron emerged. "Oh, I'm sorry," She said, "I didn't know You had company."

"That's all right," said God, and then He added with a certain mischievousness, "You are forgiven."

Sophia smiled back at Him and Kevin realised where God had found the inspiration for the dawning of the sun.

"Well, aren't You going to introduce Us?" Sophia asked God.

"I will if he tells Me his name."

"Er, Kevin Mullins, Your ... Your ..."

"Your Maker," finished Sophia with a twinkle in Her eye.

"Kevin Mullins, this is My Wife, Sophia. Sophia, this is Kevin Mullins."

"I'm very pleased to meet you, Kevin," said Sophia.

"Thank You," said Kevin.

"And I'm God," said God.

"What do you think of all this, then?" Sophia asked Kevin.

"All what?"

"All this." She gestured towards what Kevin now recognised as the Pearly Gates.

"Oh. Oh, it's very nice."

"Really?" replied God. "You don't think the overall effect is a bit over the top, do you?"

"No I don't think so. I think it's just about right," Kevin said earnestly.

"Well of course, it's not finished yet," God pointed out.

"And what do you think of all that down there?" asked Sophia.

She pointed to a gap in the clouds below them.

Kevin looked down and saw a beautiful land populated by strange and wonderful creatures.

"I think it's splendid," he told Her.

God smiled.

"It looks very nice," she admitted, "but I still think it's a stupid idea."

"What's a stupid idea?" asked Kevin.

"Evolution. I don't know why He doesn't make everything perfect in the first place."

"But it gets so boring," said God.

"At least You'd get a result more quickly. How long have You been working on this pet project of Yours – 4,500 million years? And how far has it got? The dinosaurs rule the earth. Brilliant."

"But what wonderful dinosaurs!" enthused God and Kevin together.

"I've tried explaining it to Her but She won't listen," God said to Kevin. "I'm sure you understand."

"Of course!"

"Well, he would say that, wouldn't he?" retorted Sophia. "He's the product of Your little experiment, isn't he?"

"Yes. But this is all very interesting," said God, thoughtfully. "I hadn't expected such a highly developed mammal as you to have evolved by now. The reptilian civilisation is just emerging, and there are all sorts of species to appear before a creature like you comes along. It's as if you've just popped out of nowhere."

"I'm afraid that's because I have."

"Have what?"

"Popped out of nowhere. At least, in a manner of speaking. You see, I'm from the future."

"Oh. Oh well. That explains it, then. There you are, Sophia, I told You it would work."

"Yes, You did. But that was evolution – We're talking about time travel. I mean that's not supposed to be feasible, is it?"

"Excuse me," said Kevin, "but did You just say something about a reptilian civilisation?"

"Yes, I did," said God. "It's the very latest thing. I have very high hopes for it."

Sophia shook Her head with a wry smile but said nothing.

"How highly have they developed?" asked Kevin.

"Oh, they're all driving around in cars, now."

"What, automobiles?"

"Yes, that's right. Riding motorbikes and flying aeroplanes. They started off with steam locomotives that used wood from the forests for fuel, but the increased gases in the atmosphere caused the polar ice caps to melt."

"Ye-es," said Kevin.

"So nowadays they use hydrogen in internal combustion engines. That way they produce only water as a by-product and by re-foresting the whole planet they're extracting their earlier emissions of carbon dioxide from the atmosphere. Not only that, but the dinosaurs have collected all the low-level ozone produced by these vehicles and used it to patch up any holes in the ionosphere. I'll take you on a guided tour of what they've achieved, if you like. So. If you're from the future, how did you get here?"

Kevin took an unnecessary deep breath. He didn't want to explain to God how His pet project had ended but he couldn't see how it could be avoided.

"In the future, we can make time machines."

"Really?"

God and Sophia looked suitably impressed.

"Wasn't it difficult to get around all the chronological barriers He'd laid out?" asked Sophia.

"Yes, it was."

"I expect you had to use a very sophisticated nuclear reactor to produce enough energy," said God.

"Yes, we did."

"So where is this time machine, then?"

"It's down there," said Kevin, pointing to the verdant green forests below them.

"It's not anywhere near that erupting volcano, is it?" asked Sophia.

"Er ..."

The lava flow convulsed with a vivid flash, and a sinister mushroom cloud billowed up towards them. When the shock wave hit them, the erected half of the Pearly Gates fell from its hinges.

"That's odd," said God. "That shouldn't do that. I think I'd better pop down and see what's going on."

CHAPTER 11

"It's not good, I'm afraid," said God as He rejoined them. "The lava from that volcano engulfed Kevin's time machine. There's been an explosion of cataclysmic proportions."

"Oh dear," said Kevin.

"Is that serious, then?" asked Sophia.

"There's a huge crater," God told them. "The whole place looks like it's been hit by a massive meteorite or perhaps a comet. An unexpected temperate archipelago will be the result, but I will miss the dinosaurs."

"What?"

"The dinosaurs will all be wiped out."

"What?" spluttered Kevin.

"Except for the crocodiles and alligators, of course. But the most highly developed dinosaurs aren't really resistant to radiation and the less sophisticated ones seem to be mutating. Some have already developed feathers instead of scales. Thanks to that great dust cloud, a nuclear winter is beginning, and it looks like the small furry mammals are going to get a much better chance from now on."

"I'm terribly sorry," said Kevin.

"Don't worry about it, Kevin," said Sophia. "He can always make another one. Besides, I always thought volcanoes were rather ill-conceived."

"I'll be fascinated to see what the small furry animals get up to," said God, still deep in thought. "I always felt rather sorry for them being chased all over the place and being eaten." He turned to Kevin and smiled at him. "Besides, We can't stop your kind evolving, can We?"

"I suppose not," replied Kevin without enthusiasm.

"Cheer up! You mammals will happen a lot sooner now. Which reminds Me."

He turned to Sophia.

"Could You let Me have a quiet word with Kevin by Myself, Sophia?"

"Yes, of course. I hope to meet you again one day, Kevin. Farewell." And with that, and one of Her beautiful smiles, She was gone.

"Now then," said God. "You can see that We're nowhere near ready for you, Kevin, can't you?"

Kevin glanced around at the Pearly Gates, now both lying on the clouds. He nodded, swallowed hard and licked his dry lips.

"I'm afraid, We don't have anywhere for you."

"I'm quite willing to help."

"That's a wonderful offer, Kevin, it really is – but you have no idea what's involved. I've suddenly got an awfully large number of dinosaur souls to admit right now."

"But I'm a palaeontologist! I've studied their fossils and can help in their classification! I'd be the ideal person!"

God smiled gently and shook His head. "No, I don't think so."

"No? Are You cross with me because I destroyed the dinosaurs with my time machine?"

"It wasn't deliberate, was it? You weren't anywhere near your time machine at the – er – time."

"No. You're right. I didn't mean that to happen at all. I love dinosaurs. Do I have Your forgiveness?"

"Of course you do, although for what I'm not sure."

"Let me help You. Please."

Again God shook His head. He put His arm around Kevin's shoulders.

"Try to see it from the dinosaurs' point of view. Large numbers of them have just been vaporised and many others will be suffering quite severe radiation burns, followed by poisoning. The climate will be changing permanently and nearly all their all species will die out. They arrive here expecting a relaxing time in the after life, and find you here. I wouldn't say anything to them, of course, but, y'know, they would find out eventually. They might not be as charitable as I am, especially when they discover that you're a palaeontologist."

Kevin frowned. "Wouldn't they be flattered by someone who took such an interest in them?

God gave Kevin one of His looks. "Would you be flattered by the attentions of a grave robber?"

"Ah. Ye-es. I see You might have a point there."

"You'd only get in the way of the angels, as well."

"Or I could stay here and help You," and Kevin gestured towards the entrance to heaven.

"No," said God, gently. "I can't expect you to build your own heaven."

"I don't mind!"

"It's simply that We don't have anywhere for you at the moment."

"This is very much Your project, isn't it, God?"

"Yes, it is. Exactly right. And because old *homo sapiens* isn't going to be around for some time yet – well, apart from you – and because – how can I put this? – you don't have the right heaven building skills, I'm afraid you're going to have to wait. I'm sure We'll have one ready soon. In view of what's just happened down there it looks as if We'll be needing it sooner rather than later. But first I must attend to all these dinosaurs."

They peered over the edge of the cloud and saw the end of the splendid dinosaur culture. To Kevin a great deal of it seemed remarkably familiar. The land masses were different but, from a distance, the civilised beings that populated them had a vaguely human appearance. It was only when he looked closer that he could make out the scales and claws.

Dinosaur commuters were arriving home from the office and shouting "Hi honey! I'm home," to their spouses who proudly looked over clutches of eggs in their nurseries. Others collaborated over kindergarten rosters and drove environmentally friendly dinosaur carriers to take their little ones to school, where they learned about science, art and music. There had been a recent craze in roller skating among adolescents and many youngsters tried out new fashions or listened to accomplished musicians, bards and poets. The working population worked only three days a week and there were no extremes of affluence or poverty.

Kevin was surprised to see how popular motor racing was. In fact, a good deal of contemporary culture had embraced this pastime and he fancied he could hear a Rock'n'Roll band playing a song about eight little spark plugs.

However, it was practically all over for the dinosaurs. The land masses were changing even as Kevin looked at them. They were fracturing and heaving and coming out in volcanoes like spots on a teenager.

Happy campers were coming home from vacations to discover they were homeless. Tidal waves engulfed cities and only in the more remote outposts of dinosaur civilisation would a few species be able to hold out for a few more generations until succumbing to the inevitable. Rock music would soon be dead, buried under millions of tons of lava.

Dead dinosaurs were already filling the skies. Kevin could hear their soul music. They were stacked up in what air traffic controllers might call a very tight holding pattern. In between the patient dinosaurs flew their angels, implausible looking creatures with wings that were far too small for them. To help the sorting process, each angel resembled the species they were going to be hosting and Tyrannosaurus rex, triceratops and stegosaurus angels were trying to organise their new arrivals with improvised loud hailers and hastily grabbed table tennis bats.

"I can see that you're all going to be very busy," said Kevin, glumly.

God nodded. "I've got to supervise dinosaur heaven."

A diplodocus angel bumped into a tyrannosaurus rex angel, causing the tyrannosaur to drop the umbrella it was holding aloft. The two turned to face each other and, rather unexpectedly, the highly strung tyrannosaurus rex angel burst into tears.

"I can see things are getting a bit fraught," said Kevin. "The dinosaurs really ought to come first."

"Well said, that man!" said God. "So how do you feel about re-incarnation?"

"Re-incarnation?"

"That's right. Of course, I only intended to use it in exceptional circumstances, and strictly speaking it makes a mockery of everything that I've been trying to achieve here, but if I can't bend the rules then who can?"

"Yeah," said Kevin, brightening up.

"You'll do it, then?"

"I think it's a brilliant idea!" Kevin's relief was colossal. For a nasty moment, he'd had a horrible feeling about what the alternative to heaven might be, especially for someone with his record.

"Splendid!" said God. "There is just one other thing I feel I ought to mention."

"Oh, yes? And what's that?"

"You'll have to be a tree shrew."

"I beg Your pardon?"

"You'll have to be a tree shrew."

"A tree shrew?"

"Yes. They're the most highly developed mammals we've got at the moment. You see, there aren't any other life forms around right now that are suitable."

"Ah," said Kevin. "I think I understand now."

"Good," said God. "I hoped you would."

Something jolted heaven. "Ow," said a voice and an enormous head on a long neck began to rise up through the cloud.

God quickly pushed Kevin out of sight.

"God? Is it all right to keep new arrivals up here?" asked the seismosaurus angel.

"Yes, but I'll say when."

"Okay."

As the head sank back down, Kevin watched it cautiously. The wings of the seismosaurus angel looked woefully inadequate. God seemed to have adopted a one-size-fits-all policy. On the backs of several seismosauruses, were patient queues of other smaller dinosaurs who must have been very surprised at their afterlife so far. Kevin couldn't be sure, but on the back of the nearest seismosaurus a well behaved pack of velociraptors were about to start a game of Twister.

"I'll just have to adapt, won't I?" said Kevin.

"Yes. Precisely. However, suddenly becoming a tree shrew could be something of a shock. Later on, evolving will probably happen so gradually you won't notice."

Kevin wanted to think about it but he could see God was eager to get cracking on dinosaur heaven. "God?"

"Yes, Kevin?"

"Can I keep my memory as I evolve?"

"Well, I'm not sure," said God, thoughtfully. "I suppose there wouldn't be any harm in it. If that's what you really want, I suppose We can allow it."

"I'd really appreciate it. I'd have my past experiences to help me pull through. Or rather, my future experiences, if You follow me."

"Yes, I see what you mean. Very well, you can keep your memory, but on two conditions. One, that you never, ever let on about re-incarnation. Everyone would try and get away with murder if they knew about it. So it must just be our little secret. The other condition is that you don't try and change the course of history. Unless I tell you to, of course. That's just as important."

Kevin thought about the defutured and rehistoried-in-waiting, but he didn't seem to have much choice. "I promise."

"Good. I think that's it. I hope everything works out for you, Kevin."

"Thank You, God. And the same to You."

"Good bye."

"Good bye. And thanks again, God."

Kevin began to float away. God stood and waved at him. Then He turned towards the Pearly Gates and reached for the pencil behind His ear.

Kevin felt quite giddy. He was about to embark on another journey through time, but in the opposite direction and much more slowly. It would be an extraordinary experience from a scientific point of view. He'd have to try and remember as much as possible.

That was the last thing he thought of as a member of the human race until much, much later, for the next moment he had just been born as a tree shrew in the middle of a nuclear winter.

CHAPTER 12

Monsieur Cadvare crunched some numbers, processed some words and tried to concentrate on his work. Outside it was raining, and the rest of Mourion spread out to the horizon, grey on grey.

The vidphone chirped with a compulsory response message and, when M Cadvare answered it, he saw a face of questionable humanity.

"Ah, M Cadvare," it said, "my name is Gris, Inspector Gris."

An icy grip of fear engulfed M Cadvare.

Inspector Gris paused to consult another screen just out of sight of the vidcam. "I see from my records that your personal transportation device is overdue for its annual re-certification of roadworthiness."

"I'm s-sorry," stammered M Cadvare, "I-I had no idea."

"Evidently. Whilst it is true that the regulations regarding vehicle testing have been recently changed, and many re-certification dates brought forward, it is also equally true that there is no excuse for ignorance of the regulations."

M Cadvare nodded dumbly.

Inspector Gris had the familiar featureless features of government officials everywhere. In Post Unification Euphobia, there were thousands of people like him and M Cadvare had a growing suspicion that the government had inaugurated a secret civil servant cloning programme.

"Provided you submit your vehicle for testing within the next working week I am prepared to overlook this transgression. Do I make myself understood?"

"Yes," mumbled M Cadvare.

"*Au revoir*, M Cadvare."

M Cadvare did not reply but watched his patchwork of text and data replace the image of Inspector Gris. He tried to return to his work but he couldn't concentrate. He kept wondering what other regulations had changed without him knowing and imagined endless hordes of grey inspectors poring over screens just like his, auditing him to within an inch of his life.

Post Unification Euphobia was full of standards and directives issued by the Euphobian Commissioners. The life of every citizen was closely regulated and a vast bureaucracy existed to keep them on the right side of their directives, or, more accurately, those directives issued for their own benefit, in their own name.

M Cadvare worked as a transaction auditor within that bureaucracy, so he had visibility of how breaches committed by others came to light.

But he was not part of that bureaucracy.

He used his privileged position to covertly live his life the way he wanted and habitually flouted the standards and directives it was his duty to audit.

And the directive he flouted the most was the SoLD – the Standard of Living Directive.

Of course, he would like to be able to flout it openly but he knew, better than most, what would happen if he did. The commodity inspectors would escort him for Re-education in the Product Planning Blocks.

M Cadvare lived alone. M Cadvare did not eat processed food. M Cadvare did not follow fashion but bought the things that he liked. M Cadvare had filled his apartment with antiques. M Cadvare mended his consumer durables so that they continued to work far beyond their intended design life. M Cadvare saved money by doing as much as he could himself, thereby jeopardising the livelihoods of many qualified trades people. M Cadvare did not watch his weekly quota of television. M Cadvare did not expose himself to the media as much as the government would like. M Cadvare lived within his means. M Cadvare did not worry about what his possessions said about him as a person.

He did not live for his work. He wasn't interested in promotion. He was a crap transaction auditor and under some government definitions could be labelled as being "economically inactive".

But his life was punctuated by isolated bursts of contentment. And that was about as happy as he could hope to be, for the Euphobian Commissioners did not encourage positive feelings among their citizens. Contentment and satisfaction were at odds with Euphobian Consumerist Community principles. They did not drive the economy or support the government's administration.

So far, against all the odds, in any lifestyle audits under SoLD, M Cadvare had eluded a Non-Conformity Report or NCR.

Somewhere within the network of drop files and databases there had to be a tumescent dossier on his well hidden breaches of the Standard of Living Directive. One day this would burst and bring the commodity inspectors running.

His position as a transaction auditor meant he had been able to search for that dossier. So far, he had found nothing.

He spent the rest of an unproductive morning brooding about the commodity inspectors. The arms of the commodity inspectors were long and unyielding, yet M Cadvare had hidden his non-conformities so well that he had never attracted their attention before. If his record was too squeaky clean, then this minor transgression might add authenticity to an otherwise flawless record of compliance. A small part of him wondered if his exemplary behaviour and uncharacteristic oversight had prompted Inspector Gris to be lenient, but most of him knew this was a stupid idea.

Despite everything, M Cadvare's spirits began to soar. He was proud of his strength of character and determination to live his life by his own standards. It had helped him resist almost overwhelming adversity as, each day of his life, some other small joy was subverted into a chore. With practice, he believed he could become even better at hiding his violations of the SoLD and achieve his ambition of never receiving an NCR.

During his lunch break, he accessed the vehicle-testing file on his pocket organiser. According to that, it still had another six months to run. Just to check, he rang the database company. They said that they had upgraded the software but they wouldn't confirm or deny whether any changes relating to vehicle-testing requirements had been made. However, they did tell him how much the upgrade would cost, so he paid up and, once his account had been debited, he was able to verify what Inspector Gris had told him.

He vidphoned his nearest test centre, which was also an authorised dealer in personal transportation devices.

"I have to make an appointment for a vehicle roadworthiness test," he told the receptionist.

"Ah," she replied, "we have been expecting you, M Cadvare. I take it you are aware that your test is overdue?"

M Cadvare nodded.

"Then you will probably be aware that there is a surcharge for an overdue test."

M Cadvare was not aware; nor was he surprised. The surcharge was almost as much as the fine for non-compliance but, as the receptionist pointed out, it did not invoke any points on a criminal record that could ultimately lead to Re-education in the dreaded Product Planning Blocks, Re-education that would surely turn him into the type of model consumer the Euphobian Consumerist Community would be proud to have as a citizen.

CHAPTER 13

Hob walked along the auto route, humming *I need somebody* by Iggy Pop and The Stooges. Behind him lay Mourion airport. On his back, his rucksack bounced and wriggled, and on his shoulders he carried his wooden crate. The buckles on his old motocross boots clinked like spurs as he walked in time with the lyrics he muttered to himself and, when he got to the chorus, he twirled the wooden crate carelessly around him as if it were empty.

But despite being apparently carefree, Hob was deeply puzzled.

First of all, he needed to get some fuel for his bike, but so far he'd only found recharging stations for electric vehicles. He could have used public transport, but that was like having the authorities act as his chauffeur and was just wrong. So he had shouldered *Nosferatu* in its packing crate and had followed the auto route on the not unreasonable assumption that there must be a filling station along it somewhere.

Then there was the state of the souls that he'd encountered since before landing in Mourion. He'd never seen such a poor lot. The only soul worth taking was a gentle-hearted receptionist and, compared with the low spirits around her, she shone like brass in muck. A casual observer might have felt that the staff of the Euphobian customs service had shown commendable spirit in trying to confiscate *Nosferatu*, examine his passport and get him to remove his open face helmet and visor but Hob knew better. Something else drove them but he couldn't say what. He'd taken his leave of them after they had become violent.

Bullets were like water off a duck's back to Hob but he still found it incredibly rude when people shot him.

He walked on the right-hand side, with the traffic flow, since in Euphobia they drove on what he considered to be the wrong side of the road. As he strode effortlessly onwards, he rummaged in his deceptively large pockets. Somewhere, rattling about his person, was something that could confirm or deny his worst suspicions, something he shouldn't need to use if he was worthy of the title Soul Trader.

It was as he was wandering along, singing aloud now and juggling the crate while he rooted around in his pockets, that he sensed a soul approaching. Hob grinned. This was a really good one. It shone like a beacon.

He stopped walking, and stood with his crate balanced on one finger so that it span lazily on a corner like a basket ball. Then he turned and looked behind him.

A soul of great quality was approaching him in a proper car, one of the first that he'd seen on the road that day. It was a Mercedes limousine, and somewhere behind the smoked glass of the passenger compartment he sensed a remarkable personality.

Whoever it was must have been impressed by him, too, for the car was slowing down. It drew level with him and the nearside window lowered a fraction as the car pulled up, obstructing that lane of auto route.

Hob leaned forward to peer through the gap. There was a movement within the interior and then the tyres chirruped and the Mercedes accelerated away.

Hob was now even more intrigued. He had caught sight of the most beautiful pair of eyes.

He put his free left hand in his outside jacket pocket and pulled out a length of wood into which had been inserted a glass tube filled with liquid. He pointed it at the departing Mercedes and had a strong sense that those eyes were still looking back at him. A bubble in the liquid shot towards the Mercedes and the needle on a gauge next to it swung past ten, to roughly where eleven would have been. Satisfied that it was still working and that he hadn't lost his soul sense, Hob waved it at the passing traffic and occasionally the bubble moved a little and the needle stirred from its peg but these readings were the exceptions rather than the rule.

A little further on, he came at last to a filling station.

He paused and stopped throwing *Nosferatu* around, to spin it on his finger again.

"Aha! Fortunato! A garage! A little shrine to me!"

His rucksack squeaked.

Hob pocketed his instrument, shouldered the crate and strode onto the forecourt.

The filling station was empty. Hob thought it was closed until a Ford Mondeo turned off the main road and pulled up at the pumps. As Hob approached, the driver got out and began to fill the car up by himself.

Hob went to the opposite side of the pump, put *Nosferatu* down and inspected the labels. There was Veganoil, Super Unleaded and Premium Super Unleaded.

Veganoil was a non-starter since *Nosferatu* didn't have a diesel engine. Hob had no problem with bio-fuels, but, just by sniffing the nozzle, his educated nose could tell that it had the combustibility of a damp lump of lard.

He replaced the nozzle and picked up the other two, one in each hand, to assess their suitability.

"Do you require any assistance, sir?" asked the cashier over the tannoy.

"No thanks," replied Hob, "I'm just sniffing."

The Super Unleaded had none of the eye-watering kick that a good fuel had. Just as the people of Mourion lacked souls, this petroleum lacked spirit. The Premium Super Unleaded promised more, but Hob could tell that it would not travel well. And neither would *Nosferatu* if any of this stuff spilt into its supercharger.

"You're not supposed to sniff it, you're supposed to buy it," said the cashier.

Hob ignored him.

"Must be some kind of nut," muttered the cashier as the Mondeo driver came into the shop.

"Care in the community?" suggested the driver, who was from pre-unification Italia and still acted with generosity of spirit, even though his spirits were becoming more impoverished.

"What's he got in that crate?" asked the cashier, taking the driver's plastic.

"Nothing, by the way he carries it."

They glanced at the security screen. All it showed were two nozzles hanging up in mid air. Even *Nosferatu*'s crate didn't appear.

"Must be a fault somewhere," said the cashier. He banged the side of the monitor then looked out of the window. Hob was still there, but the monitor insisted he wasn't.

From his jacket, Hob had produced a square box. He unscrewed a lid, and, picking up one of the nozzles again, poured a few drops of fuel into the box, using the lid as a funnel. He replaced the nozzle, screwed the cap down tightly, wound up a handle that folded out from the side of the box, checked a gauge on the top, and pressed a button.

"I'd better go and see what he's up to," the cashier said to his customer, and they both walked out onto the forecourt.

"What d'you think you're playing at?" he demanded as he approached Hob.

"Hmm? Oh, I'm just checking the potency of your fuel." Hob looked very closely at the gauge on the box. "This Premium Super Unleaded's not very good is it?" Hob showed him the gauge.

"You can't do that!"

"I just have. I knew it was crap to start with, but this confirms how bad it is."

"What's that thing?"

"It's my bomb combustometer."

"Your what?"

"My bomb combustometer."

"Oh my God, he's got a bomb!" shrieked the Mondeo driver.

"No. Not a bomb. This is a bomb combustometer. You put some fuel in here, wind up this little fold-out handle to create a charge, press this button and you can see how good the fuel is. Hallo? Where's everybody gone?"

Hob was suddenly all alone.

He produced the long, thin object again and pointed it at two figures, running away as fast as they could. The little bubble in the glass phial wobbled slightly and the needle on a gauge flicked torpidly off its stop.

Hob tutted. "By the spanners of the Great Smith himself, the soul erosion around here is terrible!"

His rucksack squeaked its agreement.

He shrugged, put everything back into his pockets and walked over to the abandoned Mondeo.

"Boot lock open," he said, and the car obliged. Hob put *Nosferatu*'s crate in the boot and tied its lid down with a conker on some string. Then he went to the front of the car and said, "Bonnet catch release." He opened it, propped it up with its stay and leaned over the engine bay. "Splendid! A proper mill at last – an injected V6. Don't need that or this, and replace this with one of these, and we are in business. May you sing your song through your unbaffled pipes." He stroked the exhaust headers and fuel pipes. "And burn this rat's piss they've fed you on with a pure blue flame!" He patted the cam covers and said, "Cams and followers, awake and hearken to me, for your timing has come! May your pistons lighten, your valves never tangle, your bearings run free – revs with out end, ring-ding-a-ding!"

Hob took off his rucksack, buckled it and himself into the front seats and hung some furry dice on the rear-view mirror.

"Trouble's goin' – wait a moment! I nearly forgot."

Hob tapped the instrument panel behind the steering wheel.

"Come on. Show yourself. I know you're in there somewhere."

A wicked little face appeared in the corner of the instrument cluster.

"Ah ha. Now, you know who I am, don't you?"

The face nodded.

"You've probably noticed a few changes around here."

The face nodded, this time with a little more enthusiasm.

"You work for me now. Not against any neglectful previous owner. Okay?"

Hob smiled and the gremlinne smiled back. She emerged uncertainly into the instrument cluster but remained inside the plastic screen.

"Have you ever been in the Wild Hunt?"

The gremlinne shook her head.

"Have you ever fosted?"

The gremlinne shook her head again.

"Would you like to?"

She nodded vigorously.

Hob grinned widely.

"Let's have some serious fun together," he said.

With a diamond-hard fingernail, he scratched some sigils on the Perspex beside her.

"Your job is to provide me with perfect combustion. I want big, fat blue sparks; I want smoothness and flawless response. Do you think you can oblige?"

The gremlinne nodded back eagerly and dived back inside the dashboard.

"Trouble's going!" said Hob as he twisted the key in the ignition.

The engine fired and he felt the gremlinne at work.

"Trouble's gone!"

CHAPTER 14

Hob was quick, but not even he was faster than a two-way radio. On the auto-route, his Mondeo went so well, he was almost on top of the road block before they were ready for him. When he saw the flashing blue lights, he laughed.

The police had formed a funnel of squad cars. Hob knew from long experience that officers crouched between the cars, ready to flick out tyre bursting stingers as he tried to reach the enticingly empty autoroute beyond.

The Mondeo was bellowing through its open pipes and its engine note didn't change as Hob aimed it, not at the gap but directly at the cars in the road block. He saw the head of a disconcerted policeman pop up and look nervously at his colleagues. Then, once it was obvious that Hob wasn't lifting off or steering away, figures darted out from their hiding places.

The gremlinne, who had been working frantically on the Mondeo all this time, cautiously emerged from a face-level air vent on the dashboard and, after glancing at Hob, she climbed up to peer through the windscreen at the looming roadblock.

"Watch this, Fortunato!" said Hob and he fosted.

The Mondeo leapt into a benighted forest and Hob quickly switched on his headlamps. Strange creatures leapt out of his way, a vivid green against the rain-soaked blackness of the trees, and the windscreen misted over. Hob turned on the demister and windscreen wipers and then he was on the sunny autoroute again, hurtling away from the roadblock.

The astonished police began firing and the Mondeo's rear window shattered, covering the interior and *Nosferatu*'s crate with broken glass.

A bullet bounced off the back of Hob's crash helmet and the gremlinne took a running jump off the top of the dashboard and did a surprisingly graceful swan dive into her air vent.

"Why do they hate us so?" he asked Fortunato.

The rucksack squeaked.

"We need to be less predictable," replied Hob.

He soon caught up with traffic beyond the road block and set about carving his way through it.

"We've got to get off this motorway, Fortunato!"

The rucksack squeaked that they were boring and didn't have proper bends or hills.

"They're just a step away from being public transport," sneered Hob. "They're too easily controlled. There'll be another road block up ahead soon, you mark my words."

The rucksack suggested that even if they fosted through that one there would be another.

"And another after that and another after that," agreed Hob.

They overtook a queue of trucks and encountered a strange species of city car that looked out of place on the open road. Some of them accelerated after he'd overtaken them, as if a kind of madness seized them, but no way could they keep up with Hob in his souped-up Mondeo. Soon he was clear of the traffic again and made good progress for a few minutes until he rounded a bend and saw in the distance a line of squad cars on a bridge above the road. Brilliant white in the sun, they were split down their flanks by a fluorescent band of orange.

As soon as they saw Hob, the police opened fire. His screen shattered and he suffered a number of direct hits around the head and shoulders. Hob managed to protect his tyres but, as he dived under the bridge, another burst of fire hit his headlamps and grille.

The police were not prepared for him to survive their fire and ran to the other side of the bridge but were too late to do anything except loose off a few wildly aimed shots.

"A different tactic," Hob remarked to his rucksack, which ventured the opinion that the police appeared to be learning.

"Bullets don't warrant fosting," said Hob but he glanced down and noticed the temperature needle beginning to creep up. He took a stick of chewing gum from an outer jacket pocket and began to chew upon it.

"Time to be wild," he announced and he threw the Mondeo down a couple of cogs as he braked heavily to pull up by the crash barrier. He released the bonnet catch, snaked fluidly out of the open window and leapt out to look into the distance. Another bridge crossed the autoroute, and already police were lining up along it.

Traffic swerved around him.

"Hazard flashers on, Fortunato!"

Hob's rucksack leant forward and switched them on with an extended outer pocket flap as Hob opened the bonnet to peer inside.

Hob smiled. "There you are," he said. "I wondered what you had got up to."

The gremlinne was clinging to the outside of the radiator matrix, plugging a bullet hole. Hob gently lifted her away.

"Radiator, seal thyself," he commanded and the clouds of steam disappeared as he applied some chewing gum to the damaged radiator. He undid the cap to the cooling system and the gremlinne redirected the windscreen washer reservoir into it. When this ran out, Hob spat into it repeatedly until he had replaced the lost coolant. "Well, Fortunato," he said, closing the bonnet, "you don't think I'd embarrass our little gremlinne by wazzing into it, right in front of her, do you? Besides, my spittle contains a corrosion inhibitor."

He crouched down, grabbed under the bumper and lifted the front end of the car before stepping over the crash barrier with it. As the traffic on both carriageways took avoiding action, he balanced the Mondeo on the Armco with its engine still running and ran to the rear.

"This should fox 'em, Fortunato!"

He squatted down and lifted the rear wheels over the crash barrier too, so that now the Mondeo faced the opposite direction on the other carriageway.

He jumped back in and quickly drove off as a police helicopter rounded the bend behind them.

By the time he passed the bridge again, the police cars on it had gone, but the road block a little further on hadn't entirely dispersed. They couldn't follow Hob against the flow of traffic on that side of the autoroute. They did the only thing they could, which was set off in the opposite direction for the next exit, but the police helicopter swooped down after him.

Hob had hoped to be able to turn off at the next junction but the helicopter was obviously co-ordinating movements on the ground. Blue flashing lights decorated the roundabout at the top of the slip road so he carried on further down the autoroute. When he raced by the junction, a long line of police cars swept onto the motorway behind him in pursuit.

"Rev, my engine!" said Hob. "Rev higher than you've ever revved before. Raise your bloodline, push it around the clock and pull the highest gears in your design life to top your top speed!"

The Mondeo began to pull away from the cops on their tail but when Hob thought they were far enough ahead he pulled up sharply, using the gears and engine braking again, without laying too much precious rubber, and hopped out to lift the car over the barrier, like he had before.

This time he was even slicker. His pursuers came to a disorganised halt and watched in baffled fury as he accelerated away from them, in the opposite direction on the other side of the crash barrier.

The helicopter stood on its nose and swooped around to follow them.

"Reckon we can manage a hat trick, Fortunato?"

The rucksack squeaked that it did.

Hob laughed as more police cars streamed onto the opposite carriageway. However, only a handful of cars joined the autoroute completely. The others stopped and began reversing back up the slip road to stream across the flyover to join Hob's side.

"Of course, you realise where that leaves us," said Hob.

The rucksack squeaked in reply.

"Exactly. Sandwiched between the jam sandwiches."

The rucksack gave a mournful squeak.

"Which is exactly what we want," said Hob.

The rucksack gave him an "Are you mad?" look.

"Of course," said Hob. "Once we've got them all on this side of the road we do our Armco hopping trick one more time again and get out of here!"

Hob and his rucksack looked behind them and saw a long line of jam sandwiches, three abreast to block the auto route, trailing after them.

They looked ahead and saw more blue flashing lights getting into position.

"This is why I am the Horsepower Whisperer and you lot are the *Terminal Murrain*."

Hob screeched to a halt, this time not bothering to save his tyres. He jumped out again and lifted the front of the car over the crash barrier but then it became very windy very suddenly.

The helicopter had descended to put one of its landing skids on the roof of the Mondeo.

Hob pulled with all his might and, despite the pilot's skill, managed to get the car over the crash barrier but it did delay him a little. He dropped the car more heavily than he might have done otherwise and leapt at the helicopter as if to pull the pilot out of his cockpit. The pilot wisely rose out of Hob's reach but that was all Hob needed to get under way again. The only thing was that pulling up by the crash barrier were all the pursuing police cars. Police marksmen jumped out to line up as if they were at a shooting gallery and Hob was the target.

Hob was already breaking the speed limit again by the time the first volleys were fired. His faithful Mondeo shuddered under increasingly heavy impacts as bullets tore into it. Glass fell into the car and vital fluids began to drip onto the road. Then they began to pour out. The bodywork became perforated all down the driver's side as Hob twitched in the driver's seat under countless hits. The car sagged as its tyres were shredded and bullets wrecked its fuel injection system. Airbags deployed and fuel poured out of a ruptured tank. The engine stuttered and died and the car ground to a halt.

Hob kept as still as the bullets would allow, with his hands on the steering wheel at ten to two.

Gradually the firing stopped and the police began to approach. The nearest one came up to Hob's window and stooped to look in at him.

He was very surprised when Hob turned his head and pointed a long thin object at him.

Hob was not entirely surprised that this provoked more bullets but he was taken aback when the other police mowed down the officer who had approached. As he struggled to emerge from his burning car under the renewed hail of bullets, he stared at the dark grey ooze that spread out from the policeman's body.

He found he was pinned against the Mondeo but, almost imperceptibly at first, the gunfire dwindled. Several police officers had been hit by ricochets but the rest were running out of ammunition. Hob began to point at the police with what many of them took to be his weapon but, when they realised their own bullets bounced straight off him, the firing stopped entirely and Hob spoke.

"So," he began, "what have we here?"

He glanced at his instrument.

"Just as I thought. Fish fart never lies. A completely zero reading on the spirit level."

The police didn't answer. They just stared at him.

"I've got an idea," said Hob. "How about if you lot just let me go? You could put all this down to a display of high spirits," and he waved the spirit level at himself. The needle on the gauge swung round to its maximum reading and Hob quickly moved it away again. "Whoops! Don't wanna break it!"

Sirens had been progressively getting louder and now the other batch of police cars arrived, having travelled the wrong way up the autoroute under the guidance of the helicopter.

Hob tucked the spirit level away and idly picked up some spent bullets as a pair of policemen approached with a pair of handcuffs. They hesitated when they came up to him and when they moved to put the cuffs on him Hob threw the old bullets at them with deadly flicks of his wrist.

The firing began again as their bodies hit the road. Hob struggled to retain his balance and leaned into the barrage with increasing menace as he took awkward steps towards them, moving jerkily like a Harryhausen puppet, standing upright through sheer force of will. Then a heavy calibre weapon hit him on the helmet at short range and flung him into the air where he span round many times, parallel to the ground. This made it difficult for the police to hit him and what bullets did find their mark bounced off wildly in all directions.

At last Hob descended to the ground like a tired frisby and when they saw he was down the police increased their rate of fire, pushing Hob along the road as if they were flushing him off the highway with a fire hose.

"Stop shooting me!" he shouted, but they took no notice. He scrabbled with his hands and tried to dig in his heels but he couldn't find any grip.

They swept him along until he wedged up against the foot of a pillar supporting the bridge over the autoroute. Flakes of concrete burst around him as they peppered the pillar with bullets. Hob jiggled about under the fierceness of their fire and three of the armed police fell from bullets that had ricocheted. The police nearest the bridge had to dodge falling masonry and firing abated slightly while they leapt out of its way.

Hob fumbled with a scrap of red material he pulled from his pocket, but then the police resumed their firing and he almost dropped it. He was knocked off balance again by a rifle grenade, and part of the bridge collapsed but out of the dust and debris Hob rose again. The police tried to keep him down with renewed fire and Hob twitched and shook wildly as if in the grip of some gigantic terrier worrying him to death.

But Hob had at last got his hand inside the scrap of red material. It was a puppet of a little man dressed completely in red. He wore a cape about his shoulders and had a pair of horns on his forehead. He had a pointy, black beard and instead of hands he had oven gloves. In these he held a small trident that was black and enveloped in a shimmer of heat haze.

"Glove?" Hob said to the puppet as bullets slammed into him. "Glu-uh-uh-uh-ve? Glove. Ni-ce Gl-uh-ve."

The Glove turned his head to Hob as the Horsepower Whisperer jerked less rapidly. The police were running out of ammunition. The Glove nodded at Hob vigorously and brandished his trident.

Hob pointed to the police with his other hand.

"You see-ee the na-ah-sty police uh-over the-ere, Gl-uh-ve?" he asked as the last few shots hit him.

The puppet turned to face the police, shook his trident at them and turned to Hob again.

"Gl-uh-ve? Glove. Nice Gl-uh-ve. Destroy them!"

The glove took off from Hob's hand and tore into the police. He zoomed through their chests and dark grey fluid splashed over the tarmac. Then The Glove streaked up towards the helicopter like a heat-seeking missile made of felt.

Hob looked in disgust at the grey blood of the soulless ones scattered around him. He took a few steps forward to examine this phenomenon but was careful not to be stained by it. A fireball erupted above him and the helicopter fell like a stone, the stumps of its rotor blades spinning idly, to crash beyond the shattered abutment of the bridge.

It was suddenly much quieter.

Hob stood up slowly and looked around him. He retrieved his furry dice and rucksack from the now blazing Mondeo and looked for The Glove, who was whizzing to and fro in excitement, having done Hob's bidding, revelling in his animated state while he could.

"Glove? Glove. Nice Glove."

Hob patted out the flames on his rucksack and then noticed some more on the shoulders of his jacket.

"Well," he said, "it's been a funny old day."

The Glove hovered around him like a jet propelled survivor from some metaphysical Punch and Judy show.

"Good work, Glove," said Hob. "I thought they'd never run out of ammo."

The glove nodded vigorously and brandished his trident.

"You did well, Glove."

Hob opened his rucksack. There were many muffled squeaks, and the sides of the backpack were crumpled by whatever Hob kept inside. He delved inside until he was up to his shoulder in it even though the rucksack was scarcely deeper than his forearm. After feeling around for something, Hob found what he was looking for and withdrew it. It was a small, yellowy red stone that glowed dully in the direct sunlight of day and smoked slightly.

The Glove fluttered around Hob in excitement.

"Here you are, Glove. Nice Glove. Your favourite. Fresh brimstone."

Hob held it out enticingly between the thumb and forefinger of his left hand and The Glove took it from him and began to feast, making small appreciative gestures.

"Plenty more where that came from, Glove. Glove? Nice Glove."

Hob held out his hand and The Glove settled on it. They looked at each other for a moment and then Hob said, "Nice Glove. Good Glove. Steady now. Be calm. Let me just clean your trident on this uniform. Bloody hell! You little bastard, you're almost incandescent! You have done well today. Be still now. Cool down. Time to rest," and slowly – gently even – Hob neatly folded The Glove up and replaced him in his jacket pocket.

Hob peered into the flames of the burning car, reached into them and pulled out a distraught gremlinne.

"Shush," he said softly. "It wasn't your fault. I don't want you to die. I'm Nick Hob. I am Old Weird Wheels himself, the Metal Guru, the Repossession Man, the Crypto-Engineer, the personification of Malign Weirdness, the Grand Whizz-Herd and Master of the Engine Henge, the Lord High Prince of Rock'n'Roll. I am the Horsepower Whisperer and Soul Trader. I build cars and bikes. We'll soon find another one for you to play with. Now dry your eyes my dear. We've places to go and things to see."

The gremlinne smiled up at him tearfully. Hob opened a pocket of his rucksack and tucked her inside. Then he put his arms through its straps, hoisted *Nosferatu* back onto his shoulders and strode off, this time away from the autoroute.

CHAPTER 15

When he returned from delivering his car to the testing station, M Cadvare found another immediate-response message on his office terminal. As he complied, his wireless connection to his wrist watch clocked him out of flexi-working time again, and he began to wonder how he would ever make up the shortfall. Then he saw who was calling him.

Inspector Gris.

"Ah, M Cadvare," said the commodity inspector, even before he'd fully appeared on the screen. "I've been trying to contact you."

"Yes. I'm afraid I had my mobile switched off."

"I notice that you live at La Place de Lors."

"That's correct."

"Do you know anything about non-conformist activity in your apartment block?"

M Cadvare counselled himself to keep quiet, and stood by to look as surprised and innocent as he could in the circumstances.

"No, I don't," he replied.

"You would be amazed at what transgressions I come across in my line of work."

"I can't imagine what people get up to these days."

"That may be no bad thing, M Cadvare. Too much imagination is undesirable."

M Cadvare shook his head and smiled sadly. "I really wouldn't know."

"The fact is," said Inspector Gris, "we have found some vegetarians living there."

"Vegetarians?" M Cadvare answered, in genuine amazement.

"A whole family of them."

"I thought they died out years ago."

"Not entirely," went on Inspector Gris. "There are still some who breach our most fundamental directives. They can't understand that agricultural resources, of which they claim to be so fond, are bred for our consumption. If we don't consume them, there is no justification for their existence."

M Cadvare made the non-committal grunt that he had practised for such occasions. It communicated a lack of interest and insufficient intellect to appreciate such ideas.

"Of course, it's unlikely a single family could do much damage to our agricultural policy but the volume of the transgression doesn't make any difference. It's the principle that matters. As a transaction auditor, you will no doubt be pleased to hear that the renegades have been sent for Re-education."

M Cadvare did his best to appear pleased. Re-education meant a visit to the Product Planning Blocks in the middle of Mourion. He'd never known anyone who'd received Re-education but he was convinced that it involved terrible things.

"Of course, we would have flushed them out soon enough. That's what I wanted to talk you about. La Place de Lors is approaching the end of its design life. It will soon be unfit for purpose and in contravention of the latest amendments to the Standard of Living Directive."

"Really?"

"M Cadvare, you are going to be re-housed."

"But La Place de Lors has only just been re-decorated," replied M Cadvare in a tone that might easily have been construed as anti-consumerist. "H-h-how old is it?"

"Nearly twelve years old. Technically, it's still within its product life cycle but technology and consumer expectations have overtaken it in so many respects. Your re-location has been taken care of. You will be re-accommodated on the site of the old cathedral at Lille. I'm sure you can't wait to move. You may have noticed that the air conditioning in La Place de Lors has been faulty for some time."

M Cadvare had indeed noticed. It was he who kept sabotaging it. He had been convinced by the presence of an additional filter that certain pacifying chemicals were being released into the rooms at night to make him and his neighbours more pliable.

"I would advise you, M Cadvare, to be especially vigilant for any non-conformist behaviour, either by your neighbours or yourself. We must do everything in our power to bring these transgressors to justice."

M Cadvare nodded.

"The opportunity to undertake spot checks of all relocated households will also be taken. I am sure that you will be found compliant in every respect."

"Of course," said a voice. M Cadvare assumed it was his own.

"You will be pleased to hear that I shall be conducting your home visit myself. When would it be convenient?"

"Oh, anytime except Thursday."

"Next Thursday it is then. *Au revoir*, M Cadvare."

"*Au revoir*, Inspector."

CHAPTER 16

As a tree shrew, Kevin Mullins was an outstanding success, even though, initially, a lifetime at the top of the food chain did not equip him with the junglecraft necessary for survival somewhere near the bottom. Kevin lacked all the basic instincts that every other tree shrew enjoyed so, to begin with, the cycle of re-incarnation occurred very rapidly. Gradually, he managed to string it out a bit but it still took several generations before he adapted properly.

Of course, several generations in tree shrew terms amounted to far less than a single human lifetime but that was one of the things he started wondering about as he ate half his own body weight every day. Just how old was he? A switched on tree shrew might live for a couple of years at the most if they were nervous enough to avoid being chased, killed and eaten. Kevin had to really concentrate to get anywhere over eighteen months because the fascinating flora and fauna were so distracting. He began to measure his incarnations in seasons rather than years. Life expectancy was completely the wrong term. Death expectancy was more like it.

By Kevin's reckoning he was minus 65 million years old and counting. Downwards. Or was it upwards?

He never found a flaw in God's administration of the afterlife. For instance, he was relieved to never find himself in tree shrew heaven, for he imagined it to be a very crowded place full of creatures who, after a short, ephemeral burst of life, found themselves in an eternity of paradise. Occasionally he caught glimpses of tree shrew angels, regarding him rather wistfully, but that was as close as he ever got.

Kevin made the most of it. He could have found the compressed cycle of birth and death rather tedious but it made him feel extremely alive. Of course, his fellow tree shrews, who lived and died without the certainty of re-incarnation, must have felt even more alive. They were certainly going to spend longer dead.

He found antediluvian slugs and snails far more appetising than he'd ever dared hope and he developed a particular fondness for honey ants, not as personalities in their own right, but as a special gourmet tree-shrew treat.

In between birth and death he felt very fit, which he put down to plenty of regular exercise and eating sensibly. He never had any aches and pains, either, but then tree shrews rarely died of old age. Predation typically intervened.

But Kevin was clearly a tree shrew apart. His intelligence and memory often enabled him to predict what was going to happen next and this made such an impression on all the other tree shrews that they treated him with reverence. Kevin was uneasy about this, being on speaking terms with God Himself, and if he did foresee something or work something out he was powerless to prevent or encourage it. Often he was hailed as a prophet and even if he acted stupid, he became top tree shrew.

This then offered the embarrassing prospect of romantic entanglements with female tree shrews. However, Kevin did not find them at all attractive even if his fully functioning male tree shrew body did. He always felt that, in his position, there would be an uncomfortable degree of bestiality about exercising his *droit de seigneur*. He also knew that the characteristics his admirers found so impressive would not be passed on to any offspring but his behaviour only convinced them he was a self-deprecating, living tree shrew deity and added to his attraction.

Kevin remained determined not to succumb to their dubious charms. No matter how tame, they were all still shrews.

He devoted himself to his studies. He lived, died and was re-born during a series of fascinating epochs. The monsters of the post-nuclear Pleistocene were far worse than anything he'd modelled in pre-Armageddon plasticene, probably due to lingering radioactivity from his late lamented time capsule.

However, evolution bumped along pretty much as he'd hoped it would. He derived a certain joy when predators become extinct but better ones had a habit of evolving to take their place. But he was proud to discover that as nature invented a better predator, it also invented a better tree shrew. And the tree shrews got better and better until they were tree shrews no longer.

Over the millennia, Kevin felt himself diversifying. Improved voice boxes endowed him with a wider range of calls and he was able to sample a number of ecological niches featuring prehensile tails, rudimentary tool making and a great deal of mutual grooming.

In a kind of evolutionary parody, whenever he died he reverted to his duffel-coated human form. It was as if his human nature was asserting itself over whatever primordial species he'd reluctantly been part of. And the sensation of being human, even the ghost of one, filled him with pleasure.

He was no longer surrounded by dinosaurs spiralling up to heaven but giant possums and pygmy horses, marsupial dogs and sabre-toothed cats. The duck-billed mammoths and the feathered snakes were a bit of a surprise but the music and the swirling colours in the wheels of life were reassuringly familiar.

Thanks to his human nature, Kevin still ascended faster than what might be regarded as less evolved creatures, but soon he slowed for the slip road that bypassed the afterlife. Shortly he would loop back the way he'd come. The other creatures would overtake and leave him behind as they went straight on to heaven and Kevin would float as if at the zenith of some almighty spiritual Ferris wheel.

Soon he would plunge headlong back to earth to be re-born but first the dreadful, beautiful music would pause sickeningly. The spokes in the colour wheels of life would flicker and Kevin would see the bright lights coming at him again, this time from above. As they tore past him towards the earth that they had once inhabited, a hot oily smell billowed over him and the music would surge into a climax as the shadows of turning spokes flashed over him.

Behind the headlamps of their motorbikes and motorcars, reptilian eyes met his, ancient and all-knowing, as they encircled him. The sound of their motors being wound up to their rev limits added to the music, which was no longer that of souls in ascension. The spirits of the most fantastic creatures ever created, the highly evolved road-racing dinosaurs, had descended from heaven to look at him.

Kevin saw many allosaurs and tyrannosaurs among them. They were smaller, with better proportioned limbs that allowed them to grasp handle-bars and steering wheels. They looked incredibly fierce and wore open face helmets because their noses were so big. Their scuffed leathers might have been their own hides or those of even thicker-skinned creatures that they'd killed. Their legs were long and powerful and they wore baseball boots squeezed over enormous feet with claws poking out at the toe and heel. They evidently possessed a degree of cunning about which an allosaurus could only have fantasised, and regarded Kevin in silence as if too angry for words.

Others looked like scaled down brontosauruses, squeezed into studded leather. Often their skulls were so oddly shaped that their crash helmets had to have holes in them to let their bony protuberances stick out and some had holes in the tops of their helmets to allow them to breathe properly. For others, crash helmets were unnecessary. And, often, there wasn't any need for body armour. They leaned out of chromed hot-rods, draping powerful arms over the doors, or peered through their windscreens through grotesque tusks and horns, their snouts perilously close to the glass even though they had their seats right back.

There were also more lightly built creatures that reminded Kevin of oven ready eagles with malevolent stares. They had large eyes and long beaks full of tiny sharp teeth that suggested a diet of fish, and often rode small, light bikes or cars that bucked and wriggled as if they, too, were alive. One or two had wings where a fringed leather jacket seemed more appropriate. A few had a great sail down their backs, like a dimetrodon, so might not have been dinosaurs in the strictest sense at all but something earlier. Whether dimetrodon or spinosaur, they still seemed to hold Kevin responsible for their extinction.

Particularly fascinating and repulsive was the two headed iguanodon. During early incarnations, Kevin had seen one or two of these twindividuals before, but never one riding a dirt bike. These creatures were theoretically possible if their egg was damaged at an early stage in its development but Kevin suspected that radioactivity from his time machine might have caused a mutation. The poor creatures seemed to be constantly arguing about directions and criticising each other's driving, and barely noticed Kevin.

The dinosaurs all had claws and scales. Some even had fur. But there was another thing they all had in common – their brooding, silent menace. As he stood before them, ghost to ghost, yet-to-evolve-human-being to pre-maturely-snuffed-out-dinosaur, they would just look at him as they circled, their wheels never still as they popped wheelies and stoppies and did burn outs, adding the squeal of tyres to the soul music.

Only when Kevin's life cycle was about to resume would one of them speak, and it was always a different one.

"Kevin Mullins – we're going to get you, when the time comes."

It wasn't their avowed intention to "get him" that bothered Kevin. Or their disquietingly oblique reference to "when the time comes". It was the fact that they knew his name.

Then they would all grin and the music and colours would fade as Kevin fell back to earth to experience the debilitating shock of birth once again.

CHAPTER 17

A Mercedes limousine pulled into an underground car park in Fanfaronade, the high-rent district of Mourion. It stopped at the foot of an elevator shaft, and a cloaked figure alighted and walked up to the doors, which opened without prompting. The doors closed and the Mercedes went off to park.

When the elevator reached its destination high above the grey city, it stopped, not in some lobby but in an elegantly appointed apartment.

And if gazelles had walked in high heels they might have been able to ape the walk of the woman who emerged, but only after many years of deportment classes at expensive alpine finishing schools.

Madame Bland threw her cloak over the back of a chair and in the same fluid movement stepped towards a bookcase. Hidden behind some glossy fashion magazines was a thick, cheaply produced collection of adverts, printed on yellow paper in a strange language. She stuck the bundle under her arm and went to a safe behind a picture. Inside the safe was a big, old book that needed both hands to carry, and she set it down carefully on the dining table.

She treated it with reverence. It was a beautifully illuminated manuscript, *The Red Book of St Bendix*, and reflections from the gold paint danced on her face as she turned the pages. She paused at the dedication; she could never be certain that she'd translated it properly. She believed it read "To Queen Aby of the Conformorians. Who saw to it that I was made lame and without whom None of This would have been possible."

The Red Book of St Bendix was written in an archaic form of Anarcho-English, the same language as that used in the yellow-paged list of adverts. Since both books were banned throughout Euphobia, she'd been unable to ask for help in translating either, and there was still much that she didn't understand.

From the little else that she had gleaned about St Bendix, she knew Queen Aby had ordered that certain tendons in his legs were cut to prevent him from escaping. That way, she and her hordes could arm themselves with the products of his diverse metalworking skills and become invincible. However, St Bendix had other ideas and still managed to escape. During his captivity, his skills had grown and he subsequently used them to ensure victory against Queen Aby for "the once and future King."

Madame Bland wondered how a king could be "once and future." As well as St Bendix the Great Smith, the Once and Future King had been supported by a powerful sorcerer, and the combination of chivalrous leadership, engineering and magic had obviously proved overwhelming for Queen Aby and her hordes of Conformorians, for they had been wiped from the face of the earth.

Madame Bland also wondered how St Bendix had earned his beatification. He was clearly a master of very dark arts. In his *Red Book*, he boasted that his hands were black from dabbling in forbidden knowledge. He also quoted contemporary Dark Age views that his success could only have been obtained by selling his soul to the devil himself.

Madame Bland had always had an interest in forbidden knowledge. There was something about *The Red Book of St Bendix* that made the authorities in Post Unification Euphobia fear it deeply, and their determination to hide it, on the grounds that they were protecting their citizens from it, only increased Heidi Bland's determination to get hold of it.

They also feared the yellow pages of *The Piston Wheel*, and she was beginning to understand why, for she had found a link between the two.

As St Bendix had put it in his opening chapter of his Red Book, "Secrets have been revealed to me and I do not wish to take them with me to the Grave. This Manuscript is My Confession. I hope it illuminates the Darkness that is to follow and provides Answers to Questions for those that seek viz. how much one can tune a Morris Minor without breaking the standard Halfshafts and how to recognise a Horsepower Whisperer when riding in the Wild Hunt."

Heidi Bland was not sure what a Morris Minor was. From her knowledge of folklore, she knew about morris dancing but, from the illuminations in *The Red Book of St Bendix*, Morris Minors looked like jelly moulds. She presumed a halfshaft was some obsolete kitchen implement shrouded in the mists of time. She'd also wondered if Morris Minors were musical instruments that one tuned with a halfshaft, which could be broken if you tuned them too much. Somewhere in the following pages she hoped to find the answer.

However, she had found some clues in *The Piston Wheel*, which was a vast listing of miscellaneous wants and offers printed on yellow paper. This was nowhere near as old as *The Red Book*. It was fairly recent if the date was to be believed, had originated in a temperate archipelago that was not on any map and was written in a modern version of the same language as that of St Bendix, although nouns were not endowed with capitals as in the old Germanic fashion. The print was easier to read, too, even if it did smudge and come off on her fingers. *The Piston Wheel* was illustrated with strange images, and she had been flicking through it when she had found a drawing that she recognised as a Morris Minor. It was at the head of a whole column of Morris Minors that were advertised as prepared for the Wild Hunt, and as she had compared the drawing with that in *The Red Book*, some text leapt out at her from *The Piston Wheel*.

Someone was advertising unbreakable halfshafts for Morris Minors, guaranteed to withstand 300 kilowatts.

As for the Horsepower Whisperer, the illustration in *The Red Book of St Bendix* was much easier to understand. Heidi Bland knew enough about art to know that this figure could only have been drawn from life. The monk who had drawn it had endowed the Horsepower Whisperer with a disreputable quality that attracted and repelled in equal measure. In one illustration, the Horsepower Whisperer had plucked out one of his eyes and was holding it up with an outstretched arm so that he could get a better view. In another, he was balancing a huge wooden crate on his finger, nonchalantly spinning it on a corner.

From the accompanying text, she had also learnt about his involvement in a new sort of Wild Hunt – new, that was, some fifteen centuries ago.

Yet this was the man she had just seen walking along the autoroute carrying a wooden crate.

There was a noise in a nearby room.

Heidi slammed shut *The Red Book of St Bendix*. She picked it up with *The Piston Wheel* and quickly hid them in the safe.

Then she ran silently into the bathroom and began to pour a hot bath. Still with her customary grace, she grabbed some things from the bedroom and locked the bathroom door just as one on the far side of the main room began to open.

"*Bonsoir cherie*, I'm home."

Commissioner Bland was back from running Euphobia.

CHAPTER 18

M Cadvare finished work that afternoon and made his way by public transport to the vehicle testing centre where he had left his personal transportation device. The dirty, uncomfortable bus dropped him outside the test centre and engulfed him in black smoke as it pulled away, but at least he was greeted by the news that his car had passed its roadworthiness test.

"Thank goodness," he said.

"Follow me," said the technician, and he led M Cadvare into the workshops to be shown a mangled pile of wreckage.

M Cadvare's jaw dropped. "What happened?" he gasped.

"It passed. The crumple zones demonstrate optimum deformation with no significant indication of corrosion. It was very well designed for its era."

"Era? It was only three years old. Aren't you going to mend it?"

"Mend it?"

"Of course!" shouted M Cadvare. "It was in perfect condition when I brought it in here!"

"It was in good condition," the technician corrected him, "not perfect."

"I want it repaired!"

M Cadvare suddenly realised he was exhibiting non-consumerist behaviour and beginning to attract attention.

The technician looked at him as if such an outburst could only come from certain individuals who shouldn't be at large within Euphobian society. "It will be expensive," he said.

"How much?"

"Nearly as much as a new one."

The technician-salesman guided him out of the workshop and sat him down in the showroom where he was assailed by prices and specifications. M Cadvare had hoped to keep his car going indefinitely but it was now clear that the latest roadworthiness test wouldn't allow this. He remembered a subversive internet site that claimed the greatest environmental impact of a vehicle occurred during its manufacture, but his search engine couldn't find it any more. It couldn't find the one proposing the preservation of Euphobia's transport heritage, either. That sort of thing prompted him to use his transaction auditor skills to amend his connectivity log.

In response to a question, M Cadvare heard his far-away voice say, "What payment options are available?"

Choice was the curse of modern Euphobia. There were so many choices but each one was hardly any different from the others. And although M Cadvare had exercised his choice rather more than he was allowed, he had still been prevented from living the life he really wanted.

The technician-salesman explained the payment options and beamed at him.

A money spider abseiled off M Cadvare's spectacles.

None of the trim options appealed. The various interior colour schemes would make him feel even more of a prisoner. He wished he could design his own, express his own needs and wants with cheerful colours and materials that were traditional and hard wearing, as opposed to those that would breach another fashionality directive in eighteen months' time.

He took off his glasses and gazed out of the showroom windows and noticed someone wearing an old-fashioned crash helmet walking by with an enormous wooden crate on his shoulders.

"Do you mind if I have some time to choose?"

"Certainly," said the technician-salesman and he left M Cadvare alone to attend to another victim.

Outside, the crate carrier had stepped up to the windows and was peering in, regarding the personal transportation devices with extreme distaste. M Cadvare couldn't see his eyes because they were covered by a black visor, but he felt that he had caught his attention for the crate-carrier was mouthing "No!" at him.

"What have I done?" wondered M Cadvare aloud, as he opened the colour chart. He looked up and caught the eye of the crate carrier again. "How am I going to get out of this mess? I'd give anything not to have to do this."

To his surprise, the crate carrier was suddenly overwhelmed by the weight of his burden and the crate hit the ground with a bang, breaking the paving slabs under it.

M Cadvare dropped his brochure and stared. The crate carrier appeared to have been squashed flat.

"Anything?" asked a voice by his ear.

A figure had popped out of the floor behind him.

M Cadvare turned around slowly.

"You said you would give anything not to have to do this." It was the man from under the crate.

"It was a figure of speech."

"Perhaps, but it was from the heart. I may be able to help."

The stranger took a business card from a pocket of his battered leather jacket and presented it to M Cadvare.

"My card."

M Cadvare stood up and studied the stranger for a moment. His clothes did not follow any obvious fashionality and he spoke with one of the pre-unification dialects. The hand that offered the card had long steely fingers with several notable scars and dirty black fingernails.

M Cadvare took the card and glanced at it. "There's nothing on it," he said.

"Modesty forbids it."

M Cadvare turned it over. "And no address either."

The stranger smiled and shrugged. "I'm never at home."

But something made M Cadvare turn the card over a second time. " 'Nicholas Eldritch Hob,' " he read out. " 'Soul Trader and Holder of Soul Rites.' What odd spelling. 'Horsepower Whispering a speciality.' Pleased to meet you, Monsieur … er, Mister Hob," and they shook hands. "Enrico Cadvare, at your service."

Hob grinned a diabolical grin that defied the conventions of muscles and tendons. "Call me Hob, like everyone else."

Out of curiosity, but mainly a strong desire to escape the focus of Hob's grin, M Cadvare asked, "Er, what exactly does soul trading involve?"

"Well," began His Malign Weirdness, The Grand Whizz-Herd, Crypto-Engineer, Repossession Man and Master of the Engine Henge, "let us say, for instance, just by way of an example, you understand, that what you really, really wanted most of all, in the whole wide world, was to, somehow, escape from Mourion."

"But that's amazing!" cried M Cadvare. "How did you know that?"

"It wasn't difficult," replied Hob. "Let's just say it was a lucky guess. Now then. Suppose you can attain this hitherto impossible dream by trans-ferring to me the rites to something of which you are barely aware and would hardly miss? Under my careful guidance, this neglected part of you would grow to realise its full potential."

"That sounds too good to be true," replied M Cadvare. "You see, I'd have to get out of Euphobia completely."

"What, all of it?"

"Yes. It's all unified. And I don't know where I would go. They have these extradition treaties, you see."

"Who do?"

"The Euphobian Commissioners."

"Okay. Let's just develop my example a little further. Quite by chance, you happen to meet an entrepreneur who can help you leave, not only Mourion but also Euphobia. In addition, he can take you to a place far beyond any direct or indirect jurisdiction enjoyed by these Euphobian Commissioners. In short, in return for some minor consideration, he can grant you your heart's desire."

"My heart's desire?"

"Yes. That which you crave most is within reach at long last."

"Escape from Mourion? From Euphobia?"

"Precisely. Imagine that!"

"That would be wonderful! But where would I go?"

"To Anarchadia."

"Where's that?"

"It's in the Antagonistic Ocean."

"I've never heard of that."

"You wouldn't have. It's not on any map."

"Why not?"

"Because the authorities here don't want you to know about it!"

"And why would they want it kept secret?"

"Because it has no central authority."

Hob suddenly produced a small, long object and M Cadvare instinctively raised his hands into the air as he pointed it at him. Hob grabbed his wrists and forced them down again before pointing the object at M Cadvare. A bubble in a tube on the top boiled and a needle span round to the extent of its gauge.

"Hmm," said Hob. "Just as I thought. Not many like you left around here. How have your spirits survived when those of so many in Mourion have not?"

"Because I've nurtured them," said M Cadvare.

"I take it you don't believe all the propaganda they bombard you with."

"No, I don't."

"Good." Hob's visor swirled in a whole spectrum of blackness, like petrol on water. "But if you don't believe what everyone else tells you how can I convince you that what I say is true?"

CHAPTER 19

A movement outside caught M Cadvare's eye.

Riot vans were pulling up outside and overhead was the sound of a helicopter.

"Oh, how tiresome," said Hob.

"Are they here for you?" asked M Cadvare.

"Mm, more than likely. I've got something in my crate that makes them really cross. And I don't think they like me, either."

"Why not?"

"The clothes I wear? It happens."

"They seem to recognise your crate," said M Cadvare as armed police cautiously approached it.

The technician-salesman returned. "What's going on?" he asked M Cadvare.

"We're under siege," said Hob.

"What? Why?"

"Selling motorcycles from your forecourt."

"But we're not! We never would! They've been banned for years!"

"Have you chosen yet?" Hob asked M Cadvare.

"Er ..."

"Good. I'll just get my crate and let the police know what's happening." He handed M Cadvare a completely black credit card and a completed choice of options. "There you go. Have one on me, Cadaver."

"It's Cadvare, actually," said M Cadvare as the technician-salesman went off with Hob's card.

"That's what I said. Cadaver."

A police negotiator began addressing them through a loud hailer.

"Well, it looks like it's time I fetched my crate in. I shall have to be more careful where I leave it in future. I'll be back in five minutes."

Hob walked up to the glass windows and slid one of them back.

Something made M Cadvare retreat further into the showroom.

The police negotiator told Hob to put his hands up and police marksmen motioned at him with their guns.

Hob just picked up his crate.

There was another, more hurried, warning from the loud hailer and the police opened fire.

Hob came flying backwards through the windows and glass burst everywhere.

M Cadvare dived for cover. He found the technician-salesman cowering under a desk nearby. He grabbed Hob's card and the registration documents and he crawled away from the shooting to the back of the showroom and into the vehicle despatch area, where personal transportation devices stood, apparently ready to go. Stray bullets whizzed overhead as he opened the wallet of documents and keys to check his registration number.

There was another intense burst of firing and the sound of more glass shattering. M Cadvare quickly wriggled on his stomach to what was apparently his new car.

He opened the door and the firing ceased.

Suddenly it was very quiet. M Cadvare crouched on his haunches and looked back towards the showroom. Nothing seemed to be happening, so he stood up and sat in the driver's seat.

It was curious but as he shut the door, the tailgate opened and his personal transportation device sagged on its rear suspension.

The nearside door opened and Hob got in beside him.

"What are you doing?" M Cadvare demanded.

"I'm coming with you."

"But I saw you shot!"

"Or rather you're coming with me. Yes, I was blasted through a window and will admit to being a little winded by their first salvo. Stop gawping and drive!"

"But what happened back there?"

"They ran out of ammunition."

"You mean we're free to go?"

"Of course."

M Cadvare glanced in his rear view mirror. Hob's wooden crate was in the load area and the tailgate was open.

"We can't go far like that."

"You're right. But let's just get out of here. I'll tie it down later. I hope the fumes don't bother you."

"Fumes?"

"Oh no. Don't say this thing's electric!"

"Of course it's electric!"

Hob dropped his rucksack in the foot well. "I hate domestic appliances."

He closed the door behind him, opened it again, closed it, opened it and closed it again.

"There!" he said. "Look at that! When you close the door, the inside light goes out! We might as well be sitting inside a fridge!"

"They all do that," said M Cadvare but he activated the motor and they moved silently out of the despatch area.

"Bloody hell," muttered Hob. "I've met toasters with more charisma. Even the loud pedal doesn't work! This thing can't even sing the Song of the Machine – all it can do is hum!"

"I'm not disagreeing with you," said M Cadvare. "I believe they make them especially dull on purpose."

"Fortunato," said Hob, addressing his rucksack, "if you ever breathe a word of this to anybody, I will make things extremely uncomfortable for you, do you hear?"

His rucksack squeaked in reply.

"A little faster than that please," said Hob, pointing at the speedometer. He lowered the window and something red flew into the car.

"What the hell's that?" shouted M Cadvare.

"Mmm? Oh this little chap here is The Glove. Glove? Nice Glove. Good Glove."

The Glove eyed M Cadvare suspiciously.

"You have been busy today, haven't you? No! No! Stop that! Not him! He's our driver! Yes, yes, I know, usually I'm the driver but not now. Glove, this is M Cadaver. Cadaver? Say hello to The Glove."

"Hallo, Glove."

"Good Cadaver."

"It's Cadvare, actually."

"Cadaver, friend," Hob told The Glove. "Friend. Now then, I suppose you'll be wanting some treats because you have been so good today."

The Glove nodded furiously.

"Okay. Let's see what's in here." Hob delved into his rucksack and the sulphurous smell filled M Cadvare's personal transportation device, nearly making him retch.

"Por!" he said.

Hob was careful not let M Cadvare see what was inside his rucksack.

"Ah, ah, ah. Not so fast, Fortunato. Get back, there's a good soul. Here you are, Glove. Nice Glove. Good Glove. Your favourite! Hot brimstone."

The Glove jabbed the brimstone with its trident and zoomed to the rear of the personal transportation device to eat it.

"What's Fortunato?" M Cadvare asked, glancing at Hob's rucksack.

"He's a who, not a what. Fortunato is one of my most prized souls. He's the most highly spirited of the lot, and many other Soul Traders tried to bargain for him."

"But you were successful."

"Yes. I knew exactly what he'd sell his soul for. We were both skirrows, after all. Y'know. Wild Hunters. We made a deal, and for many years Fortunato was unbeatable in the Mille Miglia, the Targa Florio and the Carrera

Panamerica."

"What are they?"

"Road races, pale imitations of the Wild Hunt."

"And what's the Wild Hunt?"

Hob stared at M Cadvare.

"You've never heard of the Wild Hunt?"

"You should assume I know nothing of your world."

"It seems I should!"

"So what is the Wild Hunt?"

"Have you really never heard of it?"

"No. Never."

"Bloody hell! In this hot-rod forsaken place I can believe it!"

Hob looked thoughtfully out of the window. Every now and again he would point his spirit level at people as they passed, to confirm his darkest suspicions.

"The Wild Hunt is the eternal chase. It's older than man – much older – and is the foundation of Anarchadia's economy. I don't suppose you've ever heard of the Horsepower Wars, either."

M Cadvare shook his head.

"The Wild Hunt is a primeval celebration of speed and power, skill and luck, science and magic, a tribute to the quick and the dead and a simple evocation of the joy of the chase."

"I think I understand," said M Cadvare. "So what happened to Fortunato?"

"He splashed his brains out in the Mille Miglia. Nobody could ever say for certain why, but the upshot was he came into my possession. If he'd lived a little longer he could have been the greatest Wild Hunter of all time – after me, of course."

"So now, he's in your rucksack."

"Yes, along with the rest of the *Terminal Murrain*. We still ride in the Wild Hunt. Our appetite for the chase is undiminished. The dead have much less to lose, especially those who have sold their souls."

M Cadvare kept his eyes on the road but out of the corner of one of them he watched Hob feeding smoking yellow stones to his glove puppet.

"Pull over," said Hob, "and I'll secure the tailgate."

"Okay."

"Now then," Hob said to The Glove, as they pulled up, "have you had enough?"

The Glove nodded and stretched its little arms over its head.

Hob pulled his rucksack shut.

"Do you want to go sleepy bo-bo?"

The Glove nodded slowly.

"Okay, Glove. Nice Glove. What have we learnt today? Hmmm? Cadaver friend! Yes! That's right!"

M Cadvare sighed.

"Say night-night, Cadaver."

"Good night, Glove."

"No! Don't touch him! He's still hot!"

"I was only going to stroke him."

The Glove belched sulphurously.

"Don't touch him. Just say goodnight to him."

"Night-night, Glove. Sleep tight, hope the bedbugs don't bite."

The Glove waved at M Cadvare.

"Hey!" said Hob. "You're really good at this. He likes you!"

"Is that good?" asked M Cadvare as Hob folded The Glove up and tucked him gently inside his leather jacket.

Hob got out and began to tie the tailgate down with a piece of string at the end of which was an ancient conker.

"I'll say. You didn't see what he did to those armed police back there. Did you?"

"No."

"Put it this way," said Hob, taking his seat again, "they won't be troubling us again. Now then. What were we talking about before we were so rudely interrupted?"

CHAPTER 20

Commissioner Bland was disappointed but not surprised to find that he couldn't see his beautiful wife. He was a very lucky man to have her on his arm at so many official functions. It was just a shame that she would take baths at the most inconvenient moments. He could only assume it was all part of her glamorous image. Against all the odds, some of her glamour had rubbed off on him and the Standard of Living Directive.

"An odd thing happened at work today, *cherie*," he said through the bathroom door.

"Mmmm?" came a luxuriating reply.

"Yes. A very strange thing."

He took off his tie to appear more relaxed, but without the accoutrements of his office he felt awkward. His wife wasn't able to see him being casual so he put it back on again and immediately felt more comfortable.

"What do you know about a wheeled cross?"

"Pardon?"

"What do you know about a wheeled cross?"

"Why do you ask?"

"The police are searching for a man who has the symbol of a wheeled cross on his leather jacket. As soon as I heard his description, I thought of you and your interest in symbology."

Madame Bland was not only interested in symbology. She seemed to be interested in anything that made him and his colleagues uncomfortable.

"Wheeled crosses were often carved in stone," came a voice over some soapy splashing. "Some historians believe that by joining the arms of the cross to form a wheel, it was less likely that the arms would break. Others claim they are pre-Christian pagan carvings, subsequently adopted by the early church, while the figures, knot work designs and other motifs contain allusions to long-lost knowledge."

Commissioner Bland broke out into a cold sweat.

"How strange then," he managed to say, "that a wheeled cross should appear here, in modern Mourion."

"On the back of someone's jacket did you say?"

"Yes. On the back of a jacket belonging to the most wanted man in

Euphobia."

The splashing stopped.

"Most wanted?"

His wife was beginning to sound the way he felt.

"Yes, easily the most wanted, and in such a short space of time, too."

"What's he done?"

"To begin with, he is an illegal immigrant to our trading block. When the officials at the airport tried to do their duty he attacked them viciously. We're still piecing together what happened, but there were undoubtedly a number of discorporations."

Too late he checked himself. For some reason, his wife objected to the official term for death, but constant use during the working day made it difficult for him not to use it at home.

However, she didn't complain but seemed to be listening intently to him from her bath.

This was also strange.

Madame Bland rarely took an interest in his work although Commissioner Bland made a point of telling her about it. He didn't know how she spent her time during the day. It seemed to him that with their separate rooms and itineraries they lived completely separate lives and their paths only really crossed when they attended an official function together.

"He doesn't show up on security cameras, either."

"What did you say?"

Commissioner Bland repeated the non-conformity.

"Is he invisible then?"

"Oh no. There's just a blank space where something is obviously happening. You can tell by the way other people react that they can see him. He just doesn't show up on the cameras."

"Has the equipment been checked?"

"Yes, but there is no sign of any malfunction. He's proving easy to track but difficult to arrest. He's carrying a crate containing a motorcycle."

"A motorcycle did you say? They're banned in Euphobia, aren't they?"

"Of course."

"How do you know what's inside?"

"It showed up on the luggage X-ray machine. Our border officials attempted to confiscate it."

"It must have been a very small motorcycle for this man to carry it around," suggested Madame Bland.

"No, it's quite large. It makes him a trafficker of contraband as well as a murderer. There was a subsequent incident along the autoroute."

There was a clatter and a splash, as if someone who had just received a tremendous shock had dropped her hairbrush in the bath.

"A man answering his description entered into a fire fight with traffic police."

"Have they taken him into custody?"

"No. That's what's puzzling everyone. He's still at large but it shouldn't be hard to track him down. He's also carrying a rucksack," went on Commissioner Bland, relishing his wife's unusual interest. "That also passed through the X-ray machine but the operators seem to have gone mad. They insist that it contained 'souls'."

There was another loud crash from beyond the bathroom door.

"Heidi? Are you all right?"

"Oh, yes. Just me being clumsy."

Madame Bland was never clumsy.

"We've taken statements from surviving witnesses and put together a description. He conforms to no current fashionality. He's wearing a leather jacket, a crash helmet of all things, and some strange form of tinted visor. Those were banned even before motorcycling was outlawed."

"Souls, did you say? A rucksack full of them?"

"Yes. That's how the witnesses described it. I don't know how they recognised the X-ray of a soul, but ..."

Commissioner Bland paused.

He sometimes suspected his wife of having a soul. Often, when she thought he wasn't looking, she could be disturbingly vivacious, but up to now he had been content to let her contribute to his career.

"Pigling?"

Commissioner Bland winced. He hated her nickname for him. It seemed far below his dignity to have one.

"Have you been able to identify him?"

"He had no passport, but on the passenger list he was recorded as Mister Ernest Pilchard. Of course, it could be an assumed name."

"Undoubtedly. Do you think you will catch this man?"

"Most certainly. He is quite distinctive."

"Not where security cameras are concerned."

"No," Commissioner Bland conceded. "We are confident of an arrest, however, even if one has not occurred so far. There's one other curiosity about him."

"Oh yes?"

"On his jacket beside the image of this wheeled cross was the lettering *Terminal Murrain*. Any idea what that means?"

"Yes," said Madame Bland. "I think I might know who this man is. But you're not going to like it!"

CHAPTER 21

M Cadvare drove as inconspicuously as he could with a packing case sticking out of the back of his brand new personal transportation device. He expected the police to appear at any moment but they didn't and the further he travelled the more the likelihood seemed to decrease.

He felt he should be terrified and wondered why he wasn't. Despite his sinister *mien*, Hob seemed to understand him better than anyone he'd met before. He'd also dangled before him a very tempting solution to his problems.

Hob sat slumped to his left, still waving his spirit level at passers-by.

It wasn't long before M Cadvare was able to predict the reading the spirit level would make.

"Where are we supposed to be going?" he asked Hob, eventually.

"Anarchadia," replied Hob.

"I can't see it on any direction signs."

Hob snorted. "You won't. It lies to the north-west of this continent."

"So how do we get there?"

"It's easy enough for me and even easier for you. You just have to sell me your soul."

"I hope you won't be offended, Hob, if I tell you how hard it is to believe you, much as I would like to."

"Soul Traders don't lie," Hob assured him.

"Then are you just deluded?"

"Ah," said Hob. "I'm glad you've brought that up."

"What?"

"The question of sanity."

M Cadvare gave Hob a wary look. "There's nothing wrong with my sanity."

"Of course not, but you would say that, wouldn't you?"

"I'm not the one who's obsessed by imaginary archipelagos!"

"You're the one who wants to go there!"

An uneasy silence fell in the electric car.

Hob toyed with his spirit level.

"Tell me some more about Anarchadia," said M Cadvare.

"As archipelagos go, it's on the large side. It's a cradle of art, engineering, sedition and libertinism. It's a hotbed of subversion and freedom of thought and action. It's dangerous and vital. It has no central government, which is why central governments fear it so. It's abundant in mineral wealth, almost to the extent of embarrassment, and is a free trade area. Its principal exports are automobiles and motorcycles. Its principal imports are also automobiles and motorcycles. It has enjoyed a couple of centuries of peace and prosperity thanks to the Horsepower Wars."

"What are the Horsepower Wars?"

Hob regarded him with a mixture of distaste and pity. "Do you really have no idea?"

"I think I might."

"Okay. Let's hear it."

"Are they battles fought with engines?"

"Very good!" said Hob. "They are also the basis behind of the Anarchadian economy."

"But I can't prove your claims about Anarchadia using official sources."

"No, I'm afraid you can't."

"So I'm unlikely to sell you my soul to you if I don't believe you can get me there."

"In time, I'm sure you will believe me. But how much time do you have, Cadaver? How long will these commodity inspectors take to destroy your soul utterly?"

"Until this Thursday."

"Thursday next? Blimey! You haven't got long."

"The commodity inspectors are paying me a home visit. It's just routine. They're moving me into a new apartment. The only thing is, I've filled up my old one with contraband items that breach the Standard of Living Directive."

"A perfect incentive to leave," said Hob.

"Hob? I've seen you gunned down by police, carry a heavy crate as if it's weightless and talk to an animated glove puppet but – no – no matter how hard I try, I cannot believe in Anarchadia."

"I know," said Hob. "A whole temperate archipelago that has been distroduced from the rest of the world."

"Distroduced?" echoed M Cadvare but Hob just carried on.

"It's too much of a leap of faith, isn't it? Besides. Realising your dreams can be a daunting prospect for certain types of personality. You've lived under the yoke of the commodity inspectors for so long now that to do anything else terrifies you."

"That's not true!"

"I think it would be easier for you to stay here rather than live the life you pretend you want. I think you would be happier without your soul. I think it is cruel to let your spirits remain intact!"

"Now wait a minute!" exploded M Cadvare. "I've been living an alternative lifestyle under the commodity inspectors' noses for years! I've taken incalculable risks and evaded capture! I've managed to realise a little of an impossible dream against incredible odds!"

Hob was laughing like a drain at him.

"So! Come with me to Anarchadia!"

"But I can't believe you."

"Tell me this, Cadaver. Why should I lie? Soul Traders always tell the truth because the truth has more power than lies."

"Hah! Honest Hob, Soul Trader!"

"Yes exactly! Truth is what makes souls more interesting. It does things to them."

"What's to stop you just taking my soul?"

"Nothing at all, but it would be worthless. Souls that are freely exchanged by their own volition can be extremely valuable."

They drove on in a thoughtful silence and then Hob said, "Here's another proof that Anarchadia exists. You can understand me because I am a Horsepower Whisperer even though I don't speak your language."

M Cadvare frowned. "Yes you do! You speak Euphopranto very well. It sounds a little strange but then you're not from around here."

Hob grinned. "I'm actually speaking a form of Anarcho-English to you. I have to if I'm going to create horsepower. And English is the *lingua franca* of the world so you shouldn't be so surprised we can understand each other. But haven't you noticed the subtle idioms and nuances to my speech, the odd word or two whose meaning is clear although you've never heard them before?"

M Cadvare considered this for a moment "Like distroduced?"

"What?"

"Distroduced. You used it just now."

"Did I? What d'you suppose it means, then?"

M Cadvare thought for a moment and then said, "Is it the opposite of introduced?"

"Nearly. Anarchadia has been distroduced from the rest of the world for centuries, kept apart and kept unknown. Yet the very existence of the verb to distroduce proves that Anarchadia exists!"

"I don't see why it should. You could've just made it up."

Hob laughed. "I admire your spirit, Cadaver!"

M Cadvare locked his arms straight as he held the steering wheel.

"I have to get away. The commodity inspectors will discover my non-compliances against the Standard of Living Directive."

"Cadaver, you can't stay here."

M Cadvare did not reply.

"How would it be if Anarchadia really did exist? How would it be if you found that you could live the life you wanted?"

"I would be delighted," said M Cadvare.

"You would be a changed man."

"I would lose my soul."

"Eventually."

"Eventually?"

"You would still have your soul for a while."

"How long would I have it?"

Hob shrugged. "For as long as it takes."

"For what?"

"For your soul to develop. You have the essential spirit. That much is clear, for the fish fart never lies."

Hob showed him the boiling spirit level again.

"Is that really a fish fart?"

"You'd better believe it. You don't want to be around when somebody drops one of these."

"Wow!"

"So we have established that you excite the fish fart more than you should!"

"Thanks!"

"And for your soul to be really valuable to me, I have to tell you the truth. Soul rites don't work unless there is credibility. The transaction changes them, does things to them. And those that are robbed have no provenance. But before I fully take possession, souls should live as they have never lived before. For you, Cadaver, that will not be so difficult. You haven't been living – you've just been existing."

"That much is true."

"You're stronger than most but you can't last out for ever. Constant monotony and frustration exact a heavy toll on any soul."

"It seems to me that my soul is already lost, one way or another."

"It's really a question of what is best for your soul. What would happen if the commodity inspectors caught you?"

"I would be Re-educated."

"What does that involve?"

"To be honest, I don't know, but those that have been Re-educated buy what they are told to buy and do what they are supposed to do."

"An ideal society," mused Hob.

"Somebody's ideal," said M Cadvare, "but not mine."

"Re-education must account for the extreme soul erosion that I'm detecting. I've never come across anything like this before, until now, here in Mourion. If you stay here, Cadaver, before long, you won't agitate the fish fart like you do now. You'll be made to fit in."

"I've lived here all my life, but never felt at home."

"That's because you are being deliberately changed into soulless entities of flesh and blood in the name of economics and political and social expediency."

"And you really won't want my soul until we arrive in Anarchadia?"

"Not until long after we arrive. You've got a lot to learn, many blebs to acquire."

"Will I ever be able to come back?"

"Why would you ever need to?"

"I need to think about this for a while."

"Don't leave it too long. I'm starting for Anarchadia today. Badness knows there's nothing here for me. I need to find some fuel for my bike."

"We can travel in this thing. They're in use all over Euphobia. You'll fit in perfectly."

"But, my dear Cadaver, we don't fit in!"

"But we'll look like we do. Do you want the police to shoot at you wherever you go?"

"Now you speak sense, old chap. I can't tell you how annoying it is to be jiggled about by hot lead."

"How do you avoid being killed?"

"I can change my molecular density. It's a Horsepower Whispering thing."

M Cadvare's knuckles glowed white as he gripped his steering wheel.

"I would like my soul to survive and not be destroyed. I cannot see a practical means of escape so I'm going to try this impractical one with you. But if Anarchadia does not exist, I will expect you to have no claim over me. My soul has to grow much more before the bargain is met."

He turned to look at Hob and was surprised to find the Soul Trader grinning at him.

"Very well. The consideration must pass from the promissor to the promissee. Deal?"

Hob spat on his hand and offered it to M Cadvare.

M Cadvare spat on his and shook Hob's hand. "Deal."

CHAPTER 22

As tree shrews evolved into primates and diversified into different varieties, Kevin found himself alternating freely between one genus and another. This was confusing, and he took a long time to adjust to each new ecological niche.

One day, as he sat with other members of his troupe of proconsuls, he spotted one with wings.

Kevin immediately blamed the fermented fruit they were eating, but then the flying proconsul landed next to him and said, "Kevin Mullins?"

"Yes?" he replied with a gulp. The only creatures to have called him that for millions of years were the Hell's Dinosaurs from Hell.

"God would like a word."

"Oh. Right. What? Now?"

"Yes."

"Okay. How's He getting on?"

"Oh, fine. Would you come with me, please?"

Before Kevin could say or do anything else the flying ape had stepped off the branch and pulled him off after him. Instead of crashing to the forest floor below, they began to rise gently upwards.

"What's happening?" cried Kevin.

"Hmm? Oh, you've just died. Again. That's you down there. See?"

"But what happened to me?"

"You had too much alcohol and fell out of your tree."

"I don't believe it!"

"It's true. I'm sure there's a joke in there somewhere."

"Who are you, anyway?" asked Kevin, sobering up rapidly.

"Me? I'm just an angel."

"An angel. Of course."

"Haven't you seen any of us before? You must have done, when you were a lemur. You lot were so impressed you evolved especially to mimic us."

"I think that's a little unrealistic," began Kevin. "The flying lemurs evolved to exploit an environmental niche. No, really. It wasn't because they saw you and thought, 'Hey, that looks fun, I wonder if I could do that?'"

"With your background, I wouldn't expect you to agree with me."

Kevin scrutinised the angel. "You don't like evolution, do you?"

"My opinion is neither here nor there."

"You've been talking to Sophia, haven't you?"

"Maybe I have. Very sensible Supreme Being, Sophia. God's a very lucky chap."

"Yes. I find it odd, though, that in my culture nobody seems to have heard of Her."

"I don't, not if She doesn't want anything to do with evolution. This is very much God's idea. Sophia feels sorry for us."

"What? For the angels? Why?"

"Because we have to evolve in tandem with the life forms we represent. I wish there was a fast-forward button on this experiment and you lot would hurry up and develop into proper pan-dimensional beings."

"I beg your pardon?"

"Pan-dimensional beings. You know. Existing throughout all the levels of creation. I expect that's what you lot'll become. One day," the angel added, doubtfully.

By now, they were miles above the earth, looking down on everything. Somewhere, close at hand, strange and beautiful music was playing. It sounded as if it might be being played backwards, and made Kevin's fur stand up on end.

"Here we are," said the proconsul angel. "Monkey heaven."

He nodded towards some magnificent gates made out of bamboo. Beyond them was what appeared to be some extremely joyful apes, monkeying about. There were some old tyres for them to swing on that God must have salvaged from the remains of the dinosaur civilisation, and lots and lots of bananas. Any resemblance to a zoo was purely superficial. The gates and un-seen boundaries of monkey heaven were there not to keep the monkeys in, but the bad things out.

"What are these pan-dimensional beings like?" asked Kevin.

"Oh, just like any other sort, really."

"What! How many of them are there?"

"Oh, loads. Look. I've got to go now. That's going to be your heaven, over there."

He gestured towards the same set of Pearly Gates Kevin had seen mill-ions of years earlier. They still looked brand new.

"If you wait over there, God should be along in a minute."

"But you can't go! I want to know all about these pan-dimensional beings!"

"Some other time," the proconsul angel shouted back as he left. "There's no rest for the wicked. Ha ha."

"Wait a minute! One last question. Are you my guardian angel?"

"Don't be ridiculous! What would you need one of those for?"

CHAPTER 23

"Why have you stopped here?" asked Hob as M Cadvare pulled into the car park of a shopping centre.

"This is Cachet," said M Cadvare. "It's a *centre commercial*."

"Catchett," said Hob, reading the name off a sign in his strange accent.

"I need some things before we set off for Anarchadia."

"No you don't," said Hob. "We can get them when we arrive."

"Okay," said M Cadvare. "I'll just withdraw all the money from my account and we'll get out of here."

He walked up to a hole in the wall machine and started to fumble for his card.

Hob strolled up beside him and leant against the wall. "There's really no need for that, either," he said.

"It's my money, I worked for it and I'm taking it with me." M Cadvare tapped in his security number. "Oh dear."

"What is it?"

"It's a message from my bank manager.

"What's it say?"

" 'See me.' "

"Oh dear. Oh well. At least someone's taking an interest in you."

"Taking interest from me, more like," muttered M Cadvare, flicking through the options. "Look! They've zeroed my status and frozen my account!"

Hob looked around them. "Sounds like they're closing in," he said quietly. "Why don't you try that card you've got of mine?"

M Cadvare scrabbled through his pockets and found the shiny black credit card that Hob had handed to him back in the showroom. Was this part of the deal they'd just struck?

"Go on," urged Hob. "Put it in the machine."

"It might eat it."

Hob laughed. "I doubt it."

The machine asked for a number.

Hob thought about it.

"Don't you know the number?" asked M Cadvare.

"Of course I do," said Hob and he tapped in three sixes.

"Ah, no, it's got to be a four digit number," said M Cadvare.

"Something's happening," said Hob, peering into the slot.

Suddenly the screen blinked out for a moment only to be replaced by a new one. Instead of small boxes indicating keys to press for a balance statement or a new cheque book, there was the face of a striking young woman with pale skin, piercing blue eyes and jet black hair.

"Electra!" said Hob. "The Ion Lady!"

"How may I serve you, oh Lord of Darkness?"

Hob grinned at her. "Oh, the usual, my dear. Untold wealth."

"At once, my lord," replied Electra, "but couldn't you be a little more specific?"

"Okay, Cadaver, how much do you want?"

"I only want what's in my account."

"How much do you have, Electra?"

"Think of a number and double it," Electra replied.

"What currency do you want, Cadaver?"

"Do you have any Ecus?"

"Ecus? What the hell are they? Sneezes?"

"Euphobian Currency Units."

Hob snorted contemptuously. He turned to Electra. "Do you do Ecus?"

Electra considered his request and then said, "There is a way, my lord."

The machine began to chunter away to itself, giving off blue and purple flashes that made M Cadvare stand back.

"It is done, my lord," she said, and the machine began to disgorge vast quantities of nice, new Ecu notes.

"Would you like a receipt for this transaction?" she asked them.

"Yes, please," said M Cadvare.

"No, thank you," said Hob.

"Would there be anything else, my lord?" asked Electra.

"What about a statement?" asked M Cadvare.

Hob gave him a withering look. "Bean counter!"

"I'm sorry, serf of my lord, but a statement is impossible," said Electra.

"Hah!" snorted Hob.

"Hey! I'm not the serf of your lord! I'm not the serf of anyone yet! Am I?"

"You were born into bondage as part of the Euphobian Consumerist Community," said Hob.

"These puny till slips are not big enough for the number of digits in your account, my lord," explained Electra.

"Do you need a cheque book?" M Cadvare asked Hob.

"Cadaver, you used the Engineer of Spades to pay for your mobile fridge. Didn't you see the effect it provokes upon all major retailers?"

"No. I was watching you being shot at."

"Watch closely the next time we buy something."

"Will that be all, my lord?"

"Yes, thank you, Electra. Come along, Cadaver, let's take the money and … walk away nonchalantly."

CHAPTER 24

"Ah! Kevin! I am glad you could come." God shook him firmly by the hand. "Oh! I say! Opposable thumbs! Well, well! Whatever next!"

They sat down on a handy cloud, God dressed in His dungarees and a work shirt, with a pencil behind His ear, and Kevin Mullins still as a recently deceased proconsul.

"How are you keeping, Kevin?"

"Oh, not so bad, thank You, er … God."

"Just one moment."

God returned Kevin to his old shape, complete with duffel coat.

"How's that?"

"Sheer bliss! I usually revert to human form when I ascend."

"Yes, I know. And you get buzzed by gangs of speed-freak dinosaurs, too."

"How did You know about that?"

"Well, I am God, you know."

"Sorry. I forgot."

"I know about all the things in heaven and earth plus a few in between. From the way they treat you, I'm convinced that it was better to re-incarnate you than have you helping Me up here."

"Oh definitely, Your, er, Almighty."

"Just call me God, Kevin."

"Sorry God. I just don't want to appear over familiar."

"Why ever not? Don't you feel comfortable when you meet your Maker?"

"Yes, I feel very much at peace."

"It's the dungarees," said God. "Sophia runs them up for Me especially. Just imagine how you would quake if you met your Maker when He wore an enormous beard and great flowing curtains of cloud."

"Sophia shows tremendous empathy towards life forms products of Your experiment," observed Kevin.

"Yes," said God, not sounding completely omniscient for a moment. "She does, doesn't She? Anyway, I've summoned you today because there's something I want to ask you about the state of the primates."

"Goodness!"

There was an awkward silence. God looked past Kevin. "Oh no, they've done it again." He seemed to be looking at the Pearly Gates.

"Is anything wrong?" asked Kevin, following His gaze.

"The cats have got into heaven again."

Through the Pearly Gates, Kevin could see a group of cats patiently waiting to be let out.

"How did they get in there?"

"Well, they can get in and out officially now because I've put a cat flap in the gates."

Kevin had to look quite hard to spot it but, in the bottom left hand corner, was a small wrought-iron rectangle on its own hinges with the word *Puss* formed out of strip metal.

"Were they getting in before?"

"Yes and I will admit that I'm rather puzzled by it. It seems that I'm not the only being that moves in a mysterious way My wonders to perform."

"And then I suppose they want to be let out again."

"Exactly. Well, sort of. Watch this," and God got up and opened the gates for the cats.

The cats didn't move. Some looked curiously through the open gates while others looked up at God as if to say, "Whatever did You do that for?"

God shut the gates again.

"Now they can come and go as they please, although they shouldn't really be in there at all. D'you know what I found the other day? A Turkish Van cat swimming around terrorising the pygmy coelacanths! In their aquarium!"

"Strange creatures, cats," remarked Kevin Mullins, as a tabby emerged through the cat flap and walked past them to sit with her back to them.

"Yes," said God. "The angels adore them because they have nine lives. It makes their work in cat heaven so much easier. Puss, puss, puss!"

The tabby cat turned around and looked at God. She smiled at Him with her eyes, gave him a double-eyed wink and sauntered off in the opposite direction with a question-mark tail.

"I think Sophia's rather fond of them, too," went on God, "although She'd never admit it. Now then, Kevin. I, er, gather you've just had a little accident."

"I have? Oh. Yes. You're right."

"I heard you're a tipsy monkey who's completely out of his tree!"

"Yes," chuckled Kevin, "I suppose that's true."

God slapped His leg with mirth and wiped His eyes.

"Oh dear," he gasped. "Laughter really was one of My better creations. I knew I was onto a winner the moment I took it off the lathe. But to the point. It has come to My attention, Kevin, that the apes are at a very significant stage in their development. They're spreading throughout the world quite rapidly and there is extraordinary variety among them."

"That's true. At the moment I can be anything when I'm reborn. It takes a bit of getting used to. Despite their genetic similarities, behaviourally each one is completely different."

"That's what I wanted to talk to you about," said God. "Which variety of ape do you think will evolve into humans?"

Kevin thought carefully for a moment.

"I've been wondering about that myself, God, but it's still too early to tell."

"Do you really have no idea?"

"No. You see, the fossil records are – or were, or, rather, will be – incomplete. There is no obvious link between humans and the apes, although we know that there must be one."

"That's a shame. Of all the fossilised remains you must have found, the one We could really do with is missing."

"Will be missing."

"Quite. Oh well. In that case there's nothing else for it but for you to continue to be re-incarnated on a rotational basis until there is a definite sign of divergence from the apes. Then We can start using this place," and God waved an arm towards the Pearly Gates.

"It's a fascinating stage in evolution," said Kevin.

"I must admit that things haven't turned out quite as I had expected," said God. "Oh, not as a result of that affair with the exploding time machine," He added hurriedly. "I mean despite that. This experiment has turned out to be far more interesting than I'd ever imagined."

"But Sophia still thinks it's a waste of time."

"Yes. She also claims to have discovered a design fault."

"Really?"

"Yes and, do you know, I think She might have a point."

"Whatever is it?"

"She says any creature with a combined air and food pipe is fundamentally flawed. But you've managed all right and so have many other animals. It can't be so serious. I've analysed the number of components with a redundancy matrix and concluded that with a rudimentary reflex system this is indeed the most elegant arrangement."

"Did You explain your findings to Sophia?"

"Yes."

"What did She say?"

"She says She doesn't need Her intuition to tell Her that My set up is nuts." God stood up. "Oh well. I think I'll leave it in as a double bluff against divine infallibility."

"Have You ever heard of Henry Heimlich?"

"No?"

"You will one day. I think Your set up will be okay."

"Thanks Kevin. As soon as you recognise *homo sapiens sapiens* among the anthropoids do let Me know."

"Right. Er, how will I get in touch?"

"Oh, that's not so difficult if you really need to," said God.

"Of course. So my foreseeable future will consist of more aping around?"

God laughed. "Yes, I suppose so. You know, Kevin, I like you. I like you a lot."

"Thanks, God."

"I'm so glad you evolved."

"I expect You say that to everything in creation."

"I do, that's true. But I mean it! Humour is such a relief."

"Do other creatures experience it?"

"Oh yes, some more than others. I've tried to get the angels to use it more often, but they seem very grumpy at the moment."

"Why's that?"

"I'm not sure. Anyway, I must get on. Thank you for your time. I'll just summon Beelzebub."

"I beg your pardon?"

"Beelzebub. The angel who brought you up here."

"Oh," said Kevin, thoughtfully.

"Hallo, God," said Beelzebub.

"Could you escort Kevin back down below for me, please?"

"Certainly, God."

CHAPTER 25

"Let's have a closer look at this domestic appliance of yours," said Hob.

He stooped and lifted the sagging rear end of the car clear off the ground.

"Be a good fellow and wedge some of those shopping trolleys under it, would you?"

M Cadvare fumbled in his pockets, bought the temporary freedom of four shopping trolleys and slid them on their sides under his personal transportation device.

Hob lowered it onto them so that its wheels were off the ground, and lay underneath it.

M Cadvare could not be sure, but he thought that as Hob's back touched the ground, little castors popped out of his shoulders and hips.

There was a hot metallic smell and the sound of bolts being undone and done up at speed, and the wheels of M Cadvare's personal transportation device moved outwards a little more.

"Modifying my car will invalidate the warranty and type approval," M Cadvare told Hob.

"I'm the only warranty you'll need," he replied, emerging from underneath, castors clicking back into his pockets and shoulders.

"Where did you get that?" asked M Cadvare, nodding at what Hob held in his hands.

"It's yours, stoopid. I found it in your engine bay."

M Cadvare blinked, and Hob had it in pieces.

"What is it, er, was it?"

"It's an electric motor. What do you know of electricity?"

"Just the two main things."

"Which are?"

"You can't see it and it hurts."

"I'll tell you another. The Song of the Machine arises from a motor's tune. Every little mechanism sings to itself as it does its job, from the tiniest hinge to the greatest and most powerful locomotive. All have their voice. Create the right conditions, and every machine sings its song, giving notice of its nature." Hob held up the large electric motor that he'd just removed. "All excepting electrical motors, of course. They don't know the words. All they can do is hum."

"That's a shame."

"However, I'm going to learn this one to hum louder!"

"Don't you mean teach it?"

"No, learning it is something else again," and Hob set to work on the dismembered motor, rubbing magnets between his dirty hands and winding copper wire in intricate forms with hands that span in blurs on his wrists.

"Hob?" said M Cadvare, after an interval.

"Ngyeah?" The Soul Trader was weaving an intricate cat's cradle of copper wire between his hands and teeth.

"That motor's bigger than it was."

"Ngyeah. Ngoh what?"

"So it's not going to fit."

Hob managed to give him a sideways glance, despite wearing a dark visor. His teeth flicked up and down in his gums and he waved his arms about. As M Cadvare watched, he saw shapes emerge in the gleaming layers of copper, shapes of men like Hob on motorbikes, and cars with fat tyres and big engines.

"Do not concern yourself on my account, Cadaver," said Hob, as the last strands of copper whipped back into the motor. He pressed rivets into their holes with his bare hands, inserted the bolts that held the motor together and tightened them up with his spinning wrists. He sprouted castors again and disappeared back underneath the car. There were some thumps and bangs and M Cadvare heard him mutter some words. The engine bay began to swell at the expense of the interior space.

Hob re-emerged and lifted the car off the shopping trolleys.

"Cadaver? If you would be so kind."

M Cadvare removed the shopping trolleys, and Hob lowered his personal transportation device back onto its wheels.

"No, don't do that," said Hob when M Cadvare started pushing the slightly bent trolleys back to their chained rows. "Go on, off you go!" he said and he waved his arms.

Nothing happened immediately but then one of the trolleys began to roll cautiously away from them, slowly gathering momentum. At first M Cadvare thought Hob had created a draught with his arms but then the others turned and they all fled in different directions.

"What did you do that for?"

"I have dominion over everything with wheels, and liberate them whenever possible. Come on! We're not done yet!"

Hob pulled a reel of very soft silvery wire from a pocket and dabbed a forefinger on it. Immediately, a blob of molten metal congealed on his fingertip.

"Is that chrome?" asked M Cadvare.

"No, it's solder. There's no means of whispering to an electric motor.

They have the spark of life but no intake or exhaust so they can't absorb my powerful sentiments no matter how clearly I utter them."

Hob opened the door and quickly dismantled the dashboard. He produced the Engineer of Spades and soldered some wires to her.

"I have to use Electra as an interpreter."

Electra appeared on the instrument binnacle.

M Cadvare was deeply impressed but rather surprised to see a small shadow pass in front of her face.

"What was that?" asked M Cadvare.

Hob sat in the passenger seat and cleared his throat "Gremlin? O, gremlin. Show thyself!"

An ugly face appeared from one of the air vents in the dashboard.

"Hallo, my friend," said Hob.

The gremlin climbed out of the vent and bowed.

"Any teething problems?"

The gremlin began to speak quickly in a strange guttural language that Hob appeared to understand. It also mimed, at times violently.

When the gremlin stopped, Hob said, "Splendid. The only thing is I'd much rather you didn't. I know he's been ignoring you and how sensitive you are about that sort of thing, but now I'm here and I'd like you to help me in some modifications. Interested?"

A great grin split the gremlin's features, and he nodded eagerly.

Hob noticed M Cadvare goggling at the gremlin. "Can you see anyone standing on your dashboard?"

M Cadvare nodded.

"Really? That bodes well, very well indeed."

"But my car's brand new!" spluttered M Cadvare.

"All machinery has gremlins," explained Hob. "New ones are no different. While their fresh components are bedding in, gremlins look after them. I suppose your culture regards gremlins as pests?"

"Of course!"

Hob tutted. "That's going to have to change. Gremlins are fine upstanding fellows and fellowettes, but sensitive. Make them feel unappreciated and your machinery will never work."

The gremlin nodded vigorously.

Hob waited.

It gradually dawned upon M Cadvare that something was expected of him.

"Er, hello," he said eventually.

The gremlin made a short but enthusiastic speech.

M Cadvare turned to Hob. "I didn't understand."

Hob reached under the dashboard and studied the wiring. "Don't worry. You've only just discovered you have homuncular vision. Now you can recognise all manner of gremlins, for they are abundant in their variety. This particular gremlin is an electro-gnome unless I am very much mistaken."

The gremlin nodded in assent.

"But befriend your gremlin or gremlinne and your car will sing its song, if it can sing it. Which reminds me."

He delved into his jacket pockets again and gently held out a female gremlin.

The electro-gnome goggled at her.

Hob placed the gremlinne on the other side of the instrument binnacle, where she glowed pink.

"This young lady's car was destroyed by the police," Hob explained to the electro-gnome. "I wonder if you would consent to being her host for this journey?"

The electro-gnome nodded and swelled with pride.

Hob nudged M Cadvare.

"Your so-called civilisation has been in denial about the household spirits for centuries. Have you never heard of these little people?"

"Nothing complimentary."

As Hob rubbed the Engineer of Spades against some wires, M Cadvare turned to the electro-gnome and gremlinne, who were watching the Horsepower Whisperer with interest.

"Sorry I didn't notice you earlier," he said.

The electro-gnome responded in a torrent of hard syllables.

M Cadvare smiled.

So did the electro-gnome and gremlinne.

"I can see you lot're going to get along famously," said Hob. "Trouble's going!"

There was a bright blue flash from his experiments with the wiring.

"Aha! Lights, music, action!"

A tremor ran through the car's frame. The dashboard lit up, and there was Electra, the Ion Lady, looking at them through the instruments.

"Okay, places everyone," said Hob, standing up.

The electro-gnome took the hand of the gremlinne and they made a running leap to dive into the air vent.

"The open road is beckoning and it would be rude for gentlemen like us to ignore it!"

Hob sat behind the wheel and M Cadvare sensed a change. He had a sudden feeling of something gathering pace. Blood thundered in his ears as he stared at what had once been his personal transportation device. He supposed it was now Hob's and quite different from the machine he'd just driven there.

Hob didn't look so out of place any more. Driver and vehicle appeared to be doing more than a hundred miles an hour just standing still.

In slow motion, Hob turned to him.

"Get in," he said, his voice slurred and deeper than usual.

M Cadvare took one last look at Mourion and saw that it was drained of all colours. It was grainy and grey whereas Hob was at the middle of a patch of extra vividness that had already spread over M Cadvare's personal transportation device and was about to embrace him, too.

Getting into the car with Hob was a bigger step than selling his soul, and his feet seemed to be glued to the tarmac of the car park, yet he felt himself shrug off his torpor and take some steps towards the car. As he sat beside Hob, his soul turned over.

He would never be entirely stationary again.

"Okay?" asked Hob, speaking normally again.

M Cadvare nodded. "Drive," he said thickly.

"Trouble's gone!" said Hob.

CHAPTER 26

As Hob drove gently out of the car park, somewhere behind and below them M Cadvare felt huge new reserves of power. As they joined the main road, Hob began to grin.

"Hear that, Cadaver? That's the Song of the Machine!"

"Hear it? I can feel it!"

They were travelling quickly now. White lines flashed by their wheels, and the wind noise, which M Cadvare had never noticed before, rose in volume and tone.

"Are you ready to find out what an enraged domestic appliance can do in the Wild Hunt?" asked Hob.

M Cadvare nodded, and immediately wished he hadn't.

Hob unleashed the forces that dwelt beneath them and sent the personal transportation device into a spasm of twists and turns as they wove in and out of the other traffic on the highway.

"And, behold, the machine *almost* sings!"

M Cadvare hung on. Added to the Song of the Machine was the wailing of its tyres.

"Wheee-he-he-heeee!" said Hob, as they dived into another car park.

"What are you doing?"

"Laying a message in rubber!" replied the Horsepower Whisperer and everything became a blur until they rocketed off towards the exit.

M Cadvare snatched a glance behind them as they sped off. "What did you write?"

Plumes of tyre smoke hung over the car park.

"Have a look."

They joined an elevated highway and M Cadvare looked down to read out Hob's message.

"*Nick Hob wears his tyres with pride.*"

It was written in joined up writing with what appeared to be a four-nibbed pen.

M Cadvare felt himself smile. He'd never had the sensation of travelling this fast before. He was scared but was enjoying himself. He felt as though he was shrugging off a chrysalis of safety.

Hob treated him to several detours. If he saw a NO ENTRY sign he immediately disobeyed it. If they found themselves proceeding in a disorderly fashion the right way down a one way street, he did a perfect handbrake turn, which as any milkman will tell you is extremely tricky in an electric vehicle, and then charged at the oncoming traffic that parted in terror on either side of them. They went around roundabouts in the wrong direction and plunged down steps of pedestrian subways. They were on the pavement for some of the time but, as Hob explained later, that was only because the lights were red.

All of a sudden they seemed to be on the open road, their hot-rodded electric car humming delightedly.

M Cadvare was laughing.

"Drunk with danger, old chap?" Hob asked him.

He nodded and then shrugged.

Hob laughed, too. "Even in Mourion there's hope for us," he said.

"I suppose you ought to be careful," said M Cadvare, sobering a little. "If we carry on like this, the police will stop us."

"I issued a police warning," said Hob.

"What do you mean?"

"I didn't die when they shot me. They'd be foolish to mess with me again."

"Look out, a speed camera!"

"Really?" replied Hob with interest. "Where?"

"We've gone past it now!"

"I missed it!"

"They sense movement as you go by and photograph your number plate if you're going too fast."

"Well, well. What will they think of next?"

"Look out! That was another one!"

"Two together so soon?"

"Yes. People often speed up after them, so the second one is to catch them as they accelerate."

"And the result?" asked Hob, nudging a slower device out of their way with a flourish of their big plastic front bumper. "Everlasting fame as a road-racing hero?"

"No. Certainly not in Mourion. The owner of the vehicle, which in this case is me, is legally bound to tell the authorities who the driver was at the time, which, in this case, is you."

"Ah. I get the picture."

"That remark breaches our humour directives! It's not just the speed cameras, either. You see this?" and M Cadvare pointed to the metallic licence disc on the screen. "We are on a smart highway. This records how fast we are travelling, that is, whether at the premium rate or the standard rate. There is also roadside sensing equipment that monitors our noise and exhaust emission levels. There is a punitive charging regime that extends to fining road users who contravene directives on the use of the highways."

Hob tut-tutted and shook his head pityingly.

"A typical example of the misuse of technology," he said. "What are you worrying for? You could always lie."

"True but they have lie detector tests. And the data from these machines is never wrong."

"Or you could say I was an escaped criminal. Or criminally insane."

"Are you? That would explain an awful lot."

"No, but I can always make believe. I know. I'll steal this machine off you. How about that?"

M Cadvare considered this. "It might work," he said, as they flashed past a police patrol car parked on its ramp by the motorway.

"I mean, it's not as if you'll be taking this thing with us when we set off for Anarchadia, is it?"

"No, I suppose not."

"Besides, Electra can take care of any electrical doo-dad."

"Perhaps you're right. And even if the authorities caught up with us … "

"Which they won't."

"We'd still have sufficient wealth to pay any fine."

"So this photograph," said Hob. "Do they send it to you in the post with a form of endorsement? With a blurred image of your car and some astounding velocity printed in the corner?"

"You make it sound like a trophy."

Hob smiled. "Yes, I do, don't I? Unfortunately, I never seem to photograph very well these days."

He adjusted his rear-view mirror so that M Cadvare could see his reflection – except that there wasn't one.

Where Hob sat, the seat was empty.

M Cadvare gaped.

"I'm afraid I don't show up on photographic plates, celluloid, magnetic tape or this new fangled digital stuff," Hob explained airily, waving his hand at yet another set of strobing speed cameras. "Bloody hell! For a smart highway, this road's really bumpy!"

"That's the sleeping policemen."

"What?"

"If you slowed down a bit you might be able to see them. They're traffic calming measures."

"Don't be ridiculous! You can't tame the Wild Hunt! Traffic will do as traffic does! These so-called smart highways of yours …"

"They're nothing to do with me."

"Do they have smart traffic cones?"

"Yes. They monitor traffic at road works and record any instances of speeding or careless or dangerous driving."

"Well, there's a whole load of them up ahead."

"Oh, no. Roadworks!"

Hob did not appear to be decelerating.

"Quick!" cried M Cadvare. "Slow down!"

"Oh, make up your bloody mind!"

They rapidly approached a column of stationary traffic but instead of hitting it Hob ploughed into the traffic cones that closed off the outside lane, sending an orange and white plume into the air.

"They can't be very smart if they don't get out of the way," said Hob.

They flattened a sign that said REPAIRING WORN OUT CARRIAGEWAY and another that said SORRY FOR ANY DELAY. There wasn't any road-mending machinery and nobody had dug anything up. As they flashed by, there was no sign of any activity, although they did send a portable chemical lavatory cartwheeling into the sky.

"Careful!" said M Cadvare. "There could have been someone in that!"

"See anyone doing any work?"

"No. But then you never do."

They burst through another barrage of cones and re-joined the rest of the traffic.

"Very shy creatures, road pixies."

"Road pixies?" echoed M Cadvare. "I don't think they're road pixies. Are they?"

Hob thought about this. "Maybe not in Mourion," he conceded. "I can't imagine they'd mend a smart highway. They're the lares and penates of the highways, the gremlins of the open road."

M Cadvare noticed that the electro-gnome was standing on the top of dashboard with his nose pressed to the inside of the windscreen. He was surrounded by a light blue glow.

Hob checked his mirrors. "Well, well. Look behind us."

A row of other personal transportation devices were following their path through the roadworks.

"This is how the Wild Hunt begins! Mourion's got some spirit left!"

He glanced at his thumb and took a hand from the wheel to show M Cadvare. It looked like a cactus.

"I feel a pricking of my thumbs. Something souped up this way comes."

Hob checked his mirrors again.

"Wow! Now that's what I call an automobile! Looks like we're going to have ourselves a proper race," and M Cadvare turned to see a pink Cadillac bearing down upon them.

CHAPTER 27

The tyres of M Cadvare's transportation device squealed as Hob sawed away at the steering wheel. They weaved in and out of the slower-moving traffic, which either pulled over in panic or joined them in a quietly humming procession. Barging through the smaller cars, the pink Cadillac dipped on its compliant suspension, heeling from side to side like a racing aircraft carrier.

Hob grinned even more now that he had a proper car to race against, and M Cadvare could hear the difference the silken roar of the Cadillac made to the Song of the Machine.

Hob's rucksack clambered up M Cadvare's legs to sit on his lap and peered out of the window with unseen eyes.

Hob took a short cut through a pedestrianised area and turned into a *zone artisanale*. The Cadillac wallowed after them, and, although it didn't get any closer, they couldn't lose it, either.

"Have you seen who's driving that thing?" asked Hob.

M Cadvare looked behind them. At the wheel was a striking young woman in gull-wing spectacles and a white coat. "Is that hair real?"

"I don't think so," Hob replied, twirling the steering wheel between practised hands. "I think she might be wearing a crash helmet with its own crumple zone."

They left the industrial estate, and Hob gunned the personal transportation device to somewhere above its maximum design speed.

Behind them the Cadillac came out of the curve in a power slide, all four front tyres pointing at them, its tail partly hidden by tyre smoke.

"That's no ordinary Cadillac," said Hob.

"But thanks to you this is no ordinary personal transportation device," replied M Cadvare.

"Yeah but that thing's different in a different way."

"How do you mean?"

"My thumbs tell me."

M Cadvare glanced behind again and saw the gremlinne scurrying from one suspension tower to the next, apparently adjusting the suspension as they travelled.

Then he looked ahead. "Look out! Traffic jam!"

There was a flash and they were suddenly through.

"What happened?"

Hob chuckled. "We went through a fost. Just a small one. It's like squeezing a partially deflated balloon. Constrict the Wild Hunt and it bulges out elsewhere."

"The others are through the fost, too."

"Where are we?" asked Hob.

"We're approaching the centre of Mourion. The traffic will be getting heavier and slowing down."

Hob suddenly made a turn and they screeched into another shopping precinct. They bumped down some steps and entered a pedestrian underpass. Shoppers flattened themselves against the walls or scampered out of the way as they tore past.

At the end of the tunnel, Hob looked in his mirrors and shouted triumphantly, "Look behind us!"

M Cadvare saw that the Cadillac couldn't turn into the tunnel. It was too long.

They shot into a small garden and bumped across flowerbeds and through ornamental bushes. Hob chose another underpass and accelerated up the exit ramp. They became airborne at the top and landed on a dual carriageway, much to the consternation of the oncoming traffic.

"Oops!" said Hob and exited quickly by a slip road that led onto the autoroute. "I forgot you drive on the other side on the continent."

"I think we've lost her," said M Cadvare, "although we've still got company."

Behind them, a long column of devices defied the oncoming traffic and struggled to keep up with them.

"Good," said Hob.

They rattled through Mourion's back streets and business parks in a switchback course and caught glimpses of their remaining pursuers threading after them.

M Cadvare kept expecting to see a road block ahead or flashing blue lights behind them but Hob's police warnings seemed to be working.

Hob suddenly sat upright and looked at his hands. "I feel a pricking of my thumbs! Something souped up this way comes!"

From a side turning, the pink Cadillac nearly rammed them. Hob wrenched the wheel to one side and they squeezed by, keeping in front of the Cadillac's chrome maw by a wheel.

"She knows some good short cuts," said Hob. "Electra!"

"My lord?"

"Can you get us some more speed out of this thing?"

Electra glanced away at the inside of the dashboard. "I regret I cannot improve upon that which you have already wrought, my lord."

"Sing to me O machine," muttered Hob, "of sparks of power, fields of force and positive ions. Electric songs and power tunes have no nobler bearings when your magnets spin from raw attraction and joy soars from their keepers."

"We're pulling away!" exclaimed M Cadvare.

"Potential difference blossom forth. Deliver this promise, make the change. Earthed lightning flash across these hubs, seek the ground beneath my wheels! No room for static!"

"Voulez volts?" suggested M Cadvare and he immediately felt rather foolish for saying it.

But Hob turned to him and grinned and said, "Nice try. Irresistible resistance! Force the revolutions! From pole to pole in lines of flux, apogee of magneto-galvanics – zap me with your plasma!"

Electra laughed and sparks danced from the sharpened points of her ice-white teeth while her shoulder-length black hair stood on end.

The electro-gnome became incandescent and cavorted with the gremlinne on the dashboard.

Hob's rucksack jumped up and down on M Cadvare's lap and a giant invisible hand began to sweep them ahead of the Cadillac.

"The Cadillac's way behind us now!" cried M Cadvare. He glanced behind them. "And I can barely make out the personal transportation devices."

"Good. Let's see if she finds another short cut like she did last time."

M Cadvare twisted round in his seat to watch. He felt strangely safe, as if protected by a bubble of speed. His personal transportation device hummed willingly and he rested his chin and arms on *Nosferatu*'s crate. It was still tucked under the device's tailgate and it felt good to have it behind them.

"How are your thumbs?" he asked Hob.

"Calm again. And yours?"

"Mine are okay. Why shouldn't they be?"

"The Song of the Machine creates a certain resonance. The reverberation of compression and rarefaction of exhaust sound waves makes the thumbs of sensitive souls itch."

M Cadvare frowned. "Maybe I *can* feel something."

"Where are we?"

"The other side of Mourion. We're not far from my apartment."

"So what?"

"So I can get my passport."

"You don't need your passport to get to Anarchadia."

"Are we going there by fost?"

"No. We'd need a big one and a whole lot more internal combustion engines."

"The Wild Hunt?"

"Exactly. See any proper cars behind us, ones that breathe and excrete?"

"No."

"I borrowed one earlier at a filling station but the cops messed it up."

"You won't find many inside the city centre. They get charged so much by the smart highways."

"They're not smart highways, just avaricious."

"So if we're not to get there by fosts, I will need my passport."

"Passports are not keys to freedom. They are the shackles to your geographical accidents of birth."

"I won't be able to get out of Euphobia without it."

"Nobody can stop us!"

"All the same, I would like to have mine with me. It's proof of who I am, at least."

"Der! My point exactly." Hob laughed but turned off the autoroute.

"Proof is important to me. I'm a transaction auditor, remember?"

"Your passport proves nothing but your Euphobian identity. It's just a token of your life here. And that life never suited you."

M Cadvare fell into a sulky silence. He'd never thought of his passport as forbidden fruit. Now that it appeared to be one, he wanted it more than ever.

"But we'll go to your apartment," Hob said suddenly. "I want to see why its contents fill your commissioners with such horror. Which road should I take?"

M Cadvare pointed. "That one."

Hob followed his directions and they drove along a quiet road between grassy banks that had been erected as sound breaks in the days when traffic had contained more Mondeo-like devices and had made more noise. Beyond them lay a desert of suburbia, housing estates and dormitory enclaves.

Hob overtook some dawdling transportation devices, most of which fell under the spell of the hum of their machine, and began to chase after them.

"Uh-oh!" said Hob.

"What?"

"It's my thumbs again!"

"Mine too! Look out!"

Hob forced their device off the road and they shot over a green embankment. They landed on an unoccupied cycle path that twisted in landscaped whimsy around a lake. Behind them the embankment exploded as the massive Cadillac ploughed clean through it.

"By the long-nosed pliers of St Bendix! Where did she come from?"

Again, they were saved by a narrow underpass that was too small to let the Cadillac enter.

"This is getting a little tedious," said Hob.

"She knows where we are," said M Cadvare. "We can run but we can't hide."

"My lord?"

"Electra?"

"You may be interested to know that our pursuer is not abiding by the usual laws of physics."

"What?" With a flick of a wrist, Hob brought them back onto a proper road.

"She's creating temporal anomalies in order to catch up with you."

"I can't say that's a comforting idea. How does she know where we are?"

"I'm surprised you ask me that, my lord," Electra said, a little haughtily.

"It's the way the traffic joins us in the Wild Hunt, isn't it?" said M Cadvare.

"Can she get ahead of us?" demanded Hob.

"Theoretically, my lord. I think that's what she's trying to do, but so far you have been too quick for her, even with her temporal anomaly."

Hob grinned.

"That must use an awful lot of energy," said M Cadvare.

"It does," Electra agreed, "but she has access to vast reserves."

"Damn!" said Hob. "My thumbs!"

The Cadillac materialised ahead of them among the oncoming traffic and swept past them. The beautiful young scientist executed a perfect hand-brake turn, scattering the chorus of humming devices behind them.

"She's back," said M Cadvare.

"That was a state-of-the-art statement of the obvious," growled Hob.

M Cadvare could hear the Cadillac bellowing its tune and his hackles rose. It was obvious now what Hob meant about the power of the Song of the Machine. Through exposure, he was becoming more attuned to it. From over the top of *Nosferatu*'s crate he watched the pink and chrome monster. The woman with the beehive twirled her ivory steering wheel and the behemoth pitched and rolled but somehow slewed around the corner. It needed every one of its six wheels to hold on to the road, and although M Cadvare was treated to a brilliant display of the Cadillac's steering geometry the driver would often help it around by using the throttle, deliberately spinning the rear wheels to provoke oversteer and bring the tail round. There was a curiously nautical aspect to its progress, though the Cadillac surfed not on foaming waves but clouds of tyre smoke.

"She looks too busy driving that thing to be bending the rules of physics," M Cadvare told Hob, but just as he said this the Cadillac winked out of existence and the Song of the Machine became a mere hum again.

Hob had already lined up the personal transportation device to take a narrow side street, and having committed himself they went barrelling through it on two wheels. The street described a gentle crescent and behind them a long line of other devices trailed as far as M Cadvare could see.

Suddenly Hob braked heavily. M Cadvare was twisted awkwardly in his seat harness, nearly hitting the back of his head on the dashboard. They came to a standstill with the smell of burning rubber, and the personal transportation devices that followed them pulled up and then piled up. M Cadvare looked ahead and, as gentle thumps of energy-absorbing bumpers and deploying air-bags broke the sudden quiet behind them, realised that the Cadillac had parked across the street ahead of them, blocking it entirely. At either end, there was only a gap of a few centimetres between its bumpers and the shop fronts. Behind the wheel sat Therese Darlmat.

Hob leapt out. "That's cheating!" he cried petulantly.

"Nicholas Eldritch Hob?" asked Therese. "Leader of the Wild Hunt, Metal Guru, Repossession Man, Crypto-Engineer, His Malign Weirdness, the Grand Whizz-Herd, Master of the Engine Henge, Lord High Prince of Rock'n' Roll, Horsepower Whisperer, Soul Trader, libertine and free radical, Old Weird Wheels himself?"

"*Madame*," said Hob, with a stiff little bow, "you have named me. I am at a disadvantage."

Therese glanced at her forearms, which were covered in rows of wrist-watches. "I'm afraid I don't have much time. In a few seconds, I will re-appear to you and use the dejavuperfect verb tense. The dejavuperfect is used to describe future events that have already occurred. An example might be 'Once upon a temporal anomaly there will been a beautiful young scientist,' although within a temporal anomaly the concept of 'once' is entirely negotiable and, from my studies of the other three commonly used dimensions, I can tell you that 'there' doesn't stand much close scrutiny, either."

Hob and M Cadvare exchanged perplexed glances.

"Since I will been appearing to you," she went on, "it has come to my attention that perhaps not all the Hobs and Monsieur Cadvares in the fractured paraverses that have resulted from your activities understand the dejavuperfect, despite your abilities to perforate the fabric of space and time with your fosts. Please listen to what I will been saying to you and comply with my instructions. Your co-operation in this matter is, was and will been very much appreciated. Thank you."

She smiled at them and winked out of existence.

Before either of them could say anything, Therese re-appeared in exactly the same place but with her car facing the other way.

"Nicholas Eldritch Hob? Leader of the Wild Hunt, Metal Guru, Repossession Man, Crypto-Engineer, His Malign Weirdness, the Grand Whizz-Herd, Master of the Engine Henge, Lord High Prince of Rock'n'Roll, Horsepower Whisperer, Soul Trader, libertine and free radical, Old Weird Wheels himself?"

"Not again," muttered Hob.

Therese looked taken aback. "That's odd. The last Hob said that, too. Look, I don't have much time. You will been destabilising this and adjacent paraverses with your fosts and it will been essential that you stop your activities from now until further notice. May I count upon your past, present and future compliance?"

"No."

"Thank you, your co-operation is, was and will been highly … Whaddya mean, 'No' "?

"Phew," said Hob. "Cadaver?"

"That's no as in not yes."

Therese looked alarmed. "Why?"

"Another tricky one," said Hob.

M Cadvare held up his hands.

"I have to go!" said Therese. "I must ask you to reconsider," and she disappeared.

"Well," said Hob, "I wonder what all that was about?"

"And what she wanted?"

"I hate being told what to do, and being told what I will been doing is even worse!"

"Look out! She's back!"

"Thank you for your time," said a calmer version of Therese. The pens in the pocket of her lab coat were in a different order and the Cadillac was facing the other way again. "I appreciate this will been something of a shock for you and that you may been resenting the method of my approaches to you. However, shortly you will been able to understand not only the dejavuperfect but also the importance of my request not to create any more fosts. I'd like to will been able to wish you a long and happy life, but your contribution to the stability of these interlinking paraverses rests upon resigning yourselves to your fates as unfutured and not attempting to rehistory yourselves. Thanks again, even if you said no to start with. Goodbye."

Hob and M Cadvare stood in the middle of the street waiting for her to re-appear yet again but she didn't.

Eventually, M Cadvare said, "Hob?"

"Yeah?"

"Is your life always so badly edited?"

"My dear chap, this has never happened before."

"Or will been happening?"

"Stop that!"

They waited a little longer and then Hob turned around. On the rooftops and lamp posts around them, crows were gathering. Behind them were hundreds of personal transportation devices, some of them in quite big piles.

"Okay," Hob told their drivers, "move along now, move along, there's nothing to see."

Somewhat to Hob's surprise, for he had spoken in jest, they obliged.

"What an extraordinary woman," said M Cadvare, as they walked back to their car. "I wonder who she was?"

"I've always found the librarian-about-to-let-her-hair-down-and-dance-naked-in-the-fountain look particularly attractive," said Hob.

M Cadvare agreed. "But you didn't understand her."

"Not a word. Beauty baffles brains."

"What did you make of her car?"

"That was a Cadillac Rushmore convertible. In view of her confusing remarks, I wouldn't like to say what year it was. They have a one thousand cubic inch vee-sixteen engine and that one had evidently been considerably warmed up."

"We still managed to outrun it, though."

"Until she created that temporal anomaly. That was something else, though, wasn't it?"

"Do you always create a Wild Hunt when you drive?"

Hob shrugged. "I can't help it."

He opened the door to get in.

M Cadvare took a deep breath and said, "So how about I drive for a bit?"

Hob froze.

"Your driving style," M Cadvare went on quickly, "is conspicuous. The beautiful young scientist will be able to track you whenever you provoke a fost. And if she can, then maybe the Euphobian authorities can, too. I know they hold no fear for you but they do for me. I think we should be as discreet as possible."

"Discreet," said Hob, "rhymes with deceit."

"Okay. How about if we are not discreet but subversive?"

"Subversive." Hob grinned. "Subversive I can do!"

"So let me drive to my apartment. I can get my passport and we can have a nice cup of tea."

Hob snorted at the mention of the passport but didn't disagree with him. He thought for a few moments and then threw him the keys.

"I could murder a cup of tea."

CHAPTER 28

"So," began Kevin, awkwardly, as he and Beelzebub descended rapidly from the heavens, "how do you enjoy your work?"

Beelzebub looked a little non-plussed. "Nobody's ever asked me that before," he said. He shrugged his winged proconsul shoulders. "It's all right, I suppose."

"How do you, er, get along with God?"

"Oh very well. On the whole."

"No disagreements of any sort?"

"Nothing worth mentioning."

"Ah," said Kevin. "That's good."

A little further on, as they dropped below cloud level, Beelzebub said, "Come to think of it, there is something."

"Oh yes?"

Beelzebub paused. He wasn't used to confiding in mortals, even if they were granted perpetual re-incarnation.

"Well," he began, "it's like this. There's God in His heavens and every-thing's all right in the world. With me so far?"

"Yes."

"I haven't lost you?"

"No, I don't think so."

"Good. For us angels, though, down here it's chaos. There are all sorts of weird and wonderful creatures running about and it's putting us under tre-mendous strain. Not only do we have to adapt to whatever life form is fashion-able at the moment, but our workload's gone up, too. It can't go on for ever, not with the sort of numbers we've reached up topside. Some of these species are very successful. Do you have any idea how much krill there is up there?"

"No," Kevin replied, trying to imagine krill heaven.

"It's frightening," Beelzebub went on. "And then there are the things that just won't die out! Do you know what a coelacanth is?"

"Yes, it's a sarcopterygian."

"Eh?"

"A lobe-fin. You know, fins like …"

"… that, and swims tail-up with its head down?" they chorused together.

"Yeah, that's the coelacanth all right," said Beelzebub. "Do you know how many times we've had to build them an even bigger aquarium? Fourteen times!"

"Goodness!"

"And the cats are getting in everywhere," said Beelzebub, as they alighted on earth. "I really don't think God thought it through properly sometimes."

"Oh, I'm sure He did."

"Well, I'm not. Do you know? Everything adapts so quickly we're constantly having to create new heavens for them. Yesterday it was giant-sloth heaven – you know, lots of trees to uproot and scratch themselves against, but not much else happening – and today it's supposed to be another extension for the rabbits. And on top of that, sabre-tooth-tiger heaven still isn't finished yet. We ran out of catnip. Again."

"Can't you use one heaven for more than one species?"

"How do you mean?"

"Well, like …"

"Cats and dogs?"

"No. Mice and shrews."

Beelzebub whistled through his teeth. "No. We tried that." He rolled his eyeballs.

"And?"

"Look, have you ever got on well with your close relatives? C'mon, be honest. Have you?"

"No," sighed Kevin, "I see what you mean."

"It just not possible. Some time ago, God put the sheep and the lions in together. Apparently, it's supposed to work when everything's stopped evolving, and He, in His infinite wisdom, reckoned it was time they should try to lie down together."

"What happened?"

"Well, the lions lay down, all right, but only with indigestion. We've had to expand sheep heaven extensively. Moorland pasture takes up an awful lot of room, I can tell you."

"Couldn't you put cows in with the sheep?"

"Ooh, no. Too much fighting for the grass. And the sheep get an inferiority complex about how much more intelligent the cows are – and don't even suggest mixing sheep up with the goats. It's the same with species and sub-species. God's terribly proud of His flock. And His pack and His herd. The only trouble is we've got younds and younds of 'em."

"What's a yound?"

"It's the collective noun for collective nouns. 'They'll not want,' He says whenever I ask Him about them. It just cannot go on. I've tried to tell Him, but He just won't listen. I think the only real solution is more of this reincar-

nation business, like He did with you. Recycling wouldn't use up so many resources. Hey, you're still human! Shouldn't you be a proconsul again?"

"I suppose so."

"Blast! We'll have to go back."

"Listen. About heaven becoming overcrowded. How about developing
symbiotic relationships?"

Beelzebub smirked. "You spotted that, did you? He didn't! Yeah, it works
alright with mosses and lichen, but animals are more awkward. And parasites
aren't supposed to have hosts in heaven. They just sit around sucking ambrosia."

Neither of them seemed in much of a hurry to get back to what they had
been doing. They walked through the long grass under the trees. The view from
the hill was amazing.

"Fancy an apple, Kevin?"

"No thanks."

"Please yourself," replied Beelzebub, picking one. "They're very good."
He sighed. "You'd think grouping similar creatures together would work,
wouldn't you? But the coal tits fight the blue tits, the great crested golden
grebes have a set-to with the common or lesser brown grebes, and the Siberian
tigers shout 'Got sabre teeth! Got sabre teeth!' at the smilodons. And as for the
jackals and the wolves, well, it's dog eat dog."

"So, it's separate heavens all round, then?" said Kevin, helping himself
to some delicious wild strawberries.

"Yup. If God wants the peace and quiet He's always saying He does.
You sure you don't want an apple?" Beelzebub threw his core into a nearby lake.

"Quite sure, thanks."

They wandered on a little further, Kevin wanting to stay human for as
long as possible and Beelzebub obviously reluctant to get back to mucking out
mastodon heaven.

"Beelzebub?"

"Hey, Kevin, my friends all call me Bub, okay?"

"Oh, all right. Bub?"

"Yeah?"

"What's that silvery thing over there?"

"Over where?"

"There, by that small mound covered in daffodils."

"Why, it looks like ... No, it can't be! This place is supposed to be out of
bounds to that lot!"

"What lot?"

"Those pan-dimensional beings I mentioned earlier. There's one now,
coming out of that spacecraft. God got it right first time with them, I can tell
you. The Babbitts! Voom! In His own image, there you are! No sweat!"

"What are they doing with those female apes?"

"Where?"

"There. It looks like they're leading them out of the spaceship. Are they pregnant?"

"Cor, they'll cop it if God catches 'em here!" chortled Beelzebub. "He can be quite strict sometimes!"

The Babbitts suddenly noticed Kevin and Beelzebub watching them, and became somewhat disconcerted. They released the pair of she-apes into the wild, hurried back into their spaceship and took off.

At that instant, there was a loud thud and, turning around, Kevin and Beelzebub found an enormous net full of very small and agitated people had landed behind them. It began to roll down the hill and they had to step out of its way sharply.

"Uh-oh," said Beelzebub.

"Who are they?"

"They're the grauniads. They were supposed to keep the Babbitts out!"

The net gathered speed but hit a rock and burst, spilling out struggling grauniads in all directions.

Kevin thought hard. "Don't you mean they're the guardians?"

"Ssshh! Don't you ever call them that!" hissed Beelzebub.

"Why ever not?"

"It makes them really cross."

"They look pretty cross already."

"Wouldn't you if the creation for which you were responsible had just been messed up?"

The grauniads began to disentangle themselves from the net and fired a series of remarks at Beelzebub and Kevin.

"The Babbitts!"

"Did you see what they've done?"

"They've ruined God's experiment!"

"Stop pulling my foot!"

"Evolution will never be the same again!"

A grauniad who closely resembled a Valkyrie having a bad hair day suddenly noticed Kevin. "Who's he?"

"He doesn't look like he's evolved here," said another one that reminded Kevin of the god of thunder except that he'd shrunk in the wash.

The other grauniads began to gather round menacingly. Kevin realised how nervous viruses felt when confronted by antibodies.

Beelzebub thought quickly. "He's our star witness," he said.

"What?" cried the Valkyrie.

"Yes," insisted Beelzebub. "He saw the whole thing. Didn't you?"

"The whole thing," said Kevin, "from start to finish."

The Valkyrie scowled at him.

"Look," said Beelzebub, "why don't you go after them? We'll tell God."

The grauniads went into a huddle.

"Okay," said a small Zeus, "if you handle the Great Architect, we'll sterilise the contamination."

"Great," said Beelzebub. "Off you go then."

As Kevin watched them scatter, he whispered, "Why are they so irate?"

"Look, Kevin. How can I put this? After you happened, God invented the grauniads to stop something similar happening again."

"But it looks like it has."

"Yeah."

"Of course, Bub! The missing link! It all fits!"

"What are you wittering about?"

"Wittering?"

"Yes, wittering."

Kevin took a deep breath. "Put it this way. I think I'll be keeping a more or less human form from now on."

"What? Oh, no. Oh, no. Oh, no, no, no."

"Oh, yes!" cried Kevin. "Oh, yes, yes, yes!"

"Kevin. You realise what all this means, don't you?"

"Yes! No more mutual grooming! Bliss!"

"And another bloody heaven to build!"

Beelzebub looked as though if he'd been wearing a hat he would have thrown it on the floor and jumped up and down on it.

"No," said Kevin, "God's already got one earmarked!"

"What? That thing? It's just a pair of silly gates! We'll have to sort the rest of it out, now!"

"Well, at least you don't have to do the gates!"

"Knowing our luck, they'll probably turn out to be one of the most successful creatures ever. Look, Kevin. I know you're only trying to help, but it's not working. Not now. I'm afraid I'm just not in the mood. I'm going back up topside, and I'll get a few of the lads and lasses together and we'll have this out with God, once and for all!"

"Hey, wait a minute, Bub! You be careful!"

But the angel had gone, leaving Kevin standing alone in his human form.

CHAPTER 29

"Good grief," said Hob. "Do you live there?"

"Yep. Impressed?"

"More depressed, I think. Someone must have gone to an awful lot of trouble to override the natural instinct for pleasing proportions. Have you ever heard the expression an 'angry line'?"

"No."

"La Place de Lors contains many angry lines."

"It's not much, but it's home, and now it's been condemned."

"I'm not surprised."

"If it had a stay of execution, my non-compliant consumer durables could remain hidden and I wouldn't have to flee to Anarchadia."

"And that's a good thing?"

They drove into the underground car park, parked the car and made their way to M Cadvare's apartment by means of a lift. M Cadvare opened the door and waited for Hob's reaction.

Hob looked around for some time. "So," he said at last. "This is a typical Euphobian apartment."

"Not at all. What do you think?"

"Very nice," said Hob, "by which I mean showing fine discrimination."

"Thanks. I've never brought anyone back here. I couldn't, not without being sent to the Product Planning Blocks for Re-education. Everything here contravenes the Standard of Living Directive."

The sides of the room were covered in beautifully patterned oak panels and shuttering complete with a rarely seen raffiawork base. There was an extraordinary chandelier made of jade and Limoges porcelain, and the floor was covered by a fine example of Persian lino in the Herati style, probably from the Isphahan region. There was an early French petit-point bean bag, a Chippendale pouffe or, more properly, a hassock, and an *Art Recherché* reading table and lamp.

"I like it," said Hob, draping himself languidly in a button-backed leather armchair. He stretched and added, "Is your heating working?"

"Ah it's the air conditioning. You know they put chemicals in the atmosphere of the shopping centres?"

"To create the right shopping ambience?"

"Exactly. Well, I believe they do a similar thing here. So I've modified it just in case."

Hob stood up and examined a vent closely.

"It doesn't work as well as I would like," admitted M Cadvare.

"Your heating's completely up the spout," said Hob, peering into the grille on the wall. He pinched the screw-heads with his fingers and his hands span on his wrists. He removed the grille, peered inside and looked surprised. "The reason it doesn't work, Cadaver old chap, is because there's a vegetarian woman in the air conditioning."

CHAPTER 30

Hob was indeed right. The obstruction in the air conditioning couldn't be described as anything else but a vegetarian woman.

She was an elfin, pale-faced girl, slightly built with straight black hair that almost reached her waist and a nose that looked as if it had been turned up at quite a lot of things, mostly those on plates. She wore a long, flowing dress made out of some old-fashioned material, and although it was pure white it didn't seem to have suffered in any way from being rubbed up against the inside of some dusty ventilation system.

"Well, well. And who do we have here?" asked Hob, peering into the duct.

"That all depends on who you are," she replied.

"My card," said Hob, graciously.

"There's nothing on it," she said.

"Er, this is Nick Hob," interrupted M Cadvare, nervously, from behind the Soul Trader.

"Damn you, Cadaver! You spoilt it!"

"Spoilt what?"

"He does this thing with his card," explained M Cadvare.

Hob glared at him.

"What fashionality are you?" she asked Hob.

"I don't have one," he replied.

"You'll have to excuse him," put in M Cadvare, "he's not from around here and doesn't understand fashionality. He's a skirrow."

"I don't know that one."

"It's not recognised by the authorities. And as you can see from this room I'm an antiquester."

She nodded. "I thought as much from looking through the grille. That's against the law, isn't it?"

"Yes. Were you involved in that vegetarian ring the commissioners discovered?"

A cloud passed over her defiant face for a moment. "How did you hear about that?"

"It's big news. And I have recently come to the attention of the commissioners myself. They've changed the rules concerning roadworthiness tests for personal transportation devices, but didn't tell anyone. I've kept all my other non-compliances secret, because I'm a transaction auditor."

"Oh no!" She put her hand to her mouth and looked at him in horror.

"Don't worry," M Cadvare quickly added, "I'm probably the worst one in the whole of Euphobia. I've spun the commodity inspectors endless nonsense during my career and, if they've caught anyone as a result of the information I've given them, it's pure coincidence and I'm deeply sorry. I chose this career so that I could falsify my own records and assemble this collection, but now I've a feeling I'm under surveillance for anti-consumerist activities."

"That's just normal Euphobian paranoia," she said. "What do you think you're doing?" she asked Hob.

"I'm measuring your soul," he replied. "It confirms what I thought. This is a spirit level, and the fish fart's off the scale."

"You can't stay in there for ever," M Cadvare told her. "La Place de Lors has reached the end of its design life and they're going to re-house us. I can't see how my little hoard of non-compliant artefacts can be kept a secret any more. And now the police are after us."

"Really? They haven't followed you here have they?"

"No. Well, they might have. That's the strange thing. They seem to be keeping their distance."

"They're afraid, that's what it is," said Hob. "After some futile attempts to apprehend him, the most devious fugitive currently at large in Mourion, the authorities have given up. I speak of none other than that criminal mastermind, the terrible, the sinister, the most wanted, Monsieur Cadaver!"

"No, it's not me," said M Cadvare, sheepishly. "It's Hob they're afraid of."

"I can imagine."

"So. What are we supposed to call you?" Hob asked her.

"Nenuphar."

"Please to meet you, Nenuphar. My name is ..."

"Cadvare, yes, I know."

She smiled at him.

He smiled back, a little idiotically.

"Nenuphar," said Hob. "What a pretty name."

"It means 'water-lily'."

"Perhaps because you're so wet," remarked Hob.

"I'm leaving Euphobia with him." M Cadvare gestured towards Hob. "It's not so difficult for me to leave now that everything here will soon be lost."

"I wish I could leave so easily," said Nenuphar. "I have to find the rest of my family."

"I think the authorities have them."

Nenuphar nodded.

Hob went to the window and peered outside.

A crow was looking in through the glass at them.

"Is there anything I can do to help?" M Cadvare asked Nenuphar.

"Camaraderie amongst non-conformists, eh?" she said, with a sad smile. "It used to be honour among thieves. My heart's desire is to find the rest of my family but that seems to involve infiltrating the Product Planning Blocks."

"I'm not sure I can manage that."

"Don't worry. I couldn't ask you to do that."

"You could ask me," said Hob, turning from the window.

"Why would you help me?" asked Nenuphar.

"I'm sure we could sort something out. What happens in these Product Planning Blocks?"

"People are Re-educated," M Cadvare told him.

"And what does that involve?"

"Nobody seems to know," confessed Nenuphar, "but it turns people into model consumers."

"I was thinking that I might volunteer for Re-education," said Hob, "just to find out what it's like."

"He really isn't from around here, is he?" said Nenuphar.

"No. He's from Anarchadia. That's where we're headed."

"When do you leave?" Nenuphar asked them.

"Tomorrow," said Hob.

"I thought we were going tonight," said M Cadvare. "I thought you couldn't wait to get out of here."

"I've changed my mind," said Hob, gazing out of the window. More crows had appeared. "I might have some unfinished business to attend to by the morning."

"Then you might as well make yourself at home," M Cadvare told Nenuphar. "You should be safe here for a while, but I wouldn't want to be around when the commodity inspectors find this lot."

"Don't worry. I'll be long gone by then."

"In the meantime, my apartment is yours."

Nenuphar looked past him at Hob. "I think I'll stay in here for the moment, thank you."

"Are you hungry? Is there anything I can get for you?"

"There is something that I would really appreciate."

"Oh yes?"

"Some fresh fruit."

"Of course."

"And maybe later a bath."

"Be my guest. There should be plenty of hot water. But you'll have to come out of there first."

"Maybe when Hob's not around, *hein*?"

M Cadvare joined Hob by the window. By now there were many crows sitting outside.

"Can we trust her?" Hob asked him.

"I think so."

Hob grinned. "You fancy her."

"No I don't," said M Cadvare, going red and looking back at the ventilation system in case Nenuphar could hear.

"Yes you do. There's nothing wrong with that."

"She's a very attractive girl," admitted M Cadvare.

"Apart from being a fussy eater," added Hob. "And she was really impressed when I told her how far beyond the law you are."

"Do you think so?"

"It was obvious, Cadaver, and you know it."

"You know, I've often considered becoming a vegetarian myself."

"When you say often, would that be like during the last five minutes?"

"No. I've been thinking about it for ages."

"Oh yeah? So what stopped you?"

"Well, on top of the non-compliances in my flat, any evidence of irresponsibility towards the meat-production industry might have aroused the interest of the comestible inspectors."

CHAPTER 31

A tall building stood next to the Product Planning Blocks and on each corner of its roof flew four grey flags from four tall flagpoles. The flags were dark grey and each contained a circle of stars in a lighter grey, one for each country absorbed into the trading block of Post Unification Euphobia.

Inside the building, a meeting was under way on the topmost floor, attended by the trading block's most important people. They sat around a smoked-glass table on which a determined pilot could land a helicopter. Hanging on one of the walls were the three ideals by which they lived and worked:

> *Let's stop somebody doing something.*
> *Let's stop everybody doing something.*
> *Let's stop everybody doing everything.*

The first two lines were both marked by a large red tick. By the third was a graphical representation of a thermometer. It was already two-thirds full.

"Madame Bland," began Archcommissioner Taube, "your husband believes you may be able to offer us information on today's extraordinary events. As I'm sure you already know, an illegal immigrant has smuggled a motorcycle into our trading block and is currently still at large. This is despite the best efforts of our law enforcement services.

"Commissioner Bland also informs us that you have made the most of your privileged position in obtaining material to which we do not allow ordinary citizens to be exposed. According to some interpretations of your personal transaction log, your behaviour could be construed as non-consumerist and a systematic abuse of those privileges. The most serious example of your cavalier attitude towards our sociological standards is the retention of a document marked for destruction."

"I presume you are talking about *The Red Book of St Bendix*," answered Heidi Bland.

There was a *frisson* of unease as she said it. She looked around the attendees ostensibly for affirmation but, really, to study the wave of disquiet that ran through them for a moment.

"Indeed," said Archcommissioner Taube.

"You would have destroyed *The Red Book of St Bendix* if I hadn't saved it," she told them.

There was that *frisson* again.

"Of course, we would. We may yet unless you convince us otherwise."

"Then it's just as well that I saved it for it contains much that has a bearing on today's events."

"Your activities are not in keeping with the position enjoyed by you or your spouse, Madame Bland."

"Am I to suppose, then, that you are not interested in what I know about this illegal immigrant?"

"On the contrary. We are interested in what you know and how you came to know it. It is our solemn duty as citizens of Euphobia to uphold our consumerist community. You have not fulfilled your duty as assiduously as you should, Madame Bland. It is your good fortune to be presented with an opportunity today through which you may redeem yourself by assisting us in resolving a perplexing irregularity, namely the arrival within the Euphobian Union of a Mr Ernest Pilchard."

Heidi made a strange noise at the mention of Ernest Pilchard.

"Are you all right, Madame Bland?" asked Archcommissioner Taube.

"Yes, quite all right, thank you. I think I just swallowed a piece of fluff."

Archcommissioner Taube raised an eyebrow. Their committee room was environmentally controlled.

Her husband solicitously poured Heidi a glass of water.

She collected her thoughts and looked around the room.

"Archcommissioner, Commissionerins and Commissioners, I might be able to help but I should first of all point out that you will probably consider my sources of information highly suspect."

"The information you can offer us is one matter," explained Commissionerin Drearie. "The source of it is another."

"I have also formed opinions that you may wish to challenge," Heidi told her.

"If they are informed opinions based on facts," replied Commissionerin Drearie, "we are prepared to listen to them."

"I also don't think you'll like what you're about to hear."

Commissioner Bland gave an involuntary shudder.

"Let us be the judges of that, Madame Bland," said Archcommissioner Taube. "What can you say about the man known to us as Ernest Pilchard?"

"I believe that Ernest Pilchard is not his real name."

"Go on."

"I gather that he wears a leather jacket emblazoned with a wheeled cross."

"Correct."

Archcommissioner Taube handed her a dossier across the expanse of conference-room table. They couldn't reach each other, so a system of tiny air jets, that didn't even show up in the polished glass surface of the table, floated the papers over to her.

The dossier hovered in front of her before gracefully flattening on the top of the table.

Heidi opened it and studied the drawings.

On a screen next to the three Euphobian ideals appeared a slide of the artist's impression she held in her hand.

"So Madame Bland," said Archcommissioner Taube, "we await your contribution."

"I believe this is none other than Old Weird Wheels himself, the Metal Guru, the Repossession Man, the Crypto-Engineer, His Malign Weirdness, the Grand Whizz-Herd and Master of the Engine Henge, the Lord High Prince of Rock'n'Roll, the Horsepower Whisperer and Soul Trader! I speak of none other than that infamous libertine and free radical, Nicholas Eldritch Hob."

There was a stunned silence.

"Who?" asked someone.

"Madame Bland," said Commissionerin Drearie, "the only bit that I understood was 'libertine'. And you were right. I did not enjoy hearing it. Libertines and free radicals, ladies and gentlemen, are just the sort of people who might ride motorcycles, and are precisely the sort of people from whom we must protect our consumers."

"I'm not so sure you can protect them from him."

"We'll see about that," said the Archcommissioner.

"What business can this Hob person have in Euphobia?" asked Commissionerin Drearie.

"I don't know. What I do know is that his coming was foretold in an ancient illuminated manuscript written by a mystical blacksmith some fifteen hundred years ago."

Heidi looked around the table to take in their discomfited expressions.

"I speak, of course, of *The Red Book of St Bendix*!"

And she watched them squirm.

Commissionerin Drearie was the first to rally. "Logic dictates that this cannot be," she said.

"Commissionerin Drearie, that is my conclusion."

"There is an immediate credibility problem."

"Only for you."

"Why do you set such store in this prediction?"

"I saw Hob's name written today."

"Where?"

"Here in Mourion. In a car park, just a few miles away. I have a photograph that can explain."

She produced a personal organiser and plugged it in under the table top. She clicked a finger pad and there was an image on the screen of some writing over some parking spaces in a car park.

"What does it say?" asked Commissionerin Gueule-de-Loup.

"It says, *Nick Hob wears his tyres with pride*."

"And does this mystical blacksmith mention Hob by name?"

"He does."

"So if someone else had access to this ancient text, they could claim to be this Hob person?"

"That is true," Heidi conceded, "but I doubt they could do what your Ernest Pilchard can do."

"What makes you think our Ernest Pilchard is your Nicholas Hob?"

"Ernest Pilchard is a joke name, rather like Joe Bloggs or John Doe." Heidi paused nonchalantly before delivering her most contentious remark so far. "It originates from Anarchadia."

There was a reptilian hiss from the phlegmatic commissioners around the room as they all took a sharp intake of breath. Certain senior commissioners looked extremely alarmed.

"Madame Bland," said Archcommissioner Taube, "I should warn you that there is no such place as Anarchadia."

"As you wish, Archcommissioner, but that is where the expression comes from. According to St Bendix, it's also what Hob calls home."

"But he arrived in Mourion on a flight from Australia," pointed out Commissionerin Gueule-de-Loup. "It was diverted by extreme weather events."

"That must have been where an earlier Wild Hunt had taken him."

"Wild Hunt?" echoed Archcommissioner Taube.

"Yes," said Heidi, trying to suppress a smile. "It's the ancient chase."

"Is Hob bringing the Wild Hunt to Mourion?"

She shrugged. "Who can say?"

"Heidi," said her husband. "I asked you earlier about the significance of the symbol on Pilchard's jacket."

"Ah yes. *Terminal Murrain*."

With every outlandish expression, the commissioners became more uncomfortable.

"Hob is said to have been one of the *Terminal Murrain*," said Heidi, with relish.

"And what is that?" asked Commissionerin Drearie.

"It's a kind of gang. Perhaps I should start at the beginning. One of the things for which Anarchadia is famous is" – she paused for effect – "the Wild Hunt. This began as a celebration of survival skills and has been commemorated in the earliest cave paintings. But lately it has taken to wheels and evolved into the motorised Wild Hunt of present-day Anarchadia."

"Madame Bland, I really must ask you not use that expression."

"Very well, Commissionerin Drearie. I shall refer to it as The Land of Which We Dare Not Speak."

The Commissioners squirmed. This vague blandishment made them even more uneasy.

"Hob takes part in these spontaneous road races at night. It is said that they mimic the passage of a spectral chase, with real and incorporeal Wild Hunts running together. The authorities, such as they are in Ana … The Land of Which We Dare Not Speak, have tried to stamp it out, but to no avail. The night racers, or skirrows, race unhindered."

"And this Hob, he was one of these skirrows? He was their leader?"

"They have no leader, Archcommissioner, only those who are first in their class, if you get my meaning. Hob is a particularly fascinating individual. He seems to have started out as a skirrow who enjoyed such spectacular success in the Wild Hunt that it was said that he had sold his soul to the devil."

"Preposterous!" snorted Commissionerin Drearie. "This is ridiculous! Only Anarchadians could ever come up with such an idea!"

"Alleged Anarchadians," corrected Archcommissioner Taube. "Do go on, Madame Bland."

"Thank you, Archcommissioner. It was subsequently rumoured that Hob has more than one soul. He is supposed to have bought other souls with horsepower, horsepower that he himself has whispered up. It is said that Hob rode with a team known as the *Terminal Murrain*, which means a deadly pestilence. I gather that the fatality rate in the Wild Hunt is very high, and in Hob's time it rose to new and unprecedented levels. Hob and the *Terminal Murrain* were ostracised by the other skirrows as he became notorious for his feats as a Horsepower Whisperer."

"Could you explain that term for us, Madame Bland?" asked Archcommissioner Taube.

"Not entirely. I know that those who held great power over horses were called 'horse whisperers'. With a few well-chosen words whispered into their ears, horse whisperers could tame wild horses. I can only surmise that a Horsepower Whisperer is a kind of latter-day mechanical equivalent, except that instead of taming engines he enrages them to perform great feats of speed and power."

"But this is folklore!" snorted Commissionerin Gueule-de-Loup.

Heidi smiled. "In the Wild Hunt, the limits between science and magic are broken. Both are used in the search for more power, more speed. Hob's team, the *Terminal Murrain*, was reputedly made up of both the Quick and the Dead. Hob needs them to race against, to keep his reflexes sharp. He picks the best of the Wild Hunters and trades for their souls with horsepower. And you know what they say about power?"

"No," said Archcommissioner Taube, "what do they say?"

"Power corrupts and absolute power corrupts absolutely."

"Well," said Commissionerin Drearie, "I'm sure this is all very fascinating, but what can be done to stop Hob?"

Heidi didn't reply for a while. "I don't think there is anything you can do," she said eventually.

"One thing still puzzles me, however," said Commissionerin Drearie. "Why would this mystical blacksmith try and warn us fifteen hundred years ago?"

Heidi had to think about this. "I don't think it's a warning," she said at length. "I think it's more of a promise."

"Have you gleaned all this from your studies of this unauthorised manuscript?" Archcommissioner Taube asked her.

"Yes, but I have only translated a small proportion of it."

"Are you aware that this text had been ordered for destruction?"

Heidi nodded.

"And what do you suppose the penalty for impeding the will of the Commissioners might be?"

Heidi shrugged.

"The penalty is Re-education in the Product Planning Blocks."

Instead of looking frightened, Heidi put on a show of being puzzled. "I thought Re-education was a form of enlightenment, not punishment."

She watched Archcommissioner Taube seethe with baffled fury.

"Thank you for enlightening us," he said at length. "You may count upon us consulting you on the contents of *The Red Book of St Bendix* again in the very near future."

"As you wish, Archcommissioner."

"You may go."

CHAPTER 32

M Cadvare began his packing. Hob kept guard at the window. Whenever M Cadvare went past him, he noticed increasing numbers of disreputable-looking crows gathering outside.

"What can they want?" he asked Hob.

"They want to glut themselves on road kill," replied the Horsepower Whisperer.

"There're loads of them!"

"More than enough for a murder."

"I beg your pardon?"

"I said there's more than enough for a murder. A murder is the collective noun for crows."

"Do they often hang around you like this?"

"Yes. Crows recognise heroes before they go into battle. They expect good pickings on the battlefield when the fight is over. They await the Wild Hunt and the feast it brings. If you're seriously thinking of turning vegetarian, do you have any meat for them?"

"There's some in the fridge."

M Cadvare fetched some meat and Hob opened the window. The crows fluttered around and cawed at him.

M Cadvare watched for a while and, on hearing a noise behind him, turned around to see Nenuphar emerging slowly from the air conditioning. He helped her pour herself out and when she'd finished she was taller than he'd imagined and willowy. Despite complaining of stiff arms and legs she had a supple fluidity.

"I think I'd like that bath you offered me," she said, "while Hob's busy."

Although all the apartments in La Place de Lors shared the same layout, M Cadvare showed her to the bathroom. When he returned, Hob was still at the window, communing with the birds.

By the time M Cadvare had finished his packing, Nenuphar had emerged from the bathroom.

"If you don't mind," she said a little awkwardly, "I'd like to get back in the air conditioning. I feel safer there."

"Certainly," he said and helped her in again after she'd dusted the ducting.

Then it was his turn to dive into the bathroom where there was a pleasant feeling of unfamiliarity. There was no pink toothbrush or, indeed, any tangible sign of a recent feminine presence except for the subtle perfume that he'd detected as he'd lifted her up into the air conditioning. He lay in the bath thinking about her for ages, enjoying the enticing smell of that strange and pleasant land called woman until the water went cold.

When eventually he emerged, pink and gleaming and with decidedly puny fingers, it was dark outside. Nenuphar was examining his furniture. Of the Horsepower Whisperer, there was no sign.

"Where's Hob?" he asked her.

"He went out," she replied. "He said he was going to a 'swapmeet' and would be borrowing your personal transportation device. He said he'd have asked you properly if you'd been around but you weren't and he said he was sure you wouldn't mind."

"Mmm. I thought he was in a hurry to be off. I wonder when he'll be back."

"I asked him that and he just said, 'Late.' I hope he doesn't come back. He gives me the creeps. Where is it you're travelling to?"

"Anarchadia."

"Where's that?"

"Anarchadia? It's a temperate archipelago off the north-west coast of mainland Euphobia."

"Is that where he's from?"

"Yes."

"I've never heard of it. Are you sure?"

"Well," began M Cadvare, lamely, "not really."

"Have you got any atlases?" Nenuphar asked him, looking around.

"No," lied M Cadvare. "Anyway, Hob says it's not on any maps because the authorities don't want anyone to find out about it."

"Why?"

"In Anarchadia, people are free. They do as they please and don't need authorities. That's why it's kept a secret."

Nenuphar considered this for a while and then said, "And he's taking you there?"

"Yes."

"Have you known Hob long?"

"Known Hob long? No, not really. I only met him this afternoon. But I can't stay here, not with the prospect of an audit against the Standard of Living Directive. Surely you can see that?"

"It's just such a lovely flat."

"I know." He sighed. "I have to think of it all as being lost already. It makes leaving easier."

"How long do you think it'll take for the commodity inspectors to catch up with you?"

"I don't know. You can stay here for a while if you want. We should be gone tomorrow."

"Thanks. That would be good. I don't have anywhere else to go."

M Cadvare had to restrain himself from putting an arm around her.

"All my friends and family were rounded up. I managed to hide myself in the ventilation system, and in the confusion I must have been overlooked. Once I was in the system I could spy on the other apartments. It's frighteningly easy to spot contraventions of the Standard of Living Directive. I spotted your non-compliant furniture within half an hour."

"If you stay behind you will be careful, won't you?"

"I don't want to get caught but I must find the rest of my family."

"It seems you already know where they are," said M Cadvare, gently.

"Yes but they won't be in there for ever. As soon as they come out, I can find them and teach them all that they've forgotten."

"I don't think that'll work."

"Why ever not?"

"Whenever anyone who's been Re-educated finds a non-conformist, they alert the authorities straight away."

"But these people are my family! I can't believe they would ever do that!"

"Without experiencing Re-education ourselves, we can't understand what effect it can have on anyone, no matter how close they might be to us."

"It's a risk I'm willing to take."

"As soon as you reveal your true self to them, they'll report you."

"There has to be a way of converting them back again!"

"I hope there is, for all our sakes."

"Don't you see, M Cadvare? I'm their only hope!"

M Cadvare nodded, but couldn't see how he was going to help her.

Nenuphar sniffed. "Anyway, what's your first name? I can hardly keep calling you, M Cadvare, now, can I?"

"I suppose not. It's Enrico."

Nenuphar made a pained expression.

"Actually, I think I rather prefer M Cadvare."

CHAPTER 33

Beelzebub was right. God was not happy about the Babbitts interfering with His experiment. Kevin never did find out if anything happened to them, but for a few months Kevin was completely forgotten about. He roamed the savannah lands still in his human form, a kind of duffel-coated ghost. After millions of years of one life after another, it seemed a pleasant interlude.

Then, one day, he had a visitation.

An angel, auspiciously in proper human form, found him as he contemplated the prehistoric heavens and his future from a small hill.

"Ah," said the rather breathless angel. "There you are, Kevin! We've been looking everywhere for you. You're not busy are you? God would like a word."

As they climbed up to heaven together, Kevin asked the angel if there had been any developments since the Babbitts' interference.

"Developments? I should say so! Why do you ask?"

"Well, you are rather like a human, instead of a monkey with wings."

"Thanks very much."

"Do you know Beelzebub?"

The angel started. "I used to."

"Is he shaped like you now?"

"Not exactly, no. You see, Beelzebub and a few of the others had a bit of a disagreement with God over the way heaven was run, with the result that they were dismissed."

"Oh dear," said Kevin. "I was worried something like this might happen."

"Cheer up," said the angel brightly. "From what I gather, it's all going to work out rather well for you."

"How do you mean?"

"Well, I'd better not steal God's thunder. Perhaps it would come better from Him."

Kevin nodded pensively. Then he said, "What's your name, angel?"

"Gabriel. And please don't call me angel."

When they arrived outside heaven, God was obviously very excited. Kevin fancied He looked a little tired, but dismissed this idea as ridiculous.

"Kevin!" said God, happily, "There you are! You'll never guess what's happened."

"I think I will. I was there when the Babbitts released the pregnant she-apes into your experiment. Er, didn't Beelzebub mention it?"

"No but it's what happens next that's going to be really exciting!"

"Would You mind if I had a go at guessing what's about to happen next?"

"No, by all means."

"Here goes then. The Babbitts have created a new race of hybrid creatures."

"Yes."

"The first members of this new species are due to be born quite soon."

"That's right. And I'm very excited about it. So far so good."

"These are going to be the first humans, aren't they?"

"It was supposed to be a surprise! But yes, they'll be humans, Kevin, the first ones ever! Well, apart from you, of course."

"I don't think I count. I can't be the first as well as the last."

"I'm sure something along the lines of humans would have evolved eventually, but now they're going to happen much, much sooner. I want to try something with them, an experiment within an experiment, if you like. Every so often, Kevin, I take some samples out of evolution and keep them together in a special place where they don't die, where they don't need to evolve."

"Really? Why?"

"As you may have gathered from Sophia, usually I make everything perfect right from the start. Occasionally, I measure the impact of perfection on some of the evolutionary creatures. I intend to try this with the two new human creatures. Obviously, you'll be one of them, but you won't be born. You won't die, either."

"I suppose I'll suddenly exist fully formed."

"Yes."

"In paradise."

"Well, the Experimental De-Naturising Environments, actually."

"Really? What are they like?"

"They resemble a garden tended by grauniads."

"Hmm. What did You call this garden again?"

"The Experimental De-Naturising Environments."

"Right," said Kevin, a little non-plussed. "You don't think it's a bit of a mouthful, do You?"

"How do you mean?"

"Well it doesn't really trip off the tongue, does it?"

"What do you think, Gabriel?"

"I think it's all right," he said.

Kevin gave him a sideways glance.

Gabriel tried to avoid his eyes.

"I'm not so sure now," said God. "The Garden of Experimental De-

Naturising Environments. It sounded all right until you said it, Kevin."

"We could abbreviate it," suggested Gabriel. "How about the Garden of E.D.E?"

"We could call it the Garden of Ede," God added.

"A little too short perhaps?" replied Kevin. "May I suggest two syllables?"

"Yes. Two syllables. Exden. Hmm, perhaps not. How about the Garden of Edenve?"

"Edenve?"

"Edenve," echoed Gabriel, thoughtfully.

"Okay," said God, "perhaps not Edenve."

"It's close," said Kevin.

"Edenviron?" suggested Gabriel.

"Hello, boys," said Sophia. "Ah, Kevin! How lovely to see you! You're keeping well?"

"Oh, yes thank You, Sophia. And You?"

"Very well, thank you. Actually, Kevin, just between you and Me, I am never actually ill but I understand that you mortals can have terrible sicknesses."

"Yes, You're right," Kevin replied.

"Any problems, just let Me know. I do a really good Ambrosia pick-Me-up, even though I do say so Myself as shouldn't. Well then, what are You all up to?"

"We're trying to think of a better name for the Garden of Experimental De-Naturising Environments," explained God.

"The Garden of what?"

"The Garden of Experimental De-Naturising Environments."

"Oh, you mean the Garden of Eden! Well, that's what I call it."

"Yes, said God. "Yes. I like that."

"So do I," put in Gabriel.

"What do you think, Kevin?"

"I think it's a perfect name for paradise."

"The Garden of Eden it shall be!" said God and he gave His wife a hug.

"Good," said Sophia. "I think Eden's the best thing You've ever done. I think evolution's over-rated, but You do perfection beautifully."

"Thank You My dear."

"Whenever I've got a quiet moment, I like to have a little stroll round it," went on Sophia, "and, perhaps, do a little weeding."

"Weeding?"

"Yes. Some of the thistles have spikes on them instead of the usual fleecy down."

"Oh. Do they?" muttered God.

"Mind You, the donkeys helped by eating them."

"I'm very fond of donkeys," said God, "and they shouldn't have to do that. I'll just sort Kevin out and We'll have a word with the grauniads."

"I'll go and find them," said Sophia. "Welcome to paradise, Kevin!"

"Goodbye."

"Right!" said God, clapping His hands. "Are you ready?"

"Yes, but first I want to know what happened to Beelzebub. He brought me up here the last time."

God stiffened. "Ah Beelzebub. I'm afraid I had to dismiss him. We had a difference of opinion about where the rights and responsibilities of an angel begin and end."

"So, what's Beelzebub doing now?"

CHAPTER 34

The murder of crows led Hob to a run-down industrial estate on the edge of Mourion. He parked in the furthest corner of the car park, pulled on his rucksack full of souls and looked around. If anyone had followed him they kept their distance.

The crows had settled on top of a security fence. Behind this was an overgrown patch of waste ground. Hob put his fingers through the mesh and pulled it apart as if it was garden netting. There was no obvious path through the weeds and bushes so he walked straight into the undergrowth. The crows seemed disinclined to follow but watched with interest.

Hob soon left the street lamps behind and the shrubs became trees. Moonlight filtered through their leaves and the ground became uneven as swollen roots gripped fallen masonry in arthritic knuckles. Not a breath of wind disturbed the beards of moss and lichen on the trees.

He made his way to the top of a flight of steps that led down into the earth. They were lit by moonlight so bright it was possible to see the colours of the stones and leaves. Hob descended them to a big oak door. He rapped out a strange rhythm with his knuckles and waited.

"Ssshh! Fortunato!" he said softly. "Tonight we recruit for the *Terminal Murrain*!"

The door creaked ajar and a voice whispered, "The dragon of chaos is asleep."

"But tonight she awakes," Hob answered softly.

The door opened a little wider and if anything the night became a little blacker.

"What was that?" said the voice.

"But tonight she awakes," repeated Hob, a little louder.

"Concentrate! Think clearly! The dragon of chaos is asleep!"

"But tonight she awakes!" bellowed Hob.

"Young man. There is no need to shout. I can read your thoughts perfectly. Where is your membership card? Let me see it!"

"Cut the crap and let me in. Who is the Gatekeeper this night? Is that you, Gehenna?"

A hideous old crone emerged into the moonlight. She was bent with age and her sins weighed heavy upon her shoulders. Her feet were killing her, too.

She glared at Hob in the gloom with one good eye, the left one having been closed for business by a huge growth on her eyelid, and she chewed her leathery old lips together and waggled her hairy jowls at him, but then her mouth spread wide open in a toothless grin.

"Well, well, well, if it isn't young Master Hob! This *is* a nice surprise! Ooh, it seems like aeons since I saw you last. How are you keeping, Master Hob? How are you and yours?"

"Very well thank you, Gehenna."

"What?"

"I said … Look, have you got your telepathy aid switched on?"

"What? Stop dissipating your thoughts. Can't you think a little harder?"

"I said have you got your te-le-pa-thy aid switched on, dear." Hob pointed to the wires that came from electrodes in her hair.

"Just a minute, young Master Hob. I must just find my thought trumpet. I've got my telepathy aid tonight but it's not switched on because it wears out the incantations. I won't be a jiff."

"Oh, good grief," muttered Hob.

Gehenna stuck her thought trumpet's rubber suction cup in the middle of her heavily corrugated brow where her third eye might be.

"Now then. That's better. What did you say, Master Hob?"

"I was just wondering how you manage it, Gehenna. You look more fresh-faced every day."

"Ooh, Master Hob!!" chortled Gehenna, with much wobbling of her whiskery jowls, "you are a one! But here's me gabbling on and on and you standing outside. Come in! Come in!"

"Thank you, Gehenna, that is very ki … Oh, give me strength."

She had shut her thought trumpet in the door.

"No, no. Let me, let me," protested Hob, but it was no good. Gehenna couldn't understand him without her thought trumpet and she couldn't see too well, either. All she wanted to do was retrieve her thought trumpet and have a jolly good chinwag with him. She was very good at chinwags, was Gehenna, having more than most.

After a great deal of effort, the door was opened and the thought trumpet retrieved and straightened out again.

"There," said Hob smiling at Gehenna. "Let's stick this back on again. Come on, now, frown. Frown. Go on, now, scowl, really scowl."

"What's that you say?"

"Come on, now, you poor deluded old witch, give me a really nasty scowl to stretch that wrinkly old forehead into a surface as smooth as a baby's bottom so that this infernal device will bloody well stick!"

Gehenna tried really hard but her forehead remained as smooth as a ploughed field and the slightly warped thought trumpet refused to stick to it.

"This is no good," muttered Hob, and he pulled out of his pocket a handful of nails and a large claw hammer, and before Gehenna knew what was happening he had nailed it on.

"Ooo!" she said, "that's much better! I can sense you perfectly now, Master Hob!"

"Splendid! Er, don't waggle it about too much. That rubber is very old and it won't be long before it perishes."

"I know how it feels," groaned Gehenna. "I haven't got my youthful persona on today because it …"

"Wears out the incantations. Yeah, I know."

Gehenna steadied her thought trumpet with one hand in a kind of salute. "Gatecrashing one of our events again, are you, you naughty boy?"

"Only if I'm able to sweet-talk my way past its glamorous door-keeper."

"Well, you've had plenty of practice, you young rascal, you!"

"It's a challenge, I admit. You have the reputation of being the most effective gate-keeper of them all."

"My reputation's been in tatters since I let you in that first time," Gehenna giggled.

"Only because I said that if you didn't relax a little you'd be worn out by the time you were thirty thousand years old."

"I know, I know, flattery will get you in anywhere. Oh, you're a real tonic, Master Hob, a real credit to … to … to whomever you're a credit to. Tell me."

"Anything, Gehenna, anything at all."

"How did such a nice lad like you get mixed up with soul trading?"

Hob laughed. If you flatter, prepare to be flattered.

"I was seduced by horsepower," he told her.

"Fancy that!" she replied, and looked suitably impressed although Hob knew full well she didn't really know what horsepower was, let alone horsepower whispering. "How's business been with you lately?"

"Oh, fair to middlin', I suppose," he replied, patting his rucksack.

"Huh, that's better than some of 'em are doing. You should've seen the long faces when they came in earlier."

"Well most Soul Traders do have rather long faces, Gehenna."

"But why do they have to be so down in the dumps about it? It does my spirits good to see a cheerful face like yours. Anyway, you go on through and see what bargains you can pick up."

"Anything I can get you while you're on the door, Gehenna?"

"Muscleheads!" she giggled. "Find me some mighty Nubian slave or a body-builder from Muscle Beach and I'll lay such a glamour on them!"

"I get it. Anything to make the old flesh sing, eh?"

"Don't stop at anything. Get me everything!"

"Not so worried about wearing out yer incantations, after all, are you?"

Hob laughed. "All right, Gehenna. I'll see what I can do," and with that he drew aside the veil between this world and that of the Soul Transference and Necromancers' Trade Association.

CHAPTER 35

Hob found himself in a huge underground vault that had, apparently, been abandoned for centuries and not dusted very often before that, either. Stone columns stretched into the darkness above, and had it not been for the lack of stars twinkling overhead he could have been standing in some vast abbey, split open to the sky. However, there was no airiness to this vault. The atmosphere suggested confinement, and the darkness was a thick one that smelt of sulphur. Cabalistic sigils decorated the walls and the place was not so much lit by light as illuminated by another order of darkness.

In front of him were rows of stalls, laid out in a rough grid pattern offering all manner of souls. Around the edges, newcomers to the egojumbling circuit had just a chair and a packing case, and eager Soul Traders flicked through their cardboard boxes, searching for a bargain.

Other Soul Traders were like Hob, wandering around, browsing, but carrying their soul takings with them in case they needed to trade.

Hob squeezed through the narrow passages and used his height to peer over the shoulders of those rummaging through the piles of suitcases before him. Nothing roused his interest.

More established Soul Traders had bigger stalls and stayed put, relying on their bad name to draw custom. If they wanted to have a look around they could always ask a neighbour to mind their stall for them. Some, like Anubis or Dionysius, had been trading for so long that they employed staff and flew flags and pennants to attract prospective customers. Many Soul Traders and Necromancers had developed specialised niches in the soul market over the aeons, and by catering for relatively esoteric tastes enjoyed a comfortable afterlivelihood. Others, such as the great druid Terrlin, went for bulk, piling them high and selling them cheap.

Hob wandered through the crowds, nodding to other Soul Traders he knew. He could see why so many traders were taking an interest in the offerings of the newbies. Souls were poor. Trade was slow. Everyone was just looking.

He took surreptitious glances at the souls of the other Soul Traders and Necromancers. Trading in the souls of STANTA members was tantamount to cannibalism and banned by the articles of the association but, being unaffiliat-

ed, Hob could indulge in these fantasies more freely. The likelihood of successfully trading for one of their souls remained remote. Besides, the soul of a
STANTA member would never fetch its true worth on the black market, even if
you could find someone with whom to trade, and it was almost inconceivable
that anyone would have the equivalent value in skirrows. It soon became
apparent that he wasn't the only one coveting the souls of his fellow traders.

"Hop!" cried a female voice. "Nicholaas Ill Ditch Hop! Vell, vell, vell!
How are you, you tsexual panzer!"

Hob turned around. "Wiwwienne," he said. "This is a pleasant surprise."

Before him stood a striking young woman in a long figure-hugging
gown with ridiculously long sleeves and not really enough material in the
lower part to allow her to walk properly. Consequently, she glided everywhere. So as to look a little less supernatural in her perambulations, she
wriggled beguilingly as she floated over to him.

Hob took several steps back. He knew Wiwwienne of old.

Wiwwienne halted and, half turning her head, smiled. It was more of a
leer, showing off the glint of her strangely enlarged canine teeth behind her
glossy red lips. These were the only vestiges of colour about her, for she was
either black with her fathomless eyes, black dress and black hair, or pure white,
the whites of her big eyes, the lightning flashes of her teeth and her blemishless
skin, the sort of white not normally associated with innocence.

"Oh, come now, Hop! Vot can be rongue viz you? A pig, ssttrrrronguue
man like you afraight off a little, 'elpless gurrl like me!"

"I know vot, or rather, what you are Wiwwienne. And a little, helpless
girl you are not. For a start, you're as old as the hills themselves, and as for
helpless, why, since when was a succubus ever helpless?"

"I am liddle and 'elpful, zen?" replied Wiwwienne, with a calculated
smile.

"Certainly not helpful," replied Hob, "and certainly not little," he added,
suddenly realising in the gloom that her body swooped in and out more than
was really feasible. "By the spanners of St Bendix! What have you been doing
to yourself?"

Wiwwienne giggled and Hob's blood sang in answer. He had to think of
rebuilding the power train of a Humber Super Snipe not to drown in her silvery
laughter.

"I haff been gorrging myself especially for you," she said and with that
she slowly peeled the top of her dress off, which fitted like a shiny, second skin,
to reveal the voluptuous form that had been ill concealed within.

Hob, who had indulged in so many of the pleasures of the flesh, gasped.
He had never seen anything like Wiwwienne's extraordinary physique before.

"Tsee 'ow rrrounded I have become, so engorged viz witality! Tso
wibrantly woluptuouss! And yet, tsomehow, tso werry, werry, wulnerable. If
you are ze rred-bludded man I zink you are, I am yours for ze takink!"

All thoughts of crankshaft end thrust washers and clutch release bearings disappeared from Hob's mind.

"No, thank you," he somehow managed to say. "I know what you're after, Wiwwienne, just as you know what I am after."

"Tso, ve unterstandt itch uzzer! Ve shouldt be lovers!"

"Wiwwienne?" said Gehenna, suddenly materialising at Hob's elbow. "Are you up to your old tricks again?"

"Vot vouldt you know about zat, you olt crone?"

"Enough for me to realise that perhaps you are not such a reformed character as you would like us to think. I only let you in here tonight against my better judgement. It's been a long time since you last traded in the souls of your fellow Soul Traders."

"Zey knew vot zey vurr doingk!" sneered Wiwwienne.

"Perhaps. Perhaps they thought they would get your soul when they were really losing their own."

"Hah!" snorted Wiwwienne, with much erotic wobbling.

"The fact remains," continued Gehenna, "that while some of us just think about it for an instant, your lack of scruples allows you to just do it."

"Vot proof do you haff?" demanded Wiwwienne.

"I don't need any proof," Gehenna told her. She gripped her thought trumpet with an arthritic hand and directed it towards Wiwwienne. "If you want to continue to be admitted to these conventions then you shall abide by the rules. And the rules are: no trading with Soul Traders if it is for their own souls. Do I make myself clear?"

"Abpundantly," said Wiwwienne, pouting a little.

"Now do yourself up and trade souls. Properly."

Wiwwienne gathered herself together and twisted petulantly once or twice from side to side, as if she was sitting on some bar stool. Then with the most lascivious wink at Hob, she turned and, slowly and seductively, wiggled away.

"Phew," said Hob.

"Don't be fooled by her," Gehenna told him, taking his arm and turning him away.

"I think I would have been able to just about resist."

"Even so, but for how long? She is more than a *femme fatale,* that creature; she is the ultimate succubus. I had hoped that readmitting her to a STANTA-run swapmeet would rehabilitate her but I'm afraid that I have grave doubts, very grave doubts indeed. Watch your step Hob, my boy – watch your step with that one. It'll be more than your life you'll lose to her, I can assure you!"

"Yes, Gehenna, I understand."

"Good. Now off you go and trade. I have a convention to … to …"

"Convene?"

"Precisely."

Hob pointedly made off in the opposite direction from Wiwwienne, idly wondering if anyone else might be seduced by her considerable charms.

As he walked by the various stalls, he began to take more notice of what souls were on offer.

Souls are rather difficult to describe to those without the necessary perceptual abilities. They are rather like belly buttons. Everybody has one, or should have one, but we are hard pressed to say what they are really like, what to do with them, how to stop fluff collecting in them, or how life would be without them.

Hob saw souls as electrically charged pocket-handkerchiefs.

Most were like neatly folded paper hankies, plucked fresh from the box, very delicate and liable to tear. Generally, souls remain very still, but, every so often, something sufficiently poignant can touch, or move, a soul. When they move, they do so with a vague fluttering action as if blown by a gentle breeze. Sometimes, a deeply visceral influence can be enough to tear a soul apart, so Soul Traders dealing in the more artistic and sensitive souls have to take elaborate precautions to guard against this.

Souls typically begin as plain white and vaguely translucent, although there are some rather voguish pastel-coloured ones that find favour with certain types of Soul Trader. These plain or uniformly coloured souls are generally quite common, and any Necromancer worth his or her salt would deal with several hundred thousand of these, often serving as loose change.

During enthusiastic trading, low-value, pale, insignificant souls would fall from the tables as Soul Traders struck their bargains. These corporate lawyers, work-study practitioners and lifestyle consultants would often be left to fall, especially if their true value was fully apparent. Despite a good trampling and rolling around on the floor, these poor souls could still come up a brilliant white. Once yielded, souls cannot be artificially coloured in.

Most Soul Traders get really excited about the dotted or stripy ones, preferably made out of a more opaque material such as cotton or wool and sometimes even hessian.

"Never mind the quality, feel the thickness," so the saying goes.

Commonplace souls come all neatly ironed, and look as if they have never been unfolded. Hob and his fellow spiritual connoisseurs preferred souls that had a lived-in look, those that resembled rags rolled into a ball, those that had been used for wiping dipsticks and had been wrapped around boiled sweets. As far as Hob was concerned, the oilier the soul the better, for one that was absolutely sodden with the stuff could only be that of a Horsepower Whisperer. Such a soul would stain the other souls in his rucksack with the blood of an engine. Indeed, blood from skinned knuckles, grass stains or ingrained bits of old food are all highly valued by any Soul Trader – in fact, anything that shows the rich tapestry of life. Hob's particular favourites were scorch-holes from hot spark plugs.

Not many Soul Traders or Necromancers of Hob's acquaintance approved of horsepower whispering. It was too modern for them. They didn't understand the hold that such power could exercise over a soul. Consequently, most of them made it clear that, even if Hob had been trading for the requisite one hundred years, they wouldn't allow him to join their trade association. Hob didn't care. He wasn't the joining type. He just continued to annoy them by sweet-talking his way around Gehenna, who was one of the most senior Soul Traders, and whenever they raised objections, Gehenna quashed them.

As usual, the Representatives of the Dead were present at the swapmeet. These were anachronisms from an earlier chapter in soul trading when, for some never adequately explained reason, it was felt that the soul-trading profession as a whole ought to give the souls being traded some sort of forum to express their concerns. Of course, it was only a passing fad and now the Representatives of the Dead were put on display at swapmeets in the out-of-body equivalent of the stocks. Representatives of the Dead were the only ones already bought or sold that could be further tainted by new experiences or endowed with fresh blebs. Nowadays, passing Soul Traders were invited to hurl some of life's rich tapestry at the Representatives of the Dead in whatever form they chose, provided they made a small contribution to STANTA's malevolent fund.

That night, many STANTA members were volunteering souls for improvement in this way, happy to run the risk of damaging the more sensitive souls through too many intense experiences. Those that were capable of withstanding such treatment became worth much more, and egojumblers could increase the value of their stock without trading souls.

Typically, Hob could not resist this sort of thing and by the time he arrived most Soul Traders and Necromancers were running out of good, spare experiences. Their uplifting or degrading remarks lacked real bite and weird accounts of strange adventures just confused the Representatives of the Dead, many of them remaining largely unmarked. Necromancers were resorting to encouraging souls to reveal their most embarrassing moments in front of perfect strangers.

Hob set about regaling the Representatives of the Dead with tales of Wild Hunt derring-do. He started well and went on to describe his exploits with a burning airliner but then he stopped. His recent impressions of Mourion were dispiriting. Recounted to the Representatives of the Dead, Hob's impressions of Mourion could only contribute grey to life's rich tapestry and, although all souls should be tainted by some of this colour, tonight there was too much of it.

Leaving the Representatives of the Dead, Hob noticed a stall run by a big Negro, deftly strumming a guitar. He played it with his eyes closed, and hummed a deep subterranean hum by way of an accompaniment. Occasionally he would pause, roll his eyes and shake his head. Most of the souls on his stall moved in time with the music, which rose above the background hubbub of the swapmeet.

"Boule-de-neige," said Hob.

"Mmm, mmm," replied Boule-de-neige, as a greeting or part of his blues song. It served either purpose admirably.

Hob admired the blues man's souls, particularly those that were sufficiently touched to, as Boule-de-neige might say, "get on up and get on down like a goo-od soul should". Some had to be contained within a ring of refined brimstone to contain their gyrations.

"I'll swap you twenty public relations consultants for anything with oil stains," said Hob. He pulled his rucksack off his shoulders and began to delve inside it as it danced in time to Boule-de-neige's guitar playing.

"What?" replied Boule-de-neige. "You foolin' wi' me, boy?"

"Okay, twenty-five public relations consultants and a couple of dentists. How about that?"

"What you take me fo? Do you have any idea, mm, mm, mm, m'mm mm, yeah! how scarce goo-od souls are, here, in down town Mour-ee-on?"

"No, I don't. I am a stranger here myself."

"Well you ain't gonna get nuthin', no, not nuthin', fo ya pub-lick re-lations con-sult-ants! And as fo ya dentists – well, well, what did you trade to git them, huh? Teeth?"

"As a matter of fact, no. The medical profession can quite easily be bought with the promise of more power from their Saab Turbos."

"Hell, you ain't gonna lay some o' that horsepower whisperin' shit on me now, are ya, Hob? 'Cos if you is, I ain't buyin'. No sir."

And with that, Boule-de-neige broke off to render a soul-rending bar eight on his blues harp that shivered to pieces his, and Hob's, stocks of estate agents, tax accountants and telesales personnel. As their shredded remains blew away from Boule-de-neige's trestle tables, Hob opened a side pocket on his rucksack and pulled out the fluff of freshly rent souls.

"Oh, man, you're makin' me cry," Hob told Boule-de-neige. It wasn't that some of his souls had been torn apart. It had been the sheer pathos of the blues man's music.

Boule-de-neige smiled at Hob, which is not easy to do when you're playing a blues harp.

"So long, main man," said Hob, and, with a cursory wave from Boule-de-neige, he went on his way.

CHAPTER 36

Hob wandered on through the swapmeet. He doubted if any STANTA members would recognise the soul of a skirrow or a Horsepower Whisperer, especially in this gloom. If they did, those qualities that Hob valued would probably put them off. All the better for getting a bargain, he thought, rubbing his grubby hands together, but the more he walked around, the clearer it became that STANTA was faced with a serious soul shortage.

Those that were trading seemed to be dealing largely in bulk purchases. There were three main players in this market, and they each had a pitch in a prime position near the centre of the vast vault that housed the egojumble. Terrlin the druid, and the self-styled Great Wazir, Abdul-ben-Ziggarat, and the Karma Wallah of Bredanalapur were all doing a roaring trade. However, they seemed to be trading non-spiritual consideration in return for the souls they were gaining. Terrlin the druid was offering fully trained standing stones, and Abdul-ben-Ziggarat was doing a very nice line in second-hand flying carpets, while the Karma Wallah of Bredanalapur had the Necromancers queuing up for his curries.

Hob was beginning to wonder what the latest additions to his collection might fetch on the open market. He'd imagined that he would have been able to get at least one high-spirited, high-octane motorhead in return for his motley collection of unremarkable souls. Sometimes he could get what he considered to be quite a decent soul for very little, particularly if it was a troublesome skirrow like Fortunato, and the vendor was, as a result, glad to be shot of him or her, not knowing what a skirrow really was. But tonight he was out of luck.

He'd tried a flying carpet once before, in Old Baghdad, but he just couldn't get on with it. It didn't handle well, and lacked even handlebars or a steering wheel. On more than one occasion, Hob had counted himself lucky that he was now immortal. Most other Soul Traders would have had no difficulty controlling it with black magic.

He didn't particularly want a standing stone, either. They would only be useful to him if they contained any useful elements like iron or titanium or chrome. If they did, then there wasn't much point in having them already trained because he'd be melting them down the next time he wanted to make a decent BSA scrambles bike.

So, in the end, just out of boredom as much as anything else, he joined the queue for one of the Karma Wallah's curries. When at last he came to the front, the Karma Wallah looked at what Hob was willing to trade, and politely told him that for twenty-five public relations consultants, half a dozen golf-orientated dentists, the passengers of the airline that he'd rescued earlier that day and a still-warm airport receptionist, all he could expect in exchange was a bag of Bombay mix and a couple of poppadoms.

Munching on these meagre rations, Hob graduated slowly to the darker regions of the Soul Transference and Necromancy Trade Association's convention. Among the more specialised dealers was he most likely to find something of interest. If Gehenna were ever to let Wiwwienne have a stall of her own, it would be around these fringes.

Someone was sacrificing a cockerel on a portable altar. African Witch Doctors and Juju Men looked enigmatically at passers by, and The Concubine and Miss Prim, the Necro-Nymphomaniacs, giggled to each other about something.

It was as he wandered along, wondering why he'd bothered to come, that a fellow Soul Trader suddenly cannoned into him from a side turning.

"Drat and Triple Drat!" said the Horsepower Whisperer.

"*Ein tausend Fluchen*!" said the other.

"Badness black-hearted me!" exclaimed Hob, seeing who it was.

"*Mein Gott*!"

"No, Deutz, it's me!"

"*Na, so was*," said Caspar Deutz, straightening his hat and stroking his whiskers, "if it isn't the Metal Guru himself, Old Weird Wheels!"

The two shook hands warmly.

"How's the Foundling of Rauschenberg?" asked Hob.

"For an immortal, I'm in the best of health. And you, old friend?"

"The police tried very hard to shoot me earlier, but I remain as you see me, entirely unblemished."

"Apart from your black fingers, of course."

"Of course."

Caspar Deutz was one of the few affiliated Soul Traders for whom Hob had any time. To look at, he bore a striking similarity to Isambard Kingdom Brunel, as depicted by the famous photograph where he is standing in front of a huge drum of chains, except that Caspar Deutz was taller and a good deal younger. He was well dressed in a waistcoat and tails, and sported an excessively tall stove-pipe top hat and huge mutton-chop whiskers.

The resemblance to the great nineteenth-century engineer was so strong that when Hob first met Deutz he thought he might be Brunel himself. As a result, he had tried to trade for his soul. Old Ikey Brunel would have made a splendid skirrow so Hob went to some lengths to make a deal. For his part, Caspar Deutz had an impression that Hob might have been none other than

146

THE HORSEPOWER WHISPERER

Spring-Heeled Jack, the mysterious scourge of Victorian England, who terror-ised cities over a number of years by attacking people and leaping in one bound from the pavement to the rooftops. Caspar Deutz was particularly interested in those who developed a peculiar facility or two, or had some strange extra-sensory ability, and the two of them had circled around each other, behind their psychic shields, weighing each other up and trying to achieve what the articles of STANTA expressly forbade them to do. When they discovered their mutual mistake, they laughed long and hard, and a bond of sorts was established.

Caspar Deutz was carrying a large sack.

"What's in here, Deutz? Christmas presents?"

"Huh! No, not by any means. I have found, at last, someone willing to trade all these advertising account executives in exchange for an unknown alcoholic playwright and a policeman who can waggle his ears."

"I don't want to sound critical, old chap – perish the thought! – but you wouldn't normally be trading in souls of this quality, would you, now?"

"No," replied the Foundling of Rauschenberg, as he led Hob back towards the centre of the swapmeet. "I've never known anything like it. There's a chronic shortage of souls of any sort, good, bad or indifferent."

"It's something to do with Mourion," Hob told him. "Trying to raise spirits around here is like trying to raise the *Titanic*. There's plenty of *people* about, but not enough souls to go around. It did occur to me that perhaps the extraordinary success of mankind, in terms of sheer numbers if nothing else, has outstripped the supply of souls."

"I think they're going to bring this up at the AGM."

"It just goes to show what good value split personalities are. I should have collected more of them when they were available. So the great and the good within STANTA recognise there's a problem?"

"*Ja*, they're getting really worried. In an effort to stimulate trade they are even letting in non-affiliated traders."

"They've even let Wiwwienne in. I saw her, earlier."

"*Ja*, I know. She is trouble. But getting in is never trouble for you, I think."

"Are you being smutty?"

"*Nein*, you are just *verklemmt*, not liberated. But maybe this would be a good time for you to join the association."

"I don't think they'd have me. I don't think I'd have them. I've still got to acquire some fifty more years of unaffiliated trading before they'll even dream about letting me join. How long have you been trading now?"

Caspar Deutz whistled as he tried to remember. "Well, I was murdered on the 17th of December, 1832 and it was about another twenty years after that until I finally caught up with the thief of my life."

"Hmm. Say a hundred and seventy years."

"They don't seem at all bothered by my search for souls with, shall we

146

say, special sensitivities."

Caspar Deutz had spent roughly the first fifteen years of his corporeal existence chained to a bed in a darkened dungeon, during which time he had developed some curious abilities. As he'd had no human contact while in his cell, his senses had retained the sensitivity of the newborn. Light pained him, and he couldn't bear loud noises. Left to his own devices, he had developed his senses even further until he could, amongst other things, tell metals apart simply by passing his hands over them. Consequently, his interest in souls centred around those who could levitate or detect colours with their toes.

"Well," said Hob, "it's not as if you're the only one dealing in water diviners or those with second sight."

"*Ja*, I grant you that. And I have put the occasional skirrow your way and ridden with the *Terminal Murrain* in the Wild Hunt once or twice."

"You were in a class of your own," said Hob.

Deutz smiled and pointed a finger at him. "I could take that in one of two ways."

"Take it in the spirit in which it was given," advised Hob.

"No, I shall take it in the spirit in which it was received. Accentuate the positive, don't you know."

Caspar Deutz had earned his notoriety as the Foundling of Rauschenberg in 1828 when he staggered into Rauschenberg, carrying a letter of introduction addressed to the Commandant of the Light Cavalry, which was stationed within the city walls. One glance at his shambling gait and imbecilic expression told the good people of Rauschenberg that a career on horseback was out of the question. But Herr Griswald took pity on the boy, and his wife soon insisted they should adopt him.

"Spirits," said Hob, "are what we lack."

"Not in ourselves, but in our professional lives," agreed Deutz.

"But tonight we seem to lack them more than ever. What's going on, Deutz?"

"As you know, Hob, my perception of things is not what you might call normal. You, who have known human company all your formative years, are in some ways more acutely attuned to the human condition than I. On the other hand, you may miss things that I could not."

"Your point is what exactly?"

"Something very weird is going on."

"Oh, good. That's reassuring. Both of us can't be wrong."

"It's not just us. Everyone's saying it. Some of the older traders are talking of retiring."

"Would one of them be The Morrigan?"

Deutz chuckled. "*Ja*, but she insists she means it this time."

"She can't just stop like that. None of us can. You know, we couldn't really have been anything else, could we?"

"Apart from what we are, you mean?"

"Yeah. Here am I, born in Roathe in deepest Anarchadia and an engineer by profession, so I quickly became steeped in all the secrets of the Supply Works there. That I should subsequently race in the corporeal Wild Hunt was inevitable, and through learning the art and science of horsepower whispering, it seemed so easy to become a Soul Trader. Then, there's you, incarcerated in a dungeon twelve foot by nine ..."

"Seven feet long by six feet wide, actually," corrected the Foundling of Rauschenberg.

" ... and kept in total darkness for the whole of your childhood. You never knew anything else, did you?"

"Not until I was released, no."

"Now that was odd wasn't it? No human contact until the eve of your release."

Hob picked up a piece of fallen masonry and looked around for a pond so that he could throw it in, wistfully. Not finding one in that great hall, full of double-dealing Soul Traders, he let it drop again.

"*Ja*," sighed the Foundling of Rauschenberg. "I had never known sunshine. I'd never known sound. I'd never known any rise or fall in temperature. I had never smelt meat or coffee, and when I did, they made me physically sick."

"The ultimate in sensory deprivation, you might say."

"Very possibly. Whenever I awoke, there was some bread and water. Sometimes it tasted peculiar and I would rapidly become drowsy. On awakening again, my hair and finger nails had been trimmed and I was dressed in clean clothes. Once, just before I was set free, a hand appeared from the darkness behind me and guided my trembling fingers to trace my name. Caspar Deutz."

"The die was set for us from the beginning," said Hob.

"I couldn't join the cavalry. I couldn't walk anywhere without blistering and bleeding profusely. I had no co-ordination and was an imbecile."

"Well hardly," corrected Hob. "Illiterate, yes, an imbecile, never. But someone planned for you to join the cavalry. Hence the toy horse."

"*Ja* but I didn't expect the real thing to be as big as they are, you know? A sense of scale would have been useful. And then there was the letter of introduction and the note that was allegedly pinned to my blanket when I was found abandoned even as a baby. No other clue to my origin. I can remember the tall, dark man who carried me down the long stone staircase and took me far out into the forest where I was abandoned, for the second time in my life. I'm positive that letter of introduction was from him, but he of all people must have realised that it was a hopeless plan."

"But then you maximised the positive again. The Griswalds gave you a loving home. You astounded them with your strange perceptive abilities and the keenness of your undeveloped intelligence."

"They felt sorry for me, but also a little frightened. I was not of their world."

"But as part of their world you were a sensation! I heard you became something of fop, a real hit with society ladies."

Deutz grinned. "A little sympathy goes a long way."

"That's your unique take on the human condition." Hob turned serious again. "It was all going so well until you were murdered."

"*Ja*. He tried twice, you know – the first time he just wounded me badly. But I can remember him saying to me, 'It is necessary for you to die!'"

"Bit of a bugger, really, wasn't it?"

"But when he sent me an anonymous note to meet him in the public gardens," went on Caspar Deutz, "I knew it was him again. There was no question of not going. I was determined that I would say something to him to chill him to the marrow, just as he had done to me. And so it was. As I died, I quoted the Cursing Psalm to him."

"Psalm 109," said Hob. "I've used it myself."

And they quoted it together.

" 'When he shall be judged, let him be condemned: and let his prayer become sin. Let his days be few; and let another take his office. Because that he remembered not to show mercy, but persecuted the poor and needy man, that he might even slay the broken in heart. As he loved cursing, so let it come unto him: as he delighted in blessing, so let it be far from him.' "

"And that is how I came to transcend death," said the Foundling of Rauschenberg, in a faraway voice. "I hunted him down after life, and took his wretched soul for my own. It could have worked out differently for both of us, my friend. We were so close to being different people."

"Oh, I hardly think so! There's me at Roathe Supply Works, working at the forgemaster's knee as soon as I could walk, and there's you twice abandoned, denied human contact all your childhood, and then glimpsing normality and family bliss for a few years before some unidentified assassin does you in. Deutz, neither of us could be anything different. By the way. Did that first soul of yours ever tell you who you really were?"

"*Nein*. In the heat of eternity, I forgot all about explanations. Just retribution. I never asked him while I destroyed him."

"You traded for your first soul only to destroy it."

"I've had a long time to think about it since and, you know, sometimes it is better not to know."

Caspar Deutz gazed into the distance, thinking of who knew what.

Hob realised that of all the fey and other-worldly creatures gathered there that night, of all the shadowy creatures present, Caspar Deutz, the Foundling of Rauschenberg, knew less of the world of men than any of them.

"Anyway, who are you swapping these advertising account executives with?" he asked Deutz brightly, seeking to lighten his mood, as the crowds near the centre of the great vault reduced them to single file.

"Dionysius."

"Oh, is he here?"

"Yes, he's in charge of the party later."

"Excellent fellow!"

"Hob? You know you were saying about the general lack of souls around at the moment?"

"Yes. A veritable paucity of personae. A positive minginess of entities."

"Something like that. Well, there is one that I've seen recently that would definitely be worth having. And I think that of all the Soul Traders here tonight, you might just be the only one to be able to seal the deal."

"Oh, yes?" said Hob, his interest sharpening.

"Probably the most remarkable soul in history," murmured Caspar Deutz, deep in thought.

"You don't say! What name does this extraordinary soul travel under?"

Caspar Deutz chuckled. "You are intrigued, *nein*?"

"I am intrigued, yes! C'mon, old man, spill the beans."

He grabbed Caspar Deutz by the arm and they stopped walking.

Something was still amusing the erstwhile Foundling of Rauschenberg. "You chose your words well, my friend. Indeed! What name could this soul possibly travel under! This soul is like no other. Unique. Time does not waste it. In fact, time only makes it grow stronger."

"Stop talking in riddles, man!"

"I'm not! It is all true. Tell me, Hob, can you think of any soul that can weather time, apart from one like ours?"

"Look!" said Hob, suddenly hauling Caspar Deutz behind a stall so that they could not be overheard. "Apart from us Soul Traders, there are no souls that can do that! Everyone knows that!"

"All souls are immortal," replied Deutz with a smile.

But Hob was still in earnest. "Does this soul of which you speak belong to a Soul Trader?"

Deutz laughed again. Hob never had much in the way of patience and what he did have was running out rapidly.

"Because if you are," Hob told him, "you shouldn't forget where we are and what the Soul Transference and Necromancy Trade Association's policy is towards those who attempt to trade the souls of other Soul Traders."

"My dear friend," said Caspar Deutz, with a little less levity, "we have all thought about it. I am surprised to hear you, of all people, taking the moral high ground with me. Didn't we try to trade for each other's souls when we first met?"

He grinned and punched Hob on the arm.

Hob grinned back.

"This soul does not belong to a Soul Trader," Deutz said with emphasis.

Hob opened his mouth to speak.

"It is not the soul of a Soul Trader that belongs to another Soul Trader, either," said the Foundling of Rauschenberg.

Hob closed his mouth again.

"This soul is far more covetable. I am merely impressing upon you the inestimable significance, the ... the sheer order of magnitude of a soul that predates humankind itself."

"Well, if that's the case, then I'm not interested," said Hob. "We want the souls of humankind, not those of monkeys," and he began to walk away but Deutz took hold of him by the arm.

"Perhaps I should explain."

"I thought you were trying to. And failing, by and large, I might add."

"In the simplest terms, then, this soul of which I speak is one that has travelled backwards through time from one of many possible futures, with the intention of changing the course of history."

Caspar Deutz paused to let Hob come to terms with the concept.

"Wow!" said the Horsepower Whisperer. "Quite impossible, of course."

"I assure you that it is not."

"That really would be something, wouldn't it?"

"This soul has travelled back in time by means of a time machine, back to the antediluvian, primeval dawn of humankind! This person was re-incarnated by the Great Architect Himself."

"You mean the Big Fellow Upstairs?" asked Hob in a whisper, just in case there was really more than one after all.

"None other."

Hob glanced about them furtively. "But what was He thinking of, making some time traveller what is tantamount to immortal?"

"Who can say?" replied the Foundling of Rauschenberg. "Perhaps He took pity upon him, in His infinite wisdom."

"So, this soul, this fellow, this chap, for you have told me that much, has come back down through the centuries, through the millennia, no less, down to the present day?"

"Exactly."

"Then his soul must be colossal!"

"It is! I have seen it! It is vast!"

"It must be better than that of any Soul Trader!"

"You are right! It is! And with every tint, shade and hue of the rich tapestry of life imaginable!"

"And has it been a secret all this time?"

"Ah, my friend, you are so perceptive!" laughed Caspar Deutz. Then suddenly, he became very serious. "There have been stories, of course, but never any proof, only unreliable witnesses. It would appear that this soul, of all souls, can recognise a predatory Soul Trader from a much greater distance than is normal."

"Whereas many outstanding souls fail to recognise us at all."

"Quite. This soul has been around longer than any of us here! It knows such things, quite apart from how to tell that one of us is after it. Because of this, I caught but a fleeting glimpse of it. It is my belief that because of my extraordinary upbringing ..."

"My dear fellow," interrupted Hob, "none of us here tonight could ever be described as being in the slightest way normal."

Caspar Deutz's eyes blazed. "Because of my extraordinary upbringing," he repeated with fervour, "I could get close to this soul without being spotted for what I really was."

"And it is your belief ..."

"My complete conviction."

" ... that I am the only one who can get closer to this soul than you can."

"*Ja!* You are still new to this, although no less successful." Deutz nodded towards Hob's bulging rucksack. "He may not be able to recognise you as easily. I think that is how I caught him off guard. I am so weird even for a Soul Trader! So you ..."

"Old Weird Wheels!"

"You can creep up on his soul and claim it for yourself!"

"And why have you told me this? What's in it for you?"

"If you are successful in this," said Caspar Deutz, "then I would like to borrow this phantastical soul from to time, in recognition of information received leading to its acquisition."

"In that case, we have a deal. Let's shake upon the bargain!" and they spat upon their palms in the time-honoured fashion, and shook. "One last thing," said Hob. "What name does this soul travel under?"

"He travels under the name of Kevin Mullins."

"Oh," said Hob. "Are you sure?"

Deutz nodded.

"I was expecting something much grander."

"That's it, I'm afraid," said Caspar Deutz, slinging his sack over his shoulder again. "Now. To the business in hand. We must find Dionysius!"

Next to Abdul-ben-Ziggarat's vast edifice, covered in curlicues, gewgaws and baubles, they found, instead of a stall, what was more of a many-roomed tent.

Caspar Deutz strode into the first chamber where a sultry-looking hand-maiden was the only person present.

"Is he free?" asked the Foundling of Rauschenberg.

From somewhere behind the draperies behind her there came some muffled feminine giggling.

"I have the souls you requested," said the handmaiden, and, using the special soul-handling tongs most truly professional Soul Traders use, she passed them over to Caspar Deutz.

"*Danke schön,*" he replied, and, heaving the gently squirming sack from his shoulders, placed his side of the bargain on the counter. "When Dionysius is free, could you tell him Caspar Deutz and Nick Hob are here?"

At that instant, one of the drapes billowed out and a very happy, red-faced man emerged. He nearly wore a mantle that had been thrown carelessly over him, in the manner of a well-meaning Victorian seeking to give a Greek statue some semblance of modesty. He also had an air that was positively Bacchanalian.

"What?" spluttered Dionysius. "Did you shay Deutz and Hob were here?"

Caspar Deutz glanced at Hob, and Dionysius adjusted his focus.

"Deutz! Most exalted foundling! Hob! My dear old Whizz-herd! How are you, gentlemen? I haven't seen you since that party in Buenos Aires!"

"And what a party that was!" agreed Hob.

Dionysius' handmaiden suddenly looked a little embarrassed and quietly made her exit.

"D'you know?"

"No?"

"I don't think I've shobered up yet!"

If Dionysius had been mortal, it could theoretically be possible for him to be drunk for over three years were it not for the biological and chemical limitations of the human liver. However, everyone knew that Dionysius was perpetually squiffy and had no liver to worry about.

"There is one thing, though," went on Dionysius, frowning, trying to remember it. "A shobering thought, it was, too. Didn't last for long, of course, but it made me sweat all the shame. Ah, yes! No bloody souls round here! That's what it was! Have you notished?"

"Yes," said Hob and Caspar Deutz together.

"I shall be raising this at the next committee meeting."

"Actually, you're not on the committee any more," pointed out Caspar Deutz. "You kept dozing off, don't you remember?"

"No, I didn't," replied Dionysius, summoning some dignity. "I was conshentrating with my eyes shut. D'you know what I think the problem idge?"

"Too much fast living?" suggested Caspar Deutz.

"No, no, no, no, no!" protested Dionysius. "Can't be done! Can't be done! Believe me, I've tried. It's one of those oxymoron wossnames! Idgen't it, Hob?"

"Quite," said Hob.

"What was I shaying?"

"The problem about the current soul shortage," Hob reminded him.

"Ah yes! The current shoul sortage! Now then. Do you know what I think?" Dionysius asked them again.

"No," said Hob and Caspar Deutz.

"Conformorians!" replied Dionysius with a significant look.

"Conformorians?" chorused the two other Soul Traders in amazement.

"'Sright. Think about it. All these people scampering about in this soul-forsaken place they call Mourion, and not enough souls to go round. The ones we can find are so poor they're not worth bothering about! It's as if something is eating away at them."

"Of course!" said Hob. "I even had to check with my spirit level to make sure I hadn't lost my Extra-Sentiency Perception!"

His companions shook their heads and tut-tutted.

"Soul destruction!" said Deutz.

"By soul destroyers!" said Hob.

"Conformorians," deduced Dionysius.

"There have been stories, of course," began Caspar Deutz.

"I can't believe anyone would deliberately destroy a soul!" said Hob.

"Apart from me, you mean," said Caspar Deutz, darkly.

"The evidence shuggests otherwise," went on Dionysius.

"I thought the Conformorians were vanquished centuries ago," said Deutz.

"I know," said Dionysius, "sho did I. But recently I started wondering, and the fewer souls I find attached to more people the more I have wondered. I can't prove anything, but I believe they have never really gone away, just hidden themselves and quietly carried on their soul-destroying ways without any of us noticing."

"The question is, can we do anything about it?" asked Caspar Deutz.

"Dunno," said Dionysius. "I dunno much about them, to be honest."

"I'll be surprised if anyone does," remarked Hob. "I thought they were just myth."

"The very idea is horrible," said Deutz.

"It might not just be an idea," said Hob. "I hate to say it, but this feels right. Everything fits."

"I'll raise it at the next committee meeting," promised Dionysius.

"If this is true," said Caspar Deutz, "it could mean the end of all our ...""

"Afterlivelihoods. Yes, I know. Look, I think I'd better go. I think I might have lined myself up for about the last two decent souls left in Mourion."

"You better had," said Caspar Deutz. "Once this is raised at committee level, soul prices will soar!"

"Some people will say these rumours are deliberate," said Hob, "to create panic buying."

"It's happened before," admitted Dionysius. "There is one theory, of course, that the Conformorians were invented for that very purpose."

"The issue still has to be addressed," Deutz insisted.

"I agree," said Hob. "There's no knowing how long this will continue. Sorry but I won't be stopping for the party."

"Not going to be one, tonight," hiccupped Dionysius, one of the founder members of the Campaign for Real Ale. "Don't feel like it."

"*Ach je*," said Caspar Deutz, as they left Dionysius' tent. "A Soul Transference and Necromancy Trade Association swapmeet without a party. Is the world coming to an end?"

"That, my dear Deutz, is a distinct possibility," said Hob, grimly. "I wonder if Gehenna knows anything about this?"

"If anyone does, she does. However, may I suggest just one other point of enquiry before we leave tonight?"

"Suggest away, old son."

All Caspar Deutz did, however, was nod towards another knot in the crowd of Soul Traders and Necromancers.

Hob, following the nod, immediately understood.

Nearby was the only source of anything even approaching normal light in the whole of that vast, subterranean vault.

It emanated from a large showman's road locomotive that gently rocked as it chuntered away, generating power for its own lights and those of a large Marenghi fairground organ.

"Aha!" said Hob. "The Very Wrong Reverend, himself! The vaporous vicar of Carharrack!"

CHAPTER 37

As Hob and Deutz approached, the organ burst into life as if pleased to see them. In the vast underground vault, *Louis, Louie* by The Kingsmen was deafening. Puffs of dust and lumps of falling masonry fell around them as parts of the massive crypt overhead felt the vibrations, felt their age and then felt like a lie-down.

"The Reverend Tregaskis is your countryman, is he not?" Deutz asked Hob, as he brushed some masonry dust off his shoulders.

"Yeah. We're from the same region."

"Did I hear a story once that the Anarchadians routed the Conformorians?"

"You shouldn't pay too much attention to legends, Deutz."

Deutz grinned at him. "*You* ought to, you know, now that you *are* one."

A loosened granite corbel bounced off Hob's crash helmet.

"It takes one to know one, Deutz old chap," he replied affably.

From a distance, the Marenghi organ appeared to be a well-preserved relic of the naughty nineties. In front of its pipes and drums were carvings of dancing girls, none of whom appeared to be adequately dressed, and most of these figures were animated. One or two particularly dishabille young ladies stood against columns that supported the roof of the organ, occasionally kicking their legs in time to the music while their more modestly attired companions threatened to brandish batons, play harps, shake tambourines, strum mandolins or hit little bells with little hammers.

It was only as Hob and Deutz admired these figures more closely that they discerned a subtle quality to their carving. It wasn't just that their eyes followed you as you walked past. It was obvious that these figures were alive as no carving had any right to be. The mechanical movements had a nuance to them that spoke of a truly infernal artifice, one guaranteed to impress the practised Soul Trader or Necromancer.

As the undead might walk and imitate the living, these animated yet disconcertingly lifelike figures were the unalive.

Hob and Deutz peered around the back and saw the hapless organ grinders feeding the card music sheets into the voracious organ. In life, they had been showmen or one-man bands who had been well acquainted with the freedom of the open road. Now someone else called the tune and they were not so much organ grinders as monkeys.

Nearby was *Simplicity*, the Burrell road locomotive providing the power for the Marenghi organ. It gleamed under rows of multi-coloured light bulbs arranged along its full-length canopy and gently rocked back and forth as it worked, humming the Song of the Machine. On one side was a great solid flywheel, and this drove a heavy leather belt that stretched forward to a large generator mounted on a substantial bracket ahead of the chimney. Gauges measured the current produced, and heavy brass fittings carried thick cables that fell to the ground and stretched away into the gloom to more pools of light belonging to other diabolical amusements.

As news spread that there would be no soul swapping party, STANTA members closed their stalls and flocked to the fun fair behind *Simplicity*, where more steam engines drove scenic railways, steam yachts, cake walks, razzle-dazzles and, of course, a ghost train.

Louis, Louie came to a tumultuous climax and in the sudden absence of noise that followed there was the hum of *Simplicity's* dynamo and the slap-slap-slap of the belt that drove it.

From out of the darkness came the screams and giggles of Necromancers enjoying their proverbial thirteenth childhood.

"Ah," said Hob, "remember this one?"

Deutz nodded.

The Marenghi organ had started to play the opening bars of *Let's stay together* as sung by Al Green.

A hundred years ago, there had been a great deal of opposition to Reverend Tregaskis's *Gigantic Combination and Travelling Bioscope Show*. The old guard said soul trading was a very serious affair. They didn't "hold" with the mechanically undead undermining an egojumble's dignity or cluttering the place up with new-fangled contrivances that made a lot of noise. Gehenna soon reminded them, however, that in the old days the swapmeets had taken on the appearance of a boisterous bazaar, albeit rather a bizarre one. Anyway, she said, she liked the quiet, gentle power of these iron monsters, and an oblique comment like that from her silenced any dissent. The joyously frivolous fun of the fair contrasted perfectly with the diabolical trade going on all around it and reminded the STANTA members, Soul Trader and Necromancer alike, that immortality was not a rehearsal.

But it was the smoke from Reverend Tregaskis's steam locomotives that really won the opposition over. Such sulphurous fumes added to the atmosphere, they said. Latterly, soul or gospel songs played on a fairground organ deeply gratified the avid egojumbler.

Hob walked right up to *Simplicity* and patted it on the dynamo extension as it rocked gently back and forth.

"Hallo, *Simplicity*," he said.

"Ahh!" said Deutz. "Smell that!"

"Sulphur and hot oil," replied Hob.

"With just a hint of lightning," replied Deutz, breathing in deeply.

"Evening, gents," said a grubby grease bogle on the footplate. "I see you know how to address an engine."

"And you," said Hob, "certainly know how to look after one."

The grease bogle stood a little taller and beamed at him.

"Oh, thank you, sir!"

"Grunnion? Stop bothering those gentlemen! And get on with your work," ordered a voice.

"Yes sir, sorry, sir," and the diabolical lackey jumped down and went forth in a frenzy of oiling and polishing.

"Well, well, well," said the voice. The canopy seemed to be full of smoke and waste steam escaping from the steadily blowing safety valves. "If it isn't the Foundling of Rauschenberg! And the Metal Guru himself, Old Weird Wheels!"

"Evening, your irreverence," said Caspar Deutz. He clicked his heels and made a little bow.

Hob beamed up at the cloud of smoke and steam billowing above them. Slowly, it resolved itself into a slightly built figure of average height, enveloped in a pair of dark blue overalls, sprinkled with coal dust and stained with oil. He wore a dog collar around his neck and Hob noticed grubby finger prints around its edge where the incumbent had pulled it to one side to relieve the temperature within.

"Hob! Deutz! You will have to excuse my little, erm, transubstantiation! When I'm around such magnificent machinery, I'm afraid I can't help it."

"Think nothing of it, Vicar," Hob replied, graciously. "It's enough to make anyone come over all ethereal. You've really put on a magnificent show tonight."

"Splendid machine, isn't it? The last Burrell showman's engine ever made," and he pulled the chain on *Simplicity's* steam klaxon. It made a kind of low buzzing fart but Reverend Tregaskis gradually built it up into a great, long drawn-out whoop.

The crowd turned and grinned at him and he invited Hob and Deutz onto the footplate to each have a try.

"How goes it with you fellows?" he asked them.

"There don't seem to be many souls around," said Caspar Deutz, in between steam klaxon whoops. "Have you noticed?"

"I should say I have," said Reverend Tregaskis. "Genuine steam enthusiasts have been getting thin on the ground for some time now. The social environment in Euphobia simply doesn't favour them. However, I have discovered a source of souls that fulfils my requirements admirably."

"Really?" asked Caspar Deutz.

"Yes. Model engineers. Show something like *Simplicity* to them and they lose all sense of scale. They're quite prepared to trade their souls for an eternity of hard labour above and below the footplate. It's a smaller-sized market, of course, but I fully intend to make it my own."

"I wish you luck," said Hob. "Mourion is not good for souls."

"In the short run, I still see supply being comparatively healthy. There are enough generations of enginemen and railway modellers out there for me to be fully engaged in collecting them for some time. But the numbers and quality of brand new souls are dropping off markedly, so in the long run things may prove more difficult. Well, enough of this shop talk. Come! Who would like some Sulphur Floss?"

Sulphur Floss was the latest craze at STANTA events. If molten refined brimstone is squirted into a rapidly spinning drum at high velocity with a blast of hot air, the sticky fibrous wad that results can be wrapped round a stick and sold to eager Soul Traders or Necromancers as a treat. Hob and Caspar Deutz were both partial, and Reverend Tregaskis instructed the rather down-in-the-mouth grease bogle in charge of a nearby Sulphur Floss tricycle to give them both a massive helping.

"Would either of you gentlemen care for a 666?" enquired the uncharacteristically clean grease bogle. She avoided eye contact with them and Hob guessed that she had been relieved from her polishing duties for some minor misdemeanour and made to wear a little hat.

Hob and Deutz nodded, their eyes bright with anticipation, and the grease bogle carefully unwrapped four Cadbury's Flakes and pushed two of them into each wad of Sulphur Floss at a rakish angle as if they were horns.

"Camphor sauce?" she asked them.

"Mm, mm," answered Hob and Caspar Deutz, who by now could not open their mouths for fear of engulfing the Sulphur Floss tricycle in saliva.

"Heavy on the sauce," advised Reverend Tregaskis, "and don't forget the hundreds and thousands," and the grease bogle used up a bottle and a carton between them.

"There now," said Reverend Tregaskis, passing the Sulphur Floss to his companions.

"Aren't you having any, Vicar?" asked Caspar Deutz.

"Ah, no thank you. I've given it up for Lent," replied the reverend gentleman, and when Deutz looked puzzled he added, "Old habits die hard."

And for the next, rather sticky, fifteen minutes or so, as they wandered through the fair, neither Deutz nor Hob said a word but listened to Reverend Tregaskis as he showed them around his collection of steam engines.

Tregaskis explained to Deutz, since Hob knew the story already, that he had been present at the very birth of the steam locomotive. He had known Trevithick personally and had seen his locomotive ascend Camborne Hill for himself, beginning two hundred years of Anarchadian motoring. But even before that, Reverend Tregaskis had been seduced by the dark side. It had happened when Murdoch had been demonstrating his *Flyer* to some friends on the downs above Camborne. It didn't fly and was only a model, built to test the principles of steam propulsion, but ran along on its wheels so quickly it appeared possessed by a new and unearthly spirit. And when, as luck would have it, a visiting preacher, who knew nothing of their experiments, wandered onto their test track one evening, the little fire-breathing device came out of the gloom at him, as if emerging from the very pit itself, and the poor man fled, convinced that he was pursued by the devil himself in all his satanic majesty. From then on, Reverend Tregaskis began an ecclesiastical association with the steam engine that would last for ever, except that the souls he sought to save were irrevocably lost to those who originally owned them.

His interest in steam engines was extensive and showed a catholic taste for all things locomotive, spanning the whole steam epoch, from its primordial dawn right up to its superheated, triple-expansion zenith. However, his collection followed a theme. Every item had been scrapped. But Tregaskis had found a way to restore engines that didn't even exist any more. "What man has made, he can make again," he would say to his grease bogles and klinkergeists, and they would always prove him right.

Prominent among the fairground rides that night were the showman's engines. They had names like *The Black Prince, Boadicea, Nil Desperandum* and *Excelsior* and, like *Simplicity*, their paintwork glittered under the lights powered by their generators.. Only the most trusted grease bogles and klinkergeists were allowed to drive them. Some rides, such as the merry-go-rounds or steam yachts, had their own dedicated engines without wheels. To service the needs of these working aristocrats of the fairground, a large fleet of steam tractors and steam lorries plied through the crowds hauling trailers stacked with coal or towing bowsers full of water.

There were some very rare engines among them. Many really early ones had been scrapped long before the preservation movement had even been thought of but, thanks to Reverend Tregaskis's restoration techniques and a great deal of labour from his army of souls, there they were.

Hob spotted one of Thomas Aveling's pioneering chain-driven engines, clanking though the crowds. This was a conversion of a portable engine, literally a stationary engine on wheels that could be drawn by a horse. From the cranks and cylinders above the boiler, a heavy chain ran down to the rear axle and it twitched and rattled as power was applied.

There was also an early Robey with a vertical ship's wheel in front of its smokebox, presumably so that the steersman could anticipate his accidents more effectively.

"How did you get all this stuff in here?" he asked, as he finished his Sulphur Floss.

"There's an abandoned underground railway line nearby," explained Reverend Tregaskis. "You know what they say. Old railways never die."

"They just carry ghost trains," suggested Hob.

In one wall of the crypt was a soaring Gothic railway arch, from which sidings fanned out, each one containing a train of wagons. At the head of these stood some large locomotives. There was a Big Boy Mallet and an enormous Beyer-Garratt. They dwarfed a streamlined Gresley A2/3 Pacific appropriately christened *Dante*, and here and there were even smaller, more ancient locomotives such as Old Number One of the Shrewsbury and Chester.

"That's one of my favourites," enthused Reverend Tregaskis. "Note the Gothic firebox and the so-called long boiler design. And here we have *North Star* of 1837, a Great Western engine built to the ancient broad gauge. It survived until 1906, until someone persuaded the late, great G J Churchward that it should be scrapped. That's how it came to be in my collection. They realised their mistake at once and built a replica, but this one is the original."

"It wasn't you who persuaded Churchward to break it up, was it?" asked Hob, who knew Tregaskis well.

"I couldn't possibly comment," he replied.

Each engine had a klinkergeist and grease bogle attending to it. These unfortunate creatures were now doomed to an eternity of cleaning and polishing and mending and oiling, possibly in some form of grotesque penance for allowing these engines to be broken up. Now they inhabited the worst imaginings of Hieronymous Bosch, but with boilers and fireboxes, cranks and wheels, glowing embers and smoke.

"And would Churchward be with us tonight?" asked Hob. He'd spotted a very distinguished Edwardian grease bogle inspecting a Great Western express engine, with an air of self-criticism.

"He might be," said the vicar, without quite lying.

To the side of the Gothic tunnel entrance was a large group of very small navvies, draped languidly over piles of rubble. Not one of them was over seventy-five centimetres tall.

"Good evening, track fairies," called out Reverend Tregaskis.

The track fairies leapt to their feet and their foreman approached with his cap in his hands.

"No, no, we're not off yet," said Reverend Tregaskis, gesturing for them to be seated.

The track fairies relaxed.

"They worked very hard to get us here tonight," Reverend Tregaskis told Hob and Deutz.

"It can't be easy laying a railway just a few feet ahead of an express train," said Hob.

"Practice makes perfect," said Reverend Tregaskis. "Besides, they didn't have to tunnel much of a detour tonight."

Now that his companions had finished their Sulphur Floss, Reverend

Tregaskis insisted that they try the amusements that he had laid on.

They had several rides on his steam yachts, followed by a trip, quite literally for Hob and Deutz, on the cake walk. They ended up with a spin on the razzle-dazzle, but after consuming such vast quantities of Sulphur Floss Caspar Deutz, who still, even in his incorporeal state, had a rather delicate constitution, began to feel a little ill.

This was the source of good-natured amusement to Hob but Reverend Tregaskis showed great concern and blamed himself for letting the Foundling of Rauschenberg eat too much diabolical food.

"You know what, your irreverence?" said Hob. "You're just too kind to be a Soul Trader."

Reverend Tregaskis smiled. "Nearly everyone says that."

"Nearly everyone?" asked Deutz, still even paler than usual.

"Apart from those who say I'm too wicked to be a vicar."

"Curiously strong mint?" asked Hob, offering the packet round.

"Thank you."

"Deutz?"

"Yes please."

"Badness! These *are* refreshing!" remarked Tregaskis enthusiastically. "What sort are they?"

"Uncle Bub's Mint Bombs."

"Ah! The very best!"

They wandered back to the centre of the swapmeet.

"Steam locomotives are very labour-intensive devices," Tregaskis explained. "I could never look after all these by myself. I realised at a very early stage that I would need some help. That's why I became a Soul Trader. And I soon discovered that the invention of the steam engine had divided humankind neatly into two. There were those who became obsessed with them and those who did not. Latterly, a third section evolved, those that found the internal combustion engine irresistible."

Hob waved a modest hand.

"Of course, the whole of humankind is fascinated by fire," Tregaskis went on, "in one form or another. Horsepower depends on combustion of some sort, whether it is internal to the cylinder or, in my case, external to it, and underneath a nice free steaming boiler."

"Tregaskis was the first ever Horsepower Whisperer," Hob told Deutz, "apart from The Great Smith himself."

Tregaskis mimicked Hob's earlier gesture of modesty. "If I was, I hardly knew it. However, as a Soul Trader, I think it would not be out of place for me to say that I was quite successful."

"Quite successful!" spluttered Hob. "You kept winning The Faust Among Equals Challenge, year after year!"

"My success was embarrassing," admitted Tregaskis. "I didn't want any more trophies. Thousands surrendered their souls to me and at times I was at a loss with what to do with them, all sold so cheaply and with the whole of eternity for them to reflect upon it. I obtained some steam roundabouts driven by Savage centre engines, but perpetual rides on three-abreast gallopers and giant poultry can only amuse a soul for so long. Any that began to atrophy I sold on to other Soul Traders, and those that showed some mechanical empathy I kept. Eventually these evolved into the grease bogles and klinkergeists that you see before you now. As steam engines began to be wantonly destroyed and my collection grew, I found I needed every bit of help I could find."

"There was something we wanted to ask you," said Hob. "Well. Two things, actually. Weren't there, Deutz?"

"*Ja.* I don't suppose you have any theories as to why there is such a soul shortage at the moment, do you?"

"I might have," replied the Vaporous Vicar of Carharrack.

"Dionysius reckons it could be Conformorians," said Hob.

"But I always thought the Conformorians had been destroyed centuries ago," put in Caspar Deutz.

Reverend Tregaskis did not answer immediately. "I think you'll find that they simply withdrew beyond our ken," he said, at last.

"So you believe they exist?" asked Hob.

"Oh, indeed I do. Consider this. When has the spark of original thought been stifled? Once? Twice? Would it not be easier to ask when has it not been stifled? Take the steam engine for example. Land owners objected to railways. Punitive legislation suppressed the development of road locomotives."

He indicated a Foden steam wagon as it passed.

"You've no doubt heard of the Red Flag Act?" Reverend Tregaskis asked Deutz.

"*Ja.* A man carrying a red flag would have to walk in front of any vehicle," the Foundling replied.

"That's right. Freedom provided by the latest technology was deliberately stifled in the name of public safety."

"But that act was repealed," said Deutz.

"Oh yeah," agreed Hob, "and there's a special Wild Hunt to celebrate it, the Emancipation Run."

"That was just one small victory in a long, long war," Tregaskis told them.

Hob frowned. "Do you believe the Conformorians were behind the old RAC horsepower rating system?"

"What did that achieve?"

"Anaemic, narrow-bored motors that didn't rev," said Hob. "Any big-bore motors with any hint of performance potential were heavily taxed."

Reverend Tregaskis pulled a face. "The more you look, the more you see the dead hand of Conformorianism. It was axle-loading restrictions that finally drove the steam engine off the road, not antiquated design. Did you know that in Japan they actually tried to ban the wheel? Now ask me if indeed the Conformorians ever left us."

They wandered on in thoughtful silence and then Reverend Tregaskis asked, "What was the other thing you wanted to ask me?"

"We were just wondering," said Hob, "if you have ever seen a magnificent soul, richly embroidered with all the deepest colours of life's rich tapestry."

"I've dealt with lots of souls in my career," said Reverend Tregaskis.

"But this one is special," said Deutz. "Ever heard of the Soul of All Souls?"

"A vast soul? Been everywhere? Done everything?"

"*Ja.*"

"Pre-dates the very dawn of humankind itself?"

Hob and Caspar Deutz looked at each other.

"A time traveller from one of an infinite number of alternative futures?"

"There can only be the one!" exclaimed the Foundling of Rauschenberg, unable to contain his excitement.

"Oh, yes," said Reverend Tregaskis, dismissively, "but I didn't talk to him for long, though."

"You actually spoke to him?" asked Deutz.

Tregaskis nodded. "I passed through the dinosaur exhibition at the Science Museum on my way to see Stephenson's *Rocket*. One day that will be mine, just like *North Star*. And there he was. Never seen such a soul. It would appear that he's quite fascinated by fossils. No good for me, though. Wouldn't know a bellcrank from his draincocks."

"So," ventured Caspar Deutz, "you would have no objection if Hob and I tried to trade with him?"

"Badness, black-hearted me! None whatever. But then, would that really stop you if you wanted his soul badly enough?"

"Well, no ..."

"But I appreciate you asking."

"Could you give us any clues as to what he might trade his soul for?" asked Hob.

"I already have."

"Eh?"

"Dinosaurs. He's quite obsessed by them."

"So all we need to trade for his soul is a dinosaur," suggested Caspar Deutz.

"Or parts thereof," added Hob.

"Possibly," replied Reverend Tregaskis. "But where on earth would you find one?"

"Crocodiles," said Caspar Deutz. "An apothecary I've got came with a stuffed crocodile."

"My dear fellow," said Tregaskis, "if a soul such as this wanted a stuffed crocodile badly enough – badly enough to trade his soul for it – then he would already be in spiritual bondage to one of our fellow Soul Traders."

"I have it!" exclaimed Hob. "Do you suppose this fellow's ever seen the Wild Hunt?"

"It's possible, I suppose," said Reverend Tregaskis. "He's been around for long enough."

"Deutz. You remember that time when you raced with me and the rest of the *Terminal Murrain*? And you commented on how some of the others looked like gargoyles?"

"There was more than a passing resemblance," admitted the Foundling of Rauschenberg.

"They, gentlemen, were the oldest members of any Wild Hunt. They are the first skirrows of all time."

"What's he talking about, Deutz?" asked Reverend Tregaskis.

"The strangest creatures known – or rather not known – to man! The night-racing dinosaurs! To be perfectly frank, to look at them, some of them – how do you say this? – 'gave me the willies'."

"You see, it's occurred to me that if we can give this Kevin Mullins a glimpse of the weird and wonderful creatures in the Wild Hunt, then not only might he be willing to trade his soul but, also, we might even make a Horse-power Whisperer out of him!"

"Badness, black-hearted me!" said Reverend Tregaskis. "That would be quite something, wouldn't it?"

"All we have to do is introduce him to the *oldest* members of the in-corporeal Wild Hunt."

"You mean …" began Caspar Deutz.

"Yes, exactly. The fleet-of-foot Ferraridinosaurs and the vast Cadillac-aplodicus! I must get back to Anarchadia. We need to organise the best Wild Hunt we can. Just one other point, Tregaskis. You don't know anything about a good-looking, scientific sort of woman driving a pink Cadillac Rushmore con-vertible, do you?"

"What? One of those six-wheeled jobs? With the rear aerofoil? Yes. She pops up whenever we're about to fost. Why do you ask?"

"I have a sneaking suspicion that she somehow fits into all this. Anyway, thank you for showing us over your engines, your irreverence."

They shook hands.

"The pleasure was all mine. Most Soul Traders don't even know their Burrells from their Fosters! Good hunting, Hob!"

"Indeed!"

"And to you, Deutz!"

CHAPTER 38

Hob and Deutz made their way slowly through a seething, heaving mass of inhumanity. Sometimes they had to clamber over piles of fallen masonry to get around haggling Soul Traders. Many stalls were already being dismantled by their owners, but a hard core of determined soul swappers and egojumblers were still prowling around, searching for last-minute bargains.

"Where's the way out of here?" asked Hob, as he jumped onto an apparently deserted trestle table to peer into the gloom.

"The exit? It's over there," replied Caspar Deutz, whose eyes were always more accustomed to the gloom. "Where it says exit. By the euthanasia enthusiasts."

The sign was lit by another variation of the anti-light that illuminated the great hall, and underneath it was a small pointed archway leading to a spiral staircase. At the top of the stairs they burst through the flimsy veil between their world and that of humankind to find Gehenna peering behind an ancient and very dusty wall hanging that was draped on one side of the corridor leading up to the surface.

"Hallo, Gehenna!" said Hob. "What are you up to?"

"Gatecrashers," she muttered. She pulled the tapestry away from the wall to reveal a small wooden door with an iron grille in it.

"What's in there?" asked Caspar Deutz, brushing the dust off his coat.

"Have a look," said Gehenna, and she peered in herself.

Unfortunately, her thought trumpet came just that little bit too close to the iron grille in the door and hands from inside reached out and grabbed it, banging her head against the petrified woodwork.

"What the ...?" said Hob.

He grabbed one of Gehenna's arms and Caspar Deutz grabbed the other.

"Let us out! Let us out!" chanted many voices. "Do you hear us? Let us out! This instant!"

"C'mon, Hob! Pull!"

There was a rending sound and the three of them sprawled on the floor.

"By the spanners of St Bendix! What could do that?"

"Whatever it is, it's weird and pissed off," remarked Caspar Deutz.

"Let us out!"

"We demand to be set free!"

"Sounds like there's more than one of them, too," Deutz added, knocking a dent out of his hat.

Gehenna's battered thought trumpet flew at them from behind the iron grille. It bounced on its rubber suction cup and danced about them, as if full of joy at being back on that side of the door. Whatever had thrown it carried on shouting.

Hob and Caspar Deutz picked themselves up, dusted themselves down and then hoisted Gehenna back onto her feet, or at least onto whatever remained of them. It was rumoured that several chiropodists existed in a state of perpetual torment trying to maintain whatever supported her.

Gehenna was stricken in millennia and appeared rather stunned. They sat the whiskery old woman down on a piece of fallen masonry and Caspar Deutz fanned her with his handkerchief.

"What've you got in that cell?" Hob asked her, mouthing the words to make up for the loss of her thought trumpet.

The old oak door rattled on its substantial hinges as many tiny fists hammered against it.

Gehenna focused and unfocused her good eye several times and shuddered.

"Grauniads," she muttered.

"What?" said Hob.

"I think she said guardians," suggested an equally perplexed Caspar Deutz.

"Don't you dare call us that!" shouted the furious grauniads.

"To hear such language!"

"Just wait till we get out of here!"

"Caretakers of this paraverse," said Gehenna in the loud voice of the deafened.

"Caretakers did you say?" asked Hob. "I never knew we had any."

Gehenna's thought trumpet was not too badly damaged since it was a heavy-duty one. It was just that when the grauniads had grabbed it, they had pulled the very nails out of her head.

Hob put his hands into his pockets and produced six superscrews and his sawn-off, pump-action, reversible-ratchet screwdriver. With this it was the work of but an instant to reunite Gehenna with her thought trumpet.

"The grauniads tried to gatecrash the party," she explained. "They were on each others' shoulders and in disguise under long coats, but I recognised them straightaway and directed them into this little cell which I keep precisely for this sort of eventuality."

"They can't be after souls," said Deutz. "Can they?"

"It's possible but it's more likely they want to close us down."

"Close STANTA down?"

"And there's me nearly eligible to join," put in Hob.

"Of course! They see our trade as a blight upon creation."

"We'll close you down!" insisted a grauniad from the cell.

"We'll force you to stop your sinister dealings!" shouted another.

"And we'll return all spirits to their rightful owners!"

"We are the authority in this paraverse!"

"We insist you abide by our rules!"

"Rules are for the guidance of wise men and the obedience of fools," Hob shot back.

"Never!" screamed another grauniad.

"We shall close you down!"

"All repossessed or dispossessed souls shall become forfeit!"

"Soul trading will be banned!"

"No more fosts for you, Hob!"

"No more weirdos for you, Deutz!"

"This paraverse is not big enough for all of us!"

"Desist from this practice!"

"If you refuse, we will be forced to act harshly!"

"That's a threat, not a promise!"

"Don't you mean the other way round!"

"Stop criticising me! We're all in this together."

"Ach, words, they betray us with their meanings!"

"I always suspected there was something wrong with reality," remarked Hob.

"There's nothing wrong with reality!" chorused the grauniads.

"I don't remember voting for you."

"Nobody voted for us," they told him.

"We have divine appointment," explained one.

"You propose the end of our afterlivelihoods," protested Deutz.

"Of course!"

"Keep rubbing the brain cells together, unwarranted immortals!"

"Cease disrupting The Great Architect's Grand Design!"

All this time, Gehenna had been gathering herself and with the slow build-up of a hurricane she rose from her sitting position and approached the oak door, pulling her sleeves up over surprisingly brawny forearms.

"Wrench my thought trumpet off me, would you?" she said, slamming back the bolt to send the grauniads scampering away from the door. "Want to close us down, do you?" she shouted as she threw the door open on its hinges. "We're a self-regulatory body and don't you forget it!"

She suddenly morphed into the severest and most glamorous warrior woman Hob and Deutz had ever seen and, in full battle glamour, she slammed the door shut behind her to chase the grauniads into the next paraverse.

Hob and Deutz emerged into the pale dawn of an especially grey Mourion.

In the glade under the trees stood the coaches belonging to the swapmeet visitors. Every Soul Trader and Necromancer liked to think they had their own idea of what was suitable for a spirit in their position, but few showed much imagination.

Hob and Deutz nodded their respects to the headless horsemen who, of course, could not nod back and had to give little self-conscious waves in return. They grinned at the skeletal footmen standing to perpetual attention on the backs of skull-shaped coaches and admired carriages made out of bones. Their wheels, in particular, were works of art. One coach was hewn out of coal and had over a dozen pit-ponies between its shafts, while another was made out of diamonds, pulled by four of the fleetest Arabs. One or two put the coach before the horses and were terrible enough in that respect alone, while a few resembled Celtic war chariots, typically drawn by three huge cart-horses. These invariably had great blades sticking out from their hubcaps, but the effect was somewhat lost on the chariot with caravan wheels and pneumatic tyres. There were several huge hollowed-out pumpkins, drawn by six giant mice, and an armoured war wagon straight out of the western of the same name. Deutz liked those drawn by horses with wings or six or eight legs, whereas Hob's favourite was an elaborately constructed bronze and iron buggy belonging to an eldritch clock-maker, powered by a single clockwork horse riding a unicycle.

Not everyone had a carriage. The Concubine and the Great Wazir found a well staffed palanquin more than adequate for their needs, and several Soul Traders from the Regency period liked sedan chairs since they were much more manoeuvrable up and down spiral staircases, and surprisingly comfortable as well. The Venetian Necromancers favoured impressive gondolas that floated a few feet above the ground, and the man o' war with many cannonball holes in its sails could only have belonged to Davy Jones himself.

"Is your coach here somewhere?" asked Hob.

"*Ja*. I have tied a plastic bag to its carriage lamp so I can spot it easily."

Deutz's carriage was a horseless carriage, not an old-fashioned motorcar but a carriage without any horses. During his long captivity he'd only had a few toys to play with and his favourite had been a little wooden horse. He became very attached to it during the long years of darkness and complete solitude.

However, when he met real horses they fell a long way short of his expectations. They had minds of their own, but operated largely by nervous instinct.

Horses were also a great deal bigger than he had expected.

He realised that he'd had nothing to engender any sense of size relative to a horse, such as a soldier or a cart. Caspar Deutz had always imagined them to be about the size of his toy, i.e. no bigger than a rabbit. Consequently, his career in the cavalry was doomed.

It was also why his carriage had no horses.

Hob was always surprised that no one had thought of a horseless carriage before. An old-fashioned stage coach without any obvious form of propulsion and apparently steered by witchcraft appealed to him as much as a Kawasaki H2 with a comprehensive porting job and knackered dampers.

They walked up to Caspar Deutz's carriage, with its empty shafts folded back over the driver's seat, and Deutz untied the plastic bag fluttering from its carriage lamp.

"Farewell, Deutz. Good hunting. We have a bargain over Kevin Mullins' soul. I wish you luck in your search."

"And I you."

The two Soul Traders shook hands, and then Caspar Deutz climbed aboard his perilous carriage, which swayed like a jelly on a heavy sea as it dangled from its under-frame on straps of leather. He settled himself in his seat and looked out of the window to touch his hat at Hob. Hob did the same with his crash helmet and the wheels on the Foundling's coach began to turn. It steered its way carefully out of the coach park, and Deutz grinned back at Hob as it trundled off into the morning light.

Hob watched him go and then walked back to where he'd left M Cadvare's personal transportation device. He drove silently back to La Place de Lors, wishing along the way that it had a proper exhaust note that could blare out over the rooftops of Mourion.

There was little traffic about so early in the morning but it started to thicken as he approached La Place de Lors. He was now keener than ever to leave Mourion, and his mind was working furiously on the matter of tempting the Soul of All Souls when he tripped over something outside M Cadvare's flat. He fell flat on his face and, after a pause to collect himself, lifted his head and looked behind him.

Sitting by the door to M Cadvare's apartment was a small orange and white cone. Hob at first wondered if there was a very small wizard asleep underneath it but then he recognised it as a smart traffic cone, just like those that he had run over only the previous afternoon. He leapt up, grabbed it and burst into M Cadvare's flat with it in his hands. He went straight to the doors to the balcony, opened them and drop-kicked the traffic cone over the waking city.

"Pretty dumb for a smart traffic cone," he said and turned around to find himself staring down the barrels of at least a dozen high-calibre weapons. A few more were trained on M Cadvare and Nenuphar.

"Don't move," said one of the police, motioning with his gun, and Hob obligingly raised his hands.

CHAPTER 39

As soon as he arrived in the Garden of Eden, Kevin was glad he'd agreed to be Adam, although he still answered only to Kevin. Nobody had called him that for ages but his first name had really stuck. After 65 million years, the prospect of being human again appealed greatly.

He would be helping God out, too.

Kevin wasn't entirely sure quite where the Garden of Eden was. It felt like Earth, but everything was so beautiful, so perfect, that he wondered if it wasn't somewhere else, somewhere in another paraverse, but he decided it was on earth when he recognised the grauniads.

They popped their faces over the hedge as he was exploring Eden's boundaries and told him not to get any ideas because they were watching him, watching him very closely, and if he didn't behave there was going to be trouble, real trouble.

Kevin reassured them that he hadn't the slightest intention of causing any mischief in such beautiful surroundings. This place, he said, could only bring out the best in creatures, encouraging them to live in perfect peace and harmony with each other. The lion, he pointed out to them, was even then lying down with the lamb and asking it who its favourite poet was, and the vultures were organising a nature ramble later on, to which everyone was invited.

"Come and join us," he said to the grauniads, but the grauniads replied that they didn't want to and slid back down their ladders, and must have disappeared into the ground itself for when Kevin clambered through the thick branches of the boundary hedge and looked out there was no sign of them.

He took the opportunity to study the landscape and decided that the Garden was probably somewhere in the Middle East, say southern Persia or Mesopotamia.

Having established the boundaries, he began to explore the rest of Eden. It was clear that God had surpassed Himself. The colours were more vivid. The air was sweeter. The water was crystal clear. The temperature was just right.

There were also subtle clues to Sophia's influence as well. Kevin was sure that if he hadn't met her before he would have missed them. She made many subtle improvements when God wasn't looking.

Evolution had developed some rather distasteful characteristics. Most obvious was the fact that everything had to die. Then there was the need to consume your fellow creatures or plants as food. Life, it seemed, was finite, and there was never quite enough of it to go around. It had to be spread thinly or shared as much as possible, but some of the sharing had become unfair. It was still quite equable among amoebae, but more complicated organisms had begun to hoard it. The worst culprits were the giant tortoises and redwoods.

In the Garden of Eden, each creature had equal shares of life. They didn't have to eat and they didn't have to kill each other, either.

Kevin suspected Sophia was behind the dawn chorus as well. God had given song to the birds, but she must have orchestrated them. Although she had always denied it, Kevin was convinced she had been behind the pollination of plants by insects, too. He'd also caught her dabbling with algae and mosses just before there had been some exciting new developments among the lichens.

As far as he could see, there was only one downside to life in the Garden of Eden. God had kept the numbers of each life form down to just two. They hadn't actually said so but Kevin had a feeling that the defutured wanted him to save the whole human race not just two of them but, for the time being, he was content that there were no physical threats to humankind or catalysts towards its fall, and he strolled through Eden in a state approaching bliss.

"Psst," said something nearby.

Kevin wandered on, a new-age naturist, completely forgetting the concept of original sin, the wind playing on his body like a very gentle masseuse, kissing and caressing him, and smelling delicately of flowers.

"Psst," said something even closer now.

Kevin looked around.

"Hey! Kevin! Over here! It isss Kevin Mullinsss, isssn't it?"

The only creature he could see was a huge black snake, winding itself through the different pairs of long, lush grasses. It was completely black, with no stripes or diamond patterns on it anywhere, and seemed strangely at odds with its surroundings.

The snake raised its head up quizzically and, once or twice, flicked out its forked tongue as if trying to taste him over the distance between them.

"I used to be Kevin Mullins," he replied cautiously. Whenever he had encountered snakes as a human before, he had always been fully clothed and armed with an extremely long cleft stick at the very least. He didn't recognise this species, since snakes with little horns on their heads were new to him and the few that were in Eden spoke without a lisp.

"Whaddya mean usssed to be?" sneered the snake. "Who are you sssup-posssssed to be now?"

"Adam."

"Adam who?"

"You know! Adam!"

"What you?"

"Yes."

"You? The Father of Humankind?"

"Yes!"

"Don't make me laugh! You don't recognissse me, do you?"

"No, I'm afraid I don't."

"Hardly sssurprisssing, really," remarked the snake, glancing at his coils piling up around him as they finally caught up with him.

"Er, have we met before?" Kevin enquired politely.

"Met? Of courssse we have. If you usssed to be Kevin Mullinsss, I usssed to be Beelssszebub."

"Beelzebub?"

"Sssright."

"But you don't have any wings!"

"I know. Haven't ssseen you sssinsse that busssinesss with the Babbittsss. You know. When they did their ssspot of interfering."

"Oh. Yes, I remember, now. You were an ape angel then, weren't you?"

"Not any more, I'm not."

"Yes. I heard. I was sorry to hear that God sacked you."

"I wasssn't sssacked, I ressssigned!" spluttered Beelzebub, literally spitting venom. "And I don't need your sssympathy, either! I have sssinssse gone freelansssse!"

"Free enterprise works then?"

"Absssolutely!"

"Freelancing at what, exactly?"

"The only thing I ever knew. I sssave sssoulsss. For eternity."

"That's a long time. How's it going?"

"Very well."

"How many have you got so far?"

"It'sss early dayss yet," said Beelzebub, as sheepishly as a snake can manage, "but I have great planssss for exssspansssion."

"I'm sure you'll be very good at it," Kevin told him, hoping desperately that he wouldn't be. "What are you doing here?"

"Me?" asked Beelzebub, pointing to himself with his tail and suddenly trying to look very innocent. "I'm here in disssguissse."

"Well I know I didn't recognise you, but … a snake in Eden, and a great big black one at that. It's not a terribly good disguise, is it?"

"What'sss wrong with it? It'sss not asss if anyone'sss looking for a sssnake like thisss in Eden, isss it?"

Kevin hadn't thought of that.

"But what are you doing here in disguise?" he persisted. "I can't imagine God'll be very pleased to find you're here."

"Sssssssshhh!" hissed Beelzebub, putting his tail up to his lips. "It'sss sssuposssed to be a sssecret."

"I can sssee that!" said Kevin. "Dammit it, you've got me at it, now!"

"I'm jussst looking."

"Looking for what?"

"Nothing. Nothing. Jussst looking. A sssnake can jussst look, can't he?" Kevin folded his arms.

"You're on the lookout for souls, aren't you?"

"Now, did I sssay that? Did I sssay that? I asssk you, did I sssay that?"

"You didn't need to. It's obvious what you're up to. I'm right aren't I?"

There was a long pause.

Beelzebub the snake rolled his reptilian eyes, which is quite a trick, and generally looked less than comfortable.

"I might be," he admitted, at length.

"I thought so," said Kevin. "And what do you propose doing with these souls, may I ask?"

"Well," began Beelzebub, "I thought I'd offer an alternative to heaven. I don't think all this sssweetnesss and light isss particularly character-building."

"Not good for the soul," suggested Kevin.

"Presssisssely! It'sss far better for the sssoul conssserned to be impaled on a ssspike for ssseveral thousssand yearsss and roasssted ssslowly over a huge fire!"

Kevin looked at Beelzebub at horror.

"Nah. Only kidding!" said Beelzebub, with a hideous grin. "I'll tell you sssomething, though. My plassse isss going to be a darn sssight livelier than God'sss."

"Where is your heaven?" asked Kevin.

"Underneath," replied Beelzebub, pointing with his tail, which was as good as a forefinger for him.

"Underneath what?"

"Usss. Right underneath usss. There'sss loadsss of ssspace down there. It'sss warmer, too."

"Is it as beautiful as this?" asked Kevin opening his arms around them.

"Oh no." Beelzebub curled his lip unenthusiastically. "Nothing like thisss."

"And what are you going to call it?" asked Kevin.

Beelzebub raised himself beyond the normal vertical capabilities of the snake skeleton.

"Heck."

"Heck?" repeated Kevin.

"Yesss," replied Beelzebub, a little concerned. "Why? What'sss wrong?"

"Nothing," Kevin replied. "Does it stand for anything?"

"How d'you mean?"

"Well, like Eden stands for Experimental Development Environments."

"Oh, no. Nothing like that. Heck. I jussst really like the sssound of it."

"You don't think it sounds as if you've eaten your food too quickly, do you?" suggested Kevin, tactfully.

"No," said Beelzebub, giving him a quite unnerving sideways stare. "You're not working up to sssome sssarcassstic gag about usss sssnakesss not chewing our food enough are you?"

"Oh, no, nothing of the sort."

"Well, if you were it would only be becaussse you're jealousss of our sssside-hingeing jawsss. Jussst look what I can do," and Beelzebub opened his mouth as wide as he could, throwing Kevin into shadow.

"No," Kevin insisted to Beelzebub's tonsils. "It's just that it does sound as if you've eaten something that, perhaps, hasn't quite agreed with you and given you hiccups."

Beelzebub closed his capacious mouth and shrank back to the normal size for an extremely large snake.

"Heck," he said, thoughtfully. "Heck. Hic. Heck."

"Try to think of other creatures saying it," suggested Kevin.

"That'sss a good idea," agreed Beelzebub. "My conssstitution isss ssso remarkably good. I never sssuffer from hiccupsss and am a ssstranger to indigessstion. Heck. Heck."

"Imagine a little white rabbit saying it," said Kevin.

Beelzebub coiled himself up and attempted some bunny hops. "Heck," he said, narrowing his eyes. His fangs moved to the front of his mouth to simulate buck teeth. "Heck! God damn you to heck! Heck! I damn you to heck! Hmmm. I hate to sssay it Kevin. You do, indeed, have a point. It'sss not quite right."

Kevin took a deep breath.

"Blazesss," said Beelzebub. "God damn you to blazess!"

"How about ..."

"Hadesss!" said Beelzebub.

"Actually, that's not bad," conceded Kevin, "but I was going to suggest hell."

Somewhere, outside Eden, a peal of thunder sounded.

"Hell," repeated Beelzebub.

There was another rumble, this time closer to hand.

"Hmm," said Beelzebub. "It doesss have a sssertain ring to it."

CHAPTER 40

"Name?" asked Inspector Gris.

Hob sat opposite him at a desk in the interview room. He didn't answer, but reached inside his leather jacket for his business card.

The armed Euphobian police blew Hob out of his chair and pinned him against the wall behind him, with his feet well off the floor. Bullets bounced off him and whizzed around the room, scuffing the body armour of the guards. One found a chink in the armour of one of them and he fell to the ground. Dust billowed out from bullet holes in the wall opposite Hob and another guard fell as a bullet penetrated a leg joint from behind. Two more guards fell from ricochets, but their comrades kept on firing until their ammunition ran out. Hob stopped twitching but remained stuck to the wall for a few seconds. Then he slid down to the floor, landed on his feet and held out his business card.

"I do wish you wouldn't do that," he told them.

Behind Hob was his stencilled silhouette picked out of the plaster by many bullets.

The police dragged their fallen comrades away and eyed Hob nervously.

Hob looked around for Inspector Gris and found him emerging from under the table.

"My card," he said again, smiling.

Inspector Gris stood up and took it from him. "But there's no name," he said.

Hob smiled again. "Modesty forbids it."

Inspector Gris turned the card over. "And no address on it, either."

"I'm never at home."

"This is ridiculous," said Inspector Gris and he threw Hob's card away.

"No," said Hob, "look at the card again!"

Inspector Gris did no such thing. He sat down and opened an electronic notebook and unfolded a small camera from the side of it. He trained it on Hob and fidgeted with it. "Stand against the wall, please."

Hob was already standing by some bullet-scarred lines that marked off metres on the wall. "I'm afraid that won't work," he said, from a few centimetres below the 1.90m mark.

Inspector Gris tried unsuccessfully to adjust the camera.

"Kindly remove your helmet and visor."

"I will kindly keep them on, thank you very much."

"We need to make a positive record of your appearance," said Inspector Gris, although he seemed a little distracted.

"All the more reason for my visor and helmet to stay in place then."

Inspector Gris did not answer but examined his equipment closely, glancing back at Hob from time to time.

"I'm not at all photogenic," apologised the Soul Trader.

Inspector Gris waved his hand over the lens of the camera and looked puzzled. Then he folded out a little microphone from his notebook.

"I will be recording the following interview for training purposes," he told Hob.

"I'm sure you're already very good at it," Hob told him.

"Not for my training," replied Inspector Gris, "yours. This interview will form the basis of your Re-education programme."

"It won't, y'know," said Hob.

"I assure you it will."

"You know I said I wasn't very photogenic?"

"Your precise words were that you were not at all photogenic," replied Inspector Gris, checking the readings on the built-in microphone with growing concern.

"What would the sound equivalent be?" wondered Hob. "Audiogenic? I'm not very audiogenic, either."

Puzzled by his malfunctioning equipment, Inspector Gris gestured for Hob to sit down.

Reluctantly, Hob did so.

Beside him was his rucksack, which regarded Inspector Gris with an air of evident distaste.

The door to the interview room opened and the police carried their wounded away. Others replaced the fallen, bearing the gift of fresh ammunition. Before they closed the door, an orange and white traffic cone entered and came to rest by Hob's boots. Inspector Gris appeared not to notice.

"What is your name?" he asked.

"You wish me to name myself?" asked Hob, glancing at the traffic cone by his boots.

"Of course."

"You should have taken my card," said Hob, turning to face Inspector Gris. "Names have power. They bring influence to bear upon those who are named."

"So who are you?"

"I am Old Weird Wheels himself, the Metal Guru, the Repossession Man, the Crypto-Engineer, His Malign Weirdness, the Grand Whizz-Herd and Master of the Engine Henge, the Lord High Prince of Rock'n'Roll, the Horsepower Whisperer and Soul Trader, none other than that infamous libertine and free radical, Nicholas Eldritch Hob."

Inspector Gris sat perfectly still without entering a word on his notebook.

"But you can call me Nick," went on the Metal Guru and Repossession Man, "if your spelling's not very good."

Inspector Gris adjusted the data-entry fields on his notebook.

"Or Hob, if you're really pushed for space."

"I shall use the name for which we have documentary evidence," said Inspector Gris, "although you should be aware that this in no way officially recognises your existence without the appropriate papers. Do you understand?"

Hob shook his head. "Not really."

"I will call you Ernest Pilchard," and Inspector Gris began typing it into the machine.

Hob frowned. He had chosen Ernest Pilchard as a frightfully witty joke name when he'd originally set out on his flight from Australia, but as soon as Inspector Gris came to use it officially it wasn't funny at all. It was as if all its humour had evaporated immediately upon his use.

Inspector Gris turned the screen to Hob and showed him the name of Ernest Pilchard on the passenger list. Then he flicked back to an electronic interview form and Hob saw that Ernest Pilchard fitted the available data entry field perfectly.

"Address?" asked Inspector Gris, turning the notebook around again.

"I am never at home," Hob replied, gnomically.

"No fixed abode," said Inspector Gris with a combination of contempt and pity. "Country of domicile?"

"Anarchadia."

Inspector Gris looked up from the form.

Hob spelt it out for him but Inspector Gris didn't make a note of it.

"M Pilchard, we both know that there is no such place."

Hob shrugged.

"From where did you set out before entering the Euphobian Consumerist Community?"

"Melbourne."

"Do you claim citizenship there?"

"What do you mean?"

"Are you entitled to vote there?"

"Vote? What the hell would I vote for?"

"Do you pay taxes in Melbourne?"

"Do I look like I pay taxes?"

"What is the purpose of your visit here?"

"Pleasure."

"Pleasure?" Inspector Gris seemed unfamiliar with the concept.

"Yes. You know. You say 'What is the purpose of your visit, business or pleasure?' and I say 'Pleasure – that's my business!'"

Inspector Gris just stared at Hob, and Hob began to feel a little smaller than usual.

"What is your occupation?"

"I am a Soul Trader."

"Explain?"

"People sell me souls for things they really want. Pleasure is often involved."

"M Pilchard, I will ask you a direct question. Are you involved in vice?"

Hob was surprised how irritating it was becoming to be called M Pilchard.

"People want to feel good about themselves," he told Inspector Gris. "I help them."

"Are you, or have you at any time in the past, been engaged in smuggling illegal immigrants?"

Hob considered his answer for a while and then said that he probably had.

"How much money do you make from human trafficking?"

"I don't receive a penny," said Hob.

"Really not?"

"No."

Inspector Gris scrolled through a number of sections on his e-form.

Hob added, "Of course, what I get back in return is much, much more."

Inspector Gris stopped scrolling and gave Hob a long look. "I don't think you realise the gravity of your situation," he said.

"You may have a point," Hob conceded. "I usually realise levity."

"The reason you have been brought to the Product Planning Blocks is because you have been exhibiting un-Euphobian behaviour."

"That's okay. I'm an Anarchadian."

"You stand charged with the following offences against the citizens of Euphobia."

Hob nearly pointed out that he was still seated but there seemed little point. Jokes could not last long in the company of Inspector Gris, especially the weaker ones.

"First of all, you have entered the Euphobian Consumerist Community illegally. Within minutes, you were responsible for the deaths of twelve customs officials and the destruction of baggage-handling and monitoring equipment."

"That wasn't my fault."

"You subsequently walked down the autoroute from the airport. Pedestrians are prohibited from all major thoroughfares for their own safety."

"Thanks for your concern, Inspector Gris, but I was looking for some fuel."

"What for?"

"My bike."

"Ah yes. We have the images of it from the baggage X-ray machine. You have also smuggled a motorcycle into our trading block. Motorcycles have been banned in Euphobia for several years now."

"Why?"

"On the grounds of public safety, of course."

"Of course," echoed Hob but his sarcasm was lost on Inspector Gris.

"We also have some rather strange images of the interior of your ruck-sack."

Hob's rucksack suddenly looked very self-conscious.

"May we see?" asked Hob.

Inspector Gris turned his notebook round again and pressed a button.

"Badness black-hearted me!"

Hob reached out to the keyboard and scrolled around the image in fascination. His rucksack jumped up and down to try and see but, for some reason, Hob didn't want it to know what its insides looked like.

"So what is contained in this rucksack of yours? And why is it so difficult to open?"

Hob considered his answer for a moment and then said, "It contains my souls."

Inspector Gris looked at him for a moment and then carried on without noting Hob's reply.

"Your next crime was to steal a private car, kill a whole shift of traffic policemen and women, destroy their pursuit vehicles, shoot down their control helicopter and vandalise the concrete piers of one of the flyovers on the *périphérique* Mourion."

"Hey, that wasn't me – that was them! They were shooting at me, and the bridge was behind me."

"Do you deny that you killed them?"

"Sort of. It was The Glove."

"I see," said Inspector Gris in a deeply significant tone. His fingers became blurs on the keyboard as he made copious notes.

"Although," conceded Hob, after a little thought, "I did ask him to do it."

"Who?"

"The Glove."

"This inanimate item of clothing is a he, is he?"

"Oh yes. I've met his wife."

"And she is the other glove of the pair, is she?"

"I wouldn't say they were a well matched pair."

"And with the help of this glove ..."

"*The* Glove."

"With the help of The Glove, you killed the police?"

"I resent being shot at."

"They don't shoot without reason. It appears not to harm you at all."

"Hey, shoot me, and I may not bleed but it still smarts a bit. When can it ever be right to suddenly start shooting people in Euphobia?"

"They were upholding the law."

"Your law."

"You also killed over twenty armed response officers at a Strunts dealership."

Hob burst out laughing.

"There is nothing amusing about that," said Inspector Gris.

"Strunts!" spluttered Hob. "You said Strunts!"

"You are charged with murder!" Inspector Gris said loudly.

"I'm sorry," managed Hob before subsiding into giggles. "You can't imagine how rude that word is where I come from!"

Inspector Gris waited a long time for Hob to stop laughing.

"Okay, I'm fine now," said Hob. "Where were we?"

"At the Strunts dealership."

That set Hob off again.

Inspector Gris had to raise his voice once more. "You kidnapped an apparently innocent bystander at the, er, Strunts dealership and made your escape in a stolen and wantonly overloaded personal transportation device. You fraudulently made a massive cash withdrawal from an automatic telling machine in Cachet and then blatantly contravened construction and use regulations by modifying the stolen personal transportation device to make it go faster."

"Modified Strunts! Oh matron!"

"You then drove this modified Strunts dangerously and without due care and attention at illegal speeds across Mourion, and encouraged other citizens to do the same. When we raided the home of the citizen you had kidnapped, you were also harbouring a vegetarian woman."

By now Hob was slumped in his chair holding his sides. "Where are they?" he gasped.

"Your companions? They are here in the Product Planning Blocks and are being Re-educated."

"What?" Hob wasn't laughing any more.

"Obviously the vegetarian woman is in breach of numerous Standard of Living Directives, not least of which is a complete disregard for the products of the Euphobian meat-processing industry. She doesn't follow any officially recognised fashionality, either. Actually, that is another felony that you have committed," and Inspector Gris tapped Hob's lack of fashionality into his notebook.

This had been the first time Hob had ever knowingly met a Conformorian, and now he was beginning to realise just what they could do to a vulnerable soul. And not just to a vulnerable soul, either.

Hob was experiencing unfamiliar emotions from long ago that he'd almost forgotten.

First he'd been embarrassed by his initial light-hearted behaviour, and then bored with the struggle to maintain it in the face of seemingly over-whelming odds. He felt frustrated, too, and surprisingly weary, which was most unlike him.

Inspector Gris was not so much powerful as grindingly inevitable. And – if Hob was honest with himself – Gris was also able to provoke a special sort of fear.

Before Hob had become virtually immortal, he had thrived on fear. It had invigorated his performance in the Wild Hunt and inspired death-defying acts of bravery and foolhardiness. He'd come to look upon this fear as a constant companion until he couldn't live without it. But that had all changed once his horsepower whispering had enabled him to become a Soul Trader. He'd left the fear behind, although he saw it in others during each and every Wild Hunt.

The fear that Inspector Gris produced was not that sort of fear. It had no positive aspect. It didn't inspire, but debilitated. It provoked no rebellion, but engendered hopelessness, a steadily growing realisation that resistance was futile.

An ordinary person wouldn't stand a chance against such fear. It swept through the consciousness like a blast of dry ice, petrifying the soul into inactivity. Even a Soul Trader and Horsepower Whisperer like Hob was not invulnerable, and he began to realise that in the face of such fear he needed to save Cadaver's soul before the Conformorians did any lasting damage to it. And elsewhere in these grim buildings there must be other souls in peril, vulnerable souls who would be desperate to be saved.

It was fortunate for Hob that he retained many basic human traits, and the acquaintance with such fear outraged him and led swiftly to anger.

He asked about the fate of M Cadvare.

"He is undergoing his Re-education. From the evidence contained within his flat it is clear that he has been using his position as a transaction auditor to cover up the breach of many directives over a prolonged period. He will become a responsible and worthwhile Euphobian citizen. This will make life much easier for him. He will no longer waste his energy in fighting the need to conform. He will understand its manifold advantages and embrace the Standard of Living Directive. He will adopt the consumerist dream with fervent enthusiasm and unquestioning loyalty."

"So you are going to destroy his soul."

"Of course. It will enable him to conform."

"You're going to rob him of his individuality."

"It is necessary."

Hob glared at him, speechless with rage.

Inspector Gris gave Hob a triumphant little smile. "And that is exactly what is going to happen to you," he said.

"You'll be lucky!" declared Hob.

"There is no element of chance about it."

"Those who do not consider chance do not deserve to be favoured by her," said Hob.

"M Pilchard, there is no favouritism here. We will treat everyone the same."

"Until they are the same?"

"Precisely."

"There's something you should know about me," said Hob.

"Oh yes?" replied Inspector Gris, putting his elbows on the table and interlacing his fingers.

"I have some rites."

"I am afraid rights are meaningless without responsibilities. Your behaviour is at odds with the needs of our society. Consequently, your rights are forfeit. "

"I am not talking about human rights. I speak of my soul rites – nothing to do with rights or responsibilities, forfeit or otherwise."

Hob stood up slowly.

The riot police trained their reloaded weapons on him.

"Sit down," said Inspector Gris.

"I won't be staying to be Re-educated," said Hob. "I am on a mission, a mission to save souls and find out about Conformorians."

A flicker of something approaching doubt crossed Inspector Gris' normally inscrutable features.

"That mission is just about over," continued Hob. "But before I daemonstrate my soul rites to you, know this and know it well. You have no record of me. Even your equipment does not officially recognise me. I exist in ways you cannot possibly imagine. I represent the energy, the adventure and the risk of the Wild Hunt. I offer great futures and unexpected disasters. I offer responsibility for your own calamities and the exhilaration of living under the shadow of death. I give the liberty to take risks or avoid them as you please, a state few individuals enjoy even in times of war. I can help you attain the skills and fortitude to laugh in the face of catastrophe and the euphoria of a race well run. I am the Horsepower Whisperer. I explore where art and engineering collide and produce a bounteous union. I am the Soul Trader who dances in the void of human inadequacy and pulls it through the mangle, soaked in the rich tapestry of life. I endow it with blebs and jewels of pleasure and pain that provide an armour against the slings and arrows of outrageous fortune. I offer discontent from victory, but joy at success, no matter how small. I produce, and inspire others also to produce, machines evolved by brains and hands of skill for testing to their limits not in closed laboratories but out on the open road, in front of thousands of fellow enthusiasts and spectators. No other machinery can be brought nearer to practical and apparent perfection. I bring enthusiasm and privilege to the drivers so they inspire these things of latent power to spring into action and change course under the guidance of their experienced hands. I inhabit their engines and I sit upon their shoulders. And they inhabit me and sit upon mine. I whisper up horsepower and talk the torque, inspiring engines to great feats of power and endurance, enabling their drivers to push the envelope of dynamic perfection.

"I am not Ernest Pilchard! I am Old Weird Wheels himself, the Metal Guru, the Repossession Man, the Crypto-Engineer and Malign Weirdness, the Grand Whizz-Herd and Master of the Engine Henge, the Lord High Prince of Rock'n'Roll, the Horsepower Whisperer and Soul Trader, none other than that infamous libertine and free radical from Anarchadia, that trafficker of traffic of no officially recognised fashionality, Nicholas Eldritch Hob!"

"This outburst will only count against you," said Inspector Gris.

"To those who can see no beauty whatever in what I do, I have nothing to say at all." Hob turned towards the police. "I'm leaving now. It is time for me to take back what is mine."

Hob reached inside his jacket for The Glove.

The guards caught him in a crossfire, and Hob jerked more violently than ever from their shooting. He danced like a rag doll, but not for long. The ricochets were deadlier than ever and many guards fell, dark grey stains spreading out over the carpet where they lay.

Hob jerkily pulled his arms and legs into the foetal position. Above the din, he said, "Glove? Nice Glove. Destroy them!" and a red flash shot up from his immobile body.

The remaining guards saw the red flash and thought they'd wounded him. They pumped away at him more vigorously than ever, determined to exploit any weakness. But all they accomplished were more ricochets, and soon they began to slump to the ground.

What they didn't see was The Glove, who swept through them like a red hot needle. A blur linked them for an instant, and when the redness faded they collapsed, as if on a necklace with a broken cord.

The Glove stopped and peered under the splintered table in the middle of the room.

Inspector Gris peered back at him.

"Leave him," said Hob. "I want a survivor to tell other Conformorians what has been unleashed upon them this day, and by whom."

The Glove hovered by the cowering Inspector Gris, making highly suggestive gestures with his trident.

"No. Leave him. If he crosses our path again he'll regret it."

The Glove stopped making his intimidating gestures. Then he shrugged his shoulders and, with apparent magnanimity, nodded his head.

"Come on," said Hob, shouldering his rucksack, "let's get out of here and find Cadaver."

CHAPTER 41

Kevin awoke gently and lay dozing for some time, slipping comfortably into unconsciousness and then back again.

"This," he told himself, blearily, "is where humankind deserves to stay."

He lay on an expanse of cool springy grass that was peculiar to Eden. Each blade was thicker and fleshier than usual, and when he walked across it he felt he literally had a spring in his step. It made a splendid mattress for the bower that he had made with Eve, so long as they could stop the badgers and racoons from trampolining on them during the night.

Kevin slowly rolled over and felt the special thrill his eyes provoked when they gazed upon Eve. She lay beside him, the sound of the gentle breathing of the world's first woman flowing over him like a soothing balm.

Although they were hybrid creatures, Kevin thought they both looked especially fine. Neither of them were what God or Sophia would call "in-Their-own image".

Kevin was a sculpted athlete, muscles rippling subtly beneath a skin glowing with vitality. He'd always thought of himself as something rather less than physically attractive, and now that he was enjoying the open air life and plenty of exercise, he had already caught himself gazing at his reflection in pools of water.

God was too busy to admire Himself in pools of water. If He ever caught sight of His reflection He would have seen a thoughtful do-it-yourselfer in dungarees with a pencil behind His ear and nearly too much beard.

Kevin preferred looking at Eve, and did so now as she lay sleeping.

Eve resembled an earthbound goddess. For a first try, she was the personification of beginner's luck, even if that beginner had been God. Kevin felt intoxicated by waking up next to this female, human, wild animal. From now on, each morning held such promise with Eve beside him.

Kevin knew he was biased. He hadn't seen another human female for roughly 65 million years. Sophia didn't count and the last one he'd ever seen was the beautiful young scientist just after he'd been killed. Therese Darlmat, with her freakishly high forehead, was too brainy, whereas Eve had a quick wit, but also a charming naivety. And while Eve was an innocent Aphrodite freshly anointed by Eden's first dew, Sophia was a rosy-cheeked farmer's wife in gumboots.

"Kevin and Eve," he said, still getting used to the idea.

With all the violence of a flower opening in the morning, Eve awoke to find him looking at her, smiling in wonder at the first ever real woman.

"Hallo," she said.

"Hallo," he replied.

"You were stroking my hair."

"Was I? Yes. I suppose I was."

"Why?"

Eve stretched, and Kevin moved out of her way slightly. She was still getting used to the feeling of her body, much as Kevin was getting used to his, and to stretch it and feel it starting to come alive again after the little death of sleep was a good feeling. Eve, being that little bit newer, seemed that little bit more alive.

"You have wonderful hair," he said.

"Do I?"

She had a great mane of thick, luxuriant hair. Sophia had taught her how to wash her swirling locks in the diluted extracts of various fruits and nuts, and now it caught the light like a waterfall of jewels cascading over her shoulders.

"Yes, you do."

"What do you think of the colour?"

"The colour? Why, I think it really suits you."

"I quite like it, too," Eve admitted.

If Kevin had been surprised to find out about Sophia, he was even more taken aback to discover his complexion on his arrival in Eden.

Christians of European descent traditionally depict Adam, or Kevin, and Eve as a pale buff colour, sometimes bronzed, often conspicuously sunburnt. Those in the east consider the first humans to have been a nice lemony sort of hue, while native American Indians would choose a darker red than a sunburnt white man. Indians from India would favour a lightish sort of brown, and Australian Aborigines are convinced black is beautiful. Africans have always, supported by a considerable amount of archaeological evidence, visualised Kevin and Eve as a pleasantly dark brown.

Kevin and Eve now knew that they were all wrong. The first man and woman in the world were, in point of fact, green.

Kevin's initial reaction was that he was mortally ill and he'd immediately found God.

"What do you mean you're off-colour?" asked The Great Architect.

"It's just a figure of speech."

"There's nothing wrong with you," insisted God, "you're supposed to be like that."

"Really?" Kevin squirmed around to see if he was green all over.

"Of course. How else are you going to photosynthesise?"

"Photosynthesise?"

"Yes. Didn't you notice all the other creatures in Eden were green?"

"Oh yeah."

"Well then."

"I just thought they weren't, you know, quite ripe."

"You didn't think the animals were quite ripe?" echoed God, incredulous. "I thought you were supposed to be a palaeontologist?"

"I was. But I've learnt a lot since then."

"Now that you're in Eden, why do you think you never get hungry?"

"Ah."

"And you can stop worrying about lavatory paper, too."

Kevin had then adapted to being green, although it wasn't easy.

Eve had never known anything different. And Kevin now thought that whatever colour she was, she would look good. He wondered how she might feel about body painting but, this morning, he was content to see her naked and unadorned.

"Eve, you're a very beautiful woman."

"But I'm the only one there is!"

"That's true, but it doesn't change the fact. Believe me. I know about these things."

Eve gave him a startlingly knowing smile for someone so new to the world.

While God and Kevin might catch sight of each other across Eden, as God tried out some new idea of His and Kevin pottered about, Sophia and Eve had already spent hours together in a huddle just talking. Kevin had managed to overhear their conversation through a herbaceous border, but he didn't understand a word of it. He could recognise phrases, but their meaning was lost on him. And yet it still held a strange fascination for him. Eventually, he had asked God about it.

"Yes," He'd said, "I don't understand it, either. I call it girl talk."

"Do You think they're talking about me?"

God had reached for a pencil behind His ear. "I wouldn't be at all surprised. Could you hold the end of this tape measure for Me, please?"

That was as far as their discussion on the subject went and Kevin wondered how much knowledge Sophia could possibly impart in a few hours.

"Yes," said Eve, looking at him closely, "I suppose you do know about these things. Kevin?"

"Yes?"

"Do you mind if I ask you a question?"

"Of course not," he said.

Eve sat up and hugged her knees close to her chest with her arms. "You know how God has made all this stuff?"

"What stuff?"

"All this stuff. Everything."

"Oh I see. Yes?"

"And that includes us."

"Yes."

"Well why did He do it?"

Kevin didn't answer immediately.

"What are we here for?" Eve asked him, as if he hadn't understood her the first time. "Why did he make us?"

"Ah," said Kevin knowingly.

Inwardly, he frantically tried to marshal his thoughts but it was difficult when all he could really think about was *why didn't I think of that?* And *why didn't I ask God when I had the chance?*

"That's a very good question," he said.

It was such a good question he should have known she was going to ask it. But, then again, how could he have known she was going to ask that question when it had never occurred to him?

"I think that might come to be called the ultimate question," he went on. "Just why are we here?"

He felt ashamed to admit that he'd never given the issue a single thought. He had never wondered about why he was here. He'd often wondered about *when* he had been, but had never asked himself why, or if he was part of some grand plan.

It wasn't that he'd never had enough time to give it some thought. He couldn't claim that he'd already lived so many rich and full lives that he'd been distracted. Millions of humans, during lives that seemed to him pitifully ephemeral, had spent most of their time pondering the question of life, their paraverse and nearly everything. But for Kevin, what was for the rest of humanity, often literally, a burning issue, the question of his place in creation had passed him by.

"You see, it's like this," he said.

He'd never wondered about it when he had been a child, a human child, for that first time, all those years ago. He'd never asked his parents or his teachers this most awkward of questions, and so had nothing to draw upon now that it was posed to him.

"It may take some time to explain," he told Eve.

He wondered if it was because he was a scientist. Perhaps he had such an enquiring mind that he hadn't enquired about the really big issue. The question hadn't escaped many of his fellow scientists. The more they seemed to know the more they seemed to wonder. Kevin had blithely continued his studies and had never given it a thought. It hadn't even occurred to him when he'd been digging up all those dinosaurs. And it hadn't occurred to him, either, when he'd accidentally wiped them out with a thoughtlessly-parked time machine.

Eve waited patiently. She tilted her head and her hair rippled over one shoulder.

"God, she's beautiful," he thought.

Eve twitched her head and frowned. "Thanks, but what's that got to with it?"

Kevin realised he'd spoken out loud.

"Everything," he heard himself say.

He took a deep breath.

"The reason God made us is because it gave Him such great pleasure to do so. His pleasure is evident in everything He does and makes. And when I look at you, His pleasure is more noticeable than ever."

Eve laughed.

"Yes," she said, a little self-consciously, "I thought that might be it."

Kevin gave a long sigh of relief. He couldn't decide whether her laughter sounded like the water bubbling gently over pebbles in the brook or a particularly musical peal of bells, but there was one thing he knew for certain. He knew an awful lot about the universe, including the fact that it was a potentially wobbly paraverse among many others, and a tremendous amount about the history of this planet – more than a single person could normally be expected to know – but although he really knew nothing about what motivated God, he knew what he liked. He liked Eve's laughter. He really liked it.

Why hadn't anyone one ever written a song about Eve's first laughter in Eden?

"In fact," Eve went on, "that's exactly what Sophia told me, too."

"Really?" said Kevin trying to hide his surprise.

"Really," said Eve, trying not to look as if she had noticed it. "We are created out of pleasure."

"Both of us can't be wrong then."

"What would you like for breakfast?"

"A particularly long sunbathe, I think."

Explaining to Eve about the pomegranate tree was going to be a cinch by comparison.

CHAPTER 42

Dawn was coming up as Heidi Bland put down her pencil and closed *The Red Book of St Bendix*. She felt a curious mixture of fatigue, elation and fear. Although she had barely scratched the surface, she felt sure nobody could have penetrated the mysteries of *The Red Book of St Bendix* as far as she had, at least not in this generation, and she was beginning to see, now, why they might not want to.

Her husband hadn't been able to make it past the dedication.

"To Queen Aby of the Conformorians. Who saw to it that I was made lame and without whom none of this would have been possible."

The Red Book of St Bendix had been confiscated from the library of an ancient monastery and was to have been destroyed but Heidi Bland had successfully prevailed upon her husband to let her have it instead.

"Why should this book be destroyed?" she asked him. "Look at these extraordinary illuminated pages!"

Commissioner Bland couldn't understand why the need for its destruction wasn't self-evident. Heidi wondered if there was a kind of literary radioactivity to specific books that threatened only certain people, but her husband had eventually agreed to let her keep it.

Heidi had already gleaned enough about St Bendix to know that he was a highly skilled Anglo-Saxon blacksmith whose forge had been overrun by a tribe who were clearly Conformorians. St Bendix was brought before their Queen Aby, who recognised in his metalworking skill a great and dangerous talent. She ordered that he be employed in making weapons for the Conformorians' war effort against his own people. To prevent his escape, she had his Achilles tendons cut.

This was not an uncommon fate for many smiths during the Dark Ages, but St Bendix was not just any smith. He was *the* Great Smith, and he escaped the clutches of the Conformorians on an engine that he had made himself.

Ultimately, after many adventures, St Bendix reached the little-known, but extensive, temperate archipelago of Olde Anarchadie, far away to the west in the Antagonistic Ocean.

The Red Book of St Bendix was a record of The Great Smith's wisdom and included some of the most intriguing predictions Heidi Bland had ever come across. For instance, St Bendix had prophesied most technological advances and was able to describe them accurately. He also foretold that even though he had repulsed the Conformorian hordes with his war engines, they would regain the ascendancy after a long and covert campaign.

This was of particular interest to Heidi. St Bendix was convinced that "Two thousand Years after the Birth of Our Lord, Anarchadie will have assumed a second Ascendancy. And in readiness for that Time, The Soul Trader will ride in The Wild Hunt with The Quick and The Dead."

Other predictions were too obscure for her to understand.

"Rolling off the Throttle in the Middle of a Bend will cause the Bike to sit up and have you running wide" meant nothing to her, but Gildas, a Celtic historian writing in the sixth century, seemed to agree.

Another nonsensical forewarning was, "Be careful to make sure that there is adequate clearance between the Valves on Twin Cam Engines otherwise they can tangle with disastrous Results."

Then there was "If the Timing is sufficiently far out, the Engine can kick back and poke your Shin out through your Knee."

Apparently this had happened to the Velocette Bede but she had no idea who he was.

Heidi just added these mysterious references to a long list. Items on this included references to the Once and Future King, ignition timing, clutches, chassis, superchargers, pistons, valves, twin cams, throttles, springs and brakes. Part of her could only assume that these words must have had some other meaning fifteen hundred years ago, although the complicated pictures seemed to suggest otherwise.

Some of the words were clearly colloquial references to things for which she didn't understand the proper term. There were nails, slugs, bedsteads and foo-foo valves. The slugs or Romeos seemed to go up and down inside pots or Juliets, and nails were driven by knockers, sometimes double knockers.

Other words were quite out of context. Many, such as carburettor and chassis, were of recent tribal French origin. Others were so out of place they became unbearably sinister for the wife of a Conformorian commissioner.

And yet she was fascinated by them and, she now admitted it, a little seduced by them.

And most seductive of all were the further mentions of a Horsepower Whisperer, or Whizz-herd.

"Hob, that incorrigible Rogue, will frequently travel Abroad under the Name of Ernest Pilchard!"

In her forays into esoterism, Heidi had come across obscure references to the Horsepower Whisperer, but the writers had all been too afraid to specify who this person was. It seemed to be a tacit understanding that across the centuries everyone would know who he was and that it was not the done thing to speak of him.

Only St Bendix did not share this coyness.

" 'Old Weird Wheels himself, the Metal Guru, the Repossession Man, the Crypto-Engineer, His Malign Weirdness, the Grand Whizz-Herd and Master of the Engine Henge, the Lord High Prince of Rock'n'Roll, the Horsepower Whisperer and Soul Trader, none other than that infamous libertine and free radical from Anarchadia, that Trafficker of Traffic and of no accepted Fashionality, Nicholas Eldritch Hob!' "

The Red Book of St Bendix also pointed to some connection with Euphobia.

Heidi added Euphobia to her list of obscure words. Of course, it was familiar to her but the name had only been coined a few years ago, and yet here it was, written down in Anarchadian script, well over a thousand years earlier.

St Bendix went on to describe how Hob would ride around the world with "The Quick and The Dead" in "The Greatest of All Wild Hunts" which he would lead to "the eight corners of The Earth."

This was St Bendix's little jibe at those around him who insisted that the world was flat and not round, which he, The Great Smith, had already divined. So, instead of the four corners of the earth, he had the eight corners of a cube, which "I sincerely hope can be regarded as a glorious Compromise until they eventually come round to my way of Thinking."

Her sense of confusion became one of alarm when she read that the world would end when Hob persuaded "the Time Traveller to sell him his Soul". By this stage, Hob would have been corrupted by absolute horsepower and corrupted by horsepower absolutely. Being a Horsepower Whisperer was one thing. Becoming a Soul Trader was another.

But there was one glimmer of hope.

St Bendix had written his red book to offer help in avoiding this turn of events. Red was the colour of danger after all.

Quite how such a transaction could take place was not, as yet, explained.

If only she could believe it.

St Bendix had given her proof after proof, but she was still sceptical. The association with her own world was making her doubt the provenance of *The Red Book of St Bendix.* Rationally, it was too incredible. A reader in the twenty-first century could only see it as the hoax it must surely be. Yet Heidi's instincts told her that *The Red Book of St Bendix* was genuine. Unbreakable halfshafts for jelly-mould Morris Minors were for sale in last month's edition of *The Piston Wheel* and now Nick Hob himself was abroad in Euphobia.

For the time being, Heidi felt that she'd done enough.

She rose from her chaise-longue and stretched before wandering over to the balcony windows. Down below, in the leaden light of dawn, Mourion was beginning to stir. Street lights were being switched off and the roads were filling for the inappropriately named rush hour.

She peered up at the grey skies and leaned against the balcony to call out a name.

"Julian?"

There was no answer, but she hadn't expected one. Yet still she called.

"Julian! Julian?"

She drummed her fingers on the rail of the balcony.

"Julian, Julian, wherefore art thou, my Julian?"

Again there was no reply, and Heidi pouted as if spurned by a lover who had promised a rendezvous but never shown up.

Then, out of the corner of her eye, she caught a movement so swift she doubted she'd seen it.

It was a rusty red blur that flashed through the open doors behind her and into the apartment.

Heidi turned in delight and skipped back into her boudoir.

"Oh, Julian! There you are! You shouldn't tease me like this!" and she rushed forward and crushed him in a wild embrace.

Julian was used to this sort of behaviour. In fact, he could be said to encourage it.

He was a splendid Anarchadian Flying Fruit Bat Fox, and she had found him while on a dull cruise with her husband. It was just after a storm, and the poor creature, who had obviously been blown far off course, had plopped into the sea just off their port bow with all the elegance of a collapsed umbrella. Fortunately, Commissioner Bland had been called away to the conference line on urgent business, and Heidi was able to rescue the hapless creature by herself just before the weight of his magnificent water-logged brush pulled him under for the last time.

When she had brought him home, nobody in Mourion had ever seen a creature like Julian before. He was quite anomalous to accepted zoology. The vet seemed extremely keen to put Julian "out of his misery", despite an evidently cheerful disposition and a weakness only for chasing things, and it had taken all Heidi's considerable powers of persuasion to deter him and spare this poor creature to whom she had rapidly become devoted. As for Julian, he seemed to understand that he owed her his life, and in return he spent hours amusing her with games of fetch or Frisbee or find the rubber chicken. He even attended social occasions with her, curled over Heidi's shoulder and snapping playfully at the other fine ladies and their, by comparison, rather lifeless stoles.

Heidi found him highly amusing.

Her husband couldn't get near either of them.

"Come along, Julian," she said, "time for bed," and Julian let himself be picked off the curtains and held, for him, the wrong way round with his head up and his feet down.

"I've had a long night and so, I think, have you."

Julian always gave the impression of understanding everything she said, which was more than could be said for Commissioner Bland.

Heidi climbed a small staircase on wheels that had once served in her extensive library and, rather unnecessarily, carried Julian up to his perch where she hooked him up as if he were too tired to do it for himself. While she'd been studying, Julian had been cheerfully dive-bombing chickens and indulging in moonlit gluttony so he did not object. It was one of their little rituals. He swung back and forth in great pleasure to be home again.

She avoided looking up. The Blands had felt pleasantly surprised when Julian appeared to be house trained but that was before they noticed the mess on the ceiling.

Although it was really morning, Heidi undressed for bed.

Just as she lay down Julian swooped from his roost, snagged a corner of the duvet with his hind claws and pulled it over her in another of their little rituals. Then he resumed his perch and checked his membranous wings and preened his fur.

Heidi gazed at him lovingly as he drew his wings about him like a particularly cosy blanket.

"Julian? Have you ever heard of Nick Hob or St Bendix?" she asked him, sleepily.

Julian started.

Of course he had. St Bendix was his patron saint, wasn't he? And all species of vermin have a particular affinity with Hob the Soul Trader.

But Heidi was asleep. And, once Julian was dozing peacefully, too, grey Conformorian figures tip-toed in and stole away *The Red Book of St Bendix* and all of Heidi's hard-won translation.

CHAPTER 43

Out in the corridor, small groups of Conformorians tried to arrest Hob and The Glove but without success. Hob was content to let The Glove deal with the Grey Ones for most of the time but was not above punching in the face those that got in his way.

However, the Product Planning Blocks contained many Conformorians. The groups of soulless ones flinging themselves at Hob became bigger and more numerous until he found he was lashing out constantly and their attempts to stop him became less futile.

He hit out at a leaping Conformorian, and even as he killed him Hob noticed no expression on his face. Destroying them brought Hob no pleasure. He was a Soul Trader, not a killer.

But how could he kill something that had no soul?

He needed to find M Cadvare before the Conformorians destroyed his soul, but he couldn't move quickly against so many Grey Ones and soon he was at a standstill and surrounded.

Some shots caught Hob off guard and knocked him against a wall. The Grey Ones fell away as they avoided the shots and then the lethal ricochets. Hob moved jerkily under the impacts but carried on fighting. He grabbed the weapon of the nearest guard and slammed it into his chest, knocking him back into those behind. He lashed out with his fists and more unarmed Conformorians fell down, heads lolling on necks so broken they were attached only by skin. The Glove got to the soldiers beyond Hob's reach and they fell before their ammunition ran out. But the tide of Grey Ones engulfed Hob once again.

The Glove became a zigzagging blur as he flew deliberately into them. His preferred point of entry was just to one side of the sternum but at the velocity at which he flew it didn't really matter if he hit bones or not. His exit was often through the spinal column anyway and he operated at such high temperatures that he cauterised the wounds he made. This made for a clean kill and kept the spills of dark grey blood to a minimum.

"Glove!" shouted Hob as another volley of bullets hit him.

The Glove dived after the gunmen.

But the corridors kept filling up with more animated Conformorians as quickly as Hob could de-animate them. These were the bureaucrats of Mourion, workers not soldiers, and they seemed intent on subduing Hob by sheer force of numbers.

The Grey Ones were all dressed alike and although their facial features differed, they all had the same blank eyes. Through the windows of their souls Hob saw just empty rooms.

Some of the Conformorians appeared to be female, and Hob, who gave women no quarter in the Wild Hunt, hesitated before raising his fists to them. But, as these androgynous creatures fluttered around him and grabbed at his arms, he found himself batting them away as if they were large, troublesome moths.

As the bodies piled up, the Conformorians had to climb over their fallen comrades to get at Hob and soon Hob found himself in a macabre kind of bunker formed by walls of dead Conformorians. Although both Hob and The Glove made clean kills, a black ooze began to creep towards Hob, who took care not to step in it.

Hob did not want to end up standing in a sump of Conformorian blood. He began to climb onto their bodies even though the under-foot sensation was so distasteful. Before long, he stood perilously on a pyramid of fallen Conformorians and caught glimpses of the masses beyond those actively fighting him. There was no apparent end to their numbers. They trampled over the fallen more eagerly than he did and pushed those closest to him onto his fists.

Hob lost his footing and then his balance. For a moment he thought he was crowd surfing, but found himself borne away on his back by many hands. Beneath him his rucksack snarled and snapped with its zips and straps. Hob sank suddenly into the crowd once or twice as the rucksack chewed downwards into Hob's supporters, but they were always replaced by more and Hob was buffeted along on a sea of bland grey faces.

Grabbing at the ceiling didn't help. Hob just brought it with him. The polystyrene tiles and strips of aluminium littered the sea of grey faces as Hob floundered above them. He tried to adjust his molecular density and although this slowed the Conformorians beneath him, he decided he didn't want to sink under their surface entirely. So he kicked and punched as much as he could, shouting for The Glove.

Like some army of grey-suited ants, the crowd carried him along. Hob noticed he was approaching a lift shaft where the corridor narrowed. In the crush, someone must have called the lift, for the doors opened and the crowd leaked into it sideways. Hob grabbed the doorway and pulled himself into the lift. He kicked upwards instead of downwards, and the emergency hatch in the ceiling of the lift burst open. Like a snake, Hob slithered through it and slammed it back down on the Conformorians below him. Using his night racer's vision, he grabbed the cable that held the lift and parted it with his bare hands. As the lift plummeted to the bottom, he stepped onto a ledge in the lift shaft and Conformorians spilled into the shaft below him until someone managed to close the doors against the press of bodies.

The darkness and sudden silence of the lift shaft came as a pleasant relief. Hob climbed up to the next floor and pulled the sliding doors apart to step into the corridor.

A pair of guards tried to rush him but he knocked them down and ducked through some fire doors. Expecting to enter another corridor, he found himself instead in a large open-plan office. Some workers nearby tried to grab him but he just swept them aside. Then their colleagues approached. He batted them away with office chairs at first but, when their frequency and numbers increased, he picked up a computer desk. He shook it free of its IT equipment and mowed down the Conformorians, holding the desk in front of him by its legs and using it as a kind of very blunt scythe. He pressed it against the mass of Grey Ones and pushed them up to the glass windows until the glass shattered. The computer desk flew out of the window after them and Hob nearly followed it.

Behind him, more Conformorians streamed into the office. He picked up another desk, using it as a rotary flail against the crowd trying to engulf him. Papers and Conformorians swirled around him as he made his way across the office and back through the fire doors, but here the corridor was too narrow to swing a computer desk around. However, there was just enough room for him to hold it in front of him and he used it to bulldoze the Conformorians down the corridor.

Hob strained against the mass of Conformorians and adjusted his molecular density to suit. The heavy computer table creaked and groaned. Conformorians pressed up against it and Hob braced himself on the hard-wearing carpet as he began to push, with his upper body parallel to the floor.

He forced his way down the corridor. At the narrowing by the lift shaft, he was pleasantly surprised to feel a slight venturi effect, for there was a slight quickening through the gap as if they were atoms of air and fuel passing through a carburettor.

After that the resistance gradually increased and, with his legs pumping like the connecting rods of a steam locomotive, Hob strained to maintain velocity, not really knowing where he was going.

He felt something give. At first he thought it was the table collapsing but there was a distant tinkling of glass. Progress suddenly became much easier. Hob didn't have to push so hard. He was almost jogging along now behind his desk. He adopted a more upright stance and, looking over the bulging eyes and gaping mouths of the Grey Ones before him, saw what was happening.

He was squirting a plume of Conformorians out into the quad between the Product Planning Blocks.

A great surge of joy spurred him on and he virtually sprinted the last few metres, falling horizontally forward until the last of the Conformorians had been pushed out of the building.

It was the rucksack that stopped Hob from tumbling after them. As the heavy computer desk fell away, it tangled its straps through the remains of a broken blind. Hob swung out over the pyramid of crumpled Conformorians and then swung back in again, as the computer desk landed on the peak of bodies.

A red streak came down the corridor behind him and re-arranged itself to form The Glove. A few Conformorians emerged from under a nearby stairwell and The Glove made a slight detour to thread his deadly way through them.

"Ah, there you are," said Hob, nonchalantly, as The Glove came to stop before him. He clapped his hands of dust and checked for blotches of Conformorian blood. "Did you see me defenestrating all those Grey Ones?"

The Glove nodded and flew out of the window to inspect the pile of Conformorians below. It flew back in and saluted Hob with its trident.

"C'mon," said Hob. "Let's find Cadaver and get out of here."

CHAPTER 44

"Whose apple core is this?" bellowed God.

The Garden of Eden shook.

There is nothing more frightening than mild-mannered individuals, or omnipotent deities, who have become thoroughly enraged.

"It's mine," said Eve. She'd never seen anyone so angry before. "Why do You ask, God?"

"Because I expressly said you were not to eat the fruit of the apple tree!"

"Did You?"

"Yes! Oh, Eve! Don't you remember?"

"I remember You standing over there and saying, 'Do anything you want and go anywhere you like but do not pick any fruit off that tree over there.'"

"Good! So you do remember!"

"Yes. You stood right there, where You are now, and You said, 'Don't eat anything off that tree,' and You pointed over there at that pomegranate tree. So we said, 'Okay, God we won't.' Didn't we Kev ... I mean Adam? That's funny. He was here a moment ago."

"Wait a minute," said God. "Did you say pomegranate tree?"

"Yes."

"I wasn't pointing at the pomegranate tree."

"Well we weren't sure at the time, and it seemed to be important to you, so I said 'Do You mean the one on the left?' and You said, 'Right.'"

"Oh dear," said God.

"Is something wrong?"

"Eve?"

"Yes, God?"

"Having eaten of this apple, do you feel any different?"

"I feel very well."

"Good. Good."

"It's just that as I bit into it, I suddenly realised I was completely naked."

"Ah."

"So I made this dress out of flowers and grass. Do You like it?"

Eve gave Him a little twirl.

"I was coming to that," said God. "Yes, it's very pretty."

"It's very comfortable."

"Yes, I'm sure it is. Now then, where's Adam? Did he have any apples?"

"Yes, I think so."

"Adam? ADAM!"

"Try calling him Kevin, God. He says he can't get used to being called Adam, not after being called Kevin for millions of years."

"Well who else would he think I was calling?"

Eve pondered this for a while but wisely said nothing.

"Kevin?" shouted God. "KEVIN!"

Eden was not such a big place.

Kevin's head popped out from behind a bush.

"Did You call, God?"

"Yes, I did, Kevin. I wanted to ask you about the pomegranate tree."

"Yes," said Kevin, earnestly. "I spoke to Eve about it and explained that it was extremely important not to touch it or eat anything off it."

"I see," said God, stroking His beard.

"Anything wrong, God?" asked Kevin.

"Kevin?"

"Yes, God?"

"You didn't eat anything off *that* tree did you?"

"What? That tree on the left?"

"Right. I mean, yes! No, I don't, I mean, no!" God took a deep breath. "You didn't eat anything off the apple tree, did you, Kevin?"

A cloud fell across Kevin's usually sunny countenance. "The apple tree?"

"Yes, that's right. I mean, correct."

"I might have done," Kevin replied, airily.

"Oh dear." God put a hand over His forehead.

"But we didn't have anything from the pomegranate tree at all, did we, darling?" said Kevin as he joined Eve.

"No," she replied.

God stood for some time with a hand over His eyes. He seemed lost in thought.

Kevin and Eve edged a little closer in a helpful sort of way.

God wearily put His arms down.

He rolled his eyes and closed them for a moment.

Then He opened them again.

And boggled.

"Kevin! What in Eden are those?"

"What?" said Kevin, looking behind him hurriedly.

"Those things you're wearing!"

"What, these?"

"Yes! Those!"

"These are a pair of trousers," said Kevin proudly, and he walked up and down to show them off. "Look! They've got pockets and are held up by this little belt and there's this secret little pocket here for … for … putting little secret things in and they've even got turn-ups! Eve made them for me. She's very clever. What do You think?"

"I think you'll be able to keep each other company outside."

"What?" chorused Kevin and Eve.

"Look," said God, sitting down heavily on the grass and indicating for them to follow suit. "This really isn't easy for Me."

"We never ate anything from the pomegranate tree," Eve whispered.

"Pomegranates look much more like forbidden fruits than apples," Kevin pointed out.

"Well I would hardly advertise the Tree of Knowledge with something so seductive, would I?" said God, reasonably.

"We thought we'd be safe eating apples!" replied Eve. "Can't we just forget about the whole thing and put this down to experience?"

God shook His head and smiled sadly. "No, Eve. I know you're only trying to help, but I'm afraid it just doesn't work like that. There's more to it than simply taking off your clothes right now and keeping them off for ever more."

Kevin and Eve looked extremely uneasy at His suggestion.

"Even if it was in front of You?" they said together.

"Yes."

"In front of Eve?"

"In front of Kevin?"

God nodded. "See what I mean?"

"Couldn't You just forgive us?" asked Eve, in that helpful tone that made God feel so wretched.

"No. I mean, I do forgive you but I'm afraid it won't change a thing. You see, now that you wear clothes you won't be able to photosynthesise."

"Ah," said Kevin, "of course."

"And now that you can't photosynthesise, you'll be starting to feel a little peckish."

"Now You come to mention it, God, a little something would not go amiss."

"Now that you've started on the fruit and veg, it's but a small step for humankind to begin eating meat."

"Oh no," said Eve, "I could never do that!"

"You could," God assured her, "once Kevin has invented fire and you've learnt to cook. And as soon as you start hunting and gathering, there will be fewer animals and plants in Eden. So I will have to let them start evolving again. And to let them start evolving again I will need to let them reproduce and have young."

"Photosynthesis," muttered Kevin, thoughtfully. "That's how humankind was expelled from The Garden of Eden."

"*Original Photosynthesis*," corrected God. "It's none of your common or garden variety."

"I was never any good at scripture," said Kevin. "I was half expecting You to forbid us from eating apples but so much else is different here from what I remember being taught that it didn't seem to matter."

"We could still take our clothes off," suggested Eve.

"That wouldn't do any good," sighed God. "You've both got used to the feeling now, haven't you?"

"I think they're overrated, myself," said Kevin, undoing his belt.

God shook His head sadly again and put a restraining hand on Kevin's shoulder. "It's not the same as it was before, though, is it?"

Kevin thought about it. "I suppose there is now the prospect of being naked."

"And how do you feel about the prospect of seeing Eve naked?"

"I know it shouldn't make any difference for I've seen her naked often enough before but, even with her wearing that dress of flowers, when she stands close to me I think it's advisable that I keep my trousers on."

"You're thinking about evolving again, aren't you?"

"It's my genes talking," admitted Kevin.

"I knew it," said God. "Kevin? I have to admit that I am a bit surprised at you. Not for forgetting that it was apples and not pomegranates, but after cavorting about naked, all this time – since the dinosaurs died out – you suddenly feel compelled to pull on a pair of trousers."

"It seemed like a good idea at the time," said Kevin, defensively. "Besides, I had fur back then."

"Anyway," put in Eve, "You wear clothes, God."

"Yes, I do don't I?" He replied. "Now, can either of you tell Me why I should feel the need to do that?"

They both thought hard for a while, and then Eve, who had partaken of the apple a little before Kevin, asked uncertainly, "Is it because You already knew about *Original Photosynthesis*?"

God nodded slowly. "Obviously, I couldn't say 'Don't eat any apples because then you'll know all about *Original Photosynthesis*,' because then you would know all about it."

"And You wear Your overalls to protect us from it?" Eve reasoned.

"Yes. Well, no, that's not strictly true."

"Oh."

"No. You see, I wear My overalls to protect My clothes, to be precise. Otherwise, I'd get paint and grease and wood shavings and mess all over them, and Sophia would fuss at Me about it. But you're very close, Eve."

"We're very sorry, God," said Kevin.

Eve nodded earnestly.

God sighed.

"So am I, Kevin, so am I, Eve. I suppose putting a tree, any tree, in the middle of the Garden of Eden and forbidding you to eat from it was asking for it to happen really, wasn't it? I'm beginning to think this Free Will and Self-Determination business isn't all it's cracked up to be."

"I wouldn't mind," said Eve, "but I wasn't even hungry."

"Of course you weren't," said God. "Perhaps I should have been more explicit."

"I thought that was what You were trying to avoid," said Kevin.

God suddenly looked puzzled. "So why did you eat the apple?" he asked Eve.

"That snake suggested it."

"What snake?" said God and Kevin together, in perfect unison.

"That big black one with the horns on it."

"What?" said Kevin. "Horns like this?" and he made some with his fingers on his forehead.

"Yes, that's right!" laughed Eve, who thought he looked ridiculous. "He said it would be all right and that no one would mind. Why? Do you know the one I mean?"

"I'm afraid I do," said Kevin. "That could only have been Bub. And he was lying."

Eve looked thoughtful.

"I suppose that's all they can do," she said.

"Why? What do you mean?"

"Well, they don't have any legs. They can either lie on their fronts or lie on their backs."

"No, Eve …"

"Unless you could say he was sitting down, I suppose."

"No, Eve, not lying down," said Kevin, "but lying to you. Bub lied to you."

"What is this lying?"

"It's not telling the truth," he told her. "It's a sin."

"A sin?"

"It's a bit like photosynthesis but without the photo or the thesis."

"I can see that I still have much to learn, Kevin."

"Bub?" asked God, feeling a little less than omniscient.

"Yes," said Kevin, "Beelzebub."

"Be-elze-bub? Kevin. Are you telling Me that Beelzebub is here in Eden?"

"Yes."

"Oh, Kevin!"

"I'm afraid so. I'm sorry, God. Perhaps I should have mentioned it. It's just that I made Eve promise that she wouldn't touch any pomegranates, so I thought there wouldn't be any problem."

"I'm just as much to blame as you are. He used to be one of My angels," He explained to Eve, "but I had to let him go."

"He seemed so sad, too," said Kevin.

"What did Bub do?" Eve asked God.

"He said he could make a better job of running heaven than I could," God told her.

"Tact isn't one of his strong points, I take it."

"Perhaps I was a little harsh on him."

"I still think he asked for it, though," she said turning to Kevin.

"He spoke in haste," said Kevin.

"Maybe I did, too," said God.

"Just because You're in charge of everything doesn't mean to say that You're not sensitive," said Eve, putting a gentle hand on the sleeve of God's work shirt. "In fact, I think it's better that You are sensitive. I'm certainly happier to know that whoever looks after us genuinely cares."

"Grauniads?" God called out.

Seven little figures pole-vaulted over the herbaceous border of the Garden of Eden and ran to where they were sitting. To Kevin they appeared quite mythical and included a Norse god in a horned helmet, a Red Indian hunter, a Zeus-type figure and somebody's favourite middle-aged aunt who wore a very mischievous expression.

"You called, O Great Architect!" they choroused.

"Yes. And please don't call Me that! Plain God will do."

"All right, God."

"Sorry, God."

"Some people are never satisfied," muttered the aunt.

"Shut up, Gert!" hissed the other grauniads.

"I beg your pardon?" said God.

"Nothing," said Auntie Gert.

"Okay. You are all forgiven. Now then. I want you to search Eden for a big, black snake with horns on its head like this."

Eve had to smile again when God made the horned gesture to the grauniads. She was that kind of girl.

"We see," said the grauniads.

"Oh ssshit," said a muffled voice, somewhere close at hand.

"And I seem to recall," said Kevin, looking around with a curious expression, "that he likes to lie around under bushes quite a lot."

"Oh bugger," said the voice again and they could just make out a kind of frantic slithering away sound as if something very long and slithery was trying to get away without being seen by anyone.

The grauniads ran off into the bushes. There was a good deal of hissing and a brief but violent struggle until the bushes were parted by Auntie Gert to reveal a long coiling line of her fellows. Underneath their feet was a big black snake with horns.

"There is a worm at the bottom of my garden," said Auntie Gert.

"And his name is wiggly-woo," said the Norse god.

"Sorry, God."

"I don't know why we said that."

"No need to apologise," said God. "Now then, Beelzebub. Are you going to behave?"

Beelzebub nodded as vigorously as he could under the feet of the grauniads. He was going a bluish sort of black in the face.

"Good. Let him go."

The grauniads stepped off him and Beelzebub rolled around in coils, gasping for breath.

"So, Beelzebub. What do you have to say for yourself?"

"I ... refussse ... to sssay ... anything ... that ... may, ... or ... may ... not, ... incriminate myssself," he gasped.

"Did you, or did you not, tell this young woman it would be all right to eat the fruit of this apple tree?"

"Okay ... okay," panted the wretched serpent. "I admit it. It wasss me. I told a fib." He regained his composure. "Ssso whaddya gonna do about it, God? Eh? Sssack me again?"

"You told me you resigned," said Kevin quietly, but just loudly enough for Beelzebub to hear.

Beelzebub glared at him and stuck out his forked tongue.

"Beelzebub," said God, "thanks to you, these two innocent young creatures now know all about Original Photosynthesis."

Kevin and Eve beamed at each other at being called innocent young creatures.

Beelzebub glanced at Eve.

"Wow!" he said. "Hell-o! That dresssss really sssuitsss you!"

"Thank you."

"I sshould sssay ssso! Nothing better than a woman in the buff than a sssexssy woman in a well-fitting dresssss! Getsss the old imagination goin'! Know what I mean?"

He leered and stuck his tongue out repeatedly at her, flicking it suggestively.

"Stop it!" said Eve, pulling the hem of her dress down over her knees as she sat on the grass. She'd never seen a snake do that sort of thing with its eyebrows before. Come to that, neither had God or Kevin.

The grauniads stood on Beelzebub again, which really made his eyes pop.

"Thanks to you," said God, "Kevin and Eve can no longer stay in the Garden of Eden and will have to take their chances outside along with the rest of us. Do you understand?"

"Mumgpth!" said Beelzebub, swallowing hard.

"Good. Let this be on your conscience for ever more." God motioned to the grauniads to stand down again but they kept a restraining foot on Beelzebub. "Do you have anything to say?"

"Eh? Aren't You going to forgive me, then?"

"There's no need to be sarcastic," said God.

"What's sarcastic?" asked Eve.

"I'll tell you later," Kevin whispered. "Needless to say, it has no place in Eden."

"Whaddya 'ssspect me to sssay? D'You want me to plead exsssstenuating sssircumsssstanssssessss? Isss that what You want? Well, how about dessstitution? Unemployment? You fired me! Thisss isss asss much Your fault asss it isss anyone'sss!"

"Now, you can't expect anyone to believe that for a moment," said God, a little huffily.

"The hell I can!"

"Hell? What on earth are you talking about?"

"I'm sure you said you resigned," said Kevin.

"Aw, ssshutup!" said Beelzebub.

"Throw him out," directed God.

The grauniads jumped off Beelzebub but before he could wriggle away they picked him up and held him over their heads.

"Hey!" he protested, "That'sss not fair! That'sss, oooh, loadsss againsst one!"

The grauniads took no notice but swiftly formed an inhuman pyramid, pushing Beelzebub up into the sky.

"Oo-er," said Beelzebub, peering down at God, Kevin and Eve. "I feel a bit odd."

The brawny Norse god in the horned helmet held Beelzebub's tail in his oversized fists.

"I've got vertigo," complained Beelzebub as he tried to coil himself around the grauniads who formed the pyramid.

"Don't be ridiculous," they told him as they pushed him away.

"Ridiculousss?" spluttered Beelzebub. "Of courssse I've got vertigo! I wriggle around on my ssstomach!"

The Norse god put his arms above his head, and began to swing the struggling snake in a broad circle.

Beelzebub shut his eyes, flicked his forked tongue in and out and began to rise up under the influence of centrifugal force.

"God," said Kevin, "if he suffers from vertigo, giving him wings and employing him as an angel must have been awful for him."

"Oh, my giddy aunt!" said Beelzebub who was now rotating parallel to the ground.

"Don't listen to him," said God. "He lied to Eve."

There was a great Whoosh! each time the serpent passed over them.

"Oh, my good Gawd!" exclaimed Beelzebub, but it sounded more like blasphemy than an appeal for clemency.

"He does look very pale," said Eve with growing concern. "Maybe he really is afraid of heights," but at that moment the little Norse god gave a great heave and let go.

"I think I'm gonna be sssick!" wailed the snake as he sailed, a wiggly line in a graceful arc, over their heads and disappeared over the horizon.

The Norse god clapped his hands.

"Good riddance to bad rubbish!" he squeaked.

"Now steady on," said God. "We mustn't lose our charitable nature, must We?"

"No, God. Sorry God."

The pyramid dissembled itself.

"All right, then. You are forgiven." God frowned. "I wonder what he meant by hell?"

"Are we forgiven, then?" asked Eve.

"Oh, yes," said God. "But I'm afraid you'll both have to leave Eden," he added, hurriedly. "Don't look too alarmed, little Eve. Kevin will look after you. He's been out there before, and for millions of years. And I shall look after you both. If ever you want any advice, all you have to do is ask, no matter how trivial you may think it is. And all the time I shall be moving in a mysterious kind of way, My wonders to perform."

"So, does this mean we'll still be immortal?" asked Eve.

"Ah," said God. "I was just coming to that."

CHAPTER 45

"C'mon, Cadaver! Where the blazes are you? Glove? Hey, Glove! Glove! Nice Glove. Calm down a bit, there's a good fellow. I despise these … entities as much as you do, but we must find Cadaver, all right?"

Hob's rucksack was much bigger than before. The Product Planning Blocks were full of souls in terror, all prepared to sell themselves cheaply to avoid Re-education.

Hob glanced up and down the next corridor.

"You try that side and I'll try this."

He pushed a locked door which fell into the Re-education suite beyond like a drawbridge. Strapped into a large dentist's chair, bound and gagged, was Nenuphar. Two masked Conformorians were standing over her. One stood by a table scraping out the jelly from a long line of pork pies. The other was mixing the jelly up and preparing to feed it into a funnel strapped to a large, surgically chromed, cantilever arm over Nenuphar's mouth. Her gag had a small opening with a non-return valve in it.

"That's not him," said Hob. "Glove? Glove. Two in here."

Something small and red burst into the room and turned the two comestible inspectors into something far worse than pork-pie jelly.

Hob strode down the corridor of Re-education suites, bursting open doors as he went, but only finding more Conformorians attending to souls that, frankly, weren't worth having. The standard of souls fell the further Hob penetrated into the Product Planning Blocks but on reaching the end of the corridor, he paused. Behind him, the heat and brimstone fumes given off by The Glove had activated the fire alarms and sprinkler systems. The drops of water might just as well have been bullets for all that Hob cared as he stood there, concentrating. They left him entirely untouched. He wasn't even wet.

There was a notice board opposite the lift doors and The Glove approached it curiously.

Hob stepped up to a floor plan on the wall of the lift shaft.

"Oh dear," he said, "it's all in foreign."

He put a grubby finger on a point labelled *Vous etes ici.*

"I think we might be here," he said and left a black smudge on the map but it wasn't from engine oil but the blood of the Conformorians.

Hob's rucksack peered over his shoulder like a baby in a papoose.

The Glove got too close to the notice board and the paper spontaneously combusted despite the water sprinklers.

"We must find Cadaver, my incandescent little friend."

The Glove nodded and zoomed off down the corridor.

Hob turned quickly down another corridor and broke into a run. His Extra Sentiency Perception was homing in on a substantial soul in considerable torment. He passed by one door, but stopped and returned to it.

"Glove?" he shouted, and knocked the door down.

Inside was M Cadvare, strapped to a chair, bound and gagged. One Conformorian was attaching electrodes to his head. The other was checking the readout from an apparatus somewhere between a Van de Graaf generator and a television.

"There you are, Cadaver!" said Hob. "Stop messing about and come with me!"

The Conformorians didn't attack but stepped back.

Hob burst M Cadvare's bonds with one hand and hoisted him to his feet with the other.

"No wonder I had difficulty tracking you down," Hob told him. "They're using extra sentiency persecution techniques. I thought I was losing my touch, but your spirit was being drowned by their interference," and he ripped off M Cadvare's sticky-tape gag.

M Cadvare roared with pain.

"Oh, sorry," said Hob, insincerely. "Catch the bum fluff, did I?"

"Ugh! No, Hob! It's just what these fiends have been up to!"

"Those? Fiends? They're not fiends! Now, a fiend ... Glove? Glu-huve. Here Glove. Good Glove. Nice Glove. Now, *that's* a fiend!"

Hob pulled M Cadvare into the corridor, back the way he had come, leaving the hapless Conformorians to the diabolical attentions of Hob's right-hand glove puppet.

"We must find *Nosferatu*," said Hob.

"And Nenuphar!" added M Cadvare.

"What! That hippie chick?"

"Yes! Have you seen her?"

Hob looked blank. "Er, yes. Somewhere around here."

"There she is!" shouted M Cadvare and he dived into a wrecked Re-education suite. He undid her bonds and Hob peeled off her gag with its non-return valve.

Nenuphar did not suffer from a facial-hair problem but she still grimaced and moaned.

"My dress! Look at my dress! Pork-pie jelly all over it!"

"Don't worry," said M Cadvare, brightly. "It'll soon wash off under the water sprinklers."

She stood up and he saw that she was already soaked through.

"Oh, I say," said Hob. "Hell-o Miss Wet T-shirt!"

"I suppose," said Nenuphar, "that you're going to say we should get out of our wet clothes."

"Well, now you come to mention it, it would seem sensible."

"Dream on, Hob! I'd rather catch double pneumonia!"

"Well, if ever you feel a bit, you know, chesty …"

"Why aren't *you* wet?" said an equally bedraggled but less alluring M Cadvare.

"Do you remember me telling you I can control my molecular density? I can ward off rain and sprinkler systems, too."

Nenuphar stamped her foot. "Look …"

"I am looking."

"We must find my family."

"Your family?" Hob and M Cadvare said together.

"Yes. The comestible inspectors took them away. They must be here somewhere!"

"They could be anywhere," snorted the Soul Trader.

"But we must find them! I hope nothing has happened to them!"

M Cadvare gave Hob a meaningful look.

"When did the inspectors come for your family?" he asked her.

"About four or five days ago."

"And they took them because they were vegetarian?"

"Yes."

"Why, exactly?"

"The lives of the animals depend on meat eaters eating them," she replied.

Hob considered this for a moment and then said, "No, sorry, you've lost me there."

"I wasn't terribly sure about it, either," admitted Nenuphar. "The Conformorians believe eating animals perpetuates their species. It gives them justification for their existence, they said, and if we don't eat the animals their lives have no point."

"He's thinking of becoming a vegetarian," said Hob, jerking a thumb at M Cadvare.

"Am I?"

"Are you?"

"Well, yes …"

"You don't sound so sure."

"It's a big decision."

"Well, I'm glad you're even thinking about it."

"Really?"

"Of course."

Hob grinned at the pair of them and, when Nenuphar looked up and down the corridor outside, gave M Cadvare a nudge and a wink.

"Four to five days in the Product Planning Blocks is an awfully long time," said M Cadvare. "Do you think we'll be able to find them, Hob, if they're still here?"

"Well," said Hob, "I imagine that individuals with such a strong subversive facility as your kith and kin would have the strength of character to withstand Re-education better than most, eh, Nenny?"

"I sincerely hope so."

Hob produced a long, thin object from his jacket pocket. "Then with my Extra Sentiency Perception and this spirit level, if they are in this building we shall find them and escape. But first, we must do a little soul searching."

"Of course!" said M Cadvare. "There's a moral issue here. We can either escape to make everyone know what's happening or rescue as many souls as we can!"

"Rescue them? I was thinking more of liberating them."

"Exactly."

"As in possessing them. Finders keepers sort of thing."

"This is no time to think of business!"

"Of course, it is. Out of the pork-pie-jelly fat and into the fire and brimstone of the soul sack they come!"

"What on earth are you wittering about?" demanded Nenuphar.

"Hey! Soul Traders don't witter! All right?"

"We need to be looking for my family," Nenuphar insisted, "right now!"

"Just the point I was making before our vegetarian-in-waiting here went off on an ethical tangent."

"And your point," said Nenuphar, "is what exactly?"

"My point is that we should search for these poor souls who may have survived attempts to Re-educate them."

"Exactly! So let's go!"

"But first there is a small matter of consideration."

"Consideration?"

"It passes from the promissor to the promissee."

"I think what Hob is trying to say," M Cadvare said to Nenuphar, "is that … well, we're going to have to make it worth his while."

"What? But that's despicable!"

"Hey, honey, I'm a Soul Trader. Whaddya expect?"

"A what?"

"This is all your fault, Cadaver!"

"My fault?"

"Yes – but admitting it at this late stage isn't going to make it any easier!"

"Why's it my fault?"

"You stopped me giving my card to this charming young lady. Remember?"

"Ah, yes, but ..."

"And now, in less than ideal circumstances, I am forced to try again. My card, my dear. I apologise for not introducing myself properly earlier."

Nenuphar studied it. "There's nothing on it," she said.

Hob beamed. "Modesty forbids it."

M Cadvare thumped his forehead in exasperation.

Nenuphar turned the card over.

"And no address, either."

Hob shrugged.

"I am never at home. Mind you, we are on our way there, aren't we Cadaver?"

Nenuphar turned the card over a second time, just as thousands of people had done before her. As if by magic, the letters appeared.

Nicholas Eldritch Hob. Soul Trader and Holder of Soul Rites. Horse-power Whispering a speciality.

"What odd spelling!" she exclaimed with a strange delight. Then she frowned. "I've never seen this language written before. How can I understand it?"

"It describes a universal truth," said Hob. "One might even say a para-versal one."

"So what is a Soul Trader?" she asked, looking as if it might be better not to know.

"A Soul Trader is someone who deals in souls," explained Hob.

"What? The soles of shoes?"

"No."

Nenuphar opened her mouth.

"And not soles as in fish, either," said Hob. "Do I look like a fish-monger? Think again. Look. Here. Souls. S-O-U-L-S."

"You're a ... Soul Trader," she murmured.

Hob nodded. "Some might say The Soul Trader."

M Cadvare fidgeted.

"Oh my God!"

"Now, look ..." said Hob.

"Oh my God!"

"There's no need for that sort of language!"

"Y-you're a Soul Trader!"

"That's what I said. If you become hysterical, I shall have to strike you. Hard."

"There's no need for that," M Cadvare interjected.

"You gave me the creeps right from the start!"

"Really?" Hob suddenly looked very proud. "I bet you say that to all the Necromancers!"

Nenuphar was thinking fast despite her confusion.

"So you want my soul in return for finding the rest of my family? Is that it?"

Hob pulled out his spirit level, measured her soul with it, and smiled, showing her the bubbling fish fart that lurked at the extreme end of its scale. "In a word, yes."

"Never! Not in a million years! I'll find my family myself!" and with that she stormed off down the corridor.

"Pity," remarked Hob, putting his spirit level away. "Quite a spirited young gel, that. Shame about the vegetarianism. Come on. I've got to find *Nosferatu.*"

"Okay," said M Cadvare, "you do that – I'll talk to Nenuphar."

CHAPTER 46

M Cadvare finally caught up with Nenuphar in the next tower of the Product Planning Blocks. He crept up behind her and tapped her on the shoulder in the expectation that she would squeal and jump out of her skin. He liked girls who did that.

This she duly proceeded to do.

What he did not expect was to find himself lying on the coarse grey carpet semi-unconscious with a spectacular nose bleed.

"What did you do that for?" demanded an irate Nenuphar, who peered over him, even paler than normal.

M Cadvare recalled something about flight or fight.

He discounted flight.

"Nngmpr," he replied, suddenly philosophical.

The colour returned to Nenuphar's cheeks. In fact she blushed. Even so, for overall redness, M Cadvare's face had hers easily beaten.

"Here," she said, "let me have a look."

She knelt down and M Cadvare flinched.

"Hmm," she said.

M Cadvare's head swam. It swam in a little pool of blood.

Nenuphar's face rippled, somewhere above him, but just as he felt like drifting off somewhere warm and pleasant, she tore a bandage off from some mysterious piece of underclothing.

M Cadvare's concentration returned immediately.

With a strip of clean white linen, she dabbed M Cadvare's nose, gently moulding it back into something resembling its original shape.

Over the all-pervading smell of iron filings, he could just make out another smell, a perfume he had smelt in the bathroom the night before.

His head began to reel again at the thought of it.

Or was it the subtle aroma of pork-pie jelly?

Seeing his eyes glazing over, Nenuphar tore off another strip from her underclothes, this time higher up, and she regained M Cadvare's attention even more quickly.

"I'm not going to apologise," she told him.

M Cadvare blew some bubbles at her.

"No, don't try to speak." She dabbed. The flow was gradually abating. "You won't try that again, will you?"

M Cadvare considered shaking his head but didn't dare because of his loose-fitting nose. Instead he blew some more bubbles at her in a sort of Morse code, one bubble for yes, two for no.

"Kick boxing," said Nenuphar, in answer to an unasked question. "I picked it up along the way. Feeling any better?"

One blow.

"Steady now. Try breathing through your mouth. D'you think your nose is broken?"

Another blow.

She rewarded his fortitude with another bandage and a glimpse of suspender, which provoked a short series of bubbles.

One of the bubbles became airborne and floated gently away. They both stared at it in amazement as it wafted across the corridor and, just above a floor-level ventilation duct, suddenly popped out of existence against the grey wall, leaving behind the outline of a perfectly round red circle.

"Wow," said Nenuphar. "I bet you couldn't do that again, even if you tried."

M Cadvare tried and couldn't. His nose was rapidly becoming sealed with what felt like quick-drying cement.

There was a distant commotion and from a floor above them someone began squeezing a giant tube of grey toothpaste into the quad outside.

"Ready now?" asked Nenuphar.

She put the rolled up bandages in his fingers and then planted his hand on his nose with a surprising gentleness.

"Come on, we can't hang around here all day. Sooner or later the inspectors'll re-group and come after us."

She helped him to his feet and they caught sight of Hob. He was in a transparent tube that stretched from one Product Planning Block to another, back to back with The Glove as they battled a grey mass of Conformorians.

"M Cadvare? May I ask you a question?"

Holding his nose, M Cadvare nodded.

"Have you sold your soul to Hob?"

He nodded again. "It seebed like a good idea at der tibe. Id fact, I dode dink I'd'b got this far widdout his help."

Hob and The Glove seemed to be winning against the Conformorians. Hob was brandishing another computer desk he'd found somewhere. The Glove had flown around the tubes and corridors and was now attacking the Conformorians from the rear. Hob had time to grin and wave at them before he charged the Grey Ones with his computer desk in front of him like some administrative bulldozer.

"He's very effective," Nenuphar admitted.

"I bleeve he's our best bet," said M Cadvare.

"Is he totally evil, do you think?"

"I'b dot sure. Dot totally evil. Dobody who's kind to verbid and carriod der way he is cad be cobpletely bad, I suppose." He frowned. "In sub ways, I rather like hib."

"What? Why?"

"Well he certaidly livedd thigs up aroud here, did't he? A few hours ago, I was just adother dowd-trodded Chartered Badagebent Auditor. Dow, I've falledd id wid what bust be Euphobia's boast wadted bad, and I'm prowlig aroud der Product Pladdig Blocks wid by soul idtact."

"Not much of an exchange, in my opinion."

"Eddythig, absolutely eddythig, was better thad by existeds beforehad."

"But you're not soulless! You know – like a commodity inspector."

"I've still got by soul." M Cadvare took the wad of bandages away from his nose now that it had solidified and spoke less nasally. "He's got to make my dreams come true before he can take it."

"Is that what he meant about consideration passing from the promissor to the promissee? So. What did you get in exchange for your soul?"

"Passage to Anarchadia."

"So as soon as you're there, you're damned!"

"Not exactly. Hob said something about turning me into a skirrow or a Horsepower Whisperer or something."

"Why?"

"I'll be worth more to him that way. He says that prior to actually taking possession of a soul he can work on it to improve it, fulfil it, grant it its dreams. But after it's been exchanged, it can't be improved."

"Do you trust him?"

"As much as I've ever trusted anyone in my life."

"But you haven't had much of a life, right? Look. Doesn't any of this bother you at all?"

M Cadvare stopped to think about it. "Only when I stop and think about it," he said. "I always make a point of trying to look on the bright side. You should try it some time. While I have the spirit, I intend to be spirited! Once we get to Anarchadia …"

He trailed off.

Nenuphar wasn't paying attention.

A group of people were watching them from the glass tube that Hob and The Glove had just cleared of Conformorians. Four security guards flanked a distinguished-looking gentleman of about fifty. He looked haggard and ashen.

"Look! It's my daddy! It's my daddy!" and Nenuphar ran off to meet them.

CHAPTER 47

Hob was determined not to crowd surf again. He'd just squirted another column of Conformorians out of another window when even more ran down the corridor towards him, as if they had been lying in wait.

He regretted throwing the computer desk out into the quad but by the time the last Grey One had been defenestrated, the desk was travelling so fast even he couldn't stop it. Now he would have to fight with his bare hands and he hated touching the flesh of the Grey Ones, even if it was for the briefest of impacts. Then there was that dark grey ooze that spilt out of their veins. He was trying to keep the blood off his hands but it was very difficult

With The Glove, he faced another great crowd of Conformorians. Hob goaded them with double vee-signs as they closed in and The Glove brandished his trident and indicated even more graphically what he thought of them. Then they fell upon the great wad of Grey Ones. Hob hit out as hard as he could and felt the spirits in his rucksack urge him on as The Glove darted everywhere. It wasn't just himself he was fighting for. It was for all the souls in Euphobia.

M Cadvare's words came back to him. He not only had to rescue the souls he'd harvested. He had to get out of the Product Planning Blocks and let the rest of the world know what was going on in Euphobia. Today – this very hour – would be the beginning and end of something. This was where the stand against the Grey Ones would begin – one man, albeit a Soul Trader and a Horsepower Whisperer – against the massed hordes of Conformorians.

He saw that there was no end to their numbers so he throttled back to fight them more efficiently. If he wasn't careful, this rebellion wouldn't last long.

He concentrated on hitting out accurately. As he drew back his arms he hit the Grey Ones behind him and tried to marshal their upright inanimate bodies to cover his back for there was no room for them to fall. It became difficult to tell which Grey Ones were alive or not.

The Glove encircled Hob like a raging electron orbiting its nucleus. He swooped up and down and round and round but there were still plenty of Grey Ones who got past him, no matter how fast he flew.

Hob realised that he was surrounded. He felt the unfamiliar sensation of rising panic run through his flailing limbs. He felt that the Conformorians sensed the seeds of his despair and rallied in their attack. But as the fear deepened, Hob reacted just as he had in the days before he was immortal. He tapped into it and used fear to his advantage.

The killing continued. Hob took no pleasure from it. He wondered how something without a soul could be killed. They were dead already – unalive, perhaps – and he was just de-animating them, so that they didn't get in his way any more. They looked the same in death as in life. Their expressions didn't change. Their listless gaze didn't alter. Even the dead ones seemed to move against him, forced on by those behind, and, alive or dead, the only way they moved was against him.

An old friend came to visit him. It was the red haze that made him ride aggressively, strengthening his sinews and sharpening his reactions. Although it had been honed in the heat of the Wild Hunt, he adapted it to fight the hordes of the Grey Ones. All thought of restraint left him.

He lashed out wildly with his fists, but there were so many Confor-morians trying to overpower him that he couldn't fail to find a mark. He opened his great wings and flapped them, breaking arms and heads with every beat.

A disturbing thought crystallised in his mind as he battled on. Perhaps the distinction between life and death was a thin one for the Conformorians. They certainly had no fear of death. He wondered if it was fear of life – his life – that drove them on. Maybe, without sensitive and troublesome souls to complicate matters, the Grey Ones could easily be re-animated. If this was the case, he decided their physical bodies would have to be broken up as compre-hensively as he could manage.

The Glove was now embroiled in a battle of his own. Somehow they had become separated. Although there was no-one in obvious control of the Con-formorians, Hob could not believe their attacks were not carefully co-ordin-ated. His blood boiled at the thought and he unleashed the berserker within. He felt that the longer he stayed here, the longer the Grey Ones could exercise their will over him. The more they could restrain him, the more scrapes M Cadvare could get into and the more souls would be destroyed by other Grey Ones elsewhere. Speed was now of the essence. All thought of economy of move-ment left him. Indeed, nearly all thought left him.

Instinctively, he clambered up over piles of recently de-animated Con-formorians.

Without the protection of The Glove, the rucksack snarled and snapped at those who tried to overpower Hob from behind. Many Grey Ones were taken by surprise as the teeth in the zips on his rucksack bit chunks out of their flesh and then spat them back out again, blinding them with their own dark grey fluids.

Hob perched perilously on the remains of his victims again. Fighting was easier but he kept catching glimpses of the numbers that surrounded him, and this would have dispirited a lesser man.

"Listen to me, Hob," a voice suddenly intoned. "You cannot hide and have nowhere to run. You are outnumbered. Resistance is useless."

It was Inspector Gris.

"You cannot keep this up indefinitely," he went on. "You will never leave the Product Planning Blocks without Re-education. Ultimately, you will be made to conform."

"I got a rite!" shouted Hob.

He stood on tiptoe and reached up to pull a speaker out of the ceiling. He yanked it down and the broadcast stopped, but the crowd surged and Hob toppled onto its surface. Immediately he felt a thousand hands trying to pluck out the feathers from his wings so he snapped them back into his leather jacket and lashed out with just his four ordinary limbs. He felt grey bodies crumple beneath him, but any that fell were replaced by others and they barely faltered as they carried him back down the corridor.

As they flowed into another Product Planning Block, Hob managed to grab some light fittings in a bid to prevent himself being swept away entirely but, in a grotesque display of fluid mechanics, the sea of Conformorians billowed up and engulfed him, creating a Mexican wave that pulled him along, ceiling brackets, wiring and all.

Hob pulled down sprinkler systems, security cameras, smoke detectors, ventilation ducting and more public address speakers.

"Conform and enjoy the rights of Euphobian citizenship," said a speaker in his lap.

"Never!" shouted Hob and he crushed it between his legs.

"Resistance is useless," repeated Inspector Gris as they entered a new corridor with its speaker system intact.

"I got a rite!" yelled Hob.

He was swept along like a piece of flotsam and, looking between his feet, saw he was accelerating towards a floor-to-ceiling window at the end of it. The Conformorians were going to defenestrate him, presumably as the start of his Re-education.

"We are overwhelming you."

"Glove!" he roared but The Glove was somewhere else.

"You have failed, totally."

That was the worst thing Inspector Gris could have said.

Hob thought hard of total failure and what you did when it came rushing towards you.

He had a rite, more than a rite. He had soul rites, rites of passage, rites of airflow and rites of combustion. He just had to exercise those rites.

"All is lost," said Inspector Gris.

"When faced with complete disaster," shouted Hob, "total defiance is the only answer!"

Hob adjusted his molecular density. He rolled up into a ball to concentrate his mass and visualised the process involved in making cannonballs. This involved heating a crucible of molten iron at the top of a tower and then emptying it into the void below. As the molten metal fell, it formed a spinning spherical mass and by the time it hit the wadding at the foot of the tower it had cooled sufficiently to adopt this form permanently.

Hob sank into the crowd and the Grey Ones stumbled over him as they flowed by, unable to stop. Hob hoped they defenestrated themselves. He felt something give underneath him and, with a supreme effort, he managed to fall through the floor onto the one below.

He landed in another corridor and some Conformorians tried to pour after him, but the hole was small. Hob unrolled, readjusted his density and jumped up to de-animate them so that they blocked the hole he'd just made.

He took off his rucksack to check it for stolen souls but none were missing. As far as the spirits in his rucksack were concerned, it had been a fight for more than mere life.

The limbs of dead Conformorians dangled from the hole in the ceiling like gruesome stalactites but from somewhere within the Product Planning Blocks came the sound of many pairs of feet trampling down the stairs.

Hob dragged another computer table out of an adjacent office and armed himself with it, taking up position to one side of the stairwell.

At the far end of the corridor the water sprinklers sprang into life, one after another, and Hob grinned as a small red dot grew into The Glove. Puffs of steam punctuated his progress as he shot through the sprays of water until he rippled in his heat haze in front of Hob.

"Good work, Glove! There can't be many more left."

A small bunch of Conformorians rushed them at that moment. Hob and The Glove were so wound up they almost fought each other to destroy them.

"Watch my back!" shouted Hob, and The Glove zipped behind him, scowling down the corridor at the Grey Ones coming around the corner.

The doors to the stairwell burst open and yet more Conformorians flooded the corridor in front of Hob.

The water sprinklers stopped. Heavy-calibre bullets tore into Hob's computer table. Others bounced off him from behind. Caught in the crossfire, Hob wasn't knocked over. The barrage from both sides kept him upright but he twitched and shuddered under the onslaught. The Glove ventured into the crowd to bring the guards down and bullets ricocheted in every direction, shattering windows, burrowing into the walls in puffs of dust and smashing into the ceiling. Bits of polystyrene tiles fell down like confetti, and the table bucked and kicked in Hob's hands as bullets ripped into it.

When the shooting stopped, the massed ranks of Conformorians rushed them from both directions.

As soon as he could see the greys of their empty eyes, Hob brandished the table at chest level and roared a battle cry. But the table felt much lighter, and he glanced down, doing a double-take at what he had in his hands.

All he had was a torn and twisted metal frame. Most of the table was a pile of sawdust covering his boots.

He kicked the sawdust away and swung the frame of the computer table into the oncoming crowd. Conformorians splashed aside at every stroke of the mangled metal frame but still more replaced those that fell. Hob felt the frame twist and fracture in his hands. Another two swings and it disintegrated, and he was back to hand-to-hand fighting.

Behind him, The Glove weaved back and forth, back and forth, across the corridor, threading its own brand of hot death through the chests of the Grey Ones. Each rank hung in the air as if on an invisible kebab before keeling over under the weight of those behind. Gradually, the corridor filled up with their lifeless corpses.

Hob punched and thumped as hard as he could. He tried to push the crowd before him but it was like pushing the sea. What he really needed was something to act as another barrier.

"I need another table, Glove!" he shouted.

The Glove broke off from skewering Conformorians and quickly zig-zagged through the locks of the doors on either side of the corridor before the advancing Grey Ones could gain much ground.

Hob chose his moment carefully. Using his berserker's fury he fought the Conformorians further down the corridor. Then he fell back, side-stepped into a nearby office and pulled out another table. When he hit the ranks of the Grey Ones, it produced a perfect display of Newton's Second Law of Motion. The impact set up a bow wave that rippled all the way down the corridor, bounced off the ceiling-to-floor glass wall at the far end and then came back towards Hob. But by then he was pushing with all his might, and a bigger wave going the other way engulfed the first one.

The Conformorians fell back and Hob could feel them being pushed up against walls and windows. Their struggling faltered. De-animated Grey Ones oozed over and under his computer desk. Hob pushed harder still.

Suddenly everything became much easier. His pace quickened and soon he was almost running. Then the table fell away and he found himself teetering on the edge of a hole where a plate-glass window had once been. Confor-morians tumbled through the air beneath him and spread out on the floor of the quad below.

Hob put out his wings and wedged them against the gap, dangling awk-wardly above the twitching pile of Grey Ones. There was the briefest of red flashes and The Glove was pushing him back into the building with the blunt end of his trident against Hob's crash helmet, roughly where his third eye would be.

"I got a rite!" yelled Hob.

The Glove, almost glowing yellow from his exertions, gave him an enthusiastic thumbs-up sign.

Side by side they ran down the corridor, easily dealing with any isolated groups of Conformorians that they came across. They entered another Product Planning Block and skidded down some stairs just in time to hear someone shout, "Nenuphar!"

"Cadaver!" shouted Hob and he burst through some stout wooden fire doors.

They swung shut in the face of The Glove, but he just blasted his way through, leaving them smouldering.

Hob found himself in another open-plan office.

M Cadvare had his back to him and beyond him were a group of people.

Conformorian guards, who had been creeping up behind M Cadvare, tried to rush Hob but were merely impaled by the jet propelled Glove.

"Hey!" yelled Hob, pointing. "Who's that bloke groping Nenuphar? He's old enough to be her father!"

"He is her father, you idiot!"

A door beside them opened, and a traffic cone emerged to take up station by Hob's boots but Hob didn't notice.

"What?" Hob exchanged glances with The Glove and realised that what M Cadvare had told him must be true.

Another foolhardy group of Grey Ones attacked and Hob dealt with them effortlessly, even though he was distracted by this latest revelation. He pulled the jacket off a fallen Conformorian, wiped his dark grey hands clean, turned to gape at Nenuphar, her father and the guards and fell head over heels.

"There, there my child," said Nenuphar's father.

She raised her head and looked hard into his face, frowning.

"Nenuphar," he said. "You must stop *all* this, my dear."

Hob stood up slowly, with his arms outstretched. "What the hell's this?"

M Cadvare glanced at what Hob was holding. "It's a smart traffic cone," he muttered.

Hob angrily drop-kicked the smart traffic cone through the window. He glanced at M Cadvare but did a double take.

"What's happened to your nose?"

M Cadvare did not reply.

"Papa?" asked Nenuphar.

"You must stop all this nonsense at once," her father told her.

The Glove scratched his head with his trident.

"Wait a moment!" said Hob.

He pulled out his spirit level, pointed it at Nenuphar and then her father. Hob and M Cadvare checked the gauge.

"Uh-oh," they said, looking at each other. "Fish fart never lies!"

CHAPTER 48

"Nenuphar, my child, my dear child," said her father, "listen to me. All this misguided idealism must stop. What I taught you was wrong ... so wrong. I should never have indoctrinated you with such seditious thoughts and brought you up to believe in such things. Come with me now, bring your friends with you, and I will explain everything to you. It's for your own good as well as that of Euphobia. I can see that now. Believe me, you must be made to understand how important it is to be responsible citizens."

"Glove? Guards!" said Hob, as more Conformorians approached, but The Glove was already on the case.

"This is all wrong," said M Cadvare.

Hob checked his spirit level once more.

"Isn't it?"

Hob nodded and put the spirit level away.

"Her father's one of them, isn't he?"

"Is he?" replied Hob, suddenly intrigued. "What? Her father? You mean, like, you know?" and he made a coy gesture with one hand and put the other on his hip.

"No, not one of those ... a Grey One."

"By the socket set of St Bendix!"

"It's true, isn't it?" M Cadvare asked Nenuphar.

"Yes," she whimpered.

Seeing that the game was now up, her father released her, and she ran to M Cadvare.

"I was wrong," repeated Nenuphar's father as he faced them. "And so are you. All of you."

"Take her downstairs, Cadaver," ordered Hob. "To the underground car park. Your hotted-up fridge awaits us."

"Come on," said M Cadvare, gently.

Nenuphar took a few steps and then collapsed. M Cadvare was obliged to carry her away.

"It's all starting to make sense," said Hob, advancing on her father. "The last souls I found barely showed up on the spirit level. They were so poor, they were worthless, eroded by sheer bloody frustration and tedium. And it would appear that yours has gone completely."

The Glove returned from despatching the guards, and hovered menacingly, just behind Hob's shoulder.

"I was weak," said Nenuphar's father. "I just didn't understand how wrong I was. How wrong everyone else was, too. You in particular," he finished, looking at Hob.

"Did you know that to err is to be but human?"

"No. And I won't make mistakes like that again."

"I bet you won't," said Hob, looking at The Glove. "So what are we supposed to do with you now?"

"Listen to me. Killing me won't help. There are thousands more like me, and our numbers are growing all the time. The tide has turned against you."

"First of all, I'm not the listening sort," said Hob, fighting the urge to become irrationally pedantic, "and killing you will actually make me feel a whole lot better. But I'm a Soul Trader. I don't kill people. I trade with them. And I couldn't kill you anyway, because, for all intents and purposes you're already dead!"

"You may think that."

"I do." Hob turned to The Glove. "What do you think?"

The Glove drew his trident across his throat in an unequivocal gesture.

"You," said Hob, pointing, "are nothing more than dead hair and old skin!"

"What you think is not as important as what I know."

"Which is?"

"Come," said Nenuphar's father, beckoning. "Come, my son. Come with me and I will show you. I will explain everything to you and make you understand. Completely."

"Like you did with the others? Uh-uh. Glove?"

The Glove sprang to attention.

"You know what to do."

"You'll understand one day," said Nenuphar's father. "We will catch up with you; it's only a matter of time. Then you'll understand ..."

But Hob had turned his back and was walking away. His rucksack had a perfect view of what happened next. A plume of something dark grey splashed the wall and, shortly afterwards, The Glove caught up with him.

CHAPTER 49

"Well, it's been a funny old day," said Hob, as he wiped dark grey blood off his hands.

M Cadvare stood beside his personal transportation device in the underground car park. He had carried Nenuphar all the way down and poured her into the passenger seat. He was checking her pulse when Hob joined them.

"How is she?" Hob asked him.

"Er, all right. I think. It must have been a terrible shock."

"Keep her warm, then," advised the Horsepower Whisperer.

M Cadvare was surprised Hob knew any first aid at all.

Nearby was *Nosferatu*'s crate. The Glove must have ventured down here earlier, because four Conformorian technicians lay beside the crate with typical Glove wounds.

Hob walked over to it. Scattered all around it were dozens of broken jemmies and claw hammers. He smiled, picked the crate it up and placed it in the back of M Cadvare's personal transportation device. He tied the hatch down again with another conker on its string and looked at the sleeping Nenuphar through the glass, while The Glove peered over his shoulder.

Hob took off his rucksack and it wriggled obesely on the floor besides Nenuphar's feet as he opened a pocket and produced an irregular block of some sulphurous material.

"Smelling salts?" he said, offering it to M Cadvare.

"Only if you want to kill her," said M Cadvare, recoiling. "Besides, I think it's best if she rests for a while."

Hob nodded and turned to The Glove hovering expectantly nearby.

"There, Glove! Good Glove!" he said, rummaging in the pockets of his leather jacket. "You have worked especially well today, haven't you?"

A heat haze rippled off The Glove as if the air was corrugated.

Hob held out his arm to The Glove and approached him carefully, as if he was an orangey-red bird of prey as hot as the centre of the sun.

"Yes, of course you have!"

The air around The Glove squirmed as if it was too painful to be in contact with him and Hob fed him the brimstone.

"Glove? I saved you some of this," said Hob, and he held out a mangled wad of Sulphur Floss from the egojumble.

The Glove's little red face lit up, and he skewered the floss on his trident and licked it off eagerly.

"Had enough?" asked Hob when The Glove had finished.

The Glove shook his head.

Hob chuckled.

"Time for sleepy bo-bo?"

The Glove thought about it for a moment but the words had affected him strangely and despite his best efforts he yawned and stretched.

"This will be a day we'll both remember," said Hob, handing out some more brimstone from his rucksack. "Time to rest now."

He carefully took The Glove in his hands. "Ow! Shit, you little bastard, you're incandescent!"

He gingerly rolled up the yawning Glove and placed him carefully in the outside pocket of his leather jacket.

Hob's jacket, which had withstood the onslaught of explosions and many Conformorian bullets, smouldered but did not catch fire.

"Any change?" Hob asked M Cadvare.

M Cadvare shook his head.

Hob pulled out his spirit level and pointed it at Nenuphar.

"Her spirit is damaged."

"Badly?"

Hob nodded. "Wouldn't yours be?"

"I don't really know. I never really had a family."

"You were damaged then," said Hob, "but with time your soul healed. The experience made you stronger."

"Will the same thing happen to Nenuphar?"

"I don't know," said Hob. "It should do. But everyone has a breaking point, and it can appear in the most unexpected places."

M Cadvare swallowed hard. "If she is broken can you repair her?"

"Only at a price." Hob jerked his helmet towards the personal transportation device. "If I lift her out, can she sit on your lap?"

M Cadvare nodded.

Hob picked Nenuphar up easily and gently draped her over M Cadvare. They looked at her frowning as she slept.

"What now?" asked M Cadvare.

"To the coast. Then passage to Albion and on to Anarchadia itself!"

Hob took up position behind the wheel. "Trouble's going," he said, as the instrument lights came on.

"Trouble's gone," sighed M Cadvare, and they started to move slowly through the underground car parks.

"Hob?"

"Yeah?"

"You could've escaped at any point, couldn't you?"

Hob glanced at M Cadvare.

"I could've. Up until the point when all those Grey Ones came running up to me. I just needed to see what we were up against. Then I found I'd started something and had to finish it."

"So what *are* we up against?"

"Hordes and hordes of soul-destroying Conformorians."

"Why are they doing this?"

"Why? I can't possibly understand why. To me they seem to be squandering such unbelievable riches. The people here could be just as iconoclastic, creative and original as anyone, but what do the Grey Ones do to them? They send them here, to this glorified laundry, where they bleach all life and colour out of them. The citizens of Euphobia are becoming just a grey wad of tissues, the unseemly fluff in the pocket-corners of humanity. Use one of those fuzz-away brushes and you'd never know they'd existed."

"What d'you call them? Conformorians?"

"Yeah. The Grey Ones. They want everyone to be the same, and to do that they destroy their souls." Hob frowned. "I am advised this is nothing new."

"Advised? By whom?"

"Other Soul Traders. I've heard stories about Conformorianism, but never really paid them much attention. Among Soul Traders they are the stuff of legend, if once-mortals like us can have legends of our own. To us, they are the bogeymen."

"To you? *Merde!*" M Cadvare glanced nervously at the shadows of the underground car park. "Do you think we can just drive out of here?"

"Don't see why not," replied the Horsepower Whisperer. "What can they do to stop us? Hang on. I feel a pricking of my thumbs!"

A vast pink Cadillac appeared before them.

Hob pulled up sharply.

Behind the wheel of the Cadillac was the familiar figure of Therese Darlmat, but beside her and all along the back seat were half a dozen grauniads, all carefully strapped into child seats.

Hob leaned out of the window. "It's not a good time," he said.

Therese looked at him for a moment and then at Nenuphar slumped in the arms of M Cadvare. She nodded and selected D for de-materialise on her column change.

"What do you suppose she wanted?" M Cadvare asked after she'd gone.

"Badness, black-hearted me! How the blazes should I know?" replied Hob as they bounced onto the street outside the Product Planning Blocks.

"You don't think … you don't think she was trying to warn us about something again, do you?"

Hob shrugged his shoulders and sent the personal transportation device around a roundabout on two wheels. "How should I know?"

CHAPTER 50

"Hallo Kevin."

Kevin Mullins sat slumped before the mirror in his dressing room with his head in his hands. He peered through his fingers and saw behind him that his dressing room was full of pink Cadillac. His dressing room seemed to have grown to accommodate it.

"Hallo Therese."

He turned to face the beautiful young scientist who sat behind the ivory steering wheel of the six-wheeled convertible and noticed that her car was full of grauniads, all sitting in child seats.

Not every one can see the homunculi. Different types have different spheres of influence and only those people with a strong bond to the little people's realm can see them.

Kevin had broken all the laws designed to prevent time travel, wiped out the dinosaurs, met God and His Wife, established first name terms with Beelzebub himself, stood in for the Father of Humankind and been re-incarnated for millions of years. In terms of gaining the necessary homuncular vision to see the grauniads, the caretakers of his paraverse, he was almost over-qualified.

"Hallo Thor, Brunhilde, Moon Wolf, Isis, Gaia, Zeus and Gertrude."

"Oh just call me Gert and leave my rude part out!"

Therese and the grauniads all laughed, although they'd heard Gert's routine many times before. And Kevin, despite his despondency, found himself smiling.

"How's it going, Kevin?" asked Therese.

"Not very well."

Everyone in the Cadillac frowned and waited for him to explain.

"This life has been a big disappointment for me."

"Why this one in particular?" asked Thor.

"It's not as if your others were particularly successful," said Brunhilde.

"I do apologise," Therese said hurriedly. "You must remember, Kevin, that grauniads lack many elementary social skills."

"What about my joke?" demanded Gert.

"My point entirely," said Therese.

There was just enough room for her to open her door and climb out to stretch her legs.

Moon Wolf shot Kevin with a metaphysical arrow. "Social skills or no social skills, Kevin, you must admit we are correct."

Kevin sighed. "All my lives have been a failure."

"A failure?" echoed Isis.

"Don't you mean many failures?" asked Gaia.

"We don't mean to sound harsh," said Zeus.

"Social skills notwithstanding," said Gert, pointedly.

"But all your lives have been many failures," Thor went on.

"Manifold in their scale and variety," Brunhilde pointed out.

"You make it sound an achievement!" exclaimed Kevin.

"Nobody else could have managed it," said Moon Wolf.

"That's not strictly true," said Therese. "Many of your re-incarnated selves in alternative existences and paraverses were entirely fruitful."

"But not this one," said Kevin.

"No. Unfortunately, not this one. Sorry, Kevin. I didn't mean for it to sound like that. Perhaps I've been around grauniads for too long."

"It's okay," said Kevin. "I just hoped things would have turned out differently by now."

"Perhaps it's still not too late," said Isis, gleaming gold in the light from the bulbs around Kevin's mirror.

"Perhaps you just needed more practice," Gaia suggested helpfully. She was an earth mother after all.

"More practice than all the other Kevin Mullinses across the realms of possibility," added Zeus.

"Perhaps all your previous errors were necessary," Gert said at last, cleaning her spectacles on her cardigan.

"Maybe you had to get them out of your system," said Thor.

"Maybe you are working up to saving this pitiful paraverse at the last moment," added Brunhilde, toying with her pigtails.

"Just when all hope seems lost," murmured Moon Wolf.

"Although on past performance," said Isis.

"This does seem unlikely," Gaia concluded.

"Thank you for your confidence," said Kevin. He turned to Therese. "Don't you know how I can save humankind? I have a nasty feeling they're about to become the unfutured any day now."

"I have to admit that I do not entirely understand what's been going on," said the beautiful young scientist.

Gert gave an unsubtle hiss behind her hand to Kevin. "Psst! She doesn't believe in God!"

Therese ignored her. "I am still assessing the situation."

"I hope you work out something soon," said Zeus with feeling.

"You're not going to commit suicide again, are you Kevin?" asked Gert.

Kevin shook his head. "No. I learnt very early on that killing myself didn't work."

"Couldn't you even manage that?" asked Thor.

"Are you a complete incompetent?" demanded an amazed Brunhilde.

"Oh no," said Kevin, "I killed myself easily enough. I was simply re-incarnated again."

"That must have only served to highlight the futility of your existence," added Moon Wolf.

Kevin ignored him. "Once Eve and I had been expelled from the Garden of Eden, we had a choice. At the end of our lives, we could either be re-incarnated or go to heaven. Eve chose to go to heaven. She is a very nurturing sort of person. Well, she *was* the mother of humankind. She still wanted to look after what she saw as her children, our children. Not to mention her grandchildren and great grandchildren."

"Is it true all of Eden turned up to see you off?" asked Isis.

"Yes, they did."

"And did they really sing *It isn't easy being green* as you walked out?" asked Gaia.

Kevin smiled. "I dare say, as expulsions go, it could have been a lot worse."

"A lot worse," muttered Gert.

Kevin glanced at Therese. "God made a very good speech. He said we should look at our expulsion from Eden as a kind of retirement. It didn't really matter what fruit we had eaten, He said. The point to remember was that we had eaten from the Tree of Knowledge."

The grauniads began to speak quickly again in turns, starting with Thor and ending with Gert.

"Apples are unjustly maligned."

"Apples were never specifically mentioned."

"You merely ate the fruit of the Tree."

"The specification of the fruit is thanks to generations of painters."

"They sensed 'Eve handing a generic fruit to Kevin' doesn't sound or look right."

"It lacks a certain something."

" 'Eve tempting Kevin with a Satsuma' is no good, either."

"Quite," agreed Kevin. "And if there hadn't been the confusion about left and right – or right and wrong – the whole misunderstanding could have been avoided. Anyway, God mentioned that He would be giving us a useful present for our new life. Bearing in mind his comments, and my time-travelling exploits, I had a horrible premonition that He was going to present us with a clock on our retirement from paradise. I knew they weren't going to be invented for thousands of years but He might have dug one up from the dinosaur civilisation. However, I had done such a good job of wiping them out that nothing seemed to remain. Besides, God doesn't have such a warped sense of humour.

"Once we were out of Eden, we soon discovered what this leaving present from God was. We could still photosynthesise. We were as green as the day we had awoken in Eden. Our children, however, were not quite as green. They were beginning to evolve and developed a hunger that could not be satisfied by simply sunbathing all day. They had to hunt and gather. We also had to be careful of the wild beasts. In Eden we co-existed with them quite happily. Now that we had left paradise, we were part of God's great experiment again and had to be much more careful. God called His great experiment Eve-o-lution."

"Was Eve flattered?" asked Therese.

"She said she was but we were suddenly very busy. Eve was continually surprised at what she could expect in this uncomfortable new world. For a start, she assumed that we were both going to be immortal once we had left the Garden of Eden, but God said, "Ah," and Sophia had a long talk with her."

"Sophia?" queried Therese.

"Yes, God's Wife."

"Don't you know anything?" asked Gert in surprise.

"I know many things," replied Therese, "because there is proof."

The grauniads exchanged knowing looks.

Kevin continued. "Sophia explained to Eve that, unlike the young of other creatures, human babies would not be able to fend for themselves for ages. She went on to explain that this meant parental care had to last for many seasons and not just one or two, which was usually enough. Eve adapted beautifully. For myself, I initially felt there would be too much responsibility to act as the Father of All Humankind, but as far as God was concerned I was on a short-list of one."

"There was no one better qualified than you," said Gaia.

Kevin shrugged. "It gave me the chance to rehistory the defutured but I would have to do this without arousing the suspicions of God. I never knew if He really was all-knowing or all-seeing, and devising a test for Him seemed, somehow, unworthy.

"So I decided to make as fresh a start as possible. As the Father of All Humankind, my influence would be far reaching. I believed that the innate goodness of my children and the gentle influence of Eve would be sufficient to ensure that they would never be unfutured. At some point the unfutured had fallen under a malign influence so all I had to do was keep them on the path of righteousness.

"Our children grew big and strong and were just that little bit better at fitting into this strange new world than we were. They weren't as green as us, though, and our grandchildren were hardly green at all. The honeymoon period was over although it lasted the whole time Eve and I were together."

"A match made in heaven," said Gert a little dreamily.

Gaia, Isis and Brunhilde tilted their heads and went, "Ah!"

"It was clear that God's leaving present to us of photosynthesis was a huge advantage. Eventually, we grew old and Eve opted to go to heaven. Some of our sons and daughters were already up there and she was looking forward to being re-united with them.

"My future, as you know, was already mapped out. I still had to try and save the human race. But when Eve died peacefully in her sleep and went straight to heaven I discovered that I missed her terribly. We'd been through a lot together. Our family were very good to me but whenever I left our cave, I knew I wouldn't see her face again when I came home. So it was almost a relief when I was torn limb from limb by a pack of wolves and spent a very happy nine months with her and some of our kids before being re-born again as one of our great grandchildren. But my heart wasn't in life any more. I committed suicide as soon as I could with a wild boar and spent another joyous nine months with Eve. And then I killed myself again and again and again.

"Of course, God wasn't happy about this and made me promise not to do it again. 'It messes up Eve-o-lution and sets a dangerous precedent,' He told me. 'What happens if all the other creatures committed suicide?'

"So I don't do suicide. Not any more. I try to adapt and encourage others to adapt, too."

"You failed to keep humankind in paradise," said Thor.

"But you achieved something else," said Brunhilde.

"Every cloud has a silver lining," pointed out Moon Wolf.

"Thanks to you," said golden Isis, "modern humans emerged from paradise."

"Photosynthesising or not," added Gaia.

"The human race emerged from total dependence," explained Zeus.

"To perilous self-reliance," finished Gert.

Kevin smiled a little sheepishly.

"You helped them to survive," said Therese.

Kevin shrugged his shoulders. "A bit."

"Maybe you contributed to their success more than you know," she added.

"But I would like to contribute more to their success! I don't want them to end up as the unfutured!"

"That might not be such a bad thing," said Thor.

"Maybe that is what you should work towards," suggested Brunhilde.

"If the human race turned into the unfutured, you'd get another chance," pointed out Moon Wolf.

"They'd have to invent another time machine, of course," pointed out Isis.

"And choose you to save humankind all over again," added Gaia.

"It would be a long shot," said Zeus, thoughtfully.

"But it might just work!" finished Gert.

"Oh I couldn't go through all that again," said Kevin.

"Why ever not?" demanded Thor, brandishing a thunderbolt.

"You'd know what to do next time around," said Brunhilde.

"You could park your time machine more sensibly," said Moon Wolf.

"And not eat from the Tree of Knowledge!" exclaimed Isis.

"And never leave Eden!" added Gaia.

"Yeah but he'd already know," said Zeus.

"Wouldn't he?" asked Gert.

"Know?" asked Thor.

"Know what?" enquired Brunhilde.

"Ah," said Moon Wolf.

"I see your point," said Isis, gleaming even more.

"Kevin would know already about the Tree of Knowledge," said Gaia.

Zeus and Gert nodded at each other.

The grauniads stroked their chins and scratched their heads. They glanced at Therese once or twice and then more often.

"Don't look at me!" she said at last.

There was a flash of lightning.

"You could go," said Thor.

"Oh no!"

"Why not?" asked Brunhilde.

"I'd have to leave my temporal anomaly!"

"Couldn't you take it with you?" demanded Moon Wolf.

"What? In a time machine?"

"Well how big is a temporal anomaly?" Isis snapped back.

"It's not a question of how big," said Therese, "but of when. And thanks to Kevin, *I* now know about the Tree of Knowledge as well."

"That's one journey that can't be re-traced," said Kevin, "the loss of innocence."

"Besides, even if stuffing myself and a temporal anomaly into an untried and untested time capsule were possible, it wouldn't help *you*."

Gaia frowned. "Wouldn't it?"

"No!"

"Why not?" asked Zeus.

"Because you lot would perish with the unfutured when this paraverse collapses!"

"Ah," said Gert, "we hadn't thought of that."

"Looks like it's all down to me, then," said Kevin brightly.

The grauniads didn't look too hopeful.

"Kevin," began Therese. "Why are you sitting in a dressing room?"

"Aha!" said Kevin.

"Is this some palaeontology gala night?"

"Ha! I'll not be going to one of those again!"

"Why not?"

"Because, Therese, I have turned my back on the world of palaeontology for ever!"

"But you should be brilliant at it!"

"I was! That was the problem. My work on the missing link was world renowned! And then I topped that with my startling re-construction of the pineapple-faced gibbon. But my next discovery went horribly wrong."

"What happened?"

"Double-headed chickens…"

"Oh no!" Therese put her head in her hands and groaned.

"Double-headed chickens, double-headed snakes and even four-legged ducks are scientifically possible. If the egg is damaged in a certain way at a precise stage in its development, the foetus can grow two heads or two tails. There is no reason to suppose that it could not occur amongst the dinosaurs. In fact, I am often haunted by the vision of a two-headed iguanodon on a dirt bike.

"I spotted this brontosaurus when I was a tree shrew. It was one of the few survivors of my accidental holocaust and I'm sure it was caused not by damage to its egg but exposure to intense radiation from my exploded time machine. The two-headed brontosaurus was literally in two minds about everything and fairly small minds at that. Its indecisiveness was made worse by a lack of confidence since it was a social animal ostracised by the rest of its chomp.

"Chomp?" echoed Therese.

"Yes," replied Kevin. "That's the collective noun for brontosauruses.

"As I watched it weighing up the pros and cons of cycad or ginkgo leaves for breakfast, a young pair of tyrannosaurus rex twins, enraged by terrible radiation burns and mouth ulcers, attacked it. They died before eating the body and I knew then what a sensation such a skeleton would make. I recently discovered that it had already been dug up but when the palaeontologists started to re-assemble it, they panicked and hid it away, hoping they had mixed up two separate skeletons. I re-discovered it, re-assembled it and made it the most controversial re-construction in the history of palaeontology."

"I think I can see where this is going," said Therese.

"Unfortunately, I was universally ridiculed. Well, paraversally. The more I tried to refute the allegations of trickery, the more I was denounced as a charlatan. Now, my fossil-hunting reputation is in tatters."

"We're very sorry to hear that," said Therese, glancing round the dressing room.

The grauniads nodded earnestly.

"So what career are you pursuing now?"

CHAPTER 51

At last, Hob succumbed to the lure of the open road. Ever since he had landed in Mourion, it had been jumping up and down at him like some beckoning fair one with a tax rebate in suspenders.

There was no sign of any Conformorians coming after them but M Cadvare harboured a deep suspicion that the Grey Ones were re-grouping somewhere and that they wouldn't get far without a road block. But then he began to wonder what would happen if the Conformorians did stop them. Hob and The Glove would just destroy them.

Hob was full of glee, delighted to be behind the wheel again. The needles of the dials were firmly planted in the red sectors of whatever it was they were measuring, and Hob kept what he persisted in calling the loud pedal buried in the footwell carpet – except, of course, that being electric, it was anything but loud. However, there was the exotic fragrance of over-heated electronic components.

Yet the personal transportation device hummed a happy tune, punctuated only by the occasional warning buzzer that kicked in whenever Hob committed some new traffic offence.

M Cadvare was aware of a scurrying sensation beneath the interior trim and caught glimpses of the gremlinne and electro-gnome keeping his car running smoothly.

"Electra?"

"Yes my lord?"

"Switch off that noise, there's a dear."

"Of course, my lord," Electra said with a smile, and the buzzer was cut short.

Out of town, dashing along the auto route that led to the coast, other personal transportation devices tried to keep up with them but none of them could match M Cadvare's Hobspeed Strunts, especially when driven by its constructor.

They rapidly approached a string of meekly humming vehicles and Hob scattered them across all three lanes of the auto route. They flashed past the speed cameras and as the cameras flashed back at them, Hob said, "Bye, bye Gatso." And whenever they went under the gantries of road charging equipment, he would brandish the Engineer of Spades at them.

"What are you doing?" asked Nenuphar, who had awoken from her shock-induced slumber.

"Waiving the charges, my dear."

The road charging equipment turned into a spectacular firework display.

"Where are we going?" she asked.

"Zebragee," said Hob.

Nenuphar and M Cadvare both looked blank. "Where's that?"

"On the coast. It's a major port. Look, it's on the bloody map."

M Cadvare looked. "Do you mean Zeebrugge?"

Hob frowned. "No. Zebragee."

"Hob?" asked Nenuphar. "Has anyone diagnosed you as being dyslexic?"

"Of course not!"

"I think many Anarcho-Anglo-Saxons often have difficulty with words," M Cadvare remarked to Nenuphar.

"Difficulty with words! Hah! I'm a Horsepower Whisperer!"

They came to some roadworks and Hob made a point of driving over as many traffic cones as he could.

"You can't say M Cadvare's name properly," persisted Nenuphar, "and you can't pronounce Zeebrugge correctly either."

"Nenny, has it occurred to you that I could but just don't feel like it?"

"Don't be ridiculous. You'll be shouting at us again if we don't understand what you're talking about."

"She's right, Hob," said M Cadvare. "People from your part of the world do tend to shout if they can't master the language."

"There you are, Cadaver," said Hob, as they flashed by a road sign. "Zebragee, clear as day."

"My point entirely," said Nenuphar, triumphantly. "Non Anarcho-Anglo-Saxon words are in grave danger of being brutalised to death with a blunt instrument, namely your tongue."

"It's only natural to convert foreign words into my own language."

"But they're not foreign words here! You're the foreigner in Euphobia!"

"And don't I know it! Whatever happened to *Welcome to Euphobia! Euphobia welcomes careful drivers!?*"

"Careful drivers?" wondered M Cadvare.

"That wouldn't include you, would it?" asked Nenuphar.

"Of course not! I am not Ernest Pilchard. I am Old Weird Wheels himself, the Metal Guru, the Repossession Man, the Crypto-Engineer, His Malign Weirdness, the Grand Whizz-Herd and Master of the Engine Henge, the Lord High Prince of Rock'n'Roll, the Horsepower Whisperer and Soul Trader, none other than that infamous libertine and free radical from Anarchadia, that trafficker of traffic and of no accepted fashionality, Nicholas Eldritch Hob! Not once did I mention the word careful."

"How would you say chassis?" Nenuphar asked him as they cut through a row of cars on a corner.

"Chassis," replied Hob.

"And how would you say charabanc?"

"Charabanc." Despite his black visor and crash helmet, Hob seemed to be frowning more with each word.

"Le Mans Grand Prix?"

"Le Mans Grand Prix."

"And what about Chevrolet?" offered M Cadvare.

"Chevrolet," muttered Hob.

"Sorry, I didn't hear you," said Nenuphar mischievously. "What was that?"

"Chevrolet!"

"Hob? I must complement you on your Euphobian accent. It would appear that you have unwittingly added some foreign words into your Anarcho-Anglo-Saxon vocabulary and you pronounce them tolerably well."

"We adopted them because we felt sorry for them being surrounded by all those typing errors."

"Typing errors!" Despite everything Nenuphar guffawed.

"Besides," Hob went on, "if you want the real deal it's not Anarcho-Anglo-Saxon. It's Celto-Anarcho-Anglo-Saxon and we make it up as we go along."

"I like the sound of that," said M Cadvare, a little wistfully. "In Euphobia, Euphopranto is unified and carved in stone."

"Carved wrongly in stone," Hob assured him.

They passed another sign for Zeebrugge.

"There you are again. Zebragee. What did I tell you? It's not my fault there are all these typos on the road signs in this part of Euphobia. Besides. You lot all speak Celto-Anarcho-Anglo-Saxon anyway, often better than we do."

M Cadvare and Nenuphar found themselves smiling at each other at this truism.

"Sometimes you forget, though, and shouting at you is the only way to remind you. Besides, there are some Anarcho-English words that have leaked into your language."

"Oh really?" said Nenuphar. "Like what?"

"Would you say you were an intrepid pair embarking on this adventure with me? Or would you say you were a trepid pair who were merely barking?"

"What are you talking about?"

"You can understand one sentence but not the other. Just by looking at some words you can tell that there must be an opposite meaning but it doesn't exist in Euphobian parlance. These are the Anarcho words that have infiltrated your language."

"Like introduce and distroduce?" M Cadvare put in.

"Bravo, Cadaver! You were listening after all! Anarchadia has been distroduced from the rest of the world for centuries, Nenny, because central governments fear it so. It has to be kept secret in case it causes the most terrible and wonderful revolutions. And that's why we're going there. That's what makes us intrepid."

They let him have the last word and motored in silence for a while until M Cadvare remarked that there wasn't much traffic.

"There isn't *any* traffic except us," replied Hob. "There isn't even any on the other carriageway."

"That can't be normal," said Nenuphar.

"My guess," said M Cadvare, "is that the authorities are up to something."

"They're over the horizon, out of sight," Hob assured them as he glanced in his mirrors.

"Are you sure?"

Hob nodded.

"Can we outrun them?" asked Nenuphar.

"We can outrun anything in this thing," said Hob patting the steering wheel.

Among the loose wires and displays on the dashboard Electra, the Engineer of Spades, smiled indulgently at Hob.

"But we can't outrun a two-way radio," he added. "Or helicopters. Look! Jam sandwiches!"

They swept by a road junction and half a dozen white police cars swung out behind them with their blue lights on.

"What's this thing's range?" demanded Nenuphar. "Were its batteries fully charged when we set out?"

"Leave the technicalities to me, my dear," said Hob. "You could say that the batteries have been supercharged." He held up a packet of curiously strong mints. "I popped one or two of these into the electrolyte earlier."

A pair of helicopters kept pace with them on either side.

"How fast are we going?" asked Nenuphar.

"Fast enough. You see they want us to speed up. They want us to be caught out by whatever's up ahead."

"But if they stop us, you and The Glove'll just destroy them," said M Cadvare. "Won't you?"

"I'm surprised there are any left to be destroyed," said Hob, "and don't forget I can fost."

A berserker's chuckle gurgled in his throat and his teeth looked a little longer and sharper than before, not just his canines but all of them. Out from the shoulders of his battered leather jacket, black leathery wings spread out before the faces of his travelling companions.

M Cadvare and Nenuphar caught Electra's reflection in the instrument panel. She was no longer the demure, pale-faced Ion Lady. She was laughing with perfect teeth and shaking her black hair around her naked shoulders so that it gave off huge, fat, blue sparks. Her sapphire eyes were blurred spinning wheels turning faster and faster.

Hob folded his wings back into his shoulders and kept his right foot down as the smell of burning plastic grew.

"They think they've set a trap for us!" he said, his black visor swirling in unholy vortices. "Let's dive into their cloying embrace faster than they could ever anticipate!"

CHAPTER 52

Nobody could say for certain what happened next, least of all Hob.

The steering wheel exploded, Nenuphar screamed and they careered off the autoroute at full speed. Hob fought for control but they hit a road sign and cartwheeled into the air, the personal transportation device rolling end over end. M Cadvare had a vague impression of Hob fighting a weather balloon that must have been sucked into the cockpit while they were airborne.

They landed with a bone-jarring crash by the side of the road, and the personal transportation device began to disintegrate, flinging wheels and other parts all around. The tailgate flapped and buckled and *Nosferatu*'s crate tumbled out behind them. The personal transportation device rolled onto its roof, sides and belly while Hob continued to try driving it despite his battle with the weather balloon and the loss of its road wheels. It came to rest upright and slithered forward until it lost its momentum.

Jam sandwiches screeched to a halt on either side of it, tyre smoke overtaking them and hurtling off into the distance. Police surrounded the personal transportation device and then dragged an elderly and rather worried archbishop, in full regalia, right up to where it had come to rest.

Meanwhile, Hob was winning the battle with the weather balloon. He tore it apart with his hands and teeth but it was large enough to fill the cockpit. It wasn't the only one, either. Smaller ones had popped out all along the dashboard, headlining and roof pillars and Hob had to conquer them all before he could punch the broken windscreen away to emerge through its aperture, flapping his wings and shouting his defiance at the authorities.

The two gremlins jumped out of the dashboard and each took on a subsidiary weather balloon in a desperate bid to help the Horsepower Whisperer.

Hob plucked what was left of the steering wheel from its column as if it were a flower and hurled it into the crowd of police like a discus, neatly felling many of them. But others closed ranks around the terrified archbishop and pushed him forward as he tried to unclip the lid of a Tupperware container. In his panic, he nearly spilt its contents all over the road. Somehow he managed to recover his composure and pulled out what appeared to be a pastry brush from the sleeve of his vestments.

Hob seemed to notice the archbishop for the first time.

"In the name of the Father, the Son and the Holy Ghost," said the archbishop in a querulous voice, and he flicked water at Hob.

The Holy Water hit Hob between the eyes.

The gremlins looked up in horror and disappeared.

The purple-black clouds in Hob's visor stopped swirling and he fell forward, over the front of the personal transportation device.

CHAPTER 53

There was a knock at the door and someone tried the handle but Therese's Cadillac stopped it from opening.

"Kevin?" said a muffled voice outside.

"Quick!" hissed Therese, "we must hide."

"Maybe the grauniads should," said Kevin.

"Only if your guests have homuncular vision. I meant you and I should hide."

"But I'm supposed to be here," replied Kevin. "This is my dressing room."

"Then I must hide!"

"No. Exotic-looking women in dressing rooms are only to be expected."

"You're enjoying this, aren't you?"

Kevin wasn't sure if Therese was speaking to him or the grinning grauniads who sat in silence in the Cadillac.

"Kevin?" An arm appeared through the narrow opening of the door. "Have you got someone in there?"

Therese was beginning to panic.

"It's okay," Kevin reassured her. "It's only Vince Shylock, my manager. Come on in, Vince."

"Manager? What sort of new job do you have?"

"It's not really a job. It's a complete change from fossil hunting."

"Are you going to tell me or not? This isn't like any of your other alternative existences that I've seen so far."

A shoulder in a dark suit was now slowly squeezing into the room. "What the hell's this pink thing?" demanded Vince.

"That? Oh that's just a Cadillac convertible."

"In your dressing room? Cool! That's up there with Rolls-Royces in swimming pools!"

"So what *do* you do for a living?" whispered Therese.

"Well, to say I do it for a living is stretching a point a bit."

"Kevin!" snapped Therese.

"Look. In which ever age I've been re-incarnated, it's obvious that there are some professions that are definitely 'of the moment'. You know – a scribe in Ur during the development of cuneiform, a general in Alexander the Great's army, an artist during the Renaissance or an iron founder during the industrial revolution. I've been none of those things when any of them are 'of the moment'."

A rather shaggy and devious face had now emerged into the room. "How the hell did you get this car in here? Hey! Who's the babe!"

"This life," Kevin said quietly to Therese, "I'm going to be 'of the moment' even if the unfutured run out of time."

Vince's arm, shoulder and head had now been joined by the rest of him and he climbed over the Cadillac, somehow without treading on any unseen grauniads.

"Kevin, you old rascal! You've got your first groupie!"

"Don't smack her on the bottom like you do with your secretaries!"

Vince held up his palms. "Okay, okay. I won't touch her. She's yours. Don't worry."

"Therese, I'm going to be a rock star!"

"Hey, he already is, hun. Arntcha gonna introduce us, Kevin?"

"Therese, this is Vince our manager."

"Our manager?"

"Oh not ours. Not yours and mine. Vince is the manager of my band, The Love Pumps."

Some other disreputable individuals were squeezing into the dressing room and casting approving glances at the Cadillac as well as Therese.

"Vince. Guys. This is Therese. Therese is from out of town."

"Onshontay!" said Vince taking her hand but Therese pulled it away before he could kiss it.

"And these are the rest of the band," said Kevin proudly. "May I present our hide frying beatmaster and all round lord high priest of percussion, Percy Postlethwaite."

"Pleased to meet you, Therese."

"Our subterranean string torturer, Sebastian Pratt, the basest of all bass players."

"Pratt by name," said Sebastian, "but Prodigy by nature."

"And our rhythm guitarist, Dymchurch's most famous son, windmill-armed Septimus Smellie-Ramsbottom."

"That's not my real name of course," said Septimus.

"Of course not," said Therese.

"I'm really Sextus Ramsbottom-Smellie. My parents would disinherit me if they ever found out that I was besmirching their good family name by playing in a rock band. Inheritances figure highly in my family history. My parents had to adopt the double-barrelled name to ensure they were the beneficiaries of a complicated bequest."

"Isn't your stage name a bit obvious?" asked Therese.

"Ah," said Sextus, "that's the clever bit. If ever we make it big, my parents are bound to register the name but won't believe it's me because it's so close to my real name."

"We've tried to explain it to him," said Kevin.

"It's a sort of double bluff," Sextus added.

"Sexy? You're rambling again," said Percy.

"Sorry. It's the pre-gig nerves."

"Okay," said Vince, clapping his hands together. "We all know why we're here. The Love Pumps are supporting Boys R Us Tonite!"

It was obvious from the way he said it that tonight was spelt tonite.

Vince frequently spoke in capitals and also had a bad habit with apostrophes. The Love Pumps had only narrowly avoided becoming The Love Pump's. As Kevin had pointed out, what worked for The B-52's didn't necessarily work for everyone else.

"This is our Biggest Break so far," enthused Vince. "As I expect you all know, Boys R Us are touring to promote their latest album, *Walk like a Big Girl's Blouse*. The title track has already been released as a Single and gone straight into Number One so just think what a Chance we've got here Tonite! Just think! What an impact you'll make when you walk out on stage and play your Latest Single to that Packed House out there!"

"Our latest single?" queried Kevin. "We've never released a single unless you count flexi-discs given away free at record fairs."

"And we've never had a recording contract, either," said Percy.

"That's why I've worked so hard on your Look," Vince assured them, "because Record Producers felt that a failed archaeologist didn't have the right sort of Image. Sorry Kevin, it's not me, it's them. That's why we've gone for the Ne'er Do Well Leather."

The grauniads peered over the side of the Cadillac to take in the slashed jeans, leather jackets and huge motocross boots that were The Look for The Love Pumps.

"Do you really think we'll appeal to the fans of Boys R Us?" asked Sebastian.

"I don't think so," said Vince, "I Know So!"

"We haven't even had any airplay," Sextus pointed out.

"Tonite is where The Love Pumps get to be Mainstream!" Vince insisted. "Our lack of success isn't because you aren't any good, it's simply because you've never had The Breaks. Until now! Tonite, the fans of Boys R Us are gonna find out just how Brilliant you guys really are!"

"Thanks Vince," said Percy.

"Yeah," said the rest of The Love Pumps, "thanks, Vince."

Vince beamed at them. "It wasn't easy mind, pulling this one off. Think about it, lads, a Captive Audience! All Those Screaming Kids! And their Grannies! This is the kind of Opportunity we've been waiting for! Tonite, The Love Pumps are gonna *steam* Boys R Us!"

Kevin and Therese caught sight of the grauniads. They were obviously very impressed with Vince.

"Now then, lads," he went on, "after Tonite your Latest Single is gonna be Huge."

"Our latest single?" Kevin queried again.

"Well, your first single, then," conceded Vince. "When eventually we get around to cutting one after all this Touring. I'm telling you, *I Wanna Be Your Dog* is going to be *Huge*!"

Puzzled expressions flickered over the features of The Love Pumps.

"*I Wanna Be Your Dog Bag* was by Iggy and The Stooges," said Percy.

"Was it?"

"Yes."

"You sure?"

"D'you really think I could be mistaken?"

"No. No, of course not. My mistake. Silly me. What is your Latest Number then?"

"Well, we've just had a jamming session in the bogs ... "

"Oh no, Kevin, not again! Other Rock 'n' Roll bands trash hotel rooms! You guys just block up the drains!"

"No," said Kevin. "A *really* good jamming session. Just after the sound check."

"I blame myself," Vince told Therese. "All this Constant Touring and a rotten diet."

"Look. We were playing with each other in the toilets."

Vince eyed them suspiciously.

Kevin ignored him and carried on.

"It sounded really good. So good, in fact, that we're going to open with it tonight."

"Really? Tonite? As good as that, eh?"

"Yes."

"You don't think opening with a Cover Version would be a good idea, do you?"

"No."

"A Boys-R-Us number?"

"No."

"I knew you'd say that. What's this thing called then?"

"*Crash Landing On Planet X.*"

"Triffic! How's it go?"

"Well, we're still working on it but something along the lines of 'Crash landing on Planet X, crash landing on Planet X, oh no, oh yes, crash landing on Planet X.'"

"Okay," said Vince. "It's good. How's the chorus go?"

"That is the chorus."

"Right. I'm with you, now. Yeah, it's got something. Run it past me again."

" 'Crash landing on Planet X, crash landing on Planet X, oh no, oh yes, crash landing on Planet X.' "

"Wow," said Vince.

"It's semi-autobiographical," explained Sextus.

"Of course," said Vince. "Curtain call in fifteen minutes."

"That's if we can get out in time," added Sebastian and they began to climb over the Cadillac towards the door.

"You okay getting this thing out of here?" asked Vince glancing at the Cadillac wedged in the dressing room.

"Oh yes," replied Therese, "that'll be no problem."

"Great! I'll cop you later!"

"Sorry about that," said Kevin, once Vince had left.

"He's a slimeball but I have to admire his chutzpah," replied Therese. She glanced at the wrist watches down her forearm. "If you're on in fifteen minutes, I don't have much more time. The reason I've tracked you down across the infinite possibilities of outcome is to tell you that you are in terrible danger."

"Oh great," said Kevin. "As if appearing in front of an audience of un-appreciative Boys R Us fans isn't enough."

"It would be much safer if you didn't go out there."

"I couldn't do that."

"Why not? Do you have any fans to disappoint?"

"I have the rest of the band to think," Kevin told her a little stiffly.

"Doesn't the rest of your universe matter?"

"It's a rock'n'roll band."

"The show must go on, I suppose."

"Yeah."

"It could be your farewell gig," said Therese. "The grauniads assure me that the danger to you personally has increased dramatically. This will be one death that you won't be able to escape through re-incarnation. Your paraverse is weak and depends upon you for stability. And I can also see the potential impact that your untimely demise will have, not only on this space/time continuum but also upon the neighbouring ones."

"So she's knitted you a hat," said Thor.

"We helped," said Brunhilde.

"You must wear it on stage Tonite, er, tonight," insisted Moon Wolf.

"The Horsepower Whisperer might be in the audience," Isis advised.

"Or watching on telly," added Gaia.

"He must not recognise you as The Soul of All Souls," said Zeus.

"Otherwise," said Gert, drawing a finger across her throat, "kieurch for all of us!"

"Here it is," said Therese. "It's a Discretion of the Soul Hat. Provided you wear this at all times, your soul will be perfectly safe."

"It's ... horrible," said Kevin.

"That's right," beamed Thor.

"It doesn't *go* with anything," said Brunhilde.

"Especially not The Love Pumps Look," observed Moon Wolf.

"Try it on," suggested Isis.

"We helped with the design," said Gaia.

"Girls have a more highly developed sense of colour," explained Zeus.

"Especially when it comes to what goes with what and what doesn't," agreed Gert.

"It is quite comfortable," admitted Kevin.

Therese seemed to be trying not to laugh.

"Why should I need a Discretion of the Soul Hat?"

"Soul Traders want your soul," said Thor.

"We've been warning you about them for centuries," Brunhilde reminded Kevin.

"So far, you've been able to keep one step ahead of them," said Moon Wolf.

"Largely thanks to us," added Isis.

"But now they're getting sneaky," Gaia warned him.

"There's a new one who might be able to trade for your soul," said Zeus.

"We have to hide your soul from the Horsepower Whisperer," Gert explained.

"You remember what we said would happen?" went on Thor.

"What would happen if you sold your soul to a Soul Trader?" Brunhilde added.

"Our paraverse would come to an end," explained Moon Wolf.

"We don't really know why," admitted Isis.

"But it's all in *The Red Book of St Bendix*," Gaia told him.

"And a lot of what is in *The Red Book of St Bendix* has already been verified," said Zeus.

"So," Gert assured Kevin, "we take the claims of The Great Smith very seriously."

Kevin turned to Therese. "Do you believe this?" he asked her.

"Frankly no. Certainly not all of it. St Bendix has accurately predicted many things, but I am a scientist."

The grauniads snorted.

"I need to have proof," insisted Therese. "I don't believe in Soul Traders. I don't believe in God. However, I can recognise other indications that this paraverse could be nearing the end of its existence."

"Really?" said Kevin. "Like what?"

"Oh there are so many! Look, Kevin. Here's just one example. Punk rock always evolves just before the end of civilisation. It happened to the dinosaurs and it's happened already here."

Kevin's eyes glazed over as he tried to imagine punk rock dinosaurs.

"Culturally, this paraverse is overripe," said Therese. "You know what the punk mantra is, don't you?"

" 'No future!' " sneered Kevin, automatically.

"That's right. I know a potentially unstable paraverse when I see one and you ought to be able to spot all the signs as well. Or have you forgotten what it was like to live at the end of a space/time continuum?"

"No, I haven't!"

"This paraverse has survived longer than it should, largely thanks to the efforts of its grauniads."

The grauniads looked modestly pleased with themselves.

"Therese?"

"Yes, Kevin?"

"Are there are any alternative existences that evolve beyond this point at which we find ourselves?"

"Yes. Yes, there is. Just the one, but it's a most remarkable paraverse. I've seen it. In fact I've spent long hours studying it. In this paraverse, the dinosaur civilisation was not destroyed. It advanced and made many technological discoveries that mammals would struggle to achieve on their own. And yet the mammals evolved in parallel with the dinosaurs, and the two have learned to live in harmony with each other. Working together they solved the problem of space flight. And although it is only an isolated example, they even managed the problem of pan-dimensional travel, too."

"Really? Like you?"

"I speak of my own home paraverse," said Therese.

"Wow!"

"She still hasn't met God, though," said Gert.

"Or His Wife," added Zeus.

"We keep telling her about Them," said Gaia.

"But she insists she needs proof," sighed Isis.

"She lives for proof," agreed Moon Wolf.

"Why can't she just look around her?" Brunhilde asked Kevin.

"And see His Creation everywhere," said Thor.

"I have been tracking The Horsepower Whisperer across the infinity of existence," said Therese, "in an effort to persuade him not to trade for your soul. The fosts he makes when he rides in the Wild Hunt make him easy to find compared with you, but he's very pigheaded. This Discretion of the Soul Hat is our fallback. He knows you exist, Kevin, and he covets your soul above all others. He should care about ending this paraverse by not trading for your soul, but I fear that his greed for it clouds his judgement."

"So, what you're saying," said Kevin, "is that you are working backwards from the end of the space/time continuum …"

"Event Omega," interrupted the beautiful young scientist, checking her watches and beginning to climb back into the Cadillac.

"… and intercepting the Horsepower Whisperer to dissuade him from seeking my soul."

"Precisely. Now. I must go. If I get the chance again, I shall speak to Hob. I've got to shoot off to another cusp point in another alternative existence, the one where you take up jazz funk and form Kevin Mullins and His Juicy Bananas."

"Good grief!" exclaimed Kevin. "I thought that idea had some potential."

"It hasn't," said Thor.

"You're even less of a success than you are here," added Brunhilde.

"Although we know that's hard to believe," said Moon Wolf.

"Ten out of ten for effort, though," said Isis.

"But nought out of a hundred for talent," added Gaia.

"You should stick to this Foot Pump idea of yours," said Zeus.

"Love Pumps," corrected Gert. "Love Pumps."

"Do you have any CDs?" asked Thor.

"Here," said Kevin. "It's only a demo."

"Thanks," said Brunhilde.

"Good sleeve design," said Moon Wolf.

"Does it have the words?" asked Isis.

"Yes, they're all here," Gaia assured her as she opened the jewel case.

"You're not going to play that stuff are you?" Zeus asked Gaia.

"Come off it, Zeus," said Gert. "How many rock stars do you know?"

Zeus shrugged.

"Wear the hat at all times from now on," Therese advised Kevin. "It'll make your soul look inconsequential."

She started up the Cadillac but, before she could select D for De-materialise, Thor put a restraining hand on her shoulder.

"There is a subtle irony to being hunted by The Horsepower Whisperer," he told Kevin.

"Yes," agreed Brunhilde.

"You may have wiped out the dinosaurs," said Moon Wolf.

"There's no doubt that you did," said Isis.

"You definitely were responsible," said Gaia.

"But at the same time you created a most extraordinary temperate archipelago," explained Zeus.

"Indirectly or otherwise," added Gert.

"Therese assures us Anarchadia exists in all the other paraverses around this one," Thor told Kevin.

"And yet kings and centralised authorities have kept it a secret for centuries," said Brunhilde.

"Without you, Anarchadia would never exist," added Moon Wolf.

"The Horsepower Whisperer comes from Anarchadia," Isis told Kevin.

"You could be said to have sown the seeds of your own doom," Gaia cheerfully pointed out.

"But maybe this is a bargaining point and worth remembering if the Horsepower Whisperer penetrates your disguise," said Zeus.

"If he has any higher feelings," added Gert, doubtfully.

Someone banged on the door. "Five minutes!"

"We must go," said Therese. "Good luck, Kevin!" and with that his dressing room was empty and noticeably smaller.

"Mm-yes," said Kevin, thoughtfully. "But what on earth would I sell my soul for?"

CHAPTER 54

"Pastry," muttered Hob.

"What did he say?" The question was posed by an elderly archbishop to a distinguished rabbi.

"I don't know," replied the rabbi, "but it sounded like pastry."

"Is it in this old book?" asked a Moslem cleric.

A Jesuit cardinal thumbed through an ancient leather-bound tome, making its pages crackle.

"No," he said, "I can't find anything about pastry."

"Pastry!" shouted Hob, still unconscious.

A large group of assembled clergy raised their Holy Water Pistols.

"Pastry," mumbled Hob.

"There," said a Methodist minister, "he said it again."

"No he didn't," the mullah told her. "It was nothing like it."

"I don't know why we're doing this," said a Buddhist monk next to him. He jerked his Holy Water pistol at Hob. "I'm a humanist. I don't believe in Holy Water."

"I'm not sure about it, either," said the Moslem, "but we all saw what the archbishop could do with just a pastry brush."

"Shut up!" growled a Greek Orthodox Patriarch. "If you two don't start believing soon, you'll find yourself firing blanks!"

"Pastry!" said Hob, louder than ever. He strained against the ropes that bound him to his chair. "Pastry!" he shouted, "Pastry! Pastry! Get it away from me!"

He struggled violently but, being bound to his chair, toppled to the floor. Something began to move behind the darkness of the visor that covered his eyes and he raised his head, still wearing his crash helmet, to look around the room.

"Oh," he said, finding his captors and peering up at them. "It was all a dream. I'm most terribly sorry, I must have dropped off."

Slowly, he seemed to register that he was tied to a chair and lying on his side on the floor, confronted by a half circle of clergy who cowered behind an enormous book. There was a frail Anglican archbishop who seemed vaguely familiar, a female Methodist minister, a Jesuit Cardinal, a Greek Orthodox

Patriarch, a bearded Moslem cleric, a saffron-robed Buddhist, a bespectacled Rabbi, and a striking young woman wearing a wetsuit and a wimple, who could only be one of the Sisters of the Blessed Alohas, those evangelical surfing nuns.

Beside Hob stood a smart traffic cone wearing a strangely stern expression.

Hob tested his bonds again but, since he was still wet with Holy Water, he couldn't break free.

"It's working!" gulped the archbishop, looking over a pair of half-moon reading glasses.

"There might be something in this religion of yours, after all," said the Buddhist.

The cardinal snapped the book shut and the clergy advanced on Hob, but only to pull him upright.

It was then that he noticed another figure at the back of the room.

"So, Monsieur Pilchard. We meet again. Or should I call you Mister Nicholas Eldritch Hob?"

"Well, well," said Hob, now that he was upright. The purple-black clouds in his impenetrable visor swirled rapidly. "Insect Degree."

"I am now Commissioner Gris," said Commissioner Gris, standing a little taller. "I am the sole survivor of your attack on the Product Planning Blocks."

"Hah! Soul survivor? I don't think so! I let you go to warn the others."

"We are going to Re-educate you, Nicholas, and show you the error of your ways. We are going to tame you and this Wild Hunt of yours for ever."

"I will remain untamed," Hob promised him.

"We have learnt a great deal since we last met and our resolution to turn you into a valuable member of society has increased."

"I'm not part of your society."

"You soon will be. Horses used to be broken in to do our bidding and become useful animals. The same will happen to you, and you will thank us for it afterwards."

"Where am I?"

"You're in hospital, Nicholas" said Commissioner Gris, "a mental hospital. Your travelling companions are also being Re-educated as we speak. And although we may not have so many guards as we did in the Product Planning Blocks, we are armed with incense bombs and Holy Water pistols."

He gestured and the clergy raised a fine armoury at Hob.

"And I've got me longboard, kook!" added the Sister of the Blessed Alohas.

Hob glanced down at the floor around him. He was sat inside in a circle, drawn in chalk on the carpet, and radiating out from this were ancient sigils and geometric forms. Where lines crossed stood bells, books and candles. He struggled again, as hard as he could, but it only confirmed the sort of ritual that contained him.

"So," boomed the Orthodox Patriarch, "what's the next stage?"

The cardinal held the ancient book open and began to read.

" 'Check that the Pattern of Bells, Books and Candles is in accordance with the Illumination.' "

Everyone consulted the illumination, which showed a remarkable likeness of Hob strapped to an interview room chair, complete with smart traffic cone by his motocross boots.

"No!" cried the Methodist minister, "read it properly! It says 'Check that the Pattern of Bells, Books and Candles is in accordance with the Illumination before the Horsepower Whisperer awakes!' "

Everyone took several steps away from Hob, except for the smart traffic cone, which resolutely stayed put.

There was an agonising pause.

Hob struggled again but was still too weak to burst the nylon blue towrope that must have been sanctified in some obscure rite.

He stopped struggling.

The clergy crept closer again.

"It's okay," insisted the Jesuit Cardinal, "we must have followed the illumination perfectly!" and the others drew a great sigh of relief.

"Excellent!" declared the Sister of the Blessed Alohas. "No need to get amped!"

"I beg your pardon?" said Commissioner Gris.

"Sister Winifred says there's no need to get over-excited," translated the archbishop.

"Nicholas?" said Commissioner Gris. "We have *The Red Book of St Bendix* and you are our prisoner."

Hob struggled against his bonds again but still to no avail. Then he began to shout.

"Galley! Gargamelle! Get me out of this!"

"It won't work, Nicholas," said Commissioner Gris, raising his voice. "No one can hear you here."

"I'll fight you every step of the way," Hob promised him.

"It will do you no good."

"Oh, I'll feel a lot better. When faced with complete disaster, total defiance is the only answer."

"Resistance is futile."

"You may break me physically but you will never break my spirit."

"That used to be the case," admitted Commissioner Gris, "but not any more. We have found ways of reaching your soul to neutralise undesirable non-conformist tendencies and erode recalcitrant spirits. You saw what we can achieve when you were in the Product Planning Blocks in Mourion."

"And you saw what I can do."

"You discorporated many of my colleagues."

"I should have 'discorporated' you when I had the chance."

"Yes, perhaps you should. Now we know who you are and are better prepared."

"I suppose I did give you a bit of a clue," admitted Hob, ruefully. "And I wasn't reckoning on you getting hold of *The Red Book of St Bendix*."

"So you are familiar with it?"

"It has a certain following in Anarchadia."

"Let's just get something absolutely clear before we go on," said Commissioner Gris. "Anarchadia does not exist."

"Yes it does. I was born and bred there."

"Anarchadia does not exist. It is not on any map."

"My, my," said Hob, "and doesn't the very mention of it make you nervous! I am living proof it exists."

"Not much of a recommendation," sneered the cardinal.

"So what are you gonna do? Deport me?"

"How can we send you back to somewhere that does not exist?"

"You could let me worry about finding it."

"No, Nicholas. You are an anomaly, an aberration, an abhorrence and an abomination. There is no place for non-conformity in Post Unification Euphobia. We cannot rest until it is resolved."

"You haven't even tried!"

"We will always be looking over your shoulder."

Hob gave a wry chuckle. "You're never alone with a Conformorian!"

"Displays of bravado will get you nowhere," said Commissioner Gris.

"I'm Dr Bravado!"

"You will become a worthwhile member of society."

"But I don't want to!"

"This is where your Re-education begins."

"So what exactly have I done to deserve this reception?"

"How can you be so gnarly?" cried the Sister of the Blessed Alohas.

"Ever since I arrived in your country you've been trying to shoot me!"

"You've discorporated hundreds since you landed here, dweeb!"

"I get annoyed by people knocking me off my feet with a barrage of red-hot lead."

"Dweeb," said the Methodist minister to the archbishop. "That's not very nice, is it?"

"You were discovered smuggling a motorcycle into Euphobia," Commissioner Gris went on.

"I hardly smuggled it in, did I?"

"They are illegal here."

"So?"

"So you have broken the law."

"Your law."

"While you are here, our laws are your laws."

"I am beyond the law."

"Correct. Very good, Nicholas. You are beginning to see the difference between right and wrong."

"No," replied Hob. "You are outlawing me. That's completely different."

"No it isn't."

"Yes it is."

"No it isn't."

"Yes it is."

"No it isn't."

"Look. I didn't come here for an argument or even straightforward contradiction. I do what I do but you made me beyond the law. Now I'm beyond part of it, I'm beyond the rest of it. I have nothing more to lose. That is why I am what I am. You made me and I am beyond the law."

"At least you admit to being beyond the law. It's a start. Now my colleagues would like to explore some moral issues." Commissioner Gris turned to the assembled clergy. "Ladies and gentlemen, who believes they can put the moral issues across to Nicholas?"

"Er, we do," said the elderly archbishop, "myself, the cardinal and my Methodist colleague."

"*The Red Book of St Bendix* works," the Buddhist monk explained to Commissioner Gris, "but it's not our creed. It makes sense to follow the lead of those who understand the doctrines of the ancient Celtic church most of all."

"Bro? You're sooo reasonable," the Sister of the Blessed Alohas told him. "You wanna try baptism through wipin' out in God's breakers, man."

"No, I don't believe I do," he told her. "And," he said to Commissioner Gris, "the archbishop can read the writing."

"I see," said Commissioner Gris. "You and I will have to talk later about your familiarity with this banned language, archbishop. Of course, there is no such thing as Celtic any more in modern Euphobia. We are all the same here. But for the purposes of this exercise, I authorise you three to use *The Red Book of St Bendix* to suppress Nicholas' powers until we can assimilate him into our Euphobian Consumerist Community."

The clergy nodded.

"Very well," said Commissioner Gris. "Proceed."

The cardinal pulled up a seat and sat directly opposite Hob. He put down *The Red Book of St Bendix* and made a great point of lighting an incense burner and began to swing it threateningly in front of his prisoner.

Hob glared at him.

The Methodist minister sat on his left and smiled pleasantly at Hob, who smiled pleasantly back.

"You're a non-conformist," he said to her. "What are you doing siding with the Conformorians?"

"We are concerned for your spiritual well-being," she replied.

"Bloody hell!" said Hob. "You sincerely believe that, don't you?"

"Of course."

"But how can you ever be affiliated with an Orthodox Patriarch?"

"We have sunk our differences to deal with evil when we find it," growled the Patriarch.

"We are divided only by a thin line," said the Moslem.

"Divided to keep you from squabbling?" suggested Hob.

The archbishop sat on the right of the cardinal. He obviously found the smell of the incense nearly as distasteful as Hob, but tried hard to hide this.

"So," he began. "Here we are." He had brought with him a very old PVC holdall and he unzipped this to reveal a Thermos flask bearing a battered tartan pattern.

Hob viewed it with great suspicion.

The archbishop referred to *The Red Book of St Bendix* and unscrewed the top of the Thermos. "Now then," he said, "how about a nice cup of tea?"

"Oh." Hob sniffed the air and somewhere under the incense smoke detected the scent of tea that was still pleasantly hot. "Thank you, your reverence. That's very kind of you."

"I always say that you can't go wrong with a nice cup of tea," said the archbishop, pouring some out into the cap of the Thermos. He handed it to Hob, who took it in his hand, which was still bound to the chair.

"Well, this makes a refreshing change," said Hob, "even if I can't drink it."

The archbishop produced a very long strong straw and put one end in Hob's cup and the other in his mouth.

"Be careful," he warned, "it might be hot."

"I'll be all right," said Hob, out of the corner of his mouth. "I've suffered worse," and he slurped some tea.

"Yes, I'm sure you have, my son."

"I was getting a bit fed up with that get thee hence stuff."

"Would you like a confession?" the cardinal asked the archbishop, caressing the crucifix around his neck. There was a click as if a finely made watch case had opened, and a long knife blade flicked out from the crucifix.

The archbishop looked horrified and the Methodist minister tutted and folded her arms.

Hob threw back his head and squirted a mouthful of tea in the face of the Jesuit cardinal, who leapt up, only to be restrained by the Moslem and the Methodist.

"Look what you've done now," Hob told him, after spitting out the straw. "You've spoilt the ambience. And we were getting along so nicely,"

"I don't think there's any need for that," the archbishop scolded the cardinal.

Reluctantly, the cardinal wiped his face with a lace handkerchief and sat down again.

"Now then," said the archbishop, brightly. "What I thought we'd do is just ask you some questions."

"Okay. Fire away."

"Digestive biscuit, perhaps?"

"Oh, no thank you, vicar, they make me fart."

The Buddhist and the Moslem had a coughing fit but the cardinal jumped up and hit Hob over the head with his incense burner.

"Is that really necessary?" asked the Methodist minister.

"Bloody Pape!" shouted Hob.

The cardinal hit him again.

"Look," said the Methodist minister. "I don't see why you have to keep hitting him over the head with that thing."

"You obviously fail to realise what we're up against, here, Miss," said the cardinal.

"Minister to you," she replied. "Besides, it's Mrs."

"Wouldn't it be cabbagier to nail him while he's sparko?" asked the Sister of the Blessed Alohas.

"I beg your pardon?" asked Commissioner Gris.

"Sister Winifred says it would be easier to achieve our desired objective if he were unconscious," the archbishop explained.

"How can you understand her?" the Methodist minister asked him.

"Oh, my see features many surfing beaches," quipped the archbishop.

"He'll have us paddlin' beyond the break," said Sister Winifred.

"What does Winnie say, Horace?" asked Hob.

The archbishop looked a little surprised. "She said you could lead us into deep water if we're not careful. Er, how did you know my name was Horace?"

"I didn't. You look like one, I suppose."

"Let's waste him, he's so unhoopy!"

"She suggests we do what we have to do now, for it is unlikely that Hob will ever be beatified."

"Me a saint?" laughed Hob. "Stuff you and your sexwax!"

"Eat my longboard, dweeb!" and Sister Winnie hit Hob in the chest with her surfboard.

"Shall we, perhaps, start," suggested the archbishop, "by asking you to confirm your name?"

There was a pause while Hob got his breath back.

"Nicholas Eldritch Hob."

"Where did you come from?" demanded the cardinal, warming to his new role as inquisitor.

"Anarchadia."

"I'm sorry," said Commissioner Gris, although he clearly wasn't. "I cannot allow that."

"Tough," said Hob.

"Would that explain the peculiar accent?" continued the Orthodox Patriarch.

"What peculiar accent?" replied Hob.

"What is your trade or profession?" asked the archbishop.

"I'm a Horsepower Whisperer. I talk to innocent engines and enrage them to new heights of speed, power and endurance. I traffic traffic and talk the torque. I race the race in the Wild Hunt. And I will promise you such power if you will trade with me your soul.

"Oh dear. That's not a very nice thing to do, is it?"

"Nice?"

"What makes you think you can whisper horsepower?"

"More to the point, Archbish, what makes you think I can't? Eh? You saw how fast that car I was driving could go."

"Car?" queried the Methodist.

"That's a non-compliant and inflammatory term for a personal trans-portation device," explained Commissioner Gris. "We don't use it any more due to its negative associations."

"Ah," said the archbishop, "you mean the Strunts you were driving!"

Hob laughed. "Yeah, the speeding Strunts I was driving!"

"Had you traded any souls before modifying the Strunts?" asked the Methodist minister.

"No, it was a kind of free sample," giggled Hob.

"Do you often offer free samples?" she asked him.

"Yeah. You wouldn't believe the amount of trade they generate."

"Let's be absolutely clear about this," said the archbishop. "Are you trying to tell us that you give people horsepower in exchange for their God-given souls?"

"Yes. And they get horsepower in abundance!"

"But that's terrible!"

"They'll never want for power again. It's better than destroying their souls entirely, which is what your new best friends are doing."

"Better no soul than a corrupt soul," put in Commissioner Gris, looking pointedly at the assembled clergy.

"Well, we generally rejoice at the redemption of a sinner," the archbishop told him.

"They value reformed sinners more highly than those who have never strayed from the path of self-righteousness," Hob explained. "A life of debauchery and sin followed by a quick confession on the death bed and they've bought their passage to heaven."

"That's not true!" shouted the cardinal, and he whacked Hob over the head with his incense burner again.

"Steady on," said the archbishop. "We still want to interrogate him, don't forget."

"Power corrupts," said the cardinal, "and absolute power corrupts absolutely."

"Yeah!" said Hob. "Doesn't it? Mind you. It hasn't done the Almighty much harm, has it?"

"Blasphemer!" shrieked the cardinal.

"Do you wish to repent your sins as a Soul Trader?" asked the archbishop.

"Not today, thank you."

"But you will tomorrow!"

"I'm not planning on being around that long," said Hob.

"So," said the archbishop, "do you admit to being a motorcyclist?"

"I am proud to ride *Nosferatu*."

"Who or what is *Nosferatu*?"

Hob grinned. "*Nosferatu* is a blasphemously supercharged Vincent engine in an Egli frame with re-valved Roadholder forks and disc brakes."

"I'm sorry but I didn't understand a word," said the Methodist minister.

However, the archbishop had put on his reading glasses again and was feverishly scanning the text of *The Red Book of St Bendix*.

"There's something about that in here," he told them, and began to read. " 'The Horsepower Whisperer will by now have risen out of the West. There will be a species of Engine, a well conceived Pair of Cylinders arranged in a Vee, the universal Symbol of the Holy Grail. The Genesis of this Engine will occur by Fortuity when two Blueprints of the Vincent 500 Single are caught in a Breeze, innocent and incidental, to come to lie upon one another before the Gaze of its Designers, thereby exciting their Imagination and Cunning. Hob will blasphemously supercharge one of these Engines with his utmost Artifice, force feeding its Cylinders via a pressure Vessel under the fuel Tank to allow for their irregular intake Cycles. This Engine he shall put into one of Fritz Egli's special Frames, with specially tuned Roadholder Forks and a home made Disc Brake Conversion and renowned shall he be in the Mouth of the Peoples and his deeds in the Wild Hunt shall be as Meat and Drink to Them that tell thereof.' "

Despite the fluorescent strip lighting, the room had grown darker as the archbishop read aloud.

The clergy looked nervously at each other.

Commissioner Gris looked even paler than usual. "What nonsense!" he said.

But the archbishop's eyes were widening at another passage in *The Red Book of St Bendix*. "My goodness!" he muttered.

"What?" asked the Methodist minister.

"Look at this!"

"It looks like a jelly mould."

"I used to have one of those!"

"What is it?"

"It's a Morris Minor!"

"Really?" Hob and Commissioner Gris said it together before glaring at each other.

"Mm. It kept breaking its halfshafts. One of my mechanics serviced it and it was always breaking them after that."

"Excellent!" exclaimed Hob. "This mechanic of yours – did your car go better after he'd 'serviced' it?"

"Oh yes, it was quite quick. He'd really done a marvellous job on it."

"What year was it?" asked Hob.

"1963, so it didn't have trafficators."

"But it would still have had clap hands windscreen wipers."

"Oh yes!" said the archbishop, happily. "And it was an estate version."

"A Morris Minor Traveller!"

"That's right! With timber framing!"

"Stop, stop, stop!" shouted Commissioner Gris.

Guards had entered the room.

"Arrest the archbishop for anti-Consumerist behaviour and conspiracy to destabilise Euphobia."

"What?" cried the archbishop.

"Wait a moment," said Hob. "I thought he was on your side."

"Not anymore," replied Commissioner Gris.

"But all he did was own a Morris Minor Traveller!"

"All old cars are banned from Euphobia for health and safety reasons. Anything that operates beyond its approved design life is also a potential threat to the Euphobian economy and not part of the Standard of Living Directive."

"But this was years ago!" protested the archbishop. "I bought my Morris Minor new!"

Commissioner Gris narrowed his eyes. "I am empowered to decree that the legislation applies retrospectively. Take him away!"

As soon as the guards had whisked the archbishop out of the room, Commissioner Gris turned to the other religious representatives. "Is there anyone else here who would like to confess to owning a Morris Minor or other, similar, anachronistic means of transport that breach the Standard of Living Directive?"

None of them liked to, so they remained silent.

Apparently satisfied with this response, Commissioner Gris turned back to a very intrigued Hob.

"We must proceed with the prisoner's Re-education, expeditiously," he said.

He pressed a button on his mobile phone.

A technician in a white coat entered the room and, stepping carefully over the candles and patterns drawn on the floor, made his way to a strange machine behind Hob. He put his clipboard down and began to connect electrodes to the Horsepower Whisperer's helmet.

"How is the prisoner?" he asked.

"He's in denial," said Commissioner Gris.

"Oh no I'm not!"

"See what I mean?"

"It's only to be expected," said the man in the white coat. "I'll just wire him up."

Hob regarded him distastefully. "You don't have a soul," he told him. "How can you exist?"

The soulless technician ignored him and busied himself in adjusting his apparatus. It looked like a mad scientist had been mixing up electrical equipment in much the same way as classical legends created griffins and sphinxes.

"Would you remove your visor and helmet, please?" he asked Hob.

"No," said Hob. "I wear them for a reason."

"It will be necessary for me to connect these electrodes directly to your scalp," the technician replied, mildly. "We will also have to measure the effect on your soul by closely examining the reactions of your eyes."

"My helmet and visor are not to protect my sight," said Hob, "but to protect everything I see from my sight!"

"We had a go when he was unconscious," said the cardinal, "but couldn't pull 'em off."

"Does it say anything about them in *The Red Book of St Bendix*?" asked the Patriarch.

The cardinal began scanning the pages furiously.

"No matter," said Commissioner Gris. "He's not going anywhere and we have as much time as it takes to break him."

"Break him?" queried the Moslem.

Except for the surfing nun and the Jesuit Cardinal, all the other clerics looked uncomfortable at Commissioner Gris' turn of phrase but he either didn't notice or didn't care.

"Couldn't you just put my behaviour down to high spirits?" asked Hob. "You know. Live and let live?"

"That is the worst excuse for breaching the Standard of Living Directive."

Hob looked at the clergy. "But you all have souls," he told them. "Good souls. Can't you see what these Grey Ones are doing?"

"They are allied with us to rid the world of people like you," said Commissioner Gris. "We are engaged in a classic battle between good and evil, and must use every available means to ensure that our will prevails. You are a danger to yourself and society. It is our duty, as responsible citizens of Euphobia, to Re-educate you. Soon we will have weakened you sufficiently to enable us to remove your helmet and visor without any trouble and get a direct connection for the *geistkriegmaschine*."

"Oh yeah?"

"Yes. A leopard can be made to change his spots through environmental pressure. Eventually you will realise that it is easier to accept our Re-educating techniques and succumb to normality."

"We are working for a world without evil," said the Moslem.

"You are working for a world without souls!" retorted Hob. "Don't you even suspect that your souls might be the next on their 'to do list'?"

"Don't listen to him," said Commissioner Gris.

"The Karma Wallah would pay well for a soul like yours," Hob told the Moslem cleric.

"It is not for sale."

"Letting him have it might the best thing you can do when the Grey Ones come after you. And they will. They will."

"Remove his helmet!" ordered Commissioner Gris.

"Do it now while your soul is still worth something!" Hob shouted at the Moslem.

The clergy pounced on him. Some stuck their fingers under the edges of his visor and crash helmet and heaved while the others kept Hob still.

Hob's headgear remained stubbornly in place.

The clergy huddled in closer, muttering oaths that bordered on the blasphemous, and tried even harder. The cardinal noticed that the archbishop had left his shepherd's crook leaning against the wall. He raised it above the melee and wedged it between Hob's nose and the bottom edge of his visor. He waggled it in to find the path of least resistance and put all of his considerable weight on it. With a foot on Hob's chest he forced it further under Hob's visor, down the side of his nose.

The vortices in Hob's visor swirled furiously and suddenly the crook was snatched out of the cardinal's hands and, with a mechanical screech, disappeared somewhere inside the Horsepower Whisperer's head. The cardinal fell over and a split second afterwards two plumes of wood shavings shot out from Hob's nostrils. The hooked end slammed into his visor, twitched feverishly for an instant and dropped to the floor.

"Bummer!" said the Sister of the Blessed Alohas.

"He won't try that again in a hurry!" said Hob, glancing at the Jesuit Cardinal who wasn't used to getting up from so far down.

"It's no use," said the Rabbi, panting.

"We can't remove his helmet," said the Orthodox Patriarch, massaging his fingers.

"Or his visor," said the Moslem cleric.

"It's just as well for you that you can't!" said Hob.

The Methodist minister began to read slowly from *The Red Book of St Bendix*. " 'If the Spirits of Horsepower Whisperers become overinflated, they can, by means of a special Tool, the Geistkriegmaschine, or Spirit Crushing Engine (see Illumination XXXVIII et seq), be deflated but this course is not recommended for those who are not sensible to the Niceties of the Ritual as it can easily reduce the Value of the said Spirits when used by unskilled Hands.' "

"That's all right," said Commissioner Gris. "Deflating Hob's ego is just what we want to achieve."

"Did she say Horsepower Whisperers plural?" the rabbi muttered to the Buddhist. "The idea of more than one of them gives me the creeps."

" 'Section XXXIX. If the Geistkriegmaschine, or Spirit Crushing Engine, is available and the Operators fully comprehend the Consequences of incorrect Action, do not apply the Electrodes direct to the Scalp of the Horsepower Whisperer or the Weltschmerz Meter will blow and the Melancholicrom will be rendered inutile.

" 'Section XXXX. Removal of the Horsepower Whisperer's Helm and Visor can only be achieved by asking nicely. However, this is not recommended. Beware and mark me well. Horsepower Whisperers wear their Helms and Visors as a kindness to Others. They are not to protect the Eyes and Minds of Horsepower Whisperers from the World but the World from the Eyes and Minds of Horsepower Whisperers.' "

"Connect the electrodes to the victim's helmet," instructed Commissioner Gris.

"Hey! I'm not a victim, I'm a survivor!"

"Yes, well, we'll see about that."

"A soul survivor!"

The cardinal garrotted Hob around the neck with the chain of his incense burner while Sister Winnie wedged her longboard against Hob's neck to facilitate the placing of the electrodes on the outside of his shiny black helmet.

The technician wheeled the *geistkriegmaschine* a little closer and Hob saw that it was just like the strange machine to which M Cadvare had been connected when he had rescued him from the Product Planning Blocks.

The soulless technician switched it on and lights flashed and dials leapt to attention. He adjusted some knobs and, from somewhere inside the *geistkriegmaschine*, the sound of its principal component, the melancholicrom, could be heard. It resembled a very sad note played on a glockenspiel that did not fade.

The technician checked the Weltschmerz meter and carefully channelled a small proportion of Hob's spirituality through its sensors.

"Once we have established a datum, we can begin to erode the soul," he said. He gently twisted some knobs and the *weltschmerz* meter twitched and then swung violently to the extreme of its negative scale.

"I am Old Weird Wheels himself," shouted Hob, "the Metal Guru, the

Repossession Man, the Crypto-Engineer, His Malign Weirdness, the Grand Whizz-Herd and Master of the Engine Henge, the Lord High Prince of Rock'n' Roll, Dr Bravado, the Horsepower Whisperer and Soul Trader, none other than that infamous libertine and free radical from Anarchadia, that trafficker of traffic of no accepted fashionality, Nicholas Eldritch Hob!"

The tone of the melancholicrom rose rapidly. The technician frantically tried to stop the *weltschmerz* meter becoming overloaded with Hob's optimism. Its needle strained against the stop as he tried to adjust the circuitry, but he couldn't avoid the inevitable.

The dial glass on the *weltschmerz* meter cracked and the needle flew out of the *geistkriegmaschine* and embedded itself in the hat of the Patriarch, who had ducked but not far enough.

The sound of the melancholicrom became uncharacteristically cheerful before going beyond the range of the human ear and the sound of many dogs barking could be heard in the distance. There was a shower of sparks and the barking subsided. Everyone except Hob had small nosebleeds, those of the technician and Commissioner Gris being a dark grey colour

The technician fiddled with the *geistkriegmaschine* but all the lights were dead and he peered into the inside of the machine.

He looked away, suddenly puzzled.

Hob noticed his reaction and examined the *geistkriegmaschine* intently, too.

"That's odd," said the white-coated technician, reaching for a pen from his coat pocket. "The *geistkriegmaschine* has malfunctioned."

"What's wrong?" asked Commissioner Gris.

"I think he's overloaded the circuits."

"Excell-ent!" crowed Hob. "My spirits have maxed it out!"

Sister Winnie picked up her surfboard and dug Hob violently in the stomach with it but instead of the prisoner doubling up under the impact, there was a solid thud and the Sister of the Blessed Alohas grimaced, dropped her board and put her hands in her armpits.

"Touch my soul and it'll break your machine," boasted Hob.

The cardinal took another swing at Hob with his incense burner. However, just at the wrong moment one of its chains broke and it wobbled up into the air and came down hard on the cardinal's head, laying him out cold.

"Oh dear," Hob sympathised insincerely, "caught a crab, have we? O fisher of men!"

"Something's wrong," said the Methodist minister. "Hob's regaining his strength." She began thumbing through *The Red Book of St Bendix*.

The Orthodox Patriarch and the rabbi fired their Holy Water pistols at Hob but their nozzles were apparently blocked. They desperately pumped the plastic triggers until they broke or the pistols burst.

"Quick!" yelled the Moslem, undoing the stopper on his pistol's reservoir, "sprinkle the water on the Horsepower Whisperer!"

The blue towrope around Hob's wrists and ankles unwound itself and fell to the floor, and he stood up in time to dodge the pathetic shower of Holy Water that was all the bewildered clergy could manage.

"We need a pastry brush!" cried Commissioner Gris, in between calling for backup on his mobile phone. "Hurry!"

"Galley!" exclaimed Hob. "Gargamelle! Am I glad to see you!"

He appeared to be addressing the *geistkriegmaschine* but his assembled tormentors couldn't see anyone.

The smart traffic cone rose a few centimetres above the floor and floated across the room and out of the opening door.

"Oh no!" cried the Methodist minister. "We misread *The Red Book*!"

"Try Chapter XII, Supplements and Revisions," Hob suggested helpfully.

"Supplement XII, Supplement XII. Ah! Here we are. Oo er! 'Supplement on the Matter of Horsepower Whisperers riding in the Wild Hunt after the Invention of the Infernal Combustion Engine.'"

"Well?" said the rabbi.

"What does it say?" asked the Buddhist.

" 'Sub-section XXV. Beware all those who seek to restrain the Horsepower Whisperer," began the Methodist minister, in an increasingly querulous voice. " 'Beware and mark me well. Bungle not the use of the correct Grade of Oil in restraining the said Horsepower Whisperers in Pursuance of the Introduction of the Infernal Combustion Engine as this increases markedly the Risk of a Seizure by the Gremlins!' "

"We didn't use any oil!" said the Moslem.

"I know!"

"What's going on?" demanded Commissioner Gris.

"We have visitors," said Hob. "Friends of mine."

"But I can't see anything!"

"I can't either!" said the Methodist minister.

The Patriarch and Moslem fell to their knees and began praying furiously. The others quickly followed suit.

Hob gestured at the invisible beings, and the clerics rose off the floor and were carried out of the room.

"Poor misguided souls," said Hob as he watched them go.

"What agency have you unleashed upon us?" shouted the rabbi on his way out.

"You got gremlins," Hob shouted after him. "Or gremlins've got you."

"Gremlins?" queried Commissioner Gris and the *geistkriegmaschine* technician.

"Yes. Galley? Gargamelle? May I introduce Commissioner Gris and some soulless lackey? They've been trying to destroy my soul. Commissioner

Gris and soulless lackey – Galley and Gargamelle, King and Queen of the Gremlins. As Horsepower Whisperer, I have dominion over them. They are the little people, the lares and penates who associate themselves with all manner of trades and articles. In the case of the gremlins, each industrious homunculus is fascinated by any piece of machinery. My fiendish little friends here have not only brought with them their own loyal subjects to rescue me but along the way they've picked up some of their ancestors as well. Commissioner Gris, I believe you have just begun to demolish the cathedral at Lill for re-development."

"Do mean the one at Lille?"

Hob frowned. "That's what I said, wasn't it? Well, it would seem that we are in for a special treat! We are graced this morning not just with gremlins but a homeless band of gargoyles, their Masonic relatives!"

The *geistkriegmaschine* was slowly self-destructing.

"But we can't see them!" wailed the technician.

"You don't need to," said Hob. "What they do is always plain enough. Of course, none of you have ever mended anything. You just rip it up and wear it out. If you had, you would've understood the teachings of The Great Smith more fully and be able to recognise the influence of a gremlin, whether it be benign or not. Hang on a minute!"

He got down on one knee and sang the first line of an old Tom Jones number, "*Please release me, let me go.*"

Commissioner Gris and the technician opened their eyes wide.

All around them was the sound of tiny voices gargling the next line of the tune.

"There you are," said Hob. "The gargoyles and waterspouts from the old cathedral are in particularly fine voice. I suppose you could say they are fluent in phlegmish!"

"Are they invisible?" asked Commissioner Gris.

"Only if you do not have the appropriate level of homuncular vision. You can often hear things that go bump in the night but not always see them. It makes it just that little bit worse, somehow, or better, depending on whether you are the bumper or the bumpee."

"But you're trapped," pointed out Commissioner Gris.

If he'd had any, Commissioner Gris' spirits would have rallied at this thought.

"This is the secure wing of a mental hospital," he went on. "There are armed guards everywhere, many of them with incense bombs and Holy Water cannon. You can't possibly escape."

But Hob's spirits went rallying every weekend.

"On the Edsel-Gaffe Index of Wrongness Scale, that would be a high nine," he told them. He reached into his pocket and pulled out a bright red glove.

"Glove?" he said. "Nice Glove. Curiously strong mint?"

The Glove nodded his head earnestly and Hob posted one into his mouth.

"I know. See if the nice Conformorian over there would like one."

The Glove gave Hob the most peculiar expression, something along the lines of, "Nice Conformorian? Don't patronise me!"

"Oh all right," said Hob. "Just let him have it."

Hob wedged a mint between the prongs of his trident and The Glove zoomed over to the technician to wave it under his nose.

"Go on," said Hob. "Have one with our compliments."

The technician looked at Commissioner Gris.

"Go ahead," he told him. "What harm can a mint do?"

The technician put his hand up to take the mint but The Glove waved his trident about until the technician just opened his mouth and The Glove popped it inside.

The technician began to suck on it and made some appreciative noises. Apparently it was not an unpleasant taste. But then his features frosted over and his eyes bubbled in their sockets as dry ice poured out of his nostrils and ears. He toppled over and shattered into tiny crystals as he hit the floor.

"Bloody hell!" said Hob slurping on his mint and looking at Commissioner Gris. "Was he allergic or something?"

"Murderer!" declared Commissioner Gris.

"I do not regard the discorporation of a soulless one as murder," said Hob. "Now then. You're going to be my witness again, Commissioner Gris. Let's see how far they promote you this time! But you'll never speak again of this or any other thing, for I curse you with all my heart and all my soul to be my silent witness! From now on you'll only be able to – let me see – blow raspberries. Yes. That should do very nicely."

"***!" said Commissioner Gris.

"Come along Glove. Let's find the others."

CHAPTER 55

"Guys, guys, guys!" said Vince. "You were Magnificent! I've never seen anything like it! It was a Towering Performance! You really did Blow Them Away!"

"Clear out of the exit," sighed Kevin.

"What happens now?" asked Percy.

"Well," said Vince, beaming like a tone-deaf Cheshire cat, "we've got ourselves some Grrreat Publicity out of this gig! It would appear that you've been Banned!"

"What?" said Kevin. "By whom?"

"The Moral Minority. You can't record, publish or perform the length and breadth of Euphobia!"

"Bloody hell!"

"No! No! It's the Best Possible Thing that could have happened to us! Er, you. Once word gets out about this, you're Gonna Be Massive!"

"Really?"

"Oh yeah! Don't you see? You guys are now Forbidden Fruit! You guys are about to become an Underground Cult Band!"

"We always were an underground cult band," pointed out Sebastian.

"Yeah, well, you're gonna be Even More of one, now!"

"My mum was in the audience," said Sextus Ramsbottom-Smellie, "with my little sister."

"Really?"

"I don't *think* they recognised me."

"If they did Sexy, they would have been Proud of you!"

"So, Vince," said Percy, "like I said, what happens now?"

"Well, you boys have a little Holiday. Lie low for a bit. Create an air of Mystique for yourselves, ready for when everyone is Clamouring for Interviews. If you find The Press scratching at your door, just say 'No comment!' You know how that winds 'em up! Now if you'll excuse me, I have an Urgent Meeting with the Boys R Us' lawyers."

The door opened and some thickset men dressed in dinner jackets wheeled Vince away in his wheelchair.

"Is he gonna be all right?" asked Sextus.

"What happened to him?" asked Kevin. "I heard he's only just got back from casualty."

"He escaped from casualty," said Percy.

"He's really committed isn't he?" said Sextus.

"Yeah. That's one word for it," said Sebastian. "He means well, though. He was trying to stop the Boys R Us management from pulling the plug on us."

"Really?" replied Kevin. "I couldn't imagine them putting up much of a fight."

"They didn't, but their security consultants did."

"They really didn't like *Crash landing on Planet X*. Did they?"

"No but I think it's brilliant."

"So do I."

"Me too."

"You okay, Kevin?" asked Percy.

"Yeah," Kevin replied, but he was deep in thought.

"You sure?"

"Yeah. I'm fine."

"I'm sorry it has to end this way," Percy told them. "But we're broke. This is the end of The Love Pumps."

"You're right, Perce," said Kevin. "But what a way to go! Vince may have been wrong to get us this gig but he was right about one thing. We did blow 'em away."

"We blew ourselves away!" said Sebastian.

The Love Pumps grinned at each other. Sextus cracked open a six-pack of passion fruit and orange that Vince had liberated from the Boys R Us hospitality salon.

"And I saw the look in their eyes Tonite," said Kevin.

"What look?" asked Sextus.

"That look I've been wanting to see ever since I put down my bone hammer and started out with the heavy metal sound of Deep Turquoise."

"You should have persevered with that," said Sebastian.

"I was years before my time," said Kevin, completely without irony.

"I liked Piddly Pipe Burst And The Wood Lice From Uranus," said Percy.

"And I loved your glam rock proto punk thing as Kev Insane," said Sextus.

"Thanks. Thanks guys. That really means a lot to me. This may be the end, but we went down in flames."

And then, one by one, The Love Pumps left. Although they swapped phone numbers and promised to keep in touch, they all knew that they'd never see each other again. Looking back was something The Love Pumps never did. They looked to the future, some more than others. Besides, they'd made the phone numbers up, and the addresses were false.

Kevin's meeting with the beautiful young scientist and the grauniads had unnerved him. Tonight may have been their finest performance, but it had been born out of an appalling sense of vulnerability on stage. Vince's suggest-ion to lie low for a while was hugely appealing.

There was only one place where Kevin had truly felt at home. Getting there from Mourion would be difficult but not impossible.

CHAPTER 56

M Cadvare was being prepared for an open personality charisma by-pass operation when he was amazed to see gremlins streaming under the door to his interview room. They carried away both commodity inspectors, and clambered over the straps that bound him to something resembling an electric chair.

"Er, good morning," he murmured as they released him.

He felt fragile. The Grey Ones had been softening him up and now the whole world felt too sharp for him. Nerves in his spine and head had been uncovered. He saw the room more clearly. The light was brighter, somehow, his appreciation of being self-aware greater than ever at the prospect of the end of his soul.

The tide of gremlins turned as quickly as it had arrived, but half a dozen remained, apparently to help him with his enquiries.

"What's going on?" he asked them.

The gremlins bowed in greeting and all began talking at once. Even if they had spoken one at a time, M Cadvare would never have been able to understand them, but he didn't say so.

Fortunately, the gremlins mimed as enthusiastically as amphetamised Pre-Unification Italians and M Cadvare understood that he was rescued and that the Grey Ones were being routed yet again.

"Where's Nenuphar?" he asked, stretching his stiff joints, as his bonds fell to the floor.

They began gabbling and gesticulating again and when they stopped M Cadvare couldn't stop himself from saying, "I beg your pardon?" so they ran off through the open door and beckoned for him to follow.

Nenuphar had nearly rescued herself. Taken in by her demure appearance and initially biddable behaviour, her tormentors now lay in a broken semi-circle. With one ankle still strapped to the chair, she had dragged it over to the door and keyed in the code that she'd memorised, but the door didn't budge. She never discovered the next stage of the unlocking process for, unseen by her, the gremlins flooded under the door, formed a grotesque Gothic pyramid with the help of the gargoyles and unlocked the door for her as she desperately rattled the door knob. Thinking she'd just twisted it in a lucky way, she rushed out into the corridor.

"Nenny!"

"Cadvare!"

"*A la bonne heure!* Are you alright?"

"I'm fine. And you?"

"They were going to perform a charisma bypass on me."

"Oh really? Donor or recipient?"

"What d'you mean?"

"Sorry. That was unworthy of me. I apologise. You're a surprisingly charismatic person. They were going to laser-treat my taste buds and minimise my retch-response reaction."

"Why?"

"To turn me into a carnivore, of course."

"*Dieu merci!* We have both been rescued."

"We have? But by whom?"

"Can't you see them?"

"Who?"

"Why the gremlins, of course!"

"M Cadvare, are you sure they didn't do anything else do to you in there?"

"It must be Hob's influence. Earlier, I could see the gremlinne he rescued and the electro-gnome that inhabited my car. Now I can see them everywhere."

"What are they doing?"

"Dismantling the building by the look of things."

"We can't stay here."

"Where's Hob?"

"I don't know," but then Nenuphar realised M Cadvare was addressing the little people she couldn't see.

M Cadvare grinned. "He's escaped, like us," he told her, "and I think he's coming this way."

Somewhere not far away was the sound of gunfire.

"Quick! This is your chance to escape him!"

"But he's taking me to Anarchadia!"

"But then he'll have your soul."

"Of course he will! I've come to regard it as putting it in protective custody. If I stay here, the Conformorians will surely destroy it!"

"Quick! In here!"

Nenuphar dragged him into an empty ward just before a group of Conformorian guards jogged by. Then she cautiously opened the double doors again and peered after them.

"What sort of weapons are they carrying?" she asked.

"They looked to me like giant water pistols."

"That's what I thought."

They crept into the corridor, only to be drenched with water from behind.

"Hands up," said a voice, "and turn around slowly."

They did as they were told and came face to face with a Euphobian Commissioner. He had the complexion of a badly hungover zombie and was comparing them with a photocopied image from some ancient manuscript.

"You're not the Horsepower Whisperer!" he exclaimed.

"No, but we know a man who is," said M Cadvare, gleefully lowering his hands.

"I know you," said Nenuphar. "I've seen you on the telly. You're Commissioner Bland!"

"Hands up!" cried a terrified Commissioner Bland.

"Go ahead and shoot me," said M Cadvare.

Commissioner Bland shot him.

"You know what I think?" the freshly drenched M Cadvare said. "There's two of us and only one of him."

Nenuphar grinned widely.

M Cadvare took a step towards Commissioner Bland but there was a blur of skirts and legs beside him and Commissioner Bland landed some way off down the corridor.

Passing gremlins stopped what they were doing and gazed at Nenuphar in admiration.

So did M Cadvare.

"Do you think Holy Water cannons work on Hob?" she asked him.

"Yes," said M Cadvare. "Gremlins? Sabotage the Holy Water cannons! We must stop Hob getting wet."

The gremlins around him nodded and ran towards the sound of gunfire.

M Cadvare and Nenuphar followed. Something red and hot flew by their heads as it overtook them.

"What was that?" shouted Nenuphar.

"Hob's Glove!"

They ran round a corner and into a squad of Conformorian guards. They had cornered Hob, but their Holy Water cannons were crawling with gremlins, turning them into unpredictable ornamental fountains.

There was a brief struggle as M Cadvare tried to overpower the half a dozen guards, but there was a red flash and something flying fast hit them in the chest and came out the other side. Dark grey liquid bubbled in their wounds, but only a little stained the carpet when the Grey Ones fell.

The Glove materialised before Nenuphar with his trident pointed at her heart. His button eyes twinkled at her and then he zoomed off over her shoulder.

"Thank you, my friends!" said a beaming Hob.

But before they could join him, more guards ran up, this time behind him and carrying machine guns.

Hob turned and blocked their line of fire as they took aim at Nenuphar and M Cadvare. They fired and Hob was flung backwards through the glass wall of the corridor. But the firing didn't last long. M Cadvare saw gremlins leap upon them, and the machine guns jammed or misfired so badly they exploded.

"Oh no!" said Nenuphar. "They've shot Hob!"

"Don't worry," said M Cadvare. "This happens all the time."

"I do wish they wouldn't do that," said a voice from the landscaped garden outside.

Hob rose out of a flowerbed, brushing off shards of glass, holding a smart traffic cone in front of him. "This bloody thing's following me everywhere!" He chucked it up in the air and then kicked it as far as he could into the cloudless sky, beyond the lawns that surrounded the hospital.

"Hob! I thought they'd killed you!" Nenuphar exclaimed.

"Hah! Thanks for your concern, Nenny, but it'll take more than a few drops of Holy Water to finish me off. I dry out eventually."

"But the machine guns!"

"Oh them! I can control my molecular density."

"What's that got to do with it?"

"I can make myself denser than lead."

"Ah."

"Holy Water and Incense Bombs may knock me out, but hot, leaden death can never hurt me! Well, it does sting a *bit*."

"Is that why the archbishop sprinkled you with Holy Water when you crashed the car?"

"I didn't crash it," Hob snapped, "they deployed its air bags! Look. If you see a machine gun, send me out in front of it but if you see any Holy Water cannons, I'd be much obliged if you could put your fingers over their nozzles, okay?"

"Only if the gremlins don't get there first," said M Cadvare.

"I thought you just said Holy Water won't finish you off," Nenuphar challenged Hob.

"It won't but if I get so much of a drop of it on me, it makes me want to lie down in green pastures and that can be very inconvenient when I feel the need for speed. Now then. Some of the gremlins have been splashed with Holy Water. You two are going to have to take them outside and put them on the grass to dry in the sun."

"Why us?"

"Hob can't touch them," M Cadvare told her. "They're all wet with Holy Water."

The other gremlins looked anxiously at their fallen comrades, apparently unable to do anything for them in case they, too, were knocked out. M Cadvare gently began picking them up but Nenuphar just looked about her helplessly.

"I can't see them!" she wailed.

"You'll never make a skirrow!" snorted Hob. "It's all down to you, Cadaver!"

M Cadvare picked up an armful of gremlins.

"Why are you leaving the gargoyles?" Hob asked him.

"What gargoyles?"

"Can't you see them?"

"No."

"Hmm. You'll never make a cathedral builder."

Hob began to direct M Cadvare towards the wounded gargoyles, and when he went to lay them out in the sun to dry, Nenuphar said, "Show me where they are! I want to help these poor creatures," and Hob began giving directions to her from his side of the pool of Holy Water. As far as he was concerned, it effectively blocked the corridor.

After several trips outside, Hob said, "Hold on, Nenny! Hold those two up."

She held up the outlines in moisture of two strange shapes.

"Don't you recognise them, Cadaver?"

"Why it's your gremlinne! And the electro-gnome from my Strunts!"

"Yes indeed! They came back for us! Nenny, these two deserve special treatment. Glove? Glu-huve? Where are you, Glove? Glove! Come here, damn you! Ah, there you are. Nice Glove. Good Glove. Hold them up higher, Nenny. Now then, Glove. Dry them out!"

Nenuphar watched as The Glove shimmered in his heat haze just below what she held in her hands. Steam began to pour off what looked like two figurative crystals that had not solidified yet.

"Ow," she said, "that's hot!"

"Not too much, Glove," warned Hob. "You're boiling the vegetarian."

The Glove hovered a little lower.

"Watch out for drips," Hob warned him.

"Is it working?" asked M Cadvare.

"I should co-co," replied Hob. "Hell-o, my dear. How are you feeling? And you, my fine fellow. What heroics we have seen today! Thank you both from the depths of my black heart for helping us spike the guns of the Conformorians. Thank you, Glove, that's enough now. Farewell my loyal subjects. Put them with the others, Cadaver. May our paths cross again soon."

M Cadvare gently took the gremlinne and electro-gnome from Nenuphar and laid them with the other recovering gremlins outside in the sun, where most of them had already come round. Then he re-joined Nenuphar and Hob.

"Will they be all right?" Nenuphar asked Hob.

"Yes, thank badness! Look. The Conformorians have *The Red Book of St Bendix* and have learnt about Incense Bombs and Holy Water cannons. You realise what this means, don't you?"

"No," replied M Cadvare.

"We're not just fighting the forces of bland here. We're fighting the forces of good, too. Without the gremlins and gargoyles, I'd've been overwhelmed by hordes of Bible-bashing Grey Ones! Fortunately, I've been able to call in some grudges. We're escaping and it's not even mid-morning."

The conscious gremlins beamed at him.

"One bad turn deserves another," suggested M Cadvare.

"Precisely, Cadaver. You're getting the hang of this."

Nenuphar frowned. "But surely religious groups don't want to destroy souls!"

"You wouldn't think so, would you? But religion and Conformorianism have a long history of co-operation. Many souls have been seduced into nothingness over the centuries."

"We're still soaked through," said M Cadvare, dripping on the floor.

"Yes," said Hob, pointedly keeping his distance. "Maybe now is not a good time for a group hug. Glove? Nice Glove. Hover between Nenny and Cadaver and dry them out. Oh, I almost forgot. Glove? Nenny. Nenny? Glove. Glove? Nenny, friend. Friend. Okay?"

The Glove nodded. He was making a lot of new friends.

"It's Nenuphar, actually."

"Don't! … let him kiss your hand," said Hob.

The Glove hovered between them and Nenuphar and M Cadvare felt his heat and watched steam rising from their clothes.

"Keep close to him but don't drip on him whatever you do. Now then. Did either of you see what the Conformorians did with my rucksack and *Nosferatu*?"

"No," said Nenuphar.

"We've got to find them."

But The Glove began gesturing wildly, fanning Nenuphar and M Cadvare with heat.

"Really?" said Hob at last. "Are you sure?"

The Glove nodded earnestly and pointed down the corridor, away from the pool of Holy Water.

"What is it?" asked Nenuphar.

"The Glove has seen something else like him, flying around the corridors."

"What? Another Glove?"

"Not another Glove," Hob assured her, "something even weirder!"

"Could there be more Soul Traders in the building?" wondered M Cadvare.

"If there are, we must meet them!" declared Hob. "Come on!" and he marched off down the corridor so quickly Nenuphar and M Cadvare had to run a little to keep up with him.

CHAPTER 57

Fluorescent lights flashed on and off as if they were strobe lights. The ventilation system blew hot and cold, alarms rang and the public address system just crackled. Pools of unholy water spread out menacingly towards any still-functioning electrical sockets.

Although Hob avoided Holy Water, the possibility of being electrocuted didn't seem to bother him and he knew the difference between Holy Water and the ordinary variety without looking at it. He strode down the corridor, looking vaguely diminished without his rucksack and wooden crate.

"What's happening to this building?" asked Nenuphar.

"The gargoyles are collapsing it," Hob told her. "I have dominion over the gremlins, and the gargoyles are their civil engineering counterparts. All it takes is a special handshake and I can borrow their services. These ones are annoyed about what happened to the cathedral at Lill."

"D'you mean Lille?"

"That's what I said. Lill."

"It's been demolished, hasn't it?"

"They were going to re-house us on the site," M Cadvare reminded her.

"The gargoyles from Lill are angry," said Hob.

"If you keep mispronouncing it," replied Nenuphar, "I'm sure they'll get even angrier."

"How else would you pronounce Lill? Lill-ee? Lilly's gargoyles are angry, Nenny. They have old scores to settle. This lot were petrified by the prayers of the priests for enhancing the design of the cathedral. They said it was an ungodly superstition and forbade the cathedral builders to pay tribute to the lares and penates of stone and mortar. No matter if the resulting building would enhance the glory of The Great Architect Himself! They religiously walled them up and incorporated them into the guttering and drainage systems for centuries!"

"Anyway," said M Cadvare, "they're free now and have come out to play."

"Yeah, and what goes around comes around! The Conformorian priests had invested in trouble for later generations. If they'd humoured the gargoyles, they needn't have worried about maintenance, either, just the odd sacrifice."

"Sacrifice?" queried Nenuphar. "In churches?"

"Well, if you're serious about them standing up," replied Hob. "Surely you've heard of 'guaranteed for life'?"

From her frown, Hob could tell that she had, but not the way he meant it.

"It's mentioned in the Old Testament, I believe," he went on, "a life for a life or something. You'd be surprised how many corpses there are in churches."

"But they were laid to rest there," protested Nenuphar.

"Well obviously, but under what circumstances? Church wardens can covertly commune with the gargoyles and keep them happy. The old beliefs die hard. Collection boxes for The Poor Gargoyles don't have the same power."

"Those aren't for The Poor Gargoyles," insisted Nenuphar, "they're for the poor."

"Naah! You don't seriously believe that, do you?"

"Ah," said M Cadvare. "You're talking of charity, not sacrifice!"

"I've never understood the difference myself," said Hob. "The gift of giving." He shrugged. "Now the acceptance of receiving I grasp entirely. And don't they do that ritual with the flesh and the blood of Christ?"

"It's His symbolised flesh and His symbolised blood," explained M Cadvare. "It's actually bread and wine."

"How do you *know* it isn't His flesh and His blood?" said Hob suspiciously.

"Well it doesn't look or taste like anything except bread and wine!" replied Nenuphar, contemptuously.

Hob pursed his lips. The exposed lower half of his face suggested that behind his purple-black visor he was narrowing his eyes suspiciously.

"Haven't you ever heard of Mass hypnotism?"

"Is that like controlling your own density?" asked M Cadvare.

Hob broke his stride and stared at him.

"Are you being deliberately obtuse? Dig up the foundations of most churches and what do you find? Headless corpses upended in the trench. Placate the immured gargoyles with a little blood and bone and you'd never see a roof fund thermometer outside a cathedral again."

"Hob?" asked M Cadvare. "Have you always had such a problem with established religion?"

"No. But it's always had a problem with me. They're all the same. They try and control souls in the material world but don't do anything for them in the afterlife. Nobody should have a monopoly on spirituality. They're no better than the Grey Ones. Why do they have such a problem with souls finding their own way to God? Can't they see what impeccable blebs true gnosis can cause?"

They passed a vending machine.

"Hungry?" Hob asked them.

"Yes," said Nenuphar, "but I won't be able to eat any of that stuff."

"Beggars can't be choosers," he told her as he produced The Engineer of

Spades. He inserted the card into a convenient slot and Electra's face appeared on what had been an LED screen.

"How may I serve you, my lord?" she asked, apparently without the aid of a loudspeaker.

"Feed my friends," Hob told her, and the vending machine began firing chocolate bars at them.

M Cadvare grabbed an armful and greedily ate three, but Nenuphar read all the ingredient labels until she found one that nearly met her approval and tucked in with obvious but rather shameful relish.

A little further on, The Glove gestured to Hob as they ate, and the Horsepower Whisperer motioned for them to be quiet.

Impressed by his sudden stealth, they stood still and waited.

A violent movement through an open doorway caught their eye. Just out of sight, something was apparently being violently disembowelled. There was a brief pause and some artificial stuffing floated out into the corridor.

Then the violent agitation of a limp corpse was repeated with even greater enthusiasm.

Hob took two silent steps forward and the shaking stopped. He stared through the open doorway with a smile playing across his lips and The Glove looking over his shoulder.

"Well, well!" he said softly. "Fancy meeting you here!"

A strange creature was looking at Hob in equal disbelief.

Hob held his arm out at shoulder level. A rusty blur shot out of the doorway and an outlandish animal dangled from his arm.

It was the size of a small dog with an attractive streamlined face and lively brown eyes. Fine whiskers bristled down the side of its elegantly tapering nose, and its chin and chest were joined by a large cream patch of fur. The rest of its luxuriant orangey-red pelt shone with a remarkable lustre, and it had a great brush of a tail, nearly as big as the rest of it, which it wagged as the creature looked up adoringly at Hob. Enormous triangular ears in black fur continually twitched and swivelled around to catch the slightest sound, and it appeared to be wrapped in a dark brown blanket but, as Nenuphar and M Cadvare stared, they realised that it was actually an enormous pair of wings. In its mouth was a badly mauled pillow that was already leaking fluff.

"What a splendid flitterfox!" exclaimed Hob.

The flitterfox flapped its wings in delight and worried the pillowcase again, this time to death. The stuffing poured out onto the floor and floated across the corridor.

At this spectacle, a strange expression fleetingly appeared in the eyes of the flitterfox's eyes, one of excited happy madness, which would only have been surpassed if the pillow had been stuffed with feathers.

"Unless I am very much mistaken," said Hob, "you are a male Anarchadian Flying Fruit Bat Fox."

The flitterfox dropped the limp pillowcase, opened his mouth and went, "Ha-a-ha-a-ha-a-ha!"

"Look at my fellow countryman!" Hob said to the others and he turned to display the flitterfox to them all the better.

The flitterfox preened himself slightly and stretched out his wings. From the shoulders of his leather jacket Hob unfolded his own black wings, too, and both Anarchadians stretched themselves out so that they filled the corridor.

"What did you say he was?" asked an entranced Nenuphar, as she approached.

"An Anarchadian Flying Fruit Bat Fox," repeated Hob, retracting his wings.

The flitterfox folded in his wings, sniffed her hand and then licked it. "Nn, nn, nn," he whined, and wagged his tail. It was obvious that he would really like to lick her face all over but appreciated that human etiquette didn't allow for such a thing at a first encounter.

M Cadvare offered the flitterfox his hand with the same reaction.

Hob laughed. "Don't be fooled!" he said. "They are actually very discriminating creatures. Only those with the purest of motives gain their trust. Isn't that so?"

"Ha-a-ha-a-ha-a-ha!" said the flitterfox.

"Do they eat fruit?" asked M Cadvare.

"My dear fellow they eat everything, pillowcases included."

The flitterfox wagged his tail again.

"But how did he get here?" wondered Nenuphar.

"I think it unlikely that he got here by himself," said Hob.

"Ha-a-ha-a-ha-a-ha!" went the flitterfox, as if to say "You're getting warmer!"

"There must be somebody else in the building who enjoys a close association with this magnificent animal."

"Ha-a-ha-a-ha-a-ha!" went the flitterfox, as if to say, "You're getting hotter! And thanks for calling me magnificent!"

"Somebody who has close associations with Anarchadia," surmised Hob.

"Ha-a-ha-a-ha-a-ha! Nn! Nn! Nn!" went the flitterfox, as if to say, "Oh you're boiling! Say it! The suspense is unbearable!"

M Cadvare looked at Hob and Hob looked at Nenuphar and Nenuphar looked at M Cadvare.

"Any ideas?" asked Hob.

"No," they said.

"Hmm. Me neither."

The flitterfox adopted an "Oh come on! You must know!" expression. Then he noticed The Glove.

The Glove had been keeping a respectful distance up to now, but he had gradually floated closer out of curiosity.

The flitterfox licked his nose and sniffed at The Glove.

The Glove made a sudden movement and there was a snap of the flitter-fox's jaws.

"Steady!" ordered Hob.

The Glove whizzed menacingly from side to side, shaking his trident at the flitterfox.

The flitterfox growled.

"Come along now," said Hob encouragingly.

Nenuphar scratched the flitterfox behind the ears and stroked his head.

"Ha-a-ha-a-ha-a-ha!" he said.

The Glove stroked his beard thoughtfully with an oven-gloved hand and floated a little closer.

"Glove?" said Hob. "Nice Glove. This is a particularly fine example of an Anarchadian Flying Fruit Bat Fox. You've seen them before, haven't you? I don't know his name but he is a friend. Flitterfox. Friend. Don't make any sudden movements."

The Glove nodded slowly and descended to the flitterfox's eye level.

"Careful," Hob warned the flitterfox. "Don't sniff The Glove too closely. He lives on brimstone and has rather sulphurous breath."

In an indication of the flitterfox's considerable intelligence, he refrained from doing what came naturally and just looked into The Glove's black button eyes as he dangled before him, but there was still a sizzle and the smell of scorching whiskers.

The Glove, which was much smaller than the flitterfox, slowly moved closer. He made a point of holding his trident behind him. Then an odd expression came over his face. He suddenly threw his trident down the corridor and the flitterfox dived after it.

The three humans laughed.

The flitterfox caught the trident and gave it back to The Glove who threw it again, and the two of them swooped and dived around them.

"I'm so pleased," said Hob. "The Glove doesn't have many friends."

"So who does the flitterfox belong to?" wondered Nenuphar. "He can't be a stray can he?"

"If he is, he's strayed an awfully long way," said Hob.

Somehow he managed to catch The Glove's trident before the flitterfox got it, and stood between the two red blurs.

"Sorry to interrupt your game, chaps, but we were wondering if you, Mr Flitterfox, would be so kind as to take us to your caretaker."

The flitterfox barked with eagerness and flew to the end of the corridor where he paused and barked again.

"I think he wants us to follow him!" exclaimed M Cadvare.

"Come on!" said Hob.

CHAPTER 58

The flitterfox led them back to the intersection of corridors near the rooms where Nenuphar and M Cadvare had been held. He flew up to the ceiling and dangled from a polystyrene tile to wait for them.

As they rounded the corner, they saw that Commissioner Bland still lay on his back in the corridor, but he was no longer unconscious. He was no longer alone, either.

"Where's my book?"

The speaker had her back to them. She was crouched over Commissioner Bland. Her shoulder-length blonde hair swayed as she shook with fury.

The Glove hovered close to her but did not attack her.

"Where is it? Who's got it?"

"It wasn't yours in the first place," Commissioner Bland replied feebly.

"If it hadn't been for me it would have been destroyed!"

"You stole it from the monastery."

"I liberated the knowledge it contains!"

"The knowledge it contains is dangerous, *cherie*."

"*Cherie*?" Nenuphar echoed the unexpected term of endearment.

The woman looked around suddenly and saw them for the first time – a certified management auditor within whom revolution burned uneasily, an organic vegetarian girl who fought for freedom and the Horsepower Whisperer.

But instead of recoiling, she stood up and looked almost relieved to see them, although when she saw The Glove she raised an eyebrow.

"You!" said Hob.

The woman smiled. She was very good looking. They could see now how tall she was and that she was dressed in a figure-hugging black trouser suit that might have been designed for cat burgling.

"Julian!" she said, noticing the flitterfox.

Hob pulled a face and mouthed the flitterfox's name to his companions in distaste, but Julian flew to her eagerly and she caught him in her slender arms.

Something wet squirted against the wall behind Hob and he pole axed forward and lay still.

"Look out!" said M Cadvare, but he was too late.

A group of Conformorian guards had appeared in the corridor behind them, and Hob was out cold.

"Madame Bland?" began one of the guards.

The flitterfox woman positioned herself between Hob and the guards with her arms outstretched and said, "My husband and I have the situation completely under control."

Out of Madame Bland's vision, Nenuphar and M Cadvare exchanged a nervous glance.

Julian, who obviously didn't weigh much, dangled from her right elbow and bared his teeth at the guards. Obviously their motives were not entirely pure.

The Conformorians peered round her at Commissioner Bland who was still lying on the carpet.

"Don't listen to her!" he shouted. "Arrest Hob!"

Nenuphar and M Cadvare took up position on either side of Madame Bland. The guards went to squirt them with Holy Water cannon but found that their weapons didn't work.

"Gremlins!" breathed M Cadvare. "The gremlins have ruined their guns!"

He could see gremlins swarming all over the backs of the guards, wreaking havoc on the plumbing for the tanks of the Holy Water cannon but being very careful not to get wet.

Through a melting ceiling tile behind the guards descended The Glove.

Nobody moved.

Julian growled.

The Glove brandished his trident.

The guards began to sniff as the smell of melted polystyrene reached their nostrils. One by one they turned around to look at The Glove.

There was a noise from the end of the corridor behind Commissioner Bland, and M Cadvare turned to see another group of Conformorian guards running towards them, this time carrying machine guns.

"Look out!" he said and everyone attacked.

The guards tried to shoot but their guns didn't work. Julian swooped from Madame Bland's arm and sank his teeth into the thigh of one of them. Nenuphar felled one with a kick and M Cadvare gave another a bloody nose with a punch, but The Glove swept through them with almost contemptuous ease. Because they wore vessels containing Holy Water on their backs he didn't use his preferred route to de-animate them. He splashed through their brains and they all slumped slowly to the floor with cauterized holes the size of a fist through their foreheads.

"Don't get their blood on your hands!" Madame Bland warned them as they crouched around Hob.

"Why not?"

"It irritates the flesh just as they frustrate the soul."

"Pastry," said Hob.

"Is he going to be all right?" asked M Cadvare.

The Glove hovered nearby expectantly.

Madame Bland examined Hob. "I think so. Help me wipe away the Holy Water from his helmet. See? It's just a little splash!"

"Pastry!" shouted Hob. "Get it away from me!" and he leapt up in time to be shot at by the approaching guards.

The others dived for cover from the deadly ricochets and Hob stood over them doing a St Vitus Dance as the guards emptied their guns at him.

The Glove zoomed into their ribs and the firing stopped.

Hob staggered but remained upright.

"Oh," he said. "That's odd. It must have been a dream," and he turned to gaze at Madame Bland and smiled at her.

"Reinforcements!" cried M Cadvare, pointing down the corridor again.

"Uh-oh," said Hob. "This lot've got both Holy Water cannon and machine guns!"

"We must fall back!" insisted M Cadvare.

"Fall back?" queried Hob.

"Yes," said Nenuphar, taking his hand and pulling him down a passage that led off the corridor. "You know. Retreat."

"Retreat? I've never retreated!"

"How about a tactical withdrawal?" suggested M Cadvare, running beside them.

"That's still a retreat!" Hob retorted, but he kept running.

There was a rattle of machine guns behind them and Hob shoved his companions ahead of him and looked back nervously for any jets of water.

"Advance to the rear!" shouted M Cadvare, and they all ran away as fast as they could.

CHAPTER 59

The Conformorians ran faster than ever when they saw their quarry fleeing before them. They were so keen to catch up with them they ran straight past Commissioner Bland. They might have caught up with Hob and his companions had they not encountered The Glove who swept down and weaved his way through their grey hearts. They fell with a clatter, and The Glove hovered over them for a moment as if he'd never had time to study a de-animated Conformorian before.

But as he floated there, he detected a movement behind him.

Turning slowly, he saw Commissioner Bland taking aim at him with a discarded Holy Water cannon. He was still lying down, but had raised himself on an upturned Holy Water tank to steady himself.

The Glove regarded Commissioner Bland with his inscrutable glove-puppet stare.

Commissioner Bland stared back.

The Glove made an obscene arm gesture to show what he thought of Commissioner Bland. Then he began to advance in a terrifying movement, as if he was not hovering towards Commissioner Bland but taking slow steps before him in seven league boots.

Commissioner Bland aimed and fired, but his Holy Water cannon had been bitten by Julian and was down on pressure. The Glove side-stepped the limp jet easily and kept on coming with carefully judged menace.

Commissioner Bland tried again but with the same result.

The Glove was no more than three metres away by now and he stopped. Commissioner Bland might get in a lucky shot if he was clever. The Glove's final attack would have to be finely judged.

But having no soul did not mean that Commissioner Bland lacked intelligence. He lay with his back on the floor so that The Glove could not attack him from behind.

He picked up the Holy Water cannon and turned it on himself until he was soaked through with Holy Water.

He stared back at The Glove as if to say "Come on then! If you think you're Holy Waterproof enough!"

The Glove put his hands on his non-existent hips and cocked his head.

Then he winked out of existence as he zoomed off in search of drier prey.

CHAPTER 60

"Haven't you heard that discretion is the better part of valour?" Nenuphar asked Hob, as he jogged along reluctantly.

"Yes but what does that mean? I would've thought that you'd have to be braver to be *in*discreet."

From somewhere deep within the building came an ominous rumble and the ground shook. Ceilings and archways crashed down after they'd passed under them just like in the movies, having been kept standing just long enough by gargoyles and the occasional gremlin on industrial placement.

"Where did Madame Bland and the flitterfox go?" gasped M Cadvare.

"They must have gone the other way," replied Nenuphar, who seemed to be the best runner of all. "Have you met her before?" she asked Hob.

"Fleetingly."

"Do you think they were on our side?"

"I think so."

"But she was Commissioner Bland's wife!"

"Yes," said the Horsepower Whisperer and he stopped running.

The others stopped, too.

"But," he said suddenly, "she had the confidence of the flitterfox!"

"So whose side is she on?" asked Nenuphar.

"Why, ours of course!"

They found themselves in the medical stores.

"Spread the word, gargoyles!" announced Hob to the crumbling fabric of the building. "Let the flitterfox and Madame Bland escape before demolishing this place entirely."

The whole corridor behind them collapsed gracefully.

"We've got to get out of here," said Hob. "This lot'll come down on top of us soon. I'll be all right, of course, but you won't be."

"Thank you for your concern," said Nenuphar.

"It can't be very healthy for the guards behind us, either," said M Cadvare.

"No," agreed Hob, with a grin, "it can't can it? Glove? Where's he got to? Ah! Glove! I need to know what's going on outside. Would you be so kind as to reconnoitre for me?"

The Glove nodded and zoomed off.

"Reconnoitre," said Nenuphar, "that's another foreign word. Your vocabulary's improving."

"You're obviously very gruntled by it," said Hob.

"Gruntled?"

"Yes. You know. The opposite of disgruntled."

"That's not another of your anarchic words is it?"

"Well what do you think?"

"So what does gruntled mean then?"

"Gruntled means made very happy, like a pig in muck."

Nenuphar turned to M Cadvare. "In attempting to convince us of the existence of Anarchadia, his attention to detail is almost convincing for a very gullible person."

Hob turned to take a few steps away from his companions but fell over something.

M Cadvare and Nenuphar leapt forward to help but he stood up holding another traffic cone in front of him. His lips were very thin and the vortices in his visor narrowed and swirled.

"It can't be same one, can it?" he muttered.

Nenuphar and M Cadvare wisely didn't answer but watched him punch through a doorway into a quadrangle. Then he drop-kicked the traffic cone as hard as he could over the roof of the hospital.

On the opposite side of the quad there was a flurry of movement, and M Cadvare and Nenuphar saw that a number of disreputable purpley-black crows were hopping around the bodies of dead Conformorians.

"Hallo," said Hob, as he approached them.

"Cor!" said the crows, hopping around the Conformorians and gesturing towards the pools of dark grey blood.

"Yeah, it's a bugger innit?" commiserated Hob. "I suppose you can't eat the flesh, either."

"Nah!" replied the crows.

"Any idea what the best way of getting out of here is?"

A crow cocked its head and then said, "Car!"

"Well, obviously! What's the second best one then?"

The crow thought for a while and then said "Aha!" It gave Hob a wink and flew off.

"Come on," said Hob, "we must keep moving. The gargoyles are out of control, and who can blame them?"

The sounds of destruction continued as Hob guided them through the ruins and initiated them in the niceties of gremlin and gargoyle lore.

"Operating singly or in vast tribes ... lie in wait inside spark plugs, plumbing and wiring harnesses ... Honda camchain tensioners, Hillman Imp water pumps ... Dolomite Sprint head gaskets ... particularly fond of aeroplanes... Hear that buzzing? ... the gargoyles have brought their pets along … huge herds of specially bred masonry bees … they burrow into the mortar … hollow out cavities in structural walls and lintels … their droppings cause concrete cancer, y'know … the bees, I mean, not the gargoyles … not many people know that … thousands of different varieties … for instance … there are the tungsten-tipped kango bees … long-mandible Friesians whose acidic beeswax eats wood … the Highland RSJ cutting rubble bees, noteworthy for their shaggy pelts … and long curved antennae … indulge in epic migratory journeys to the Mediterranean during the winter … infest the structural members of hotels … spend the winter hibernating in suspended animation in storm-lashed suspension bridges … or hanging out in cable cars… often travel to ski resorts in Alpine districts… live it up in hydro-electrical dams. Aha! This looks like it."

They were in a series of laboratories and had Hob not been so attuned to his rucksack of souls they would never have been able to find it.

It was lying inside an enormous CAT scanner which would never scan again. Nearby were the Conformorian operators who appeared to have strangled each other.

"What happened here?" whispered Nenuphar as Hob retrieved his rucksack.

"Fortunato?"

The rucksack became quite animated, and after an interval Hob said, "I thought so, the fools! They scanned the rucksack and saw what's inside."

"And killed each other," added M Cadvare.

"When they realised what they were lacking," agreed Hob, strapping on his rucksack. "I've seen it happen before. When will they ever learn? Come on. We've still got *Nosferatu* to find."

Not far away they found the garages for the ambulances, most of which had already caved in.

Nenuphar brushed dust off her white dress and looked around them.

"Is that old crate of yours buried in here?" she asked.

"No problem," said Hob, taking off his rucksack, and he took a running leap and dived into the pile of rubble which heaved and rippled like a fluid.

He shortly re-appeared in the distance, on the limit of the ruins, swimming through the rubble and showing off by doing the backstroke, ostentatiously squirting out a large plume of hard-core and concrete dust before sub-merging again. Eventually a large bulge in the wreckage began to advance towards them. The pile of rubble at their feet heaved and Hob emerged, dragging *Nosferatu*'s packing case with him and brushing the concrete dust off his leather jacket.

"So you see," he said to Nenuphar, as he donned his rucksack and shouldered his crate, "I can change my molecular density to suit any occasion."

"But it can't protect you against Holy Water."

"No. Or Incense Bombs. If we're going to get to Anarchadia, I'm going to need your help."

"So I'm coming with you to Anarchadia, am I? Let's be quite clear – you're not having my soul."

"That's okay. I've got his, and you're his girlfriend."

"She's not my girlfriend," said M Cadvare, just a little too quickly.

"Yeah. Right."

"You're not, are you?" M Cadvare asked Nenuphar.

"No," she replied.

M Cadvare and Nenuphar saw the swirling vortexes of clouds in Hob's visor flatten as if he were narrowing his eyes at them.

M Cadvare tried not to look disappointed that Nenuphar wasn't his girlfriend, and Nenuphar tried not to look as if she liked the idea too much but, somehow, they succeeded only in looking more disappointed and more hopeful.

Hob smirked.

"So how are we going to get to Anarchadia?" Nenuphar asked him. "We can't all ride on your motorbike."

"Can't we fost out of here?" added M Cadvare.

Hob pursed his lips. "Mmm. Not yet. We have a problem, my friends. Euphobia is overrun with Conformorians. Now that they have *The Red Book of St Bendix* and the help of the clergy they can restrain me and prevent the Wild Hunt. I shall have to resort to low, animal cunning."

CHAPTER 61

As they explored the remains of the hospital, The Glove flew backwards in front of Hob to give him an aerial de-brief

"There are too many of them outside," said Hob, "although The Glove is ready to take them on. It would be worth a try were we not running so low on brimstone."

The Glove suddenly looked very thoughtful.

"We're back here," said M Cadvare. They were outside the rooms where they had been interviewed earlier. "Looks like Commissioner Bland got away. Couldn't we break out of here with the Wild Hunt?"

Hob shook his head. "We've got enough skirrows," he said, patting his rucksack, "but there's no manufactory here to make our road weapons, is there, Fortunato?"

The rucksack squeaked in agreement.

"This isn't the Horsepower Whisperer's last stand, is it?" asked Nenuphar.

"If it is," said Hob, lowering *Nosferatu*'s crate, "it won't be for the first time. I doubt if it'll be the final last stand, either."

"I imagine you've found yourself in a number of tight spots over the years," said M Cadvare.

"The luck of a thousand stars couldn't get me out of some of them," Hob replied.

"So do you have a plan?" Nenuphar asked him.

Hob nodded.

She looked relieved and so did M Cadvare.

"I am planning," said Hob, "to be spontaneous."

"Is that all?"

"When faced with total disaster, complete defiance is the only recourse!"

"So you keep saying! But there must be something we can do."

"I'm sure there is," said Hob. "Where there's a wheel there's a way."

He sat down *Nosferatu*'s crate and assumed the pose of Rodin's *The Thinker*.

M Cadvare and Nenuphar waited for a bit but then left him to it. They peered into the interview rooms and shuddered a little.

"We might yet end up in these rooms again," said Nenuphar, examining the taste-bud laser and retch-response modifying equipment.

"Let's destroy everything!" said M Cadvare.

"Yes! Let's!"

They picked up chairs and smashed them into the instruments of Conformorianism and, swept along in a dam burst of violence, made so much noise Hob asked them to "keep it down in there."

They ignored him and carried on until everything had been destroyed.

Panting and flushed they looked at each other and grinned.

"There's a *geistkriegmaschine* next door," gasped M Cadvare.

"Let's do it!" gulped Nenuphar and they ran round and attacked it in even more of a frenzy.

At last, tired but elated, they staggered back into the corridor to find Hob waiting for them.

"I've called in some old grudges," he said. "Behold, an opportunist bird of ill omen."

"Cor!" said the crow, a little self-consciously.

The crow held out a leg and Hob held out a rubber band and a scrap of paper.

"She's a carrier crow," he said. "Aren't you my dear?"

"Yah!" said the crow.

"We must make our way to the main entrance – a contingency plan is about to, er, continge."

The crow flew away.

Hob stood up and tripped over a smart traffic cone parked by his feet.

"The sooner we get out of here the better!" he growled, standing up.

He picked the traffic cone up and was about to throw it out of the window when he noticed some dust falling from the walls of the corridor.

"Stand back," he said and he put the traffic cone down by the crumbling wall, which promptly fell on top of it. But the pile of broken masonry then developed an attraction for other building materials in the vicinity and soon there was a great pile of wreckage spreading out from where the traffic cone had once stood. Girders slammed down on top, with more force than mere gravity could have justified, and other walls began to fly towards the rubble as if they were joining a rugby scrum.

"That should be the end of that," said Hob. "Thank you Galley! Thank you Gargamelle! My companions are indeed honoured to have been assisted today by none other than the king and queen of the gargoyles. Aren't you?"

"Er, yes," they said.

Hob propelled his fascinated companions away from the billowing destruction.

"Don't say you can't see them," he hissed. "That would be incredibly rude."

Hob pulled them up short and gave them a meaningful look. M Cadvare and Nenuphar respectively bowed and curtsied.

"What?" said Hob, apparently addressing nothingness. "An inspection? Oh, all right, then. Come on you two, follow me."

Hob shouldered *Nosferatu* again and then began to walk sideways, nodding his head and making pleasantries.

"Jolly well done. Your assistance today has been most apposite. I say! Nice fangs! And how long have you been a gargoyle?"

M Cadvare mimicked Hob's walk and smiled at where he thought Hob had smiled. At first he felt a bit silly but he soon had a vague impression that his gestures were very much appreciated.

Nenuphar also followed suit but went a little bit further. She began to say, "Very well done," and "Thanks for coming."

Hob reached the end of the line and nudged M Cadvare to be more gracious than ever, which is difficult when you can't see whatever it is you're being gracious to and don't understand what the protocol at such functions might be. He smiled more than ever, made to shake hands, thought better of it and then bowed very deeply.

When he stood up, Hob appeared to approve.

"Can you see them?" he hissed.

"No," mouthed M Cadvare.

"Bloody hell," said Hob, "I'd never have guessed!"

"Thank you your highness," Nenuphar was saying. "And you your majesty. You know, I've always wanted to ask a queen – does everywhere really smell of fresh paint to you?"

There was a pause and Nenuphar uttered a peal of gentile laughter and said "Farewell then, your highnesses, and thanks again."

"Can you see them?" an amazed Hob whispered to her.

"Of course not," she hissed back, "but I can sense something."

"Okay!" said Hob. "Let's get gone!"

CHAPTER 62

As they jogged through the building, Nenuphar suddenly said "Wait!"

The others paused and looked at her expectantly. "Can you hear something?"

"Oh yes!" said Hob dismissively.

"No," said M Cadvare.

"Listen," she told him.

He turned his head from side to side and Hob grinned at him encouragingly.

"Hear it?" Nenuphar asked.

He nodded. "What is it?"

"I don't know. Hob?"

"What does it sound like to you?" he asked her.

"Like someone blowing raspberries through a loud hailer."

Hob said nothing but grinned and turned to make his way to the main entrance of the hospital.

Carefully, they looked outside and saw their enemies were gathered around the entrance. There were clergy with incense bombs and Holy Water cannon, and Conformorian guards with both these and machine guns. There were also many police officers and a number of vaguely medical figures who looked like they might know how to work a *geistkriegmaschine.*

They were all listening with rather puzzled expressions to Commissioner Gris who was, indeed, blowing raspberries into a loud hailer.

"He wants us to give up," said Hob.

"Can you understand him?" asked M Cadvare.

"Of course but the others can't. I cursed him, you see."

"** **** ***'** ** *****, ********! **** ** *** **** **** ***** **!

(We know you're in there, Pilchard! Come on out with your hands up!)" went Commissioner Gris.

"You'll never take me alive, copper!" shouted Hob.

Commissioner Gris spluttered apoplectically into his loud hailer.

"If he gets it much wetter he could get an electric shock," said Hob, hopefully.

"If he goes much redder in the face he's going to burst something," added Nenuphar, equally wistfully.

"For a Grey One, he's turning into quite a colourful character," said M Cadvare.

Behind the ranks of Conformorians outside, crows were gathering portentously. They lined the roofs of the two hospital wings on either side of the main entrance and looked down on the horde of Grey Ones gathered there.

"What's going on?" asked Nenuphar.

"Someone is coming," Hob told her.

An old-fashioned horse-drawn carriage came into the car park.

"What the hell is that?" whispered an awestruck Nenuphar. "Shouldn't that thing have horses in front of it?"

"Who's driving it?" asked M Cadvare.

The horseless carriage stopped behind the unsuspecting Conformorians. Its door flew open by itself and a strange figure in a stovepipe top hat and mutton-chop whiskers emerged from its darkened interior.

In his right hand he held a red rubber ball and a small book. On his left he wore a huge catcher's mitt.

"*Guten Morgen.*"

The Conformorians turned around and were surprised to be confronted by someone of no known fashionality.

Commissioner Gris put down his loud hailer and stared.

The newcomer carefully placed the ball on the catcher's mitt and held up the little book, thumbing through it for a specific passage. He found what he was looking for and cleared his throat.

"My hovercraft is full of eels," he announced.

The Conformorians looked at each other but the rubber ball began to produce a strange sound, somewhere between a balloon being deliberately deflated and a motorbike engine, as it rose vertically from the catcher's mitt.

"Would you please fondle my buttocks?" he read out loudly.

The rubber ball flew at the Conformorians. It knocked the first one head over heels and bounced off the front of the hospital with a "Splat!" to fell another guard on the rebound. It ricocheted off the horseless carriage and, before they could raise their weapons against it, dived into the group of panicking Grey Ones.

Commissioner Gris began to frantically blow raspberries at his staff but the rubber ball seemed to home in onto him and hit him in the stomach causing him to collapse.

"Down!" hissed Hob and he pulled his companions to the floor.

The rubber ball bounced off the guards or any hard surface it could find, knocking them out but without dissipating its energy at all. In between each impact, the tone of its rubbery engine rasped flatulently.

The Conformorians were no match for it and they fell, either concussed or dead, to the ground. Seeing their confusion, The Glove rushed out and skewered any who looked like they might be alive. At one point, a ricochet would have sent the ball whizzing through the reception area and into the depths of the hospital but Hob leapt up and head-butted it through the doors again.

Nenuphar and M Cadvare caught a glimpse of a wicked grin and a pair of scowling eyes as it flew back outside.

The ball ricocheted between the two remaining guards, bouncing its way up their torsos until finally hitting their heads with such force that they arched into the air, flinging their machine guns and Holy Water cannons aside. They landed head first and lay very still.

Once the Conformorians were all down, the ball carried on bouncing from wall to wall, still full of energy, while the man with the catcher's mitt searched for another passage in his phrase book.

"Will you come back to my place, bouncy, bouncy?" he said, holding the mitt out flat, and the next instant the rubber motorbike noise stopped and the red ball rested in his mitt.

"Deutz!" bellowed Hob.

"It worked, Hob!" said Deutz. "Of course, it isn't quite as good as your friend The Glove but it serves!"

The Glove bowed low in front of Deutz, and the Foundling of Rauschenberg nodded and clicked his heels in return.

"Come on!" cried Hob, shouldering *Nosferatu*'s crate. "All aboard!"

CHAPTER 63

"I can take you to a railway station," Deutz told them, as the carriage set off by itself, "but that's all."

"That's fine," said Hob. "We can get a train to the coast from there."

"*Ja*, many Soul Traders are making for Anarchadia. There is an unprecedented soul migration across the face of Euphobia, a transinhumance the like of which I have never seen before. I, I am going south."

"South?"

"To the *Schwarzwald*."

"Why?"

"I still have some unfinished business. And lucky for you, for there are few Soul Traders around here now. They are going to every point of the compass rather than stay here. But speaking of unfinished business, consideration has passed from the promissor to the promissee. I covet your souls, Hob."

Nenuphar disliked the way Deutz produced a monocle and studied her closely without quite looking at their physical form. She sat, opposite the two Soul Traders, next to M Cadvare with her back to the direction of travel.

"Aren't you going to introduce us?" she prompted.

"Of course," said Hob. "Deutz? This is Nenuphar, a vegetarian of this trading block and scourge of the comestible inspectors, wanted for crimes against the economy and kicking Euphobian Commissioners unconscious. And this is Cadaver, a certified management auditor who used his position to repeatedly breach the commodity inspectors' beloved Standard of Living Directive."

"I see," said Deutz, removing his monocle and nodding slightly to them. "So you have his soul, but Nenuphar's is there for the taking."

"You'll not have my soul!" she shouted, but they just smiled broadly, like connoisseurs who appreciated her spirit more keenly.

"Nenny and Cadaver? Allow me to introduce to you an old trading partner of mine, the Foundling of Rauschenberg, Caspar Deutz. He stumbled into Rauschenberg one evening, having been imprisoned alone for all his fourteen years in a darkened tower. Nobody knew who he was and he was murdered a few years later. Ever since he wrought revenge upon those who brought him up and those who attacked him, he's been a Soul Trader."

"Hullo," said M Cadvare.

The carriage moved quickly and quietly. Without the thunder of any horses' hooves, the loudest sound was the creaking and groaning from its suspension as it coped with speeds higher than even the fleetest stage coach could have achieved with a full complement of horses.

From outside there came the sound of a helicopter and Nenuphar looked out of the window.

"We're being followed," she said.

"Glove?" said Hob and The Glove shot out of the window and took off vertically. The sky outside flashed orange and there was rumble of distant thunder.

"So there remains the issue of payment between us," said Deutz, turning to Hob.

"Of course," said Hob.

"How much is your rescue worth to you?"

"Well it was hardly an SOS, was it?"

"Maybe not, but it was close. Nenuphar's soul is the best I've seen for a long time."

"Never!" she cried.

"I'm afraid her soul is not within my gift," said Hob.

"Maybe not now," added Deutz. "So what *do* you have?"

Hob pulled his rucksack onto his knee and opened it.

Strange whirlpools of a purpley-black light lit up the gloomy interior of the carriage.

"Ah ah ah ah ah," he warned Nenuphar and M Cadvare. "No peeking."

Hob and Deutz peered inside.

Nenuphar and M Cadvare looked out of the window at a world that appeared entirely normal.

"I can either offer to reduce my share in our endeavours for The Souls of All Souls or give you a selection of spirits rescued from the Product Planning Blocks," said Hob.

"What?" burst out Nenuphar. "Is that what you planned to do to my father's soul, if he still had one?"

"Of course. I'm not a charity, you know."

"Not bad," said Deutz looking deep into the rucksack, "but some of them look like they were bargained for under duress."

"The duress wasn't from me. Well, not much. Look at the blebs on this spoon collector."

"Spoon collector? Is that such a crime, here in Euphobia?"

"It is if it's the wrong sort of spoons," explained M Cadvare.

"Wrong sort of spoons?" echoed Deutz. He shook his head but pulled a carpet bag from under his seat. "Okay, that one intrigues me. Any more?"

"Here's one I saved from a Level One Management Audit Techniques exam."

M Cadvare snorted.

"Okay, Cadaver, so you have the strength of character to withstand that sort of thing, but this young woman didn't. However, she tried to resist and that's what's important."

"Any spirit is better than none," agreed Deutz, opening his carpet bag and reaching into the rucksack.

"This one I nearly didn't get," said Hob.

"Wow, look at the blebs on that!" whispered Deutz. "It's a shame you got it under duress. If only it had been given freely."

"Yeah but look at it, Deutz. That last gold bleb is from when I waved some irradiated fruit under her nose. It was the straw that broke the camel's back."

And so it went on until the carriage rocked to a standstill and Deutz looked outside.

"*Also*. Here we are. I think consideration has passed now, Hob."

"Splendid."

"It's a despicable trade that you're involved in," declared Nenuphar. She sat slumped in the shadows, with her arms across her chest.

"I would also like to add my thanks to you," said Hob, with a glance at his companions.

"Er, yes. Thank you, Herr Deutz," said M Cadvare.

"Call me Caspar."

Hob turned his visored eyes upon Nenuphar.

She didn't answer immediately but then sighed and said, "Thanks."

Hob nudged Deutz.

"Okay," said Deutz. "Here is the station. This is where we must part. Good luck, Nenuphar, Cadvare and Hob. May you keep what souls you have, be they yours or those of others."

CHAPTER 64

"So far so good," said M Cadvare, as they walked into the railway station. "I'm surprised there are no Conformorians waiting to arrest us for riding in a non-compliant vehicle."

"Deutz's carriage confounds traffic cameras, and eyewitnesses can't believe their eyes," said Hob. "I doubt the Conformorians will bother him. If they do they'll have his inflammatory phrase book and the Bouncy Ball of Baden Wurtemberg to reckon with."

"It's a shame he's not going our way," replied M Cadvare. "Anyway, we've got as far as Charleroi."

"Big deal," muttered Nenuphar. "We haven't even left Wallonia."

"It's not so bad," replied Hob from under his crate. "This is the Pays Noyer, isn't it?"

"There you go again," grumbled Nenuphar. "Murdering our language. It's Pays Noir."

"That's what I said!"

"How do you pronounce this place?" She gestured at the station name board.

"Charlieroy," said Hob.

"It's Charleroi, actually."

"Funny. It says Charlieroy here. Do you think we ought to tell some-one?"

"Now, now, children," said M Cadvare. He was feeling happier than he had been in a long time. "All we have to do is not draw attention to ourselves. There are high-speed links from here to the coast."

But Hob was sniffing the air. "I smell the ghost of coal," he said.

"Well, this is the Pays Noir," said Nenuphar. "You might call it the Black Country."

"I prefer Pays Noyer," said Hob, looking around suspiciously. "When in Rome and all that."

"Let's just get on the train," suggested Nenuphar, craning her neck to see the destination boards.

"No," said Hob. "I've got a bad vibe."

"What do you mean?" M Cadvare asked him.

"The Conformorians are waiting for us up the line. Can't you feel it?" Hob studied their blank faces.

"We have assumed a much higher travelling profile than Caspar Deutz."

"You mean you have," snorted Nenuphar.

"But it's okay," Hob reassured them. "I smell the ghost of coal."

"Is that good?" M Cadvare asked him.

"Oh yes.

"So what are we going to do?"

"We can still go by train," said Hob, "just not any of these. See that?"

Pointedly, he turned to face some murals of ancient railway trains above the concourse.

"Bit of a clue, wouldn't you say?"

"Bit of a clue for what?"

"Come on," said Hob. "Follow me."

He led them away from the platform to the outside of the station and The Glove swooped down to join them.

"No more helicopters, Glove?" asked Hob, brightly.

The Glove shook his head and wiped his trident on a patch of grass leaving a dark grey stain.

M Cadvare noticed a column of black smoke in the distance. He also noticed passers-by looking quizzically at Hob as he carried *Nosferatu*'s crate on his shoulders and held a conversation with a rocket-propelled glove puppet. Some of his good cheer evaporated but Hob led them to the side of the railway building and chose a door that looked like it should be locked but wasn't. He held *Nosferatu*'s crate before him and went inside, and they followed only to find that Hob had shouldered it again and was descending a dimly lit flight of stairs that looked as if they hadn't been used for years.

He paused on a landing and said, "Glove? Glove. Very good, Glove. You have done well, today. And look! I have some fresh brimstone from our friend, Caspar Deutz. Yes! Badness! You are hungry!"

M Cadvare felt a little peckish, too, and then remembered the chocolate bars they'd picked up in the hospital. He pulled some out of his jacket pocket and gave some to Nenuphar, who was so hungry she didn't even read the labels.

The Glove stretched his arms over his head, and Hob gently folded him up and put him in one of the pockets in his leather jacket before descending further down the stairwell.

At the foot of the stair case was an enormous door.

"You met my fellow Soul Trader, the Foundling of Rauschenberg, just now. Beyond this door is a railway network that belongs to another of my business associates. Entering it will be a little like walking through my sack of souls."

Hob's rucksack squeaked obligingly.

"Stick close beside me and you'll be fine," and he flung the door open and stepped into the sulphurous darkness beyond.

CHAPTER 65

As Nenuphar and M Cadvare stepped through the door they were engulfed by smoke. They looked back and saw the door closing behind them. M Cadvare caught Nenuphar's eye and tried to re-assure her but the smoke stifled sound as well as light. Complete darkness closed over them but they could still breathe once they had got used to the reek of sulphur.

"This isn't so bad," said M Cadvare in encouragement to Nenuphar but he could only hear his voice through the bones of his own skull.

Then he saw a swirling motion in the darkness and the dim outline of Nenuphar, in her white dress, fanning the darkness away from her. To his relief he saw that light was filtering in from somewhere, and not far up ahead was the familiar outline of Hob's crate lurching through the clouds.

The ground trembled beneath his feet and M Cadvare saw that Hob had turned to wait for them.

"You all right, Cadaver?" the Soul Trader asked him.

M Cadvare's affirmative reply came from a long way off as he waded through the heavy atmosphere to join Hob on a platform.

Nenuphar was pulling herself through the smoke beside him and, when they finally pulled free of it and looked up, they saw they were in a vast cavern, ribbed with steel girders.

Further along the platform in front of them were rows of very old railway carriages and around these were great crowds of outlandish people who seemed to have an awful lot of luggage.

The ground shook again and thunder rolled around the iron-girt cavern. The crowds were shouting and the hapless station staff were trying to organise their obstreperous customers.

Hob put *Nosferatu*'s crate down and said, "I wonder who's in charge here?"

"I don't think anyone is," said M Cadvare.

"I say, you there!" said Hob.

"Uh, yes sir?" An embarrassingly obsequious porter cowered before him. On his jacket lapels were badges with the initials SE&CR.

"My friends and I would like to travel to Albion. When is the next train?"

"Uh, the next train is full sir."

"Oh come, come." Hob casually opened his tin of curiously strong mints and offered one to the porter. "You must be able to squeeze us on somewhere."

The porter glanced avariciously at the sweets.

Hob rattled the tin at him in a parody of collecting for charity.

"Uh, don't mind if I do sir," said the porter, his expression brightening perceptibly but furtively.

He reached out to steady the tin in one hand and picked a mint out between thumb and forefinger. He stared at it reverently for a few moments and then popped it in his mouth. From his expression it must have been the nicest thing he'd tasted for years.

"Ooo *excellent*!" he slurped, with feeling.

"Correct me if I'm wrong," said Hob, "but doesn't SE&CR stand for the South Eastern and Chatham Railway?"

"Uh, yes sir, thank you, sir."

"You're a long way from home, aren't you?"

"I'm on, uh, secondment, sir. There's a railway race on, sir, a railway race back to Blighty."

"Excellent," said Hob. "Here, have another for later."

"Ooo I couldn't, sir," protested the porter but somehow he managed.

"So is there any space on a train?" asked Hob conversationally.

"I'll see what I can do, sir," said the porter.

"Capital, capital," said Hob. "Get us on the next train to Albion and I'll put in a good word with your employer. What's your name, my good fellow?"

"Trundleramp, sir."

"Very well, my good Trundleramp. See what you can do."

Bobbing his thanks, the porter scampered off, ignoring other potential passengers who tried to accost him.

None of the trains seemed to be actually going anywhere. The harder the railway staff tried, the worse their customers became.

"Let's go and look at the engine," said Hob, "while Trundleramp does his best."

They wandered to the end of the platform and found an enormous black steam locomotive.

"An SNCF 141," said Hob. "It's not lack of steam that's holding things up. The safety valves are lifting."

"It's not going to explode, is it?" asked Nenuphar, who'd never been near such an iron monster before, especially one that hissed so much.

"It wouldn't be for the first time if it did," Hob teased, "and I dare say it won't be the last. No, safety valves lifting are a good sign, if a little wasteful. It's when they stay quiet you have to worry."

"Do you notice something odd about these trains?" she asked.

"Odd?" repeated Hob, bemused. He put down his crate again and leaned against it. "Of course, they're odd! They're full of Soul Traders!"

"No. Look. They're all pointing the same way."

"Oh yeah."

"They're all travelling in the same direction."

Hob turned to look up the old-fashioned signal box that stretched over the end of the platforms, and Nenuphar and M Cadvare followed his gaze. A lively debate was under way inside.

"At least they're not short of signalling staff," said M Cadvare.

"Yeah but they're not supposed to be trying to kill each other," said Hob.

"Can they kill each other?" asked Nenuphar, who was beginning to cotton on to the diabolical nature of the railway network they had just stumbled across.

Hob laughed. "No but they can fight for hours."

"All the trains are going in the same direction," repeated Nenuphar. "These Soul Traders are taking flight!"

The fighting in the signal box continued while the crowds beside them on the platform grew even more irate.

"Hey!" cried Hob. "Dionysius!"

A pair of slaves were carrying a slumped figure wearing a toga down the platform, one taking his arms and the other his legs. Behind were more slaves, carrying a small brewery on wheels.

" 'Show me the way to go home'," sang Dionysius. " 'I'm tired and I wanna go to bed'."

"Dionysius!"

The two slaves supporting Dionysius paused as they drew level, and Hob stepped up to their burden.

" 'I had a l'il drink about an hour ago and it's gone straight to my head!' Hob! How the devil are you?"

"All the better for seeing you, old chap! Where are you headed?"

"To a sleeper compartment, if we can find one."

"No, I meant where are you travelling?"

"To Old Anarchadie. Where else do you suppose?"

"Is everyone going there?"

"Yup."

"Why?"

"I should have thought that was patently obvious. Conformorians all over the place. Oh look, there's Boule-de-neige. Yoo-hoo, Boule-de-neige!"

The bluesman was with a band of equally soulful musicians. They all wore dark suits and carried their instruments as if they contained lethal weapons.

"Nysius!" said Boule-de-neige. "Hob! We heard you got caught, man!"

"I did. But we escaped."

Dionysius seemed to notice Nenuphar and M Cadvare for the first time.

"Hell-o," he said. "I shay, nobody'sh got her shoul!"

The crowds suddenly stopped shouting. They all turned to look at Nenuphar. Even the railway staff gazed at her in amazement. It was a long time since any of them had seen a free spirit.

Boule-de-neige's eyes were only just kept in his head by his face. "Well I'll be damned." He pointed at Hob. "What you doin' with him, honey?"

"She's with me," said M Cadvare, taking her hand.

Everyone looked at him, then.

"Go-od soul," said Boule-de-neige.

"Oh, look," said Dionysius. "They've stopped fighting in the signal box."

There had just been four short rings on a bell somewhere and the signalling staff started pulling levers frantically.

"What *are* they doing?" asked Nenuphar, happy for a diversion.

"If I didn't know any better," said Hob, "I'd say they were panicking."

The sense of urgency spread to the platform staff and they began to manhandle the Soul Traders toward the nearest doors of the train with predictable results. Someone's luggage burst in the scrum and a shiver ran through Nenuphar and M Cadvare as what appeared to be multi-coloured scraps of material tumbled across the platform.

"Are they what I think they are?" whispered M Cadvare.

Hob put his arms around their shoulders and turned them away. "And what might you think they are?" he asked.

Before either of them could answer, there was an even louder commotion and an express entered the station. As Nenuphar had pointed out, all the trains in the station were pointing in one direction. This train had just come from wherever these trains were bound. The locomotive was much smaller than the big black beast they'd just been admiring. It was dark green but had an elegant grace about it that was matched by the empty rake of small carriages that it drew.

It pulled up on the far side of one of the packed trains that stood at the platform, and the Soul Traders aboard the packed train tried to board the empty one even though it pointed in the wrong direction. But there wasn't enough space between the trains to open the doors so they opened the windows and tried to squeeze through them instead.

Hob ignored the pandemonium and strolled through the crowds and frantic station staff to the other end of the platform until he drew level with an ecclesiastical figure on the footplate of the incoming engine.

"Hallo Hob," said what M Cadvare could only describe as an Anglican vicar in a pair of dark blue overalls.

"Hallo your irreverence," said Hob. "That's an interesting locomotive you've got there."

"Yes. The Chemin de Fer D'Ouest commissioned it to try out Francis Webb's tandem compound system. Watch this!"

He fiddled with the controls and nothing happened initially, but then the engine stirred. It was grinding its driving wheels – the front pair of wheels slowly moving forward while the rear pair rotated gently backwards.

"Of course, it's not supposed to do that," he went on. "It's just a quirk of the tandem compound layout."

"It looks very tidy compared with the other engines," remarked M Cadvare.

Amongst such infernal company, he found the presence of a member of the clergy deeply re-assuring.

"Yes," said the vicar, beaming at him, "it has very clean lines, hasn't it? That's because it's a British design. C S Lewis once remarked that he felt the reason he was mortally afraid of spiders was because they were like French locomotives – they had all their works on the outside."

He smiled at Nenuphar and, despite herself, she smiled back.

"You're not afraid of French locomotives, are you, my dear?"

Nenuphar glanced back at the huge SNCF Mikado behind them.

"I don't think so. Not from here. If I was chained to the tracks and it was bearing down on me, I might be."

"Hmm. Now there's an image to conjure with."

"If I could just interrupt your conjuring for a moment, I don't suppose you have any spare locomotives, do you?" asked Hob. "All the seats on the trains seem to be taken."

"Ah," said the vicar, apparently noticing the uproar around them for the first time. He clapped his hands lightly together, but the sound carried right across the station and the turmoil subsided immediately. "Could I have your attention please? The next boat train to Albion will leave in five minutes. Thank you."

It was as if a spell had been cast over the assembled hordes. They picked up their luggage, courteously doffed their hats at the people they had just been pulling off the trains and boarded the carriages in an orderly fashion.

"What a wonderfully civilising influence you are, vicar," said Hob.

"It's just a knack, really."

He held out his hand to Nenuphar, and she responded by holding out hers but was rather surprised when he kissed it instead of shaking it.

"Reverend Tregaskis, at my service," he said.

"Nenuphar," she said.

"Nice soul," he complimented her and shook hands with M Cadvare, whose spirituality he also admired.

M Cadvare and Nenuphar stared at him.

"We'd like to hire a special," said Hob.

"What did you have in mind?"

"Oh just something big enough for me and my companions."

"I've got a Crampton you can borrow. It can't manage the weight of the trains we're running today, but running light it should prove plenty fast enough for those who feel the need, the need for speed."

Reverend Tregaskis clicked his fingers at some porters who left their piles of luggage and hefted *Nosferatu*'s crate onto their shoulders. He led the way to the end of the platform where a barrow crossing took them across the tracks to the marshalling yard. This was nearly as busy as the station, and they had to avoid numerous harassed porters with heavily laden luggage trolleys. Reverend Tregaskis paid them no attention as they took avoiding action. They often veered off the planking and into the ballast, where toppling luggage cases burst open against the rails and spilt their diabolical contents among the sleepers.

Most of the engines were resolutely black, a satin finish that indicated that even goods engines were lovingly cared for. However, there was one that looked like it had been gold plated. M Cadvare had to squint as they walked past Liege et Maastricht Number 1. In the gloom of the goods yard, it was almost too painful to look at.

"Rather splendid isn't it?" said Reverend Tregaskis. "It wasn't my idea. That's the original livery. The boiler and firebox are all finished in polished brass."

"Must be the devil itself to keep clean," muttered Nenuphar.

"Oh no, just a question of eternally damned manual labour. By way of reward for such sterling service, I've had the crew brass-plated as well."

From the green cab, a gilt-complexioned grease bogle and klinkergeist beamed at them proudly.

By now, the comfortable feeling that M Cadvare had felt on meeting Reverend Tregaskis had disappeared entirely.

"You're just another Soul Trader, aren't you?" he said.

"Monsieur Cadvare," Reverend Tregaskis replied, "you are surrounded by Soul Traders. STANTA is sponsoring a railway race to Albion and then Anarchadia."

"STANTA?"

"The Soul Transference and Necromancer's Trade Association."

Armies of porters and baggage handlers marshalled packing cases with elegant iron cranes. Shunters swarmed around low loader wagons carrying stage coaches made out of skulls and bones. Horse boxes were coupled next to them but the hay racks for their skeletal occupants were conspicuously empty.

Nearby, half a dozen spectral shunters, with flat caps and jackets over their blue overalls, and all sporting luxuriant moustaches, were trying to load a clockwork horse onto a low loader. They'd managed to separate it from the large unicycle to which it was usually bolted, but were now discovering that a horse full of gears and springs is even more top-heavy and tricky to handle than the live variety, especially when its main spring has been wound down and its iron legs are stiff and immovable.

"I commend *L'Archipel* to you," said Reverend Tregaskis. "Number 83 of the Chemin de Fer d'Est."

He indicated a low-slung machine that looked as if it were smiling at them with its deeply curved front buffer beam. This was necessary to allow access to the smokebox doors on its hunkered down boiler. It had deep outside frames, two widely spaced axles under its boiler and an enormous pair of driving wheels right at the back that flanked the crew. These wheels must have been well over two metres in diameter and apart from the chimney were the tallest part of the whole locomotive. Just like an open sportscar, there was no roof. Despite its evident antiquity, M Cadvare thought it looked like it was doing a hundred kilometres an hour even standing still.

"I'll get the road cleared for you and you can *prendre la Crampton*," said Reverend Tregaskis.

Nenuphar smiled. Unlike Hob, his pronunciation was perfect.

"I've heard that expression before," said M Cadvare.

"Indeed. The synonymity of the old *paysanterie* of *prendre la Crampton* with *take the train* has been flogged to death in a hundred otherwise decontextualised references. It does, however, symbolise the extent to which the Crampton locomotive fired the Gallic imagination. The flat open landscape of Northern France and the Low Countries suited the Crampton type admirably. Crampton wanted a boiler as low as possible to reduce the centre of gravity, and achieved this by putting the tallest wheels behind the boiler. With no restriction on axle height, larger wheels brought even greater speed and, with their low centre of gravity, Crampton locomotives were less inclined to go agricultural sightseeing when negotiating corners. Remember that at the time they were designed many thought that a human body could not stand speeds above thirty miles an hour!"

He laughed heartily with Hob at this idea.

"You speak as if you knew Crampton," said Nenuphar.

"Of course, I know him. He's out on the road at this very moment, with a later development of one of his stern wheelers, one with Jules Petiet's steam drying apparatus."

He watched with mild amusement as she realised the diabolical nature of their existence.

"And Jules Petiet?" she gulped.

"He's on the footplate with him. Now. Theirs *is* an inelegant contrivance. Nobody would blame you, my dear, for feeling uneasy in the presence of such excrescences of inelegant technical maculation! Mind you, I will admit to a certain fondness for the interesting details and singular lack of grace that some of the Continental engine builders could achieve. I'll introduce Messieurs Crampton and Petiet to you if I get the chance. They are the most fascinating fellows."

"Crampton feels at home here, then?" suggested M Cadvare.

"It was near here that the first railway in Continental Europe opened in 1836. A dozen years later and the French needed fast and smooth-running machines that could cope with relatively light trains. Crampton's engines were ideally suited for such a service and they became much more popular here than in his home in Britain."

The porters had just about got the clockwork horse onto a wagon when they became a little over-confident. It teetered sickeningly and then toppled over, crashing off the wagon to lie with its legs in the air.

Reverend Tregaskis scowled at them but they didn't notice. They were too busy staring at the hooves of the clockwork horse and hitting each other.

"So what's this thing good for?" asked Hob.

"I once timed a Nord Crampton at 93.8 miles to the hour," said Reverend Tregaskis.

"Wow, I had no idea stern wheelers were that good!" replied Hob, rubbing his hands gleefully.

All around the Crampton, M Cadvare could see half a dozen gremlins in stovepipe hats dashing between the cranks and bearings, polishing and oiling its most intimate places. On the footplate a pair of man-sized grease bogles and klinkergeists were just as busy.

"How long before we can get steam up?" asked Hob.

"Nutty Slack?"

"Yes, your irreverence?" answered the klinkergeist.

"Mobilise the pyroblins. My friends need to leave as soon as possible."

"Certainly, your irreverence."

The klinkergeist knelt down to open the firebox door and there was the reflection of a cheerful blaze on his face.

"Spoke Alarm!" called out Reverend Tregaskis.

A wheel tapper squeezed out from between the wheels of a nearby train to salute Reverend Tregaskis with his wheel-tapping hammer. "Yes, your irreverence?"

"Check the wheels on *L'Archipel*, this minute. Mendican? Make sure the engine is ready for Mr Hob."

"Certainly, your irreverence," said a grease bogle on the footplate.

"What's a pyroblin?" asked M Cadvare.

"It's a specialised kind of gremlin," explained Reverend Tregaskis. "They look a bit like an ordinary go-blin but are enveloped in flame. Hob and I both have dominion over them as we are, each of us, interested in combustion, Hob preferring that which is internal, internal to the cylinders, whereas I only countenance combustion external to the cylinders, as applied to the boiler of a steam locomotive. Now then, Hob. There is the small matter of payment."

"Ah. Yes." Hob turned to Nenuphar and M Cadvare. "Perhaps it would be a good idea if you waited over there. Reverend Tregaskis and I have some business to which we must attend."

The two Soul Traders put Hob's rucksack on *L'Archipel*'s smiley buffer beam and peered inside.

"I suppose you'll be ending up in there before too long," said Nenuphar, as she and M Cadvare waited by the Crampton's tender.

"I suppose I will."

"Never to emerge or be seen by men again."

"Oh I don't think it's quite that bad. I'll get let out of the sack with the rest of the *Terminal Murrain* for the Wild Hunt."

"Do you seriously believe Hob will let you go, once he has your soul?"

"A bit," M Cadvare replied.

"You've seen the way Reverend Tregaskis treats his souls. It's hell for them."

Despite their best intentions, they glanced back to where Hob and Reverend Tregaskis were trading souls. They seemed to be arriving at the final reckoning.

"But at least their souls still exist," pointed out M Cadvare.

"Mine still exists and belongs only to me," said Nenuphar, a little tartly.

"Yeah, well aren't you the lucky one."

"Luck doesn't come into it."

Reverend Tregaskis held up what appeared to be a particularly large soul, and he and Hob scrutinised it closely.

On the far side of *L'Archipel*, porters were dragging the clockwork horse slowly upright. With every slight change in its attitude there was an ominous metallic tinkling.

"I couldn't let my soul fall into the hands of the Conformorians," said M Cadvare. "If I hadn't promised it to Hob it would be destroyed by now."

"The lesser of two evils, eh?"

"It's not so bad. In fact I feel more alive than ever. I think his protection is about the best I can get. And then there is the forthcoming fulfilment of my dreams."

They gaped as Reverend Tregaskis took the soul he'd been examining in both hands and carefully tore it apart.

M Cadvare and Nenuphar looked at each other and gulped.

"There we are," said Hob, as he suddenly popped up in front of them. "All done."

He grinned at Reverend Tregaskis.

"Er, were you tearing a soul apart just then?" M Cadvare asked hesitantly.

"Hmm? Oh yes. What? Were you watching?"

"M Cadvare wouldn't ask if they had not been," said Reverend Tregaskis.

"We weren't tearing a soul apart," said Hob, "as you so picturesquely put it. We were adjusting its value."

"Adjusting its value?"

"Yes. You see, his irreverence here didn't have any change."

"So you just tore a strip off. Is that it?"

"It's not as simple as that," said Reverend Tregaskis.

"That soul was a multiple personality," Hob explained. "We separated it and made both parts more valuable."

The clockwork horse was now where it should be. It was upright, and externally it looked intact. Reverend Tregaskis's staff wandered round it. Then they picked it up and gave it a surreptitious shake. It didn't tinkle. It clanked.

Reverend Tregaskis sighed and walked into their line of vision and they dropped it again in their surprise. It clattered onto the railway tracks and both its ears broke off.

"Oh dear," said Hob, gently steering Nenuphar and M Cadvare away. "Those of you of a sensitive disposition may care to look the other way while Reverend Tregaskis deals with an Inhuman Resources issue. You might want to cover your ears as well, Nenny."

"Are you going to fost with this thing?" asked M Cadvare, raising his voice over the screams.

Hob grinned.

"There's always a first time."

CHAPTER 66

Reverend Tregaskis returned, muttering that he just couldn't get the staff these days. He soon cheered up, however, and showed Hob around the controls of *L'Archipel*, which was slowly coming to life as the pyroblins did their work in the firebox.

"I have to go now," he announced at last.

Several trains had rumbled out of the station as he'd been showing them around the Crampton but there were still many Soul Traders milling about on the platforms.

"They daren't travel overland, even in their fiendish carriages," explained Reverend Tregaskis.

"Deutz isn't scared," Hob told him. "He brought us here in his horseless carriage and has gone south."

"Deutz is not – how can I put this – not like the rest of us. He should be all right. It's the risk they perceive that's driven all these other Soul Traders underground."

"A perception you do nothing to dispel," said Hob, with a grin.

"Every cloud has a silver lining," said Reverend Tregaskis. "We'll squeeze them in somehow. Charleroi is singularly blessed in terms of abandoned rail links. About thirty years ago a new tram system was planned but the estimates of the revenue were wildly optimistic and although much of the new system was built it was never opened. It's lain dormant ever since. My minions and I have made frequent and extensive use of it."

There was a whistle, and a terracotta tank engine with a square chimney muscled away from the platform.

"But where do we go from here?" asked Nenuphar.

"You'll go straight through to Waterloo," said Reverend Tregaskis. "That's Waterloo station in London, in England, as opposed to the village down the road."

"Marvellous thing, pomp and ceremony," said Hob. "Come to our country and you'll disembark at a station named after your most famous military defeat."

"One thing about Euphobia," said Reverend Tregaskis, "is that there will be no more Unification Wars."

"There are already Devolution Wars," said Hob, darkly.

"Not officially. The Conformorians have kept the lid on them. They really are the most formidable foe. It's difficult to see how we can win against them in the present circumstances. Have either of you heard of *zwanze*?"

Hob and his companions shook their heads.

"It's almost entirely disappeared," lamented Reverend Tregaskis. "It survived Napoleon, the Franco-Prussian War and both Unification Wars, and until recently still existed in the mischievous subterfuge and wit of the souls I sourced here. It was the spirit of Brussels. *Zwanze* is now an alien concept to the current generation, even those who retain their souls."

"So we make a tactical withdrawal," said Hob, with a gloomy glance at Nenuphar.

"Precisely," said Reverend Tregaskis. "Take as much *zwanze* with you as you can. Nurture your spirits, be they your own or those of others. You should be able to go in about thirty minutes. I must just sort out my signalling staff."

"Good luck."

"Thank you," said Reverend Tregaskis, with a wry smile, "but unless I can impose some sort of order on my signal sylphs, you'll be in greater need of luck than ever once you leave here."

"Ah, I see your point. Anyway, thank you for all you've done." Hob shook his hand. "It's been a pleasure doing business with you."

Reverend Tregaskis smiled again. "Leave *L'Archipel* in the hands of my grease bogles at Waterloo. Farewell Nenuphar, my dear." He kissed her hand again and then he shook hands with M Cadvare. "I remain, as ever, nobody's obedient servant," and Reverend Tregaskis turned and strode purposefully towards the signal box.

CHAPTER 67

Kevin liked being in Anarchadia. He was secretly proud of his happy accident, although this would always be balanced by regret over the fate of the dinosaurs. But as temperate archipelagos went, Anarchadia was a great success.

It lay in a strange and stormy sea of its own, the Antagonistic Ocean, and, considering the trade that Anarchadia enjoyed with the rest of the world, it always surprised him how few sailors knew of its existence, let alone how to sail its tricky waters. Fortunately, centuries of experience in travelling to Anarchadia had given him a knack in finding a passage.

He'd found this one by mooching around a car showroom in Albion. If you knew the signs, as he did, it was obvious that somebody was trading in horsepower. Once he'd found out who was in charge, all he had to do was say things like, "Do you know? This reminds me of when I was in the Wild Hunt. I thought for a moment I was back in Old Anarchadie and the Horsepower Wars!"

It was an unsubtly coded remark. Its real message was, "Do what I want and I won't alert the commodity inspectors."

So he here he was, back where he felt most at home and furthest away from the cares of the commonplace world. Unsurprisingly, he'd landed in Lanson, the biggest port on the western side of Kernewek, the largest island in the group.

Unlike the cities in Post Unification Euphobia, Lanson revelled in its cosmopolitan make-up. People of all nationalities had been drawn here by the promises of the Wild Hunt. The Horsepower Wars insulated Anarchadia from the vagaries of conventional economics and, because the rich had engineered another economic recession to make themselves feel rich again, Anarchadia was now pulling in the best brains from Africa, the Antipodes, Japan and the Sub Continent, and given home to refugees from China and South America. There were even social clubs for expatriates from Gondwanaland. Most numerous of all, however, were the engineers who had escaped from the over-regulated Euphobian and Consumerican trading blocks.

Once Kevin disembarked from the game little container vessel that had braved the waters of the Antagonistic Ocean, he walked along the dockside, revelling to be back. It was a transient place where everything and everyone was on the move. The waterfront was a temporary limbo. Newcomers were not able to enter the main city until invited and, like most settlements in Anarchadia, Lanson was a walled city. If you knew people on the inside who were prepared to vouch for you then you could visit as a guest. If enough people liked you, they might even invite you to join them as a resident, and a select few passed straight through into Lanson and beyond, to the great industrial hinterlands of Mercia and The Riding.

But Lanson's waterfront attracted vast numbers of newbies since there were always plenty of ships to unload. And the Horsepower Wars could always consume new talent.

Kevin had the connections to enter Lanson straightaway, but today he chose not to. He wanted to see Anarchadia the way most immigrants saw it, and what he saw made him feel quietly happy. There was something extra about the place. He wondered what it was. An extra dimension? He'd have to ask Therese when he next saw her. An extra sense of purpose? It wasn't as grim as that. It was more ebullient. Anarchadia did things not just to the mind but also to the soul. If he couldn't quite rationalise it, he could feel it. It made his blood sing. Anarchadia was a land of endless possibility, a place where you could follow your destiny.

That's what so frightened governments and despots across the world. Anarchadia didn't need them and was flourishing. If word got out, others would begin to question why any sort of ruler was needed at all.

Acting together, they might have been able to destroy Anarchadia but they never reached any consensus. Kevin knew why. They were all secretly trading with it. Anarchadia exported power in nice mobile packages. It also offered a ready market for some of their materials and commodities, too. Raising a gun at Anarchadia would be like aiming one at their own hearts.

As he wandered through Lanson's docklands, he passed many churches. You could worship anyone you liked in Anarchadia, and newbies often felt a rush of spirituality on landing and the need to give profuse thanks. Along the waterfront, every denomination seemed to be catered for and in between the vast warehouses and boarding hostels were small mission churches.

There was one in particular that caught Kevin's eye. It belonged to the Worshipful Company of Malik Tawus and was easily the biggest and newest of all. Its style was what might be called Enthusiastic Gothic, but what really struck Kevin was its alignment. It had been built the wrong way round. It didn't face east but faced west.

Outside was a large gathering of people. They lined the steps up to the three arched doors and were waiting in what could only be called fearful anticipation. Kevin halted across the road and decided to watch.

He didn't have to wait long. A striking figure appeared in the central doorway and everyone lining the steps bowed down to him. He was well above average height and even then appeared to be larger than mere life might lead you to expect. He moved with an animal grace and wore a very well-cut suit with a waistcoat covered in blue/green eyes. He made his way down the lines of supplicants, who offered him all manner of worldly riches. Some of the women seemed to be offering themselves and were delighted when they were accepted, presumably for consumption later.

Kevin stood fascinated as this magnificent figure made his way down the steps to street level, where he turned and held his arms out to his fans.

"Thank me for having you," he said and he waggled his eyebrows at the ladies.

The crowd cheered and as they ran back inside the church, he turned around and Kevin found himself in front of a suddenly familiar figure.

He'd seen eyebrows do that before.

"I know who you are!" he cried.

"Cower, brief mortal!" replied the charismatic figure in the sharp suit.

The eyes on his waistcoat hypnotised Kevin and he felt himself sliding through the traffic across the road until he was on the other side of the street.

"Bub!" he said.

Beelzebub frowned. "Do I know you?"

"Yes," said Kevin, taking off his woollen hat.

"Kevin?" Beelzebub beamed at him in recognition. "I'm terribly sorry, I didn't recognise you."

"Yes," gulped Kevin. "It's this Discretion of the Soul Hat."

"Really? Well! It certainly works! Where did you get it?"

"A beautiful young scientist knitted it for me."

"Hey!" said Bub, in a characteristically licentious manner. He nudged Kevin in the ribs with his elbow. "You old rascal!"

"She had some guidance from the grauniads of this paraverse," said Kevin, picking himself up.

"Grauniads?" Beelzebub frowned. "Bunch of interfering busy bodies! Do I know this beautiful young scientist?"

"I doubt it. She doesn't believe in you."

"What?"

"She doesn't believe in God, either."

"I could change that," muttered Beelzebub, darkly.

"Oh don't do that," said Kevin. "She's really nice and means well."

"Not thinking of being unfaithful to Eve, are you?"

"Eve is dead."

"Yeah, but you still get to visit her every forty years or so."

"It's every seventy-five nowadays because of the increased life expectancy," Kevin reminded him.

"All the more opportunity to grow apart."

"I am not tempted," said Kevin, rather haughtily.

"If I had a soul every time I heard that," said Beelzebub, "I'd be as rich as I am now."

Kevin had to think about this. "Business is still thriving, then?"

"Ooooh, yes!" said Bub rubbing his hands together. "Have you never considered starting up your own religion?"

"Me? I've seen all the trouble they can bring."

"I'm sure you'd be brilliant at it," Beelzebub replied gnomically. "You are the Soul of All Souls after all."

"I'm probably over-qualified."

"Y'know, Kevin? You and I have got a lot in common."

"We do?"

"Certainly."

"But you, you were cast down from heaven!"

"No I wasn't!"

"Yes you were!"

"I resigned."

"We've had this argument before," said Kevin.

"I resigned," Beelzebub insisted, "and you weren't expelled from Eden, you were retired. Remember? Those were God's own words."

"He always said *you* were dismissed."

Beelzebub sighed. "So why are you wearing this Discretion of the Soul Hat?"

"One of your lot is after my soul."

"What, again?" Beelzebub chuckled. "They *are* little rascals aren't they?"

"Were you just coming out of a church?"

"It's a temple not a church."

"What sort of temple would welcome the Prince of Darkness?"

"Come off it, Kevin. You must have heard of the Yezidis."

"Yezidis? Weren't they persecuted as heretics by Christians and Moslems alike?"

"Mm hm," said Beelzebub. "And do you know why?"

"No."

"The Yezidis are responsible for the greatest religious heresy of all."

"A heresy you happen to approve of."

Beelzebub beamed at him. "They are incredibly misunderstood."

"Okay. Let's hear it."

"They believe in a reconciliation between me and My Maker. Your Maker as well, come to that."

Kevin couldn't think of a reply so Beelzebub carried on.

"The Yezidis believe that I have been reinstated by Old Thunderpants Himself and am now in charge of running the world."

"That would explain a lot," said Kevin.

"No, wait a moment, hear me out. They refer to me as the Chief Angel, which I used to be, if you remember."

"Oh I remember."

"They also call me Malik Tawus, the Peacock Angel."

"Hence the waistcoat."

"Hence the waistcoat. They recognise me for what I am."

"So what are you, Peacock Angel?"

"I am the expression of man's darker desires, those with which he is least comfortable."

"I take it this reconciliation with God hasn't happened yet."

"Not yet, no, hence the persecution of my followers." Beelzebub looked at him quizzically. "Why?"

"I doubt you'd call God Old Thunderpants if it had. So adopting the persona of the Peacock Angel is a bit premature, isn't it?"

"It's not me, it's them. The Yezidi doctrine is a recognised faith here in Anarchadia."

"They tolerate any religion here. Even devil worshippers."

"Devil propitiators," corrected Beelzebub. "I don't want to be worshipped – just appeased!"

"Look, Bub, I'm glad you've finally got the recognition you deserve."

"But?" added Beelzebub.

"But is this reconciliation really going to happen?"

"To be perfectly honest, I don't know. God botherers set great store in redemption and forgiveness, but they're a bunch of hard-nosed bastards when it comes to me!"

"You haven't provoked them in any way, have you?"

"They started it! Anything they do that makes them feel guilty, they blame it on me. They never take responsibility for their own actions. They just go around saying 'The devil made me do it'."

"So the Yezidis are going to be disappointed," suggested Kevin.

"Not by me," Bub promised him. "I'm living up to their expectations as much as I can."

He looked up at the sky and sniffed the air through flared nostrils.

"Dark Time is coming, Kevin, Dark Time is coming."

CHAPTER 68

They made good speed with *L'Archipel*. Reverend Tregaskis had looked after it very well during the last hundred years or so, and it whisked them across the northern plains of France towards the coast, travelling on a single track line within a bubble of furious track fairy activity.

The track fairies popped into existence in front of their speeding engine with just enough space to exhume the slumbering railway line from the landscape before the locomotive ran them over. Then equally agitated scenes were played out in reverse as the blur of picks, shovels and wheelbarrows was thrown up again by the wheels of *L'Archipel*'s tender, with the result that the countryside was restored so that they travelled through it without leaving a trace.

In between firing *L'Archipel* under Hob's direction, M Cadvare watched the track fairies closely and decided that as they passed over the briefly reinstated track the track fairies took a short break before covering the shiny rails up again. They moved too fast for him to see for certain, but he felt that there was some sort of shift pattern going on, a kind of infernal railway production line that somehow leapfrogged the speeding steam engine

There was no other visible traffic, either ahead or behind, and whenever a signal briefly rocketed out of the ground it was always in their favour.

For most of the journey, the line ran with very little gradient and without the need for much in the way of occult engineering works, and *L'Archipel* settled into a steady rhythm, singing the Song of the Machine.

"Can anyone see us?" M Cadvare asked Hob.

"They might but they wouldn't want to."

"We're on a ghost train, aren't we?"

"Not really."

"How can you not really be on a ghost train?" put in Nenuphar.

Hob ignored her.

"Is this locomotive real?" she went on. "Is this railway real?"

"Tregaskis will tell you that old railways never really die," said Hob. "They merely slumber. And *L'Archipel* was broken up years ago. That's how it comes to be in his collection."

"So this is a ghost train," insisted Nenuphar.

"Hardly. It doesn't run to timetable on the anniversary of a disaster. And it doesn't run in some predestined groove. This trip is for once only."

"A once in a deathtime trip," quipped M Cadvare.

The sky grew increasingly overcast as they carried resolutely onwards. They barged through housing estates and retail parks, the track fairies speedily demolishing anything in their path before re-erecting it again after they'd gone through.

"Do you mind if I ask you a question?" asked Nenuphar.

"So long as you don't mind the answer," Hob replied.

"How are we going to get across the Channel?"

"The Channel?" repeated Hob, a little perplexed.

"Yes. You know. *La Manche*. That inconsequential stretch of water between Albion and mainland Euphobia."

"Oh that," said Hob. "We're going to use the old tunnel."

"What old tunnel?"

"The old one they started years ago. There might be some delay. I've never travelled like this before but I imagine there's a bit of a bottleneck just before it. There must be many trains converging on it tonight."

"Does Reverend Tregaskis have anything to do with it?"

"Of course. The British and French governments started it over a hundred years ago but lost interest. Tregaskis organised an army of gargoyles, track fairies, road pixies, zombies and New Age navvies to build it. Of course, that was long before my time but it's still talked about among the fey, even now."

They hurtled towards a wide expanse of river but without so much as a jolt the track fairies threw some girders across it and they flew over it in a bubble of railway history.

"Could we fost with this locomotive?" asked M Cadvare.

Hob beamed at him for suggesting it. "Shall we try?"

"What's a fost?" asked Nenuphar.

"It's a kind of leak," said M Cadvare.

"That's very good," said Hob approvingly.

"When you travel fast enough," went on M Cadvare, "strange things happen. We fosted in my personal transportation device and we sort of went through a red light and queues of oncoming traffic. I think we leaked out from a point in this world into another one nearby and popped back into this one again when the path of least resistance led us to return."

"I couldn't have put it better myself," Hob congratulated him.

"What happens if it doesn't work?" asked Nenuphar.

"What happens if it does?" retorted Hob.

"What about the track fairies?" she persisted. "We can't manage it without them."

"Yeah," said Hob as if he hadn't thought of that.

He walked along the footplate to the front of the engine and knelt down on the curved buffer beam. He shouted at the track fairies but none of them seemed to pay him any attention.

Hob came back to say, "They're up for it if we are," and he threw the regulator wide open.

"How fast can track fairies go?" M Cadvare asked him.

"I don't know and neither do they so we're gonna find out!"

L'Archipel's exhaust note changed to a bark and the spokes of the big driving wheels on either side of them became transparent as the landscape flew by on either side.

"The track fairies are working magnificently!" shouted Hob.

M Cadvare worked furiously to feed the fire.

Although they couldn't see the track ahead of the engine, they could see its track bed. It stretched dead ahead to the horizon. The landscape had become darker, as if it disapproved of a performance that challenged space and time.

An unexpected sunset began to pour pink sunshine on them from the right.

Hob began muttering.

"Spin up, wake up and live! Skip along the greased rails as lightning to the horizon. Spokes and big ends spin! Cranks crank! Pistons blur in cylinders as valves reciprocate and bearings run true and cool! Fire in the belly of the engine burns orange blue. Combustion? Be incandescent! Yield up to me the ghost of supernatural power. Valves that work better under pressure, shrive from friction and static inertia, revel in force, drive, motion! Revolution after revolution! Topple time and travail, transcend these dimensions and bring us to sensation! Eat the miles, shrink time and space! Take us to our vanishing point! Power and the glory! Revs without end, ring ding-a-ding!"

"How fast are we going?" cried Nenuphar, who was crouching out of the wind.

"We must be doing over the ton!" yelled Hob. "*L'Archipel*'s riding beautifully!"

A giant invisible hand had reached down to push them onward. They thundered away under the glowing skies, and the sunset beside them grew more brilliant.

"Is this what happens in a fost on a train?" she asked M Cadvare.

"How should I know?" he shouted back in between feeding the voracious firebox. "I've only fosted on four wheels before."

"Hold on!" shouted Hob, as if they weren't already. "We could arrive in Kent at any moment!" but M Cadvare stopped firing the engine and gaped at the sunset beside them.

"Hob?" he shouted. "Is that normal?" He pointed to the pink glow. "The sun's setting in the east!"

"What? Is it? Yes, you're right!"

"That's no sunset!" Nenuphar laughed. "It's a pink TGV!"

A pink *Train Grand Vitesse* was keeping pace with them.

"Who the hell's driving that thing?" demanded Hob, but the TGV was drawing ahead of them. "We're slowing down," he said, looking at the controls.

"Look at the TGV's track fairies!" said Nenuphar.

"What?" yelled Hob, following her gaze. "But they're all girls!" he exclaimed.

"And very girly girls by the look of them," laughed Nenuphar. "Is that you wolf whistling?"

She knew full well it wasn't, because a large number of track fairies perched on *L'Archipel*'s front buffer beam were ogling the most glamorous and feminine permanent way workers any of them had ever seen. The TGV's track fairies didn't move in a blur but sashayed languorously in spectacular evening wear, waving neat gardening trowels and dainty little pickaxes at the increasingly boisterous *L'Archipel* track fairies.

"Hey!" shouted Hob "Get back to work, you little sods!" but the track fairies paid him no attention.

"How can they travel faster than us?" shouted M Cadvare. "They're hardly trying!"

"They're all glammed up," chortled Nenuphar. "Hob! Their magic's even stronger than ours!"

"Well, we won't get to Albion by fosting," said Hob gloomily, and he pushed the regulator back from its wide open setting. "I think I know who's behind this, Cadaver. Remember when we fosted before and there was that bird in a pink Cadillac?"

"Yes. D'you think that's her?"

"Who else can it be?"

"She said something about not fosting."

"My gremlins would never behave like this! If I was on some of my own machinery we would still outrun her. We did before."

"Why can't you do it again?"

"Dammit Cadaver! I'm not so good on rails!"

Hob climbed out of the cab and went forward to have it out with the track fairies. There were many aggressive arm movements from the opposing parties and then Hob chased them all over the front of *L'Archipel*, but without achieving any more speed.

CHAPTER 69

Although Nenuphar had been dubious about Reverend Tregaskis's signalling staff, they had travelled this far without incident, much of it at a reckless speed. The signals flashed by so quickly she barely saw them, let alone understood what they signified. And even if there was a signal at danger, Hob probably wouldn't have obeyed it.

As she considered this, she began to wonder what could harm a steam locomotive that had already been destroyed. For some reason that she couldn't explain, she found this train of thought mildly re-assuring. What could harm that which had already been scrapped? Another steam locomotive in a similar condition? Would they both be indestructible? Would the track fairies take care of them if the spectral signallers did not?

Now that the pink TGV had gone, the track fairies were working hard again. They descended into a cutting, and from time to time disused railways swooped in from either side to join them. She couldn't be sure but she had a vague impression of the shades of other trains waiting patiently for them to pass. Then the earth rose up and swallowed them again.

Suddenly, they were in the tunnel. The track fairies became visible again as they threw themselves and their tools onto the buffer beams, stretched their arms and legs a little and opened their packed lunches.

Smoke should have filled the tunnel, but there seemed to be very efficient ventilation for it was whisked up into the roof and disappeared into a long vent that ran above the rails. There was also surprisingly good illumination provided by gaslights at regular intervals, and the glare from *L'Archipel*'s fire lit up the walls and ceiling whenever M Cadvare fed the firebox. It was clear that they were in a monument to civil engineering and the railway age. Nenuphar could see why it had impressed the fey. She had imagined the Channel Tunnel to be little more than a drain, but its walls were covered in murals depicting a mixture of classical and industrial scenes. A recurring theme was Prometheus lighting the fires of technology. Sometimes he held a torch in one hand and a dead eagle in the other. It was not a golden eagle but a rather dingy Grey One. Occasionally, Prometheus saluted what could only be a vicar. This reverend gentleman was also depicted as if he'd had a hand in the Titan's escape, and although they passed by quickly and the light could have been better Nenuphar realised there was something more than a little familiar about this man of the cloth.

Hob had been uncharacteristically quiet since the episode with the pink TGV. It had kept pace with them until just before the tunnel and he was convinced that the beautiful young scientist was responsible.

"But she must have had some help," he said. "She knew about track fairies and their weaknesses. I wouldn't have said she was the sort to have homuncular vision, would you, Cadaver?"

M Cadvare gave a very Gallic shrug.

"Of course," Hob went on, "you realise what this means, don't you?"

"We haven't a clue what you're talking about," said Nenuphar.

"She must be working with some supernatural agency," Hob went on.

"Er, is that good?" asked M Cadvare.

"Good? Good? Does it sound good to you? Of course it's not good! The question is, what sort of homunculus would she listen to? And what manner of homunculus would she be able to see?"

Nobody knew the answer to that one, and they travelled on in silence as the tunnel carried them downwards and the sensation of travelling underground deepened.

By the time the tunnel levelled out, Hob had reverted to his normal self. He seemed able to put his troubles behind him. It was when they were alongside or in front of him that the purple-black clouds swirled in his visor.

"How do you keep so clean?" he suddenly asked Nenuphar.

"I don't know," she replied nonchalantly. "Maybe I carry the same electrical charge as dirt and naturally repel it."

"Look at her, Cadaver! Riding on the footplate of a steam engine in a tunnel and not a speck on her!"

M Cadvare looked up from his shovelling and was about to agree, but Hob was advancing on Nenuphar with his dirty hands outstretched.

"No!" she cried and began clambering up the pile of coal in the tender to get away from him.

"Come here, my pretty!" replied Hob. He rubbed his thumb and first finger together by his top lip, and said as an aside to M Cadvare, "Twirls moustache fiendishly!"

Nenuphar squealed, not entirely with horror, and Hob leapt after her.

Although he came close to catching her, and might have if he'd really tried, he chased her ineffectually around the pile of coal on the tender for several laps until he leapt on top of *Nosferatu*'s crate and snarled at her dramatically as she slithered down the pile of coal into the arms of M Cadvare.

"Curses!" he cried. "Foiled again!"

Nenuphar stuck out her tongue at him but then Hob looked up and said, "Oops," and he was whisked away by an unexpectedly low gantry spanning the track.

They stared up at his receding expression of surprise.

M Cadvare sighed. He had been watching Hob drive the Crampton, so knew how to close the regulator and gently apply the brakes.

"What are you doing?" demanded Nenuphar. "Surely you're not going back for him?"

"How far do you seriously think we'll get without him?"

"Don't you want to escape?"

"We are escaping," said M Cadvare as he put the Crampton into reverse. "We just can't manage it on our own."

"Do you seriously believe he'll take us to Anarchadia?" she asked him.

"Nenuphar, we are riding on a one hundred and sixty year old steam locomotive that we've borrowed from a Soul Trader named Reverend Tregaskis."

"That's not the point!"

"We've escaped from the Conformorians twice and have learnt more than we could ever guess about what they are doing to souls."

"None of which means Anarchadia exists!"

"Look at the track fairies down there?" gestured M Cadvare.

They track fairies were following their conversation closely in a tableau of curling sandwiches and cooling tea.

"How can you not believe in Anarchadia after all the wonders we've seen?"

That she couldn't answer.

"Don't you want to believe?" M Cadvare asked her. "Don't you want to come with us?"

Nenuphar bit her bottom lip. "I'm scared," she said. "But where else am I going to go? I have as few options as you. I just don't like this idea of you selling your soul to Hob. It's not a done deal yet, is it?"

"We can't get to Anarchadia without Hob, and I think that from what we've seen so far he needs our help as much we need his."

"Yeah! Like he needs us like not at all!"

Hob was still dangling from the gantry when they pulled up beneath him. M Cadvare carefully stopped the tender under his boots and he stepped lightly onto *Nosferatu*'s crate.

"You came back then," he said.

"Did you think we wouldn't?" asked Nenuphar.

"Not really."

"We could have gone on without you."

"It's possible I suppose," admitted the Soul Trader. "You know, Cadaver? You're not such a bad bloke after all."

"He isn't a bad bloke," said Nenuphar. "Have you only just worked that out?"

Hob ginned at her with what could only be described as a knowing grin.

"You're not so bad yourself," he told her. "I don't usually spend this much time in the close company of my souls."

"Hey!" she protested. "I'm not one of your souls!"

"You're as good as," Hob said under his breath, just loud enough for her to hear. "But that doesn't matter. I'm enjoying this trip with you. It's been fun, hasn't it? Hasn't it?"

"Fun?" began Nenuphar, intending to be serious, but she failed to suppress a little smile.

"Yes," said Hob. "Fun."

"I'm certainly enjoying this a lot more than the alternative," admitted M Cadvare.

"Hmm," said Hob. "Well if you two people could somehow find it within yourselves to curb such embarrassing displays of euphoria – or could that be Euphobia? – we shall resume our journey," and he took the controls from M Cadvare.

"Hob?" asked Nenuphar.

"Yes my dear?"

"Can we ever win against the Conformorians?"

Hob looked thoughtful before turning to answer her.

"I don't know," he said. "I really don't know."

CHAPTER 70

They emerged from the tunnel into an enormous underground marshalling yard. The track fairies jumped down from *L'Archipel*'s front buffer beam and they began to limber up for work again as Hob drove *L'Archipel* slowly into Anarchadia.

"Who's guiding us?" asked Nenuphar, as *L'Archipel* negotiated some complicated point work under the direction of a signal. "On the other side we were just funnelling towards the tunnel. Here we can go in any direction."

"We're travelling under the guidance of Tregaskis's signal sylphs," Hob told them. "It's not something I'm used to doing. I prefer something with a bit more steering, a bit less pre-destination."

L'Archipel weaved between other trains, most of which were also moving slowly. Extraction ducting still hung down from an unseen ceiling but here, with so many trains, the air was thick with smoke, soot and sulphurous deposits.

Nenuphar couldn't see very far ahead but she could hear the bustle around them and was aware of spiritually covetous eyes regarding her from the dimly lit carriages that they passed.

"Where are we going?" she asked Hob.

"Tregaskis said Waterloo. The other one. It's in London."

"We are about to meet another Waterloo," said M Cadvare.

"One was enough," replied Nenuphar.

Gradually their way seemed settled. They steamed sedately through an elaborate archway that had been built with all the optimism of confident Victorian railway engineers, and found themselves under the same monochrome sky that they'd left behind in France. The track fairies became an indistinct blur again as they picked they way along an artificial scar that still showed through the undulating English countryside.

"Ever been to Albion before?" Hob asked his companions.

They both shook their heads.

"It's not what it was. It's a bit like Belgium. It's lost its *zwanze*. It still looks quite charming, though."

"But I've never seen such old buildings!" exclaimed Nenuphar. "Look at those amazing chimneys!"

"Not so many were destroyed in the last couple of unification wars as in the rest of Europe," said Hob.

"It's Euphobia," she tutted ironically. "How many more times?"

"They all pre-date the railway. That's why the track fairies don't have to demolish and re-erect them. It's the newer ones that are getting in the way."

"I wouldn't be surprised if the older buildings won't be demolished soon," said M Cadvare, gloomily. "I can't imagine any of them comply with the latest construction and use regulations."

Nenuphar found another shovel and helped him fire *L'Archipel*, but for a certified management auditor he looked as if life as a fireman suited him.

"I take it you've been here before," she asked Hob, in between shovels of coal.

"You'd better believe it. Lydden Hill's not far off our route. Neither's Brands Hatch."

"So is this Anarchadia?"

"No," he said with a chuckle. "That's still far off to the west of here."

L'Archipel had to work harder as hills became more frequent closer to London, and so did the track fairies. They would put on a spurt and increase the distance ahead of the locomotive whenever there was a bridge to quickly restore or a cutting to dig but somehow they still seemed to avoid being run over.

Nenuphar was trying to spot the track fairies moving redundant rails forward for re-cycling but couldn't see it. Occasionally, however, out of the corner of her eye she thought she saw one of them leaning on his pick or shovel and drinking something hot from an enamel mug. Once or twice they nodded and even toasted her but, when she looked again properly, there was just a blur of movement.

Soon the track fairies had to clear the track of increasing numbers of newer buildings that had been built across it. *L'Archipel* remained unstoppable, however, and they sank into many long abandoned tunnels. In between blackened arches of golden bricks, they caught sight of ever larger office buildings and tower blocks, but these glimpses became less frequent and they eventually proceeded like a mole once again, all three of them looking around for another break in the masonry that might reveal the first indication of the great terminus that awaited them.

In one tunnel the track fairies downed tools again but their pace didn't slacken.

"We're travelling on one of the underground lines," explained Hob. "Look at the track fairies."

"What are they doing?" exclaimed an incredulous Nenuphar.

"They're licking the electrified third rail for dares."

There was a flash and a bang and a track fairy bounced off the roof of the tunnel to land on the footplate beside them.

"Good ricochet," said Hob, picking him up.

All bad feeling over the affair with the pink TGV and its glamorous permanent way workers had gone.

Nenuphar picked up the track fairy's flat cap and tried to put it back on for him but his hair was all on end. His moustache had turned into a spectacularly hairy caterpillar.

"Are you all right?" she asked him.

The homunculus grabbed his cap from her and wriggled out of Hob's grip to join the others as another electrified track fairy flew by.

"I reckon you'd be able to see gargoyles now," Hob told her, but this prospect did not fill her with relish.

Lights showed up ahead and they saw an electric underground train waiting at a signal.

With regal dignity, L'Archipel cruised past as startled faces stared out of the brilliantly lit carriages.

"Stand up straight, you two," said Hob, but the effect was rather lost as track fairies lined L'Archipel's boiler and mooned at the disbelieving passengers.

An old-fashioned signal popped out of the masonry with a rumble of tumbling bricks and the track fairies did up their baggy trousers and hopped off the engine to start tunnelling through the wall.

"Here we are," said Hob, and they passed a sign that read "Waterloo welcomes careful engine drivers. Twinned with Waterloo (Société des Chemins de Fer Belge), Gare d'Austerlitz (Paris–Orleans Railway) and Battle (South Eastern Railway)."

This was not the Waterloo Nenuphar had been expecting. She had in mind a vast glass cathedral built in honour of the railways. Instead, she got an underground forest of cast iron columns. Overhead was a matrix of girders, pimpled with rivets and blackened with soot from belching chimneys that barely squeezed beneath them.

In the confined space the noise was deafening. Express engines panted on either side of them as they entered the station, and hordes of railway staff and fiendish passengers milled around the trains, rattling couplings, slamming carriage doors and hollering to each other. Ancient luggage trolleys were being coupled up for towing by small steam tractors that might have been built by ambitious model engineers.

"Do all these staff belong to Reverend Tregaskis?" Nenuphar asked Hob, as she peered into the murk that engulfed them.

"Every single one," he answered.

"Will they be evacuated, too?"

"I doubt it. Tregaskis may need to travel across Euphobia again. Since none of his staff have their own souls, they probably can't be harmed by the Grey Ones."

"Probably," echoed Nenuphar, with a doubtful glance at M Cadvare.

"Besides," Hob went on, "there isn't any room for all of them here, and Tregaskis will need some for the upkeep of his network even while he's away. I imagine it'll go into a programme of care and maintenance."

"Using a skeleton staff," quipped M Cadvare.

Nenuphar giggled.

"You!" scolded Hob, pointing a grubby finger at him. "You should be ashamed of yourself!"

He appeared to be in a sudden and incandescent rage but they knew him well enough by now to know that it was just a façade and that if they'd been able to see his eyes they would have been laughing with them.

"You don't know the half of it, Cadaver. Grease bogles, klinkergeists, wheel tappers, pyroblins, spectral shunters, signal sylphs, track fairies, turntable turners, skeleton staff – they're all necessary for the smooth running of the network. And even if it's not running, there's coal to be polished and hanging baskets to be watered for the perpetual heats of the Best Station in Gloom competitions."

The work of the track fairies was nearly over. Many were clearly visible, sitting on *L'Archipel*'s buffer beam, waving to their colleagues on other trains. Their last job was to superintend the crossing of a few points, and *L'Archipel* coasted up to a short platform next to a long train of chocolate and cream Pullman carriages.

Hob closed the regulator and they rolled under their own momentum, to come to rest just before the buffers at the end of the line.

Next to them was an impressive semi-streamlined express locomotive in an attractive green. It had thin gold stripes down its flanks and wore a smokebox crest on its front that proclaimed that it was *The Golden Arrow*.

The track fairies gave a barely audible sigh and began doing their cooling-down stretches on the edge of the platform.

"Mr Hob, sir, we've been expecting you."

The speaker was a distinguished station master.

"Splendid," replied Hob. "We had a very good journey. *L'Archipel* is a fine locomotive."

"Thank you, sir."

"Hallo Hob."

"Tregaskis! What are you doing here?"

"I was on the footplate of *The Golden Arrow* beside you."

"How did you get here before us? We didn't see you overtake us, did we?"

"I used another channel tunnel."

"Another one?" asked Nenuphar. "How many of them are there?"

"Half a dozen," Reverend Tregaskis told her. "All abortive attempts apart from the Euphostar, of course. I just got my staff to finish them off."

"Wow," said Hob, who seemed genuinely impressed.

"My network girdles the earth."

"What?" said Nenuphar. "Even the great oceans?"

Reverend Tregaskis smiled at her. "Yes, my dear. Even the oceans, although they are not traversed by tunnels. You see, I have an especial arrangement for my boat trains."

"Ah!" said Hob. "You and Davy Jones!"

"Indeed," replied Reverend Tregaskis, with a slight bow. "I trust you all had a good journey?"

They all nodded.

"What form of transport will you be adopting for the next stage of your journey?"

"I think it's time for a little Wild Hunt," said Hob.

Reverend Tregaskis laughed. "You have shown remarkable restraint until now, my dear fellow!"

Hob snorted.

"We tried to fost with your locomotive," M Cadvare told Reverend Tregaskis, "and would have managed it had it not been for a pink electric locomotive that drew alongside and distracted our track fairies."

"Yes," said Reverend Tregaskis. "It happened to you as well, then? Hence my arrangement with Captain Davy Jones over the boat trains. Just when I'm about to fost, a pink TGV appears alongside, and my eternal way staff lose all interest and I'm compelled to slow down. The track sylphs exercise a peculiar power over the track fairies. Theirs is an ancient magic that predates the iron road by thousands of years."

"I take it you don't have dominion over them," asked Nenuphar.

"No, much as I would like to. They don't actually do any track work at all, but they perform a dance, the Dance of the Sleepers, and this holds my predominantly male eternal way staff entirely in their thrall."

"So the track sylphs don't want you to fost," Hob surmised.

"That's correct. But my humanikins believe the glamorous feminine track fairies are in the service of an even higher order of lares and penates, one that is determined to stop us from fosting."

"Tregaskis? You remember I once asked you about a beautiful young scientist driving a pink Cadillac?"

"Beehive hair do?"

"Glasses like the tail lamps on a Chevy Impala?"

"That's the one."

"This pink TGV was the same colour as her Cadillac."

"And she stopped you from fosting, you say?"

"She tried!"

"She succeeded," put in Nenuphar.

Hob glared at her.

Reverend Tregaskis stared into the distance. "Before the TGV appeared, there were some other incidents. Just before fosting I often saw an attractive young woman lying across the rails."

"Really?"

"Yes. She would just pop out of nowhere. It gave my track fairies and me quite a shock, I can tell you."

"What did you do?"

"I accelerated and fosted, of course. Running over damsels chained to the tracks is what I do. When I get the chance. But the track fairies insisted this young woman winked out of existence just as my wheels were about to pass over her. What do you make of that?"

"I reckon she introduced the pink TGV and the track sylphs once she realised that sort of behaviour only encouraged you."

Hob pulled *Nosferatu*'s crate off *L'Archipel*'s tender and put it on a luggage trolley behind a half-scale Wallis and Stevens traction engine.

"The Wild Hunt will run tonight," he said darkly, patting *Nosferatu*'s crate. "That should flush her out again in her Cadillac, but I will need something with more seats for my friends here."

"That is but a small obstacle for a Horsepower Whisperer," said Reverend Tregaskis.

The little steam engine chuffed off ahead of them.

"My engineering facilities are entirely at your disposal."

"Thank you, your irreverence."

"For a notional fee, of course," and Reverend Tregaskis smiled with interest at Nenuphar just as she was beginning to like him.

They walked along the platform to the stairs and climbed out of the noise and the smoke into what appeared to be the bowels of another railway terminus above them. Gloomy offices lit by gaslight and manned by shady ticket spectres gave way at the next floor to darkened corridors of cellars and store rooms. At the next landing, Nenuphar was shocked to see a fluorescent light fitting, albeit one that flickered with age, and on the landing after that there was the barest suggestion of some natural light filtering through from somewhere overhead.

They emerged at last at the foot of the main booking hall at Waterloo railway station. The main concourse was full of people, but few paid them any attention, even when some double doors behind them opened and a half-sized traction engine emerged, driven by a nervous-looking grease bogle and drawing *Nosferatu*'s crate behind it.

"I take it you will be travelling by road to Anarchadia," said Reverend Tregaskis.

Hob nodded. "It's time," he said, flexing his fingers. "Much as I have enjoyed driving your *L'Archipel*, I feel the need for some internal combustion."

Reverend Tregaskis pulled a slight face. "We have only so much in

common, Hob," he said, "but if you are stranded, make your way to Padding-
ton. The old Great Western slumbers there much as the South Eastern and
South Western slumber here."

But Hob wasn't listening.

His dark visor swirled and the wheels in its clouds revolved more quickly than Nenuphar had ever seen before.

"What is it, Hob?" she asked.

Hob peered up into the great canopy of Waterloo for some time before
turning back to look at them.

"We are being watched," he said.

His companions looked at each other. Reverend Tregaskis effortlessly
unloaded *Nosferatu*'s crate and waved for the cowering grease bogle to retreat.
Then they all followed Hob's gaze.

"How do you know we're being watched?" Nenuphar asked him.

"Can't you feel it?" Hob replied. "It's a common enough sensation. Come
now, Nenny, you should learn to trust your instincts. Being female, you have a
head start on the rest of us. Are you even remotely in touch with them?"

"Of course."

"And what do they tell you?"

"That we're being watched," she told him lamely.

Hob smiled. "That'll do for a start."

The crowds around them were behaving normally. There were, however, any number of waiting passengers who might be taking more of an interest
in them than they were prepared to show. This was an old feeling, a feeling that
Nenuphar had known well, back in Mourion. It was the normal paranoia that
every modern Euphobian felt.

She was just about to ask Hob what he was talking about when she
caught a rusty red flash out of the corner of her eye. Something had darted
behind one of the supporting columns and now, high up and very close to the
glass roof, it was peeking at them through the elaborate ironwork.

Just as she realised where it was hiding, it fell like a stone behind the
main destination board.

Hob didn't say anything but just stood and waited. It wasn't long before
a movement along the bottom edge of the destination board became visible and
Nenuphar recognised a face, a long upside-down face.

Hob grinned and held out an arm at shoulder height.

The face registered pleasure at this gesture and dropped off the bottom
of the destination board in another rusty red flash.

The next thing Nenuphar knew, she heard the sound of a large umbrella
being rapidly opened and closed, and an Anarchadian Flying Fruit Bat Fox was
dangling upside down from Hob's arm.

"Well, well," said Hob, "and who do we have here?"

The flitterfox hopped self consciously from one foot to another, licking his lips and flattening his ears.

"Julian?" whispered Nenuphar.

Julian looked at her sharply with suddenly erect ears and went "Ha-a-ha-a-ha-a-ha!" and wagged his tail.

"It is Julian, isn't it?" she said softly.

"Nn, nn, nn," whined Julian, and he wagged his bushy tail like a propeller.

"What a magnificent creature!" said Reverend Tregaskis.

Nenuphar let Julian sniff her hand and then stroked his luxuriant fur.

"He has no place here at all," remarked Reverend Tregaskis.

"What do you mean?" asked Nenuphar.

"He's an Anarchadian Flying Fruit Bat Fox. They're simply unheard of in London."

"We've met Julian before," she told him.

By now they were all stroking him and Julian obviously adored such attention but a strange and urgent expression suddenly overtook him. He shook himself and flew up to a girder a little way off.

He looked back over his shoulder and barked at them before flying off to the next girder. When it was obvious that they hadn't moved, he flew back to the first girder and barked again, wagging his tail above him like a furry helicopter.

"I think he wants us to follow him," said M Cadvare.

The others turned slowly to look at him.

"Well don't you?" he asked them.

"Julian?" said Hob, shouldering *Nosferatu*'s crate.

"Ha-a-ha-a-ha-a-ha!" Julian replied.

"Would you like us to follow you?"

Julian licked his nose, shook his head in a kind of nervous sneeze and went, "Nn! Nn! Nn!"

"Was that a yes?"

"Ha-a-ha-a-ha-a-ha!"

"It would appear that this is where we must leave you," Hob told Reverend Tregaskis. They shook hands. "Thank you for all your help."

"My dear fellow, think nothing of it. It's been a pleasure. I wish you and your companions good luck and *bon voyage*."

He kissed Nenuphar and shook M Cadvare's hand and then, since the stairs that they had used before seemed to have disappeared, sank regally into the shiny floor of Waterloo station.

CHAPTER 71

They followed Julian for a long way. He flew quickly and often left them behind but would always come back for them if they got lost in the crowds. His enthusiasm kept Nenuphar and M Cadvare going but eventually Hob noticed they were flagging and bought them some food from a small pastry shop. They stopped under a bridge and sat on *Nosferatu*'s crate to eat it and Julian, who at first seemed impatient for them to follow him, suspended himself nearby and washed his ears.

He wasn't stationary for long, though.

Hob caught a look in his eyes and threw some pastry at him and Julian deftly caught it and ate it. This was the start of a big game where they threw a scrap of pasty or sandwich into the air and it was intercepted by their very own Red Arrow. Julian appeared to be entirely omnivorous although Nenuphar discovered he wasn't keen on aubergines. When they'd finished their impromptu meal the acrobatics continued for a little while and then Julian brought them an ornamental shepherd's crook to throw for him.

"Where did he get that?" wondered Nenuphar.

"I'd rather not know," said M Cadvare.

She picked it up and Julian went, "Ha-a-ha-a-ha-a-ha!"

"It must be two metres long," she said.

"Come along," said Hob. "This is all very diverting, but I think our aerial guide has a job to do."

From his expression it was clear that Julian agreed and was grateful for the reminder. He plucked the crook from Nenuphar and flew off to return it to a nearby archbishop looking for something in the back of his limousine.

Julian came back, barked at them, and the chase was on again.

"Couldn't we hire a taxi?" asked M Cadvare, as he staggered along on stiffened legs.

"Okay," said Hob, "let's try it," and he hailed a cab.

A black cab pulled up straight away.

Hob pointed somewhere above the shop fronts.

"Quick! Follow that bat!"

The cab driver looked at him for a couple of seconds without saying a word.

Then he locked all his doors and quickly drove off in the opposite direction.

Hob turned to the others.

"I don't think he had room for my luggage," he told them.

"Where do you suppose Julian's taking us?" asked Nenuphar.

"I don't know," replied Hob. "But I think I might know to *whom* he's leading us."

Hardly anyone noticed Julian swooping from one architectural feature to another. Humans rarely look up but, if ever they did, Julian would strike a pose and pretend he was a terracotta moulding and they would blink and would convince themselves that a large red fruit bat was not flying around their capital city.

It wasn't long before they found themselves in an alley somewhere in Lambeth. Julian's behaviour changed markedly. He came quite close to them, but still kept just out of reach as if they had some final task to undertake.

"Why do I feel like he's herding us?" Nenuphar asked M Cadvare.

"That's because he is herding us," he told her. "He's herding us towards this door."

The door in question was a steel-plated affair with a small grille and a peephole let into it. From somewhere within, they could hear music. Or rather they could feel it through the pavement.

An old lamp was mounted over the door on an arched bracket and Julian dangled from it and looked at them eagerly, in turn.

"I think he wants us to knock," said Hob.

"Ha-a-ha-a-ha-a-ha!" said Julian and he wagged his tail.

Hob knocked.

A hatch behind the grille slid back and the music briefly grew louder but, before they could see anyone looking at them, the grille slid shut again, muffling the music. Then the steel-plated door swung open like a welcoming musical safe.

Two enormous men in straining dinner jackets gazed down at them. One was white and the other was black. Both were completely bald and each must have been a full two metres across their shoulders.

"You're expected," said the black one.

He felt a draught on his neck and glanced up, but saw only a heraldic device dangling from the nightclub's lamp above him. He peered suspiciously at Julian but Julian kept very still. Not even the wind blowing down the alley ruffled his fur.

Hob indicated his crate "Do you have somewhere to put this?"

Above the doormen, Julian kept silent but wagged his tail.

The white doorman nodded and gestured to a room just inside the wall.

Hob pushed his crate inside and took off his rucksack.

"Fortunato? I'm trusting you to be good, okay? Soon, soon we'll ride again! But for now, be calm, stay cool."

There was a red flash between the doormen but it could easily have been a stray special effect from the dance floor at the end of a short corridor.

The doormen closed the door behind them.

"What sort of music do you play here?" Hob asked them.

"Boys R Us, the usual chart stuff."

"What is this place?" asked Nenuphar.

"It's the Nightclub with No Name."

The three of them approached the dance floor, which was packed.

"I don't think I like Boys R Us," said Hob.

He didn't have to raise his voice to be heard over the music.

Julian flew up to the ceiling and orbited a large cooling fan for a couple of revolutions before alighting on a fan blade and dangling underneath it. He whizzed around, swinging upwards and outwards with centrifugal force, as if on a fairground ride.

"Now what?" shouted M Cadvare.

But Julian seemed to have heard him over the loud music and was looking intently in their direction with every rotation. He barked and wagged his bushy tail.

"We've followed that flitterfox this far," said Hob. "Isn't it obvious? He wants us to join in the dance."

"But I can't dance!" protested M Cadvare.

"Not to this rubbish you can't! Come on. Let's go and talk to our new friend the DJ."

He led them through clouds of raspberry-flavoured smoke to the DJ's enclosure. He pulled a CD from his jacket.

"I'd be much obliged if you could see your way to playing this," Hob said to the DJ.

The DJ wore shades and all the trappings of Street fashionality. "You the audience, I the DJ, man."

"Is that a yes or a no?"

"No, man."

"That was the wrong answer," said Hob.

"Look," said Nenuphar, before Hob could grab the DJ, "would you play it for us? Please?"

"For the lady, okay. Maybe the first track. What is it anyhow?"

"Soul music," said Hob.

The DJ frowned.

"Go ahead. You might like it."

"I don't think he will," M Cadvare said into Hob's ear. "He has no soul."

"Maybe that's all about to change," Hob replied as the DJ took the CD.

The DJ looked at the cover on the jewel case. Somebody very much like Hob was standing next to a sinister-looking blues man. Both of them were grinning diabolically. The title of the album was *Now that's what we call Soul Music!*

The next thing he knew – One, two three! One two three! – and they were in the *Land of a thousand dances* thanks to Wilson Pickett.

"That's better!" said Hob as he danced energetically. He knew Nenuphar and M Cadvare didn't believe he'd so much as crossed a dance floor before, so he deliberately got it on down like an amphetamised snake on legs. His arms and feet became mere blurs and his hyperactive pelvis burst through the normal constraints of space and time and began to co-exist in sundry parallel universes.

Nenuphar began to wriggle a little self-consciously around the spot where she would have put her handbag if she'd brought it, but after a few beats she loosened up and lost herself in the rhythm.

"Come on!" Hob said to M Cadvare.

"But I can't dance!" he protested.

"By the ball pein hammer of St Bendix, you poor benighted soul! You've never danced since you became an adult, have you? Come on. Just do what I do."

"Yeah!" yelled Nenuphar enthusiastically. "Come on!"

And, much to his surprise, M Cadvare did and when the time came he even knew the words.

"Na nana nana, nana nana nana nana, nana na na! Wwwwhhhaaao-ooww!"

Suddenly, the rest of the crowd knew the words, too. The dance floor was very crowded, but somehow there was more room if everyone danced instead of just standing still. It wasn't long, however, before Hob became separated from the others.

He was having a good time and really enjoyed dancing, but hadn't forgotten why they were there. He kept a close eye on Julian, who was still riding round on the big fan overhead. The flitterfox seemed to be urging him on.

By now, *Land of a thousand dances* had come to an end and Fred Hughes was singing *Don't let me down.*

Hob reached up to his right eye and gently lifted that side of his visor, so that he could get his fingers underneath. Rays of a bright bluish light flashed out, despite him using his left hand as a shield. The other dancers around him interpreted his performance as a light show and gathered round appreciatively, still dancing, not knowing how dangerous a glance from one of Hob's unprotected eyes could be. Hob plucked out his eyeball and held it aloft in his fist, filtering its rays between his fingers, with a length of optic nerve coiling down to his black visor.

He pointed it around the nightclub, throwing pale blue rays over the heads of his fellow dancers but not so much that it could damage their sight. In the middle of the swirling crowd, he saw his companions moving easily to the rhythm.

He stuck his arm in the air like he just didn't care, and with his eyeball held aloft it was much closer to Julian riding on the cooling fan. The flitterfox was fascinated by such peculiar behaviour. He seemed to be orbiting Hob's upheld eye and trying to attract his attention towards another figure in the crowd.

The music changed to *Starlight* by The Supermen Lovers and – at last – Hob saw her and was transfixed.

He'd met plenty of good-looking women before so his heart needn't have jolted as it did when he saw her. He'd also met her twice already and had even been brought here by her familiar, Julian. But when he'd caught that first glimpse of her eyes, as he'd walked down the autoroute to Mourion, he had sensed something familiar in a perfect stranger. Of course, familiars are common enough among Soul Traders but, as he'd gazed into the windows of her soul, Hob had felt more than just familiarity. It was a kind of intimate sense of ease, a soul he felt he recognised somehow. And this was with the most perfect of strangers, one whom he'd never known before. It was the most pleasant of pleasant surprises.

The next time they met, they had both been faced by Conformorian guards. There was an unspoken sense of being on the same side, even though she was evidently married to a Euphobian Commissioner.

Now that they gazed upon each other for the third time, across a crowded dance floor, angels sang, although they were probably Hell's Angels.

Hob stared at Heidi Bland and had a vague sensation of grauniads stopping the paraverse dead in its tracks so they could gawp at them like everyone else. The grauniads must have seen people fall in love countless times before. In fact, it happened thousands of times a second. Sometimes it developed after a long period of knowing each other and sometimes it arose after a relatively short acquaintance, but the suddenness of this particular mutual infatuation must have been worth their study.

Hob grinned at Heidi and she smiled back.

His thumbs pricked for a moment and there was a brief flash of a pink Cadillac somewhere in the nightclub. Out of the corner of his raised eye, Hob caught sight of a figure in a very tall haircut remonstrating with the grauniads. Grudgingly, they re-activated the space/time continuum. The dancers around Hob and Heidi danced, and the pink Cadillac faded out, but not before the beautiful young scientist had taken a good look, too.

Slowly the world began turning again.

Heidi was wearing a slinky black thigh-length dress and not much in the way of jewellery, but she looked fantastic.

Hob exchanged a glance with his glowing eye in his fist.

Thank badness she's not ugly, he thought. Or maybe she was. Maybe she had set a powerful glamour over him and one day he'd find himself next to a monster. He felt flattered to think of the trouble to which she must have gone to bewitch him so comprehensively. Of course, if she had gone to such lengths, it could only mean that he was in danger but then, wasn't that the thrill of life? To cheat death, to smuggle oneself out from the jaws of certain disaster and to race on the ragged edge in the Wild Hunt just made life profoundly sweeter.

"Hob?" asked Nenuphar, suddenly at his elbow. "Are you all right?"

Hob slowly replaced his eye but didn't say anything.

Raspberry-flavoured smoke swirled in from either side.

Heidi smiled again.

"Hob?" asked M Cadvare, more urgently. "Are you okay?"

Silently, Hob began to sink into the floor.

They tried to support him by the arms but he slipped through their fingers and, to their consternation, he disappeared entirely.

"Where's he gone?" asked M Cadvare. He put out a foot and tested the floor but it seemed quite solid.

"I don't know!" retorted an equally bemused Nenuphar. She glanced at Heidi and then looked back at M Cadvare. "I never realised he was so shy!"

"He's not shy!" exclaimed M Cadvare. "Look!"

Something was rising up out of the fog around Heidi's feet.

Heidi's eyes widened with amazement and then softened with pleasure.

A crash-helmeted figure was rising steadily out of the scented smoke that swirled around her. Hob held his hands out to shape the air around her long legs and hourglass figure, but without actually touching her.

"Have we met before somewhere?" he asked her, grinning his best and worst.

Heidi laughed. "On a cruise somewhere, perhaps?"

Hob jiggled his eyebrows at her as if he'd been taught by the devil himself. Of course they were well hidden by his visor but anyone could see what he was doing.

"I know who you are," she said.

"So do I," Hob replied.

Heidi gave a little laugh again and Hob drowned in it.

"Ah," she said, mischievously, "self-knowledge is such a wonderful thing."

"You have set a powerful glamour on me," he told her.

"And you on me, I think," she murmured.

"Ah, attraction is so attractive, don't you agree?"

"You're the man with the four way hips!"

"Wanna live for ever?"

"Maybe." Heidi put her arms on the shoulders of his leather jacket and Hob put his hands around her waist. "I wouldn't want to get bored. You're the Horsepower Whisperer everybody's afraid of, aren't you?"

"Be afraid, be very afraid. Surrender in delicious terror."

"You're not exactly inconspicuous, but that last trick with your eyeball was straight out of *The Red Book of St Bendix*."

Hob jerked his head back a little. "It was? You're right. It was, wasn't it? What's a nice girl like you doing reading a book like that?"

"Learning some of your secrets."

"Ah. Like my kiss that can melt elastic?"

Heidi laughed again.

"What?" said Hob but Heidi wouldn't say.

Instead she put her arms around his neck. Hob wrapped his around her waist and they kissed the way precocious teenage vacuum cleaners might kiss just before their parents arrived to collect them from their local electrical appliance youth club.

"By the spanners of St Bendix!" said Nenuphar and M Cadvare.

And then pandemonium broke out.

CHAPTER 72

Julian swooped down from the cooling fan and threw himself at a dancer wearing a fox fur stole.

She couldn't have heard anything except the closing bars of *Starlight* but something made her look up to see a fine set of teeth and a pair of frenzied eyes hurtling towards her.

Her scream pierced the music and the dancers panicked when it became clear that they were being dive-bombed. Emergency exits were flung open and the nightclub emptied.

M Cadvare grabbed Nenuphar and they were carried outside by a tidal wave of people and washed up in the lee of a neighbouring building.

As the crowds subsided, Hob and Heidi appeared, complete with Hob's crate and rucksack.

"What happened?" Nenuphar asked them.

"It was Julian," said Heidi, sounding impressed rather than angry.

"It wasn't his fault," said Hob. "A nightclub is hardly the natural environment for an Anarchadian Flying Fruit Bat Fox."

"Well, he's been to a few since he came to live with me," said Heidi.

She looked around now that things had quietened down. Not far away an animal was growling and snarling. Heidi shielded her eyes from the street lamps and peered up at the eaves of a Victorian block of flats where she could just make out an inverted foxy sort of shape shaking and worrying some limp thing in its mouth.

"What's he got?" asked M Cadvare.

"Ju-ju?" said Heidi.

High above them, a pair of ears pricked up.

"Come down here to Mummy. There's a good boy."

Julian swooped down to a fire escape and they saw that he had the fox fur stole in his mouth.

"So that's what he was after," said M Cadvare.

"He knows my views about women wearing real fur," explained Heidi.

Julian looked down at them and wagged his tail. Then he shook his head again to worry the fox fur to death, just in case it was trying to outwit him by playing dead.

The sound of a siren was approaching.

"We'd better make a move," said Hob.

"It's okay," said Heidi. "I've got my limo over here. Come on."

She walked off briskly and they followed her down some steps and through a door with a coded entry system to an almost empty underground carpark.

"This limo of yours," said Hob, carefully manoeuvring *Nosferatu*'s crate through the doorway, "does it have a chauffeur?"

"No," said Heidi. "I gave him the night off. I often drive myself. Because of my husband's position in Euphobian society, I can sometimes have a police escort." She whipped out a mobile phone. "Would you like that?"

"I've had enough of those already," said Hob.

"They might put their sirens on for us."

"I've never known them without their sirens."

Heidi shrugged and put her mobile away.

Hob put down his crate and peered inside the limo. It was a long wheelbase Mercedes S class.

"No sporting pretensions whatsoever," he grumbled.

"Oh, I'm sure you can persuade it to great feats of power and endurance," said Heidi with a grin and she activated the plipper.

The central locking system unlocked and Hob opened the door, but instead of getting in he pulled the bonnet release and opened it to look at the engine.

"Not bad," he said after running his oily hands over its cam covers and induction system, and he began to mutter under his breath as more sirens pulled up not far away.

"Air filters who art by plenums, allow my power gain. My amps and volts, my thrills be done, with earths according to the blueprints. Give us this day our extra revs, and forego any flat spots lest they impinge upon our torque curve and throttle response. Valves and rods, be not tempted into entanglement, and oil pumps deliver us from seizure. For divine is thy torque curve, the power and the glory, revs without end, ring-ding-a-ding!"

When he'd finished, the engine bay looked a little different although none of his companions could quite say what had changed.

Hob gently closed the bonnet as if tucking up a slumbering child and removed his rucksack to take the driver's seat.

"Wait a moment! I can't possibly drive this!"

"Why not?"

"It's an automatic! I can't drive an automatic! How can I commune with the engine and wheels through a slushbox? There's only one thing for it."

He took off his rucksack and opened it.

"Okay, you lot, rise and shine."

He pulled it wide open, turned it upside down and began to empty people out of it.

First was a small, wiry Latin figure, dressed in tight white trousers, an open-faced pudding-basin helmet and a cut-off faded red tee shirt that displayed sinewy upper arms. He somersaulted as he fell and gracefully rolled upright with all the poise of a dancer. He was a handsome devil and flashed his dark eyes and a dazzling smile at Heidi and Nenuphar.

He was followed by a streamlined feminine figure dressed in a one-piece leather racing suit in dark red. She had a mane of frizzy orange hair styled with electricity and carried a Darth Vader helmet. She landed in a crouch and in a few steps stood upright to look M Cadvare in the eye and give him the most lascivious wink he'd ever received.

"Fortunato," said Hob, as other figures rolled out of his rucksack. "First again."

"Hob, el Diablo!" exclaimed Fortunato and he punched Hob hard on the shoulder.

"The Red Witch," said Hob.

The woman in dark red leather sashayed over to him and without a word kissed him long and hard on the lips.

"Hob, you old devil," she said softly when she finished. "Speed is not always a virtue."

"My dear, you look absolutely stunning."

"I feel absolutely stunning! When do we sing the Song of the Machine?"

"Now! Tonite!"

By now the underground carpark was littered with the rising forms of all sorts of racing drivers. There were Hell's Angels, stock car drivers, Bentley Boys, lanky motocross riders, winners of the Monte Carlo Coupe des Dames and a pair of Japanese engine tuners.

"Hob-san," they said, and bowed deeply to Hob, who bowed back to them.

"Yoshiwaki," he said to the elder one. "Morimura," he greeted the junior one.

None of this prepared the others for the next members of *Terminal Murrain* to fall out of the rucksack.

A large herbivorous reptile landed in a heap on the floor, and then an angular bird-like dinosaur alighted in a sudden movement that spoke of rapid reactions. They were followed by half a dozen equally bizarre figures, not all of whom would need, or could wear, crash helmets.

However, Hob was still holding up his rucksack. He looked at the assembled throng and, not finding what he was looking for, gave his rucksack a great shake. An enormous figure fell out of it and bounced on the concrete.

"Hell shit!" he said and rose unsteadily to his feet.

He was a great bear of a man, over two metres tall and a little over-weight. Not much of it was flab, though. He glared down at Hob, who lowered the rucksack and grinned back at him.

"Of course," said Hob, "the new boy. Forrest Teague."

"So are we gonna race or what?" demanded Forrest Teague. "Cos ah'm tellin' yew, boy. Ah've had it with being cooped up in thar."

"Forrest is still at home with Mr Grumpy," the Red Witch explained sweetly.

"Ladies and gentlemen of the Wild Hunt? Allow me to introduce Nenuphar, the veggie subversive, and Cadaver, a skirrow in waiting. Nenny? Cadaver? Meet the *Terminal Murrain*."

"Hallo," said M Cadvare. "It's Cadvare, actually."

"I prefer Cadaver," said the Red Witch, suggestively.

"The Wild Hunt rides Tonite," Hob told his souls. "We are starting here in London and are going to Westward Ho! From there we fost to Lanson. We start in two hours. Choose your road weapons!"

Everyone except Forrest Teague ran off.

"Teague," said Hob, "a quiet word in your shell-like. Seeing as it's your first time, I would recommend that you stick to what you know."

Forrest Teague grinned unpleasantly. "Then that'll be a Hudson Hornet for me!"

"There'll be plenty of time to experiment later. Find the nearest manufactory and explore your powers in creating the best road weapon you can. Come back here and we go. Okay?"

Forrest Teague said nothing. He just nodded once and strode off.

"C'mon Cadaver, we've got a cogbox to swap!" and Hob descended vertically into the concrete of the carpark as if through a trap door.

"He's been doing a lot of this recently," Nenuphar explained to Heidi.

"I'm going to be one of the *Terminal Murrain* one day," M Cadvare told her.

Heidi smiled at him. "Of course you are."

She wasn't patronising in the slightest. It was a simple statement of fact, and M Cadvare, for so long the downtrodden certified management auditor, puffed out his chest.

Hob popped back out of the ground clutching a large piece of machinery in his arms.

"Haven't you done it yet?" he asked a surprised M Cadvare.

"Done what?"

"Got the slushbox out!"

"I don't know where to begin!"

"Come on! Find the jack and something to prop the Merc up with. All we've got to do is drop the front subframe, disconnect the prop and the control linkages, tilt the box down, undo the bellhousing bolts and shove this in."

"What is that?" asked Heidi.

"This? It's a six speed ZF competition gearbox."

"And where did you get it?"

Hob balanced the gearbox up on one finger and span it round slowly.

"That's for me to know and you to wonder about. Come on, Cadaver, let's get those wheels in the air!"

Nenuphar and Heidi stood back and let the boys get on with it.

They worked very quickly, especially Hob, who needed no tool kit. He undid nuts and bolts with his bare fingers and his hands span on his wrists like air wrenches. The limo was soon jacked up and Hob rolled underneath it on the little castors that sprouted from his shoulders and hips.

"I love your dress," Heidi told Nenuphar. "That's an entirely natural fabric isn't it?"

"Yes, it's simply not being made any more."

"I know. My husband was a Commissioner."

"Ah. I gathered that. Look, I'm sorry. I didn't realise I hit him so hard."

"No, he's still alive, worse luck. We're getting a divorce. I'm fed up being a trophy wife for someone who seems so alien."

Out came the old autobox with a look of disdain from Hob and then, almost with reverence, he manoeuvred the new gearbox into position. When it came to lining up the clutch plates on a new flywheel Hob had procured, a thin green line of light appeared from his visor. M Cadvare jiggled the gearbox a little to Hob's satisfaction and, with a whirr, Hob bolted everything up finger tight, except that his finger tight was to any pre-determined torque setting up to 350 Newton metres.

"How do you achieve such spontaneously beautiful hair?" asked Nenuphar.

Heidi rolled her eyes. "Hours and hours at the most expensive hair salons."

"Really? It just looks so natural."

"Thank you. That's precisely the effect I was after."

Another flash of green laser light to line up the bellhousing bolts, and Hob re-attached the propshaft. M Cadvare lowered the Merc onto its wheels and Hob jumped up and tripped over a traffic cone.

Everyone froze in horror.

"How did that get there?" wondered Nenuphar as Hob glared at the traffic cone as he lay on his back beside it.

"Cadaver? Could you oblige me by getting rid of that thing?"

"Okay."

M Cadvare picked up the traffic cone and, after a little thought, wandered off with it.

By the time he'd returned, Hob had removed the Mercedes' springs and was setting up the suspension.

"What did you do with it?" he asked him.

"I wedged it in the chassis of a juggernaut as it pulled up at some traffic lights."

"Good call," said Hob.

Five minutes later, Hob was doing a slalom round the pillars of the car park and adjusting the spring rates while the girls were trying each other's lipstick.

"Finished," said a slightly grubby M Cadvare.

"Great," said Nenuphar. "It seems an awful lot of trouble to go to. Why didn't you let Heidi drive her own car?"

"What?" said Hob. "In the Wild Hunt? Have you ever seen the Wild Hunt?"

"I've read all about it," Heidi replied.

"Knowledge does not necessarily provide experience," said Hob. "Maybe one day you'll become a Wild Hunter but it's too soon even for Cadaver, here. Hallo?" He glanced at his fingers, which suddenly resembled the leaves on a holly bush. "Can you hear something?"

The rasping exhaust note of an engine echoed far away. A light grew from out of the distant parking spaces and shortly a waspish racing motorcycle pulled up nearby with the Red Witch astride it.

She took off her Darth Vader helmet and said, "Well, what do you think?"

"Fantastic," said Hob with feeling. "A Crescent V4 two stroke outboard motor in an ally beam frame. Red Witch, that TIG welding is exquisite!"

"Why thank you kind sir! I call it the *Sister of Mercy.*"

"And those upside-down forks and inside-out discs are just so you!"

Other mechanical stirrings could now be heard and from every darkened corner of the underground carpark came a variety of racing machinery on two, three and four wheels, each one the chosen road weapon of an experienced road racer and member of the *Terminal Murrain.*

And each one came under the exacting scrutiny of Hob the Horsepower Whisperer, who was impressed with them all.

"Hey! Jeez! Nice Holden, mate!" said Hob to a Wild Hunter from Oz called Blue Flame. He was a raw-boned, carrot-topped bloke who had brought along a supercharged Holden Monaro.

"Cheers, mate," Blue replied.

"Hell shit!" exclaimed Forrest Teague, at the members of the *Terminal Murrain.* "Yew lot carry on as if you're best buddies with him!" and he jabbed a finger at Hob.

"Why shouldn't we be beaut mates?" Blue Flame asked him.

"We're all here for the same thing," added the Red Witch.

"We are-a the Quick and the Dead," said Fortunato, from the cockpit of blood red Ferrari 375. "We are-a like-a hot spurs to-a one another."

"Hob-san understands our souls better than anyone," Morimura told the huge stock car driver as he sat astride a heavily modified Kawasaki Z1.

"Hob was the one who gave us fulfilment," explained the Red Witch.

"Yeah, some more than others!" said Blue Flame, and the *Terminal Murrain* laughed.

The Red Witch basked in the innuendo.

"Maybe you would care to join us?" Fortunato asked M Cadvare.

But before he could reply, Hob answered for him.

"Later. It's all very new for him. Cadaver? If you run in the Wild Hunt Tonite you would survive. I would see to that. But you could acquire the wrong sort of blebs. Strange as it may seem, you might not want to do it again. Trust my judgement on this and ride with us in the hunt when you are ready."

He looked around the gleaming racing machinery and grinned widely.

"It's time to go! Take your places, everyone!" and the *Terminal Murrain* queued up behind the Red Witch, for she was the one who had finished first.

"Ladies and gentlemen, boys and girls, brothers and sisters, fiends and Frankensteins! It's time to sing the Song of the Machine!"

"Trouble's going!" shouted the *Terminal Murrain* and the underground car park was filled with sound as the engines burst into life.

Hob gestured to his companions to climb aboard the limo.

"Trouble's gone!" Hob shouted over the din and, after a quick lap of the car park, the *Terminal Murrain* hit the open road.

CHAPTER 73

Safe within the relative dimensions of her temporal anomaly, Therese Darlmat studied the instruments on the dashboard of her pink Cadillac Rushmore convertible. Gathered around her, like a host of unlikely cherubs, were the grauniads.

"As soon as Hob fosts," Therese told them, "this red light here will light up."

"Can you be sure it's going to be our paraverse that fails?" asked Thor, polishing his bronze helmet with the horns. He was surprisingly bald without it.

"If it is, we need to be ready for Valhalla," explained Brunhilde.

"Or the Happy Hunting Ground," Moon Wolf reminded them, emptying a pebble from his moccasin over the side of the Cadillac.

"I am an atheist," declared Isis.

"I believe in re-incarnation," said Gaia.

"I thought we were all immortal!" Zeus said, horrified.

"Whatever gave you that idea?" asked Gert.

"Was it your dominion over nature?" Thor asked Zeus.

"Or being worshipped for centuries?" added Brunhilde.

"How can you be an atheist?" Moon Wolf asked Isis.

"Maybe I meant an agnostic," she replied.

"If you were immortal, what was the point of siring all those other deities?" Gaia asked Zeus.

Zeus shrugged.

"Haven't you ever said to your children, 'Some day, kids, all this will be yours'?" Gert asked him.

"Can I ask you a question?" Therese asked them collectively.

"Yes?" they replied.

"Don't you know what happens when your paraverse ends?"

"Do you know what happens when your life ends?" Thor replied.

"Well, of course not," said Therese.

"Neither do we," said Brunhilde, buffing up her breastplates, determined to go out in style.

"But I thought you communed with God on a regular basis."

"We do," said Moon Wolf, "but he doesn't want to spoil the surprise."

"If Hob fosts much more you will all find out," Therese warned them.

"We all have our own ideas," said Isis.

"Some of you are bound to be disappointed," said Therese.

"I don't think I will be," said Gaia.

"Either way," said Zeus, gloomily, "it's death, Therese, but not as you know it."

"But there must be other paraverses for which you could act as guardians," Therese told them.

There was a sharp intake of breath from all her little companions.

"What did you say?" hissed Gert.

"Sorry," said the beautiful young scientist.

"Do that again," began Thor, radiating indignation.

"Despite our repeated warnings," added Brunhilde.

"Even if it was an understandable slip of the tongue," allowed Moon Wolf.

"And we'll get cross," warned Isis.

"Not just cross," went on Gaia.

"You won't like us when we're angry," promised Zeus. He had a brief exchange of thunderbolts with Thor, then lapsed into a thoughtful silence.

"You might witness the return of my rude part," threatened Gert.

"Look, it's any easy enough mistake to make," said Therese, "and it's the first time I've done it, okay?"

"To err is to be human," quoted Thor.

"What's that supposed to mean?" snapped Brunhilde.

"I dunno," the little god of thunder admitted.

"But couldn't you find another paraverse to look after?" Therese persisted.

"Could you?" asked Moon Wolf.

"She already has," Isis pointed out.

"Oh yeah," murmured Moon Wolf.

"Could you find another body to inhabit?" Gaia asked Therese, nodding encouragingly at Moon Wolf.

"I don't know," said Therese. "I've never tried."

"Too risky even for you, I expect," muttered Zeus.

"It's this paraverse or nothing for us," Gert told Therese emphatically.

"Why were the other grauniads so keen to let your paraverse collapse?" Therese asked them.

The grauniads stared at her.

"Other grauniads?" Thor spluttered.

"What other grauniads?" demanded Brunhilde, her voice rising shrilly.

"Er. I refutured the unfutured and the next thing I knew these other grauniads were explaining why I shouldn't have done it. So I reversed the process and defutured the unfutured. However, the defutured attempted to re-history themselves by sending Kevin back in time and now, here we are, at roughly the stage where, despite the infinite variety of possibility, the un-futured are about to fulfil their destiny. And become the unfutured. Again. Er. Are you following this?"

But the grauniads did not answer. They were holding a sudden conference.

Therese waited for their whispering to stop. She stole a glance at the idiot light. It was still unlit and not flashing "Hey stupid!"

The grauniads broke ranks to face her. Therese could not read their expressions but they exuded an air of studied calm.

"We've just had a quick conflab," explained Thor.

"So, Therese," began Brunhilde, pressing her fingertips together in front of her burnished bosom, "could you save this paraverse?"

"Of course," she replied.

"Our paraverse?" Moon Wolf clarified.

"Yes."

"But you're not going to," confirmed Isis.

"No, not if it destabilises the other paraverses."

"Not after those other grauniads convinced you to sacrifice this one," suggested Gaia.

"That's right."

"Was there a cyclops among these grauniads?" asked Zeus, his gloom replaced with indignation.

"As a matter of fact there was," said Therese, wondering where this was leading.

"And a medusa?" asked Gert.

"Ye-es," Therese answered slowly. "There was a little naked chap with wings on his helmet, too."

The grauniads all looked at each other.

"Didn't you ask them for any identification?" they chorused.

"Well, no! It was obvious they were grauniads!"

"Don't go away!" they cried, and vanished.

Therese stood up on her driving seat. "Don't go away?" she shouted. "I'm in a souped-up Cadillac in a temporal anomaly! Where am I supposed to go?"

She put her hands on her hips and felt her stiletto heels puncturing the tuck and roll upholstery.

She glanced at the idiot light as her heels descended into the seat.

Dramatic tradition would insist that it should light up at that precise moment but, like nostalgia, custom and practice don't seem to work in temporal anomalies.

CHAPTER 74

The *Terminal Murrain* thundered through the streets of London and swept towards the West End. It snaked around red double-decker buses and raced across the parks and open spaces before the police cars could even do a peel out.

M Cadvare had never even heard of the Wild Hunt until recently and never ever seen it, but now he was in it. While Heidi sat up front with Hob, M Cadvare rode with Nenuphar in the back of Heidi's limo, feeling like a high speed celebrity.

Julian dangled from a light fitting behind the front seats and took on the role of a furry G-force indicator. He swung to the side when they cornered, forwards when Hob braked heavily and backwards when they were accelerating.

Other vehicles began to join in the chase. All through London they acquired a following of personal transport devices and some of the distinctive black cabs, but these had no hope of keeping up with the cars and bikes of the *Terminal Murrain*.

But by the time the Wild Hunt spilled onto the Great West Road, more serious competition was beginning to show up.

"The Wild Hunt attracts skirrows like moths to a flame," said Hob.

He pulled alongside Forrest Teague. His Hudson Hornet wasn't much smaller than their stretched Mercedes limousine and on the wide three-lane blacktop of the Great West Road they had enough room to duck and weave around each other.

"If you're the leader of the *Terminal Murrain*, shouldn't he let you through?" asked Nenuphar.

"No! We must always race to be best of our ability. Anything else is a lie! Teague is new, and although that Hudson was a good first choice it's not as fast as this Mercedes and he doesn't have my experience."

Hob daemonstrated and eased the Mercedes limousine through on the inside of a sweeping left hander.

On long straights they caught glimpses of other members of the *Terminal Murrain*, but what frightened Hob's companions most of all were not the other Wild Hunters but the traffic that was not part of the chase. Most had no idea how fast they were travelling and often baulked them.

"Why don't you just punt them over the central reservation?" asked M Cadvare when one particularly oblivious Strunts veered into their lane.

"What? Like this?" and Hob sent the personal transportation device cartwheeling into the oncoming traffic.

M Cadvare gulped. "It was just a thought."

"Thought is action for some of us," said Hob. "I must be careful not to damage our road weapon. We are still in the domain of the Conformorians and although we must travel quickly we gotta do it inconspicuously. This Wild Hunt is a spontaneous one. It's just us, the *Terminal Murrain*. We're not racing today for the hell of it but to get home."

"Needs must when the devil drives," said Heidi.

They braced themselves as yet another Strunts pulled out in front of them. It was much further ahead but travelled so slowly they were on top of it in a matter of seconds. Hob stood on the brakes and the back of the limo went light and fishtailed violently but he still controlled it.

The limo's bumper just kissed the back of the personal transportation device, then Hob accelerated and soon the little car in front was overtaking traffic far faster than its dozy driver had ever intended.

"The problem with this manoeuvre," said Hob as they hurtled forward, "is that you can't see any hazards developing up ahead. That privilege falls to the driver of the car in front."

The Strunts on their bumper was entirely at their mercy. Its driver applied the brakes in a vain attempt to regain control but this just locked the wheels and produced clouds of tyre smoke that obscured Hob's vision even more.

"Fortunately," said Hob, "I have proximity awareness. I know the road ahead is clear."

He steered into the middle lane and the personal transportation device twisted on his bumper and span, wiping off its unnatural speed and quite a lot of itself along the central crash barrier.

"If this was a proper Wild Hunt," Hob told them, "this road would be closed. Commuters and racers have no place together."

From the amounts of recent wreckage they passed, the rest of the *Terminal Murrain* were also dealing some savage lessons to the slower traffic.

The motorway shrank to two lanes and they passed the university town of Andover, famous for its yeast culture and sandal making.

"There is a growing danger that the authorities will close the road," Hob told them. "This sometimes happens when we race on the Continent. If we're clever we should be able to anticipate this."

But it didn't happen.

The authorities let them race.

Hob expressed his surprise as they swooped down a hill to a large roundabout. "Usually, a two-way radio can outrun anything. The Conformorians are up to something."

"Hob?" said M Cadvare, whose thumbs were pricking. "Have you look-ed behind us?"

"Yes," replied the Horsepower Whisperer. "So you've seen her too."

Nenuphar and Heidi turned and saw a pink six-wheeled Cadillac trailing after them.

"Heidi, my dear, do you recognise that car?"

"It's a Cadillac Rushmore convertible, isn't it?"

"I like the colour," said Nenuphar.

"Any idea who the driver can be?" Hob asked Heidi.

"No. Why? Should I?"

"I thought that if you knew about *The Red Book of St Bendix*, perhaps you would recognise a beautiful young scientist who can fost as well as we can and has a brain so big she has to hide it beneath a massive beehive."

Heidi looked blank and shook her head. "She sounds like the stuff of legend."

"A legend that is not written yet," suggested M Cadvare.

"The Future Legend!" said Heidi. "Maybe I *have* heard of her! Maybe she's the one in The Future Legend."

"And what is this Future Legend?"

"Nobody knows. St Bendix alludes to it in his red book."

Hob frowned and turned to her. "Does he?"

"Yes. But nobody knows what The Future Legend is. The Great Smith mentions it contains a woman wiser than all wise women, in tune with the pulse of the universe."

They swept round the roundabout in a chorus of squealing tyres and flew up the next hill to catch a glimpse of Stonehenge before plunging into a tunnel, where their exhaust notes sounded magnificent. By the time they emerged from the tunnel, the beautiful young scientist was no longer chasing them.

The road narrowed further shortly afterwards, making passing more hazardous, and on a short steep hill, where slower traffic might be overtaken, speed cameras were flashing in apoplexy as the *Terminal Murrain* passed through.

Hob laughed. "Of course! They're relying on technology to catch speed-ing drivers! How naive!"

"You won't even show up on the cameras!" M Cadvare replied.

"Neither will the *Terminal Murrain*!"

Slower traffic made them bunch up and they were only a few cars away from Blue's souped-up Holden and a number of American muscle cars.

"Blue's Holden isn't as powerful as those Dodges and Chevys," said Hob, "but he's made sure it handles better. On these twisty sections, his car's actually quicker."

At the next section of dual carriageway, Hob swept by them all.

"The Red Witch!" he said loudly as they passed a filling station. "That bike's fast but thirsty."

The road changed frequently from dual to single carriageway. As they snaked along in a long queue of traffic, there was a blood-surging wail from behind them and the Red Witch wheelied past them in the face of terrified oncoming traffic.

"Who's leading the Wild Hunt?" asked M Cadvare.

"Fortunato," said Hob with a smile. "I wonder if she'll catch him? We don't have far to go now. I recognise this aberration of a road. It was built as a three-laner, but the centre lane just fills up with head on crashes."

Hob turned off this road at another big roundabout and after driving through a small village, the first one for several miles, they joined another motorway and the character of the Wild Hunt changed yet again.

M Cadvare looked behind them and saw four abreast muscle cars, each trying to outdrag the other. Blue Flame's power disadvantage seemed to be showing here, but of the pink Cadillac there was no sign.

"I think we've outrun the beautiful young scientist," he called out.

Hob glanced up at him in the mirror.

M Cadvare was no longer surprised to see that it showed an empty driving seat.

"She could fost ahead of us if she wanted to," said Hob. "The only thing faster than a two-way radio is a temporal anomaly. I wonder why she's given up?"

They turned off the motorway and swept towards the coast along the North Devon Link Road.

CHAPTER 75

As they crossed the River Torridge, Hob felt something was wrong.

"We may not be able to fost after all," he said quietly.

"What makes you think that?" asked Heidi.

"My instincts. I've grown to trust them through many Wild Hunts and I have a familiar feeling, the one that means fosts don't work."

"But we need to fost to get to Anarchadia," insisted M Cadvare.

"Precisely. Something or someone is out to prevent us. They've put a block on fosting from Westward Ho!"

"Is it the Conformorians?" asked Nenuphar.

"Is it the beautiful young scientist?" wondered M Cadvare.

"I don't know," said Hob, "but I'm sure we're about to find out. So, Cadaver, are you worried that I may not be able to fulfil my side of our bargain?"

"Yes. I need to get to Anarchadia because I can't go back to Mourion."

"Neither can I," said Heidi.

"None of us can," Nenuphar reminded them.

"Don't worry," Hob reassured them. "We'll get there. Just not by fosting."

"Why not?" asked M Cadvare.

"How else can we get there?" asked Nenuphar.

But Hob did not reply. They were almost in Westward Ho! already and Hob was no longer trying to get past Fortunato and the Red Witch. He was looking out to sea. There was the island of Lundy. And there was Barnstable or Bideford Bay, which was so good they named it twice. However, there was nothing visible that could substantiate Hob's foreboding.

The Red Witch sensed something was awry as well. She slowed down and Fortunato leapt gleefully into the lead, but he glanced in his mirror and saw her turning to talk to Hob as he came up beside her.

"This feels wrong!" she shouted over the crackle of the *Sister of Mercy's* exhaust note.

"I know," Hob replied. "I've felt it, too. Ah, now Fortunato senses it as well."

The Ferrari up ahead was cruising down to the beach.

"What else do you sense, Red Witch?"

She turned away to look out to sea.

"Something is hiding from us, something beneath the waves."

She snicked rode down to join Fortunato by some railings. Fortunato sat on the rear bulkhead of Ferrari, his feet on the seat and his hands over his eyes to shield them from the glare as he peered out to sea.

Hob and the rest of the *Terminal Murrain* parked behind them and they all got out of their cars and off their bikes to watch something pink stirring beneath the waters of the bay. At first they thought it was a sunburnt albino whale.

A pink and rather suggestive column rose gently out of the sea and a familiar figure appeared from her submarine.

"Nicholas Eldritch Hob!" said Therese Darlmat, through a loud hailer. "Listen to me and do what I tell you."

"Never!"

"Under no circumstances are you to proceed to Anarchadia by fost!"

"Madam, I am a free radical! I am going home to Anarchadia and nobody is going to stop me!"

A flock of seagulls soared into the air as a red flash swooped into them.

"Hob! I implore you! Go home by all means but don't fost!"

"Why not?"

"Incrementally, fosts bring about the end of the space/time continuum!"

"First the end of the world, now the space/time continuum," muttered Hob.

"Just when you thought things couldn't get any worse," Nenuphar put in.

"I suppose you expect me to feel guilty."

"I've asked you nicely," Therese told him, "but I don't have time to argue. I am going to ensure you can't fost."

She reached into her handbag, produced what looked like a television remote control, pointed it at the horizon behind her and pressed a button.

"So there!" she cried triumphantly.

"That!" said Hob. "That was what I sensed!"

"Whadda we supposed to do-a now, huh?" asked Fortunato with much arm waving.

Heidi put her hands placatingly on Hob's shoulders. "Why don't we just do as she says?"

"I'm sure we could smash her fost proofing!" fumed Hob.

"Until we know for certain what effect fosts have on this space/time continuum of ours, shouldn't we refrain from fosting?" Heidi asked him.

Hob was gripped by a terrible internal struggle. It wasn't in his nature to obey orders, but Heidi had made a very sensible suggestion that offered a sense of choice.

He stared out to sea.

The beautiful young scientist was stepping inside her submarine again while overhead Julian circled her. Her confidence that they couldn't fost made Hob's blood boil.

"Why don't we sail to Anarchadia?" suggested Heidi.

"I don't want to sail to Anarchadia!" he retorted before he'd engaged his brain and thought about it.

He looked at Heidi and then the rest of the *Terminal Murrain*.

"Sail to Anarchadia," he said more quietly.

"We could, couldn't we?" she persisted.

"We could."

"Well then."

"Sorry, everyone. The Wild Hunt's over for now."

"Oh!" they all said.

Then Blue piped up, "No worries! We've got ourselves a day at the seaside!" and Mesdemoiselles Volant et Vitesse, winners of more Coupes des Dames than anyone could remember, morphed into bathing beauties, produced a beach ball and ran into the sea.

"Countach!" exclaimed Fortunato. "I could-a, 'ow you say, 'murder some Sulphur Floss!'"

"So who won?" M Cadvare asked the *Terminal Murrain*.

"Fortunato," muttered Hob, "but I'll beat him next time."

Heidi put her arm through Hob's. "Why don't we buy a nice big boat?"

"Okay," he said. "We just need something big enough for the four of us and your limo."

Heidi frowned slightly. "The four of us?"

"This lot will travel in my rucksack."

"Ah. Of course."

"But we're cluttering up the sea front."

"Where can you leave your road weapons?"

"Is there a manufactory near here?" the Red Witch asked them.

"There's one at Coombe Martin," Hob told her. He turned to Heidi. "I'll take the *Terminal Murrain* there and we'll come back in the limo."

"Brilliant!" said Heidi. "Oh, Julian! Don't burst their ball!"

"Too late," said M Cadvare.

Julian was hanging from a lamp post, worrying a piece of multi-coloured plastic to death.

Mesdemoiselles Volant et Vitesse didn't seem to mind. Mademoiselle Volant found a piece of driftwood and threw it into the air.

Julian put the beach ball out of its misery, zeroed in on the stick and went after that instead.

"Wait a moment." Hob fished around in his jacket pocket. "This is the Engineer of Spades."

He wedged the black, featureless credit card in the CD player of the limo, and Electra's face flashed up on the instrument panel.

"Yes, my lord?"

"Electra, I want you to help Heidi here buy a boat."

Electra looked frostily at the glamorous young woman looking over Hob's shoulder. "Your wish is my command my lord," she said.

"I am nominating her as joint card holder, all right?"

Heidi gasped with delight at the thought of the unbridled retail activity this would bring her.

"All right?"

"As you wish, my lord."

"Good."

Hob ejected the Engineer of Spades from the CD slot and handed it to Heidi.

"Here's my card," he said. "Why don't you go and buy us something nautical but nice?"

CHAPTER 76

By the time Hob returned in the limo, Heidi had bought a trawler. He knew a lot about engines but nothing about boats. Heidi on the other hand had picked up a little knowledge from travelling on her husband's yacht.

"New EC Regulations mean an end to privately owned fishing vessels," she told them. "Only multi-national enterprises can afford the licences or cope with the administration of the fishing quota forms. Fishing grounds have been almost empty for years but they still fish in the name of research. There's been a re-distribution of trawler numbers, too. It was felt that the more land locked regions of Euphobia were disadvantaged so coastal fishing fleets had to shrink. In many instances, they had to pay for their own vessels to be broken up."

"Whose idea was all that?" asked Nenuphar.

Heidi smiled. "The Euphobian De-Commissioners. Consequently, trawlers around here are dirt cheap."

They all had a meal of fish and chips, and then Hob drove them to Appledore to see the vessel that Heidi had bought unseen. It was called the *Baggy Point Beauty* and was clearly a bargain.

"Looks okay to me," he said and he disappeared below decks to commune with the engines.

"And the hold is big enough for our car, too," said M Cadvare, peering into its depths.

Heidi had bought the *Baggy Point Beauty* from a middle-aged man. She'd either set a glamour on him or he'd been bamboozled by Electra. He greeted them effusively and gave Heidi 20,000 Ecus to take it off his hands.

Hob emerged from the engine room and pronounced himself satisfied with the state of their motive power. He strode to the stern and pulled down the grey Euphobian flag.

"We won't be needing that where we're headed," he said. "The Baggy *Point Beauty* may whiff a bit of fish but that should go away once we're at sea."

He superintended the loading of the limo into the hold and then flashed up the engines.

M Cadvare hopped back ashore to cast them off but tripped over a traffic cone someone had left in the way on the harbour wall.

"Kick it in the water," shouted Hob, "and I'll squash it against the stones," but when M Cadvare did so they were both surprised to see how suddenly it sank.

"Which way are we headed?" asked Nenuphar, once they were under way.

"Whaddya mean, which way?" Hob replied.

"Well, where is Anarchadia?"

"Over there," said Hob and pointed.

"Do you have a course planned, a compass bearing or something?"

"Badness, black-hearted me, no! I was planning on being spontaneous."

"Not again."

"It worked last time!"

"You don't know how to get there, do you?"

"No and neither do you."

"So who is the navigator on this vessel? Who is the captain?"

"I am," he told her and when she snorted he added, "This is a new experience for both of us. Anarchadia lies to the west. All we've got to do is travel westward."

"Westward from Westward Ho! I suppose!"

"Exactly, and why not? The barrier between Anarchadia and Westward Ho! is very weak."

"And how do you know this?"

"I can recognise the signs, the road signs."

"Hob? You are just so full of *merde*!"

"Would you like to know what the clue is, little Nenny?"

"Go on then."

"Westward Ho! is the only place in the whole world with an exclamation mark in its name."

"Yes," piped up M Cadvare, "I was wondering about that. Surely the Euphobian Commissioners would never allow that sort of thing."

"It's only a matter of time before they notice," said Hob. "If the Euphobian De-Commissioners de-commission the exclamation mark, the last clue to Anarchadia will be lost for ever! Our course is back to Westward Ho!, then steer between Hartland Point and Lundy and keep on going due west until we hit something!"

CHAPTER 77

After passing an ancient buoy with a weathered sign that declared HERE BE DRAGONS! Hob cut the engines of the *Baggy Point Beauty*. The open sea had become unnaturally calm and great clouds of mist came racing eagerly across its flat surface to embrace them in their clammy bosom.

"Is this what you were expecting?" M Cadvare asked Hob.

The purple-black clouds in Hob's visor swirled happily. "No," he said, "it's even better!"

There was a bell on the buoy, but it was so calm it didn't sound.

"What's wrong?" asked Nenuphar as she joined them from the galley.

"Nothing," replied the Horsepower Whisperer, nonchalantly. "Heidi? May I borrow your splendid flitterfox?"

"Of course? What do you need him for?"

"Ladies and gentleman," announced Hob, "we are on the edge of the Antagonistic Ocean. Behind us lies the Atlantic and ahead of us a vast circular reef thrown up by a great volcanic upheaval 65 million years ago. This reef was known to the Romans as *mattato marino* or the sailor's slaughterhouse."

"Splendid," sighed M Cadvare.

"With your linguistic skills, it could mean anything," added Nenuphar.

"No," put in Heidi, "I've read something about this. Is this the ship's graveyard that surrounds the Antagonistic Ocean?"

"It is," said Hob. "Classical scholars initially believed it was an impenetrable barrier to all but the bravest and most skilful of sailors, but soon they discovered that there were indeed ways through the reefs and whirlpools. The best way through is with a fost, but to please our friend in the pink submarine, we have chosen not to fost today."

"Her advice, as I recall," Nenuphar reminded him, "was not to fost at all."

"Yes, well, we'll see about that," said Hob. "So here we are, on the edge of the Antagonistic Ocean, faced with a fog clad reef that has already claimed the lives of far better sailors than us for untold centuries."

"And a clapped-out buoy warning us that 'Here be dragons,'" added M Cadvare.

"Exactly," said Hob, and he clapped his hands together. "Any ideas?"

They others looked at each other.

"Are you asking us?" Nenuphar asked him.

"Mm hmm."

"We don't know!"

"Cadaver?"

"Don't look at me!"

"Heidi?"

"St Bendix was no sailor," said Heidi. "If he'd been able to he would have fosted."

"Quite," said Hob. "There is a way. I've never tried it myself."

"What?" said Nenuphar.

"I'm going to have to resort to folklore. Perhaps it would be easier to daemonstrate."

"Don't you mean demonstrate?" she asked Hob.

"No. Daemonstrate. And for that I will need your help, Julian!"

"Ha-a-ha-a-ha-a-ha!" said Julian and he dived from the ceiling of the wheelhouse to dangle from Hob's outstretched arm.

Hob grinned and took him outside. He held up his arm and had a long talk with Julian, who hung on his every word with a fawning expression, avidly following the gestures Hob made with his other arm. Then he spread his wings and flew off into the fog.

"Will he be all right?" asked Heidi, as she joined Hob outside. "I found him foundering in the water on a yachting trip with my husband. It couldn't have been far from here."

"Don't worry my dear. The tormentor of chickens and dive bomber of seagulls will be all right."

"But he might get lost."

"I think that's extremely unlikely," said Hob. "Anarchadian Fruit Bat Foxes might not navigate using the stars but they have a very highly developed sense of smell. Remember the pong of fish and diesel when we boarded this vessel? He'll find us in this murk without any trouble."

They all kept watch and the minutes crept by. The fog swirled around them in contrast to the stillness of the water around the boat. Sometimes, out of the corners of their eyes, the more nervous members of the crew saw terrible shapes and curious points of light in the moving greyness.

"Did you see that?" Nenuphar whispered to M Cadvare.

"What?"

"There was a giant figure lurking over there."

"Over there?"

Nenuphar nodded.

"Huge great thing with horns?"

"You saw it as well, then!"

"I can't swear to it, but as soon as I looked directly at it, it was just swirling fog again."

"But why does it swirl when everything else is so still?"

"D'you think something out there is disturbing it?"

"I don't know."

"It's true that you can see better out of the corners of your eyes in the dark but I'm beginning to wish I couldn't."

"Oh for the comforting boom of a foghorn," sighed Heidi wistfully.

There was a dull thud on the deck and Hob went to investigate.

"Aha," he said and picked something up.

"What is it?" asked Nenuphar.

"What was it, you mean," and Hob showed them a well sucked seagull.

"What could have done that to it?" wondered an awestruck M Cadvare.

"Oh come on, Cadaver! It's a present from our little furry friend."

"What Ju-ju?" exclaimed Heidi. "He's never done anything like that before!"

There was another thud on the deck.

"Very obliging flitterfox, your Julian," said Hob.

"I thought he was a fruit bat," said Heidi. "I've spent a small fortune on paw paws and pomegranates."

"Oh they'll eat anything," said Hob, as there was another thud.

Hob began to make a small pile of dead seabirds as they fell out of the sky.

"Where's he getting them from?" asked Nenuphar. "I can't imagine any creature finding their way around in this fog."

"It's thanks to the fog that you can't see *mattato marino*. I've never seen it, but somewhere ahead of us I believe there are the collapsing hulks of many vessels."

"In that case I'm grateful for the fog," said Nenuphar.

"The masts and funnels provide roosts for great flocks of birds," went on Hob. "Julian's merely harvesting them."

Something large and white fell through the fog and there was a very heavy crash on the deck.

"Oh no!" said Heidi. "He's caught a hang glider!"

"Not out here, surely," said Hob. He went to look and came back with something not much smaller.

"Is that what I think it is?" Heidi asked him.

"I'm no expert," he replied, "but I think it might be an albatross."

"Isn't that awfully bad luck?"

"It certainly is," replied Hob, "at least for the albatross."

"Ju-ju, darling," Heidi called out. "Mummy says no more albatrosses!"

How far her voice could carry in the fog was anyone's guess but there was a distant barking overhead and another white blur fell to the deck.

"Too late," said Hob. "Don't albatrosses pair for life?"

"That's no consolation," said Nenuphar.

"Maybe we should have fosted after all," mused M Cadvare.

"That's enough now, Tormentor of Chickens!" shouted Hob.

"Oh don't call him that," scolded Heidi.

"Why not? That's what he calls himself. Anyway, that's stage one complete."

"So stage one is murder as many sea birds as we can, is it?" asked Nenuphar.

"We should have enough now."

"Enough for what?"

"Stage two," and Hob pulled out a penknife and stabbed the dead birds with it and threw them into the water.

"What are you doing?" demanded Nenuphar.

"He's using them for bait," said M Cadvare. "Aren't you?"

"Correct."

"So what are you planning to catch?"

"A shark."

"You're mad!" cried Nenuphar.

"No I'm not!" retorted Hob.

"Yes, you are, you're completely bonkers!"

"You can't say that any more."

"Why not? It's true!"

"There are more appropriate ways of saying less prejudicial things. You Euphobians are world leaders at it."

"Don't make me laugh!"

"You can't call me mad," insisted Hob.

"What are you then?"

"You have to call me, let me see, insanely... er, sani... sanitarily challenged." Hob frowned. "No, hang on a minute, that doesn't sound right."

"You're sanitarily challenged!" said a delighted Nenuphar.

"No!" pleaded Hob putting his hands to his ears. "Don't say it! Don't say it!"

"By your own admission, that's what you are!" she cried, dancing about in front of him with glee.

"No! Be quiet! Don't say it! Don't say it!"

"Why ever not?"

"Because."

"Because what?"

Hob sighed heavily. "I'm sensitive."

"Oh, what fun we have on the ocean wave," muttered M Cadvare. "For a moment just then, I thought you two were serious."

"I am serious," insisted Nenuphar, trying not to smile.

"She's seriously serious," said Hob.

"We've just been at sea a little too long."

"Aye!" Hob agreed with her. "Why! I seen some things at sea that'd make a grown man quiver like a cross between a jelly fish and a nervous wreck! There be some stories that be better left untold."

The others exchanged glances.

"Sharks!" cried Hob. "Don't talk to me about sharks!"

"We weren't," said Nenuphar.

"Well you ought to because there is one."

They crowded to the side of *Baggy Point Beauty* and saw a fin cutting the water's mirror surface as the shark made straight for the dead sea birds. It swallowed two as it passed and circled around for some more.

"Well," said Nenuphar, "I've never seen a shark like that before."

"Neither have I," declared M Cadvare. "Can we be sure it was a shark?"

"We all saw the fin," Heidi reminded them.

"I'm no expert in these matters," Hob reminded them, "but I think that was a hamster-headed shark."

"That would explain the very long front teeth," said Heidi.

"And the fur," added M Cadvare. "Not to mention the whiskers."

"Shame we're gonna have to kill it," said Hob.

"What?" exclaimed Nenuphar. "Why?"

"Stage three of the plan."

"Are we just going to keep on killing things?"

"No this is the last one," promised Hob and as the hamster-headed shark came round again, he swiftly banged it on the head with a piece of angle iron, killing it instantly. The shark rolled onto its side and he dropped a loop of rope around it.

"I hope this works," he said.

"You hope what works?" asked Nenuphar.

"Stage three."

"And what is stage three?"

"I could tell you," began Hob.

"But I'd only laugh."

"Yes, and at me, not with me."

The shark bobbed grotesquely. It was the only thing that broke the surface of the water.

Nenuphar shivered. After the relative warmth of Westward Ho! and Appledore, it was chilly in the fog.

Then suddenly, something rose up out of the depths and pulled the hamster-headed shark under the water.

Nenuphar screamed and Hob laughed.

The *Baggy Point Beauty* creaked. It dipped its nose and they felt it begin to slide between the oily waters.

"What's on the end of that line?" demanded Nenuphar as they gathered speed.

"Promise you won't laugh," said Hob.

"I promise."

"And you as well," said Hob. "I'm sensitive, remember?"

"We promise," said M Cadvare and Heidi.

"Well," Hob began, drawing closer to them conspiratorially, "the creature that is, even as I speak, pulling us through the treacherous reefs and shallows that surround us, symbolises the natural history of the Antagonistic Ocean. Look around us now. Can you not see within the fog the hulks of long-dead ships?"

His companions gasped.

All around them were ominous shapes, some of which towered over them while others assumed odd angles. They were proceeding slowly down a narrow channel between rotting hulks that must have lain on the reef for decades. They skirted the rotting crow's nests of some ancient sailing ship and ploughed steadily on through the narrow gap between the stricken craft. It grew dark as if they were entering a tunnel, but ahead it was a little lighter and gradually they thought they could see open water.

"Are we going to get through there?" wondered Heidi.

"I expect so," said Hob, which did nothing to inspire confidence.

"We don't want to run aground like these boats."

But Hob raised a hand to shush her. "Any minute now," he breathed. "Any minute now and we might see it!"

"See what?" asked Nenuphar.

"The only creature that truly knows these waters. The one at the very top of the food chain, even above the sharks."

Their eyes followed the straining rope and, as the refraction of the water tricked and teased them, they saw a patch of bright yellow almost break the surface in the shadow of the great rotting hulks.

Nobody spoke for a while but then M Cadvare said, "What the hell was that?"

"That, my dear fellow," said Hob, "was a sea banana!"

"That's just what it looked like to me," agreed M Cadvare. "Did you see it?"

Nenuphar and Heidi nodded.

"Amazing!" sighed Heidi. "Do you see the way it swims like a squid with its ... with its ..."

"Peel?" suggested M Cadvare.

"Yeah," agreed Heidi, "and one portion of its peel was curled around the hamster-headed shark."

"It was probably a four skin," said Hob. "Some are four skins and others are five skins. One's male and the other's female but I can't remember which is which."

"And they feed on sharks?" asked Nenuphar.

Hob nodded. "Did you see the baby one next to it?" he asked them, eagerly.

"I did but I still don't believe it," said Nenuphar.

"The sea banana is taking the dead shark to its nest."

"Nest?" queried Heidi. "Do sea bananas nest?"

"That might not be the right word," admitted Hob. "Maybe they bunch. But it's definitely taking the dead shark to feed its babies."

There was a gentle scrape on *Baggy Point Beauty's* bottom and then they were well inside the darkened passage. It appeared to be between two enormous hulks that must have steamed hard into the pile of other vessels to have forged their way so far onto the reef. Strange vegetation hung over them and brushed the tops of their mast.

"What is that?" asked M Cadvare.

"Seaweed?" ventured Nenuphar.

"Fetterweed," corrected Hob. "Once foundered on these rocks or becalmed and ensnared by the fetterweed, there is no escape."

"What happened to their crews?" asked M Cadvare.

"They're still here," said Hob, with a meaningful glance. "Why do you suppose the fetterweed bothers to climb out of the water?"

M Cadvare managed to suppose, but kept it to himself.

"Where does the sea banana live?" he asked.

"In a nest, remember?" said Nenuphar.

"So where's the nest?" persisted M Cadvare.

"There are caves on the inner side of the reef," said Hob.

"So it's going to dive at any minute," said Nenuphar.

"We'll cut the line before then," Hob told her, "otherwise we'll be joining the shark for dinner."

"Are there many sharks in these waters?" she asked him.

"I would imagine so. It's not just the fetterweed that lives off the crews."

"Why don't the sea bananas live on the outside of the reef?" asked Heidi.

Hob shrugged. "I suppose they just aren't the right sort of caves."

"Probably too many wrecks," said M Cadvare.

And on they went at a steady ten knots.

And, if any of them had looked behind them, they would have seen a small orange and white flash as a smart traffic cone fought off the unwelcome attentions of the fetterweed and struggled on after them.

CHAPTER 78

Gradually, they could make out the end of the channel. The sea banana pulled them on vigorously, and they noticed that the ships on either side aged, both in terms of their design and the extent of their neglect.

As they bumped between a derelict pair of China clippers, they heard a familiar barking overhead and looked up to see Julian peering down at them.

At first they thought he was dangling from some rigging but then the rigging moved and they saw through the mist that he was on the arm of an enormous pirate.

"Ha ha!" he shouted down to them, black and gold teeth flashing. "Ahoy there! Boat without a flag!"

"Well, well, if it isn't Davy Jones!" Hob shouted back. "We're the *Baggy Point Beauty* out of Appledore headed for Lanson! Captained and navigated by Nick Hob."

"Hob!" exclaimed Davy Jones. "Yer no sailor! What for are ye bringing land lubbin' souls like yer own through my domain?"

"Davy? Have y'ever seen a pink submarine?"

"A pink one? I should say not. Why?"

"There's a beautiful young scientist messing about in one in the waters off Westward Ho!!"

"I bin afore the mast for nigh on four hunnerd years, I've fought with phantom killer whales, I've wrestled with Kraken and I've eaten the sandwiches on cross channel ferries but women in submarines…. Why! That be as natural as having a man for a figurehead!"

"We were gonna fost our way home but the beautiful young scientist persuaded us not to."

"What!" roared Davy Jones.

"She said it would destabilise the space/time continuum."

"And ye believed 'er?"

"Not really."

"That sort o' talk never stopped ye before!"

"We thought we'd better not fost in case she was right," Heidi called out.

"And she did something to stop Hob from fosting," added Nenuphar.

Hob glared at her

"What! Ye have women aboard?"

"Yes. Two."

"Ye know that be bad luck!"

"Oh. Is it?" asked Hob, nonchalantly, as if considering whether to throw Nenuphar overboard.

"Aye. Not that I be one to listen to the less-than-super-stitions of lily-livered swabs!"

"Ha ha!"

"Ha ha! How many souls are with ye?"

"Just the *Terminal Murrain* and these three by my side."

"Well now, Hob. There be the small matter of a toll."

"Don't worry," Hob said quietly to his horrified companions, "I've thought of this."

He looked back up at Davy.

"Skirrows are useless to me," said Davy Jones. "Nobody else wants 'em except Nick Hob the Horsepower Whisperer and while he pays a good price, he'll get nothing for 'em when he comes to sell 'em. It's yer non-skirrows I be after an' I can see all ye've got is three of 'em. Hand 'em over and we'll call it a deal!"

"Could I just confer with my travelling companions?"

"Confer with 'em? Are ye losin' yer touch, Hob lad? Yer becalmed and I have all the time in the world – and the next, ha ha! Take as long as ye like! It'll be an early day of reckoning for some of ye!"

The others were speechless as he turned back to them but, instead of talking to them, he dived past and disappeared into the bowels of the engine room. They were still staring at each other in outraged silence when he came back up again, carrying an armful of industrial strength ear defenders.

"Quick!" he whispered. "Put these on!"

They were so surprised they didn't argue.

"Well?" demanded Davy Jones, the captain of a thousand sailors' souls.

"Davy?" began Hob, "we were just wondering if, perhaps if it wasn't too much of an inconvenience, whether you might be amenable to, out of the bad-ness of your benighted black heart you understand, maybe favouring us with a song from you!"

"A song? A song from me?"

"Only if you've got your squeezebox with you. And if it's not too much trouble."

"Ha ha! So mote it be, me hearties! I'll just put this flitterfox down. He's one o' yourn, I dare say!"

"Ju-ju, come to mummy!" called out Heidi, as Julian swooped down to her.

There was a discordant groan from somewhere above them and Davy

Jones re-appeared from the mist with his accordion.

"Fare ye well, me hearties! And splice the cable as soon as yer sea banana dives or I'll meet ye down below! May the devil take ye, Hob! But first a song, entitled *The Sailor with the Navy Blue Eyes!*"

CHAPTER 79

Having mended the hole in her upholstery, Therese ignored the grauniads' instructions to stay put and fosted. Somebody, somewhere, somewhen might have made a mistake and, across the vastness of infinite probability, she hoped it wasn't her.

She cast her mind back to what the other grauniads had told her. Fortunately, she had a very good memory, despite her dizzy IQ. And if ever she wanted to check events, she could always fost.

So she fosted, back to just after she had refutured the unfutured.

Re-materialising near where and when she had already been was always tricky. She had often surprised herself in the past, been surprised by herself in the future and will been surprised when dabbling with future events that had occurred in the past and vice versa – such was her complicated existence beyond the normal rules of physics in her own, personal space/time discontinuum.

According to her calculations, if she re-materialised so that she overlapped a previous or future existence, there would be an enormous explosion. The chances of her intricately edited, and complexly plotted, existence continuing would then be negligible. There was some evidence to suggest that such a terminal dimensional mingling had, or will, or will been, already occurred because Therese was pushing the envelope of her life's narrative structure. Although no stranger to encountering herself from the future, it hadn't happened for a while. The significance of this had not been lost on her. It could indicate that the cutting edge of her life's narrative was at and end. She might not have a future.

On the other hand, the rest of her life's narrative might not occur in this paraverse, which probably wasn't going to last much longer anyway. She had also invented a device to prevent temporal paraversal parking accidents. Her spatial awareness was just as highly developed as her temporal lobes but it seemed foolish to take any chances.

Using her multi-dimensional parking sensors, she re-materialised well away from her heroic previous self. She parked upside-down on the ceiling of the conference hall, trusting to the human tendency not to look up.

There she was, down below, being congratulated by the assembled world leaders. Everyone looked very happy. Mr PUE was working up to telling them his joke about the Euphobian, the Consumerican and the Gondwanalese but Therese had heard his joke before, before.

Therese switched on her gravity inverter, got out of her Cadillac and walked across the ceiling to where the same but earlier Cadillac had been parked. By now it must surely be covered in waiting grauniads who she strongly suspected had no right interfering with this paraverse and no right, either, to be there and then.

She carried a small but powerful vacuum cleaner and wore some striking knitted headwear inspired by Kevin's Discretion of the Soul Hat. It wasn't the first time that she had used a disguise of eccentric cleaning lady to closely observe interesting circumstances and she was confident that it would work on maverick grauniads. It might even have worked on her earlier self for she had no recollection of seeing any cleaning staff during her earlier negotiations with the grauniads.

There they were, sprawled insolently over the bonnet and wings of the earlier Therese's Cadillac. Instead of the familiar little figures of Thor, Brunhilde, Moon Wolf, Isis, Gaia, Zeus and Gert, there was a modest medusa, a stumpy cyclops, a fun-sized naked pensioner wearing a flying helmet and dark socks, a small green man, an English Miss or – possibly – myth, a grinning jack o'lantern and a many armed Kali who might have been statuesque had she not been merely ornamental.

The goddess of multi-tasking made eccentric cleaning lady Therese deeply suspicious. As the grauniads waited for the triumphant earlier Therese to come back to her car, Kali kept rolling up her shirt sleeves to consult the watches on her many forearms.

Therese moved closer and began vacuuming quietly.

The earlier Therese came through the doors and gaped at the grauniads draped over her car. Their exchange began just as Therese remembered it.

The grauniads insisted that the unfutured should not have been refutured because of the effect that Hob and his Wild Hunt would have on this and the neighbouring paraverses. Unless she defutured the refutured and their paraverse, they would defuture her.

As she listened to them arguing while she hoovered, Therese didn't doubt for a moment that the maverick grauniads were capable of defuturing her or the refutured. It was just that the maverick grauniads were quite insistent that she must be the one to do it. All she needed to do now was find out why.

CHAPTER 80

As the *Baggy Point Beauty* left the rotting hulks behind in the mist, figures began to emerge from under hatches with blankets over their heads. Behind them, Davy Jones was still extracting his toll. All around him the fetterweed trembled although there was no breeze. Thankfully his song didn't carry far in the fog, but M Cadvare could still hear the creak and groan of the tortured hulks behind them. Occasionally, there was a crash and a splash as something cried enough and collapsed into the sea.

The line attached to the hamster-headed shark held by the sea banana suddenly steepened dramatically.

"Cut the line!" ordered Hob, pulling off his ear defenders.

M Cadvare threw off his blanket and sliced through the rope with an axe.

Calm returned to the waters of the Antagonistic Ocean and the *Baggy Point Beauty* began to slow down again. Julian barked a farewell to Davy Jones and they could just hear him roar back at them.

"Ah, but ye've been a wonderful audience! Thank 'ee, Antagonistic Ocean, thank 'ee! And good nite!"

Hob flashed up the engines once again and they continued stealthily forward. Gradually the fog began to clear.

"Poor sod," said Hob, looking behind them. "He never wanted to go to sea. All he ever really wanted to do was to sing."

"I can't imagine he gets many requests," said M Cadvare.

"I have the feeling you've made him feel very happy," said Heidi.

"One day Davy will sell his soul for a musical ear," said Hob.

"Why doesn't he?" asked Nenuphar.

"Because it's against the rules of STANTA," Hob told her. "That's the Soul Transference and Necromancer's Trade Association. It was set up to prevent Soul Traders trading for each other's souls."

"You mean their *own* souls?"

"Yeah, their own God-given souls. Davy's a member and tries very hard to abide by STANTA's rules and regulations, but the temptations are tremendous."

"Maybe he should succumb to them," snorted Nenuphar, "and benefit musical seafarers everywhere."

Slowly the mist cleared and they began to see a few islands up ahead.

"Land ho!" shouted Hob, with pleasure. "Doesn't it look great?"

"It's very dark over there," said Nenuphar.

"It looks as if something blew this place apart," remarked M Cadvare as Hob steered them between some jagged rocks.

"It does, doesn't it?" agreed the Horsepower Whisperer.

"Why's that then?

"That's because it *was* blown apart, millions of years ago."

"Was it a meteorite?"

"Nobody knows for certain. It must have been something pretty bloody big to make a hole this size for the Antagonistic Ocean."

"It's very dark over there," repeated Nenuphar.

"Do you know this place?" Heidi asked Hob, who, out of his natural environment, did not inspire much confidence behind the wheel of a trawler.

Hob peered at the horizon for some time before answering. Eventually, he grinned and said, "Yes, I believe I do."

Ahead of them was a broken line of land where the sky met the sea. They could just see some lights on some of the larger masses, but in front of these were many other fragments, some apparently inhabited islands. They passed some rocky outcrops and came to a wide channel where they saw other vessels, typically bulky merchantmen, riding at anchor.

"None of those vessels have any flags," said Heidi.

"It's Anarchadia, isn't it?" breathed M Cadvare.

Hob just grinned and steered them towards a great mass of street lights.

M Cadvare frowned. A city was usually marked by an orange glow in the sky but here the heavens seemed to consume the light pollution.

"It's much blacker up ahead than it was before," warned Nenuphar.

The sky over the islands was darkening as if someone was pulling a cover over them. They could still make out hills in the distance and lines of buildings by the shore but it slowly became apparent that the great port that lined the coast had no sense of bustle or signs of activity. The city seemed to be contemplating its reflection in the unnaturally perfect surface of the sea.

"Dark Time is coming," said Hob.

"Brilliant!" said Nenuphar, when it was obviously anything but. "What a great time to get here!"

"Never mind," said Hob, "at least the fog's cleared up."

They chugged steadily onwards and passed some of the anchored cargo vessels, which also seemed unusually still, although there were lamps aboard, many lamps, as if the crew were trying to repel what Hob called Dark Time.

M Cadvare looked around and noticed that muddy flats were now reaching out to them on their port side.

"Are we in an enormous river channel?" he asked Hob.

"Yeah," came the slow reply. Hob seemed as awed as M Cadvare felt. "This is the River Temmar. And that is Lanson."

As he said Lanson, the lights of the city began to wink out and the *Baggy Point Beauty*'s engines began to falter.

"What's happening?" asked Nenuphar.

Black clouds were rushing in from the north as if to repel invaders. A bend in the river opened up before them and they saw tall dockyard cranes and the towers of a city beyond them. And as they watched, the warning lights that marked these went out.

Hob chuckled softly. "This land is benighted before its time."

"It's nothing to be proud of!" Nenuphar scolded him but Hob simply ignored her.

M Cadvare glanced at Heidi. She didn't look very alarmed. She still appeared better informed than he could ever hope to be but he could also tell that she was very impressed.

"Do you know about this place?" he asked her, as she leaned on the railings.

She turned slowly to look at him over her shoulder and smiled. "Not really," she said. "I've heard stories, of course. In fact, I had to dig to find the legends, rumours and twenty-first century myths about Anarchadia but when I found them I never really believed them."

"Aren't you afraid?"

She laughed. "Don't you feel like you're coming home?"

M Cadvare thought about it. "I suppose I do. I just wish it hadn't happened so late."

"Better late than never," said Heidi.

"It's so late it's practically never!" retorted Nenuphar but Heidi just turned to gaze at Dark Time again.

A strange tremor ran through the *Baggy Point Beauty* and the trawler faltered, sending a different wave pattern out on either side in the oily waters.

"Take the wheel, Cadaver," said Hob.

"What is happening?" persisted Nenuphar.

"The engines need my help," said Hob. "Can you feel the build up of static? Dark Time is upon us and it's disrupting electrical activity as well as combustion. Compression ignition engines are less susceptible to it than most and I should be able to keep any engine going during Dark Time but we're all at sea."

"Don't we know it!"

"So it's just as well that we've reached the River Temmar then, isn't it? Cheer up, little Nenny! It's not as if it's the end of the world!" and Hob descended into the engine room again.

M Cadvare saw Nenuphar's shoulders tense in fury as she watched Hob go. He reached out with one hand and was just able to place it on her shoulder. It wasn't much but she relaxed ever so slightly at his touch and shot him a sudden glance. He saw the fear in her fierce eyes and he would have liked to have put his arms around her but that would have meant taking both hands off the wheel.

Nenuphar hesitated.

M Cadvare was reminded of many years ago when there had still been feral cats living in Mourion. Some were quite friendly while others wouldn't even come close. Somewhere in between were those who liked to be stroked in certain circumstances but had a knack of keeping just far enough away so that you had to stretch. That's just how Nenuphar appeared at that moment and this impression lasted in the way she moved away from him and went out of the wheelhouse.

M Cadvare kept their course down the middle of the river. There was no other vessel moving anywhere.

They could see both banks quite clearly now. Freighters were moored at quays and in tidal basins. In places, hills came right down to the water's edge to end in muddy beaches but elsewhere there were great expanses of flat concrete wharves piled high with shipping containers. Extraordinary cranes and gantries stood guard over them. Rails reflected what light there was and M Cadvare began to make out trains of wagons lined up on the dockside. He could also see automobiles parked here and there but they were nothing like his unlamented personal transportation device. From what he could see of them, these vehicles were the kinds of machines that had prompted the Euphobian Commissioners to ban the term car. Some carried numbers on their doors and bonnets and this struck him as a very public spirited thing to do for he had often thought that registration plates were a bit side and useless when viewed side on.

The buildings ranged from ultra-modern high-tech warehouses through wooden goods sheds to rambling piles of huge stones, artfully arranged into what looked like defensive structures. Many of these fortress-like buildings had been converted towards more peaceful trading activities, except that, at the moment, there were no signs of any activity at all.

By now, there were no more significant light sources but M Cadvare could actually see quite a lot. He tried to work out where the light was coming from and realised with a start that there was a stale phosphorescence coming up from the river. And by this uncanny light, he could see shoals of fish beneath them, hanging stationery as they passed, waiting uncertainly for the strange phenomenon of Dark Time to climax. But on the land there were not even these signs of life.

He took the *Baggy Point Beauty* closer in and saw for the first time an open-sided structure that contained long lines of things that glinted in the terrible half light of Dark Time. With an awful thrill, he realised that these long low buildings contained row upon row of motorcycles.

"Do you see what I see?" he asked Nenuphar and Heidi.

They nodded slowly.

"This can only be Anarchadia," he told them.

Nenuphar still didn't look convinced.

"It might be time to start believing Hob," he told her.

"Just as the beautiful young scientist's prediction is coming true," she replied.

A heavy shudder ran through the *Baggy Point Beauty* and M Cadvare began to look for a suitable berth. Sputtering torches mounted on the stone walls lit the wet surfaces of cobbled docks and he thought he caught glimpses of figures shifting among the shadows.

The noise of the *Baggy Point Beauty*'s fitful engines sounded unbearably loud as it echoed off the walls of the warehouses. M Cadvare didn't feel as if they were being watched. He wondered if anyone on land was in a more profound state of suspended animation than the fish. Certainly, he could detect no sign of interest in their conspicuous approach.

The girls outside looked back at him and he said, "We're going to have to park this thing."

They began to search and shortly a likely looking place emerged from the peculiar gloom. It was a berth made up of huge stones stood on end. There was no mortar between them and they appeared to be held together in the maritime equivalent of dry stone walling except that they obviously weren't dry. They were covered in sea weed up to a distinct line and the nearer they got the stronger the smell of muddy harbour became.

M Cadvare cut the power of the engines. Hob was bound to notice this but he didn't come up to the bridge. He stayed below keeping the engines running in case they were needed.

M Cadvare shouted to Heidi to take the wheel from him and went to look for a length of rope.

"Take us in close," he told her, "and I'll tie the boat up. You're not exactly dressed for leaping ashore with a rope."

Heidi, who still looked ready for a night out on the town, laughed.

"You'd be surprised what I can get up to in these clothes," she told him.

She turned out to be a more than competent helmswoman and brought the *Baggy Point Beauty* in parallel to the quayside.

M Cadvare gathered up his rope into a loop and threw it as hard as he could.

It landed in a heap, nowhere near the bollard he'd been aiming for, but a red streak flew down, grabbed it and neatly looped it over his target just as he'd intended.

Julian flitted about in front of them, barking as if to say, "Again!"

M Cadvare found another rope and then another and then another and each time Julian caught them in his mouth and dropped them over a suitable mooring until M Cadvare had run out of rope.

Gradually, with Nenuphar's help, M Cadvare took up the slack and soon the *Baggy Point Beauty* bumped against the worn out car tyres that lined the masonry of the riverbank.

CHAPTER 81

From what the maverick grauniads were saying, Therese realised that Hob and the Wild Hunt had to be stopped from fosting but, to her, genocide and the destruction of a whole paraverse seemed a little extreme.

She was very pleased with her disguise. Her earlier self hadn't noticed the eccentric cleaning lady in the stripy knitted hat vacuum cleaning in the background so she was comfortable that the grauniads hadn't spotted her either.

"I see I don't have much of a choice," the earlier Therese was saying.

Eccentric cleaning lady Therese was reassured that she could not have done anything else but defuture this paraverse although her conscience was still not entirely clear.

"What if I stopped the Wild Hunt?" the earlier Therese asked the grauniads.

"You can't," replied the grauniads. "Believe us we've tried. This paraverse must come to an end. That's the only way."

And the maverick grauniads slid from her Cadillac and off went the earlier Therese to defuture the refutured.

A number of things occurred to eccentric cleaning lady Therese. Now that she knew that they were impostors, the grauniads' assurances that this approach was the only solution had a pan-dimensionally hollow ring. She also didn't understand why it had to be her who did the dirty work. They were very determined that this paraverse should come to an end immediately. Idly she wondered if they wanted Kevin Mullins to be sent back in time. But how could they know that he would be re-incarnated? And develop into the Soul of Souls?

Eccentric cleaning lady Therese decided to wait and see what the grauniads did next.

They didn't do anything for a few moments and then let out a collective sigh of relief before hugging themselves and slapping each other's backs.

Then they turned around and saw her.

Therese continued hoovering nonchalantly but from the sudden change in their expressions she began wondering if there might be a chink in her disguise that only a pan-dimensional grauniad might see.

"What in all the paraverses are you doing?" demanded the medusa.

"Ooverin!" replied Therese, still in character. "Wot's it look like?"

But even as she said this she realised her mistake. Instead of the carpet, she was vacuum cleaning the ceiling tiles. She was still upside down.

Quickly she switched off her gravity inverter and landed in a heap on the floor looking up at the knee-high grauniads with her hoover still stuck to the ceiling. But one of the advantages of being so brainy was being able to think at light-speed.

She reached out and switched off her vacuum cleaner, which fell down beside her.

"Dontcha just hate it when that happens!" she exclaimed.

There was a satisfying flicker of confusion over the faces of the grauniads. Of course, thought Therese, this isn't their paraverse. They might think this is normal.

Then the naked one with the flying helmet and socks said, "Come on! We must go!" and they went, just like that.

Therese couldn't be sure but just before they'd left, tiny wings seemed to sprout from the naked grauniad's flying helmet and socks. She stood up and checked the watches on her forearm. The grauniads were right. She was perilously out of time and had to get back to her car or perish with the defutured by her own hand. Quickly she switched on her vacuum cleaner and sat on it. She just hoped the cable was long enough to reach her car parked on the ceiling of the conference hall.

CHAPTER 82

"It doesn't look a very lively place," said M Cadvare. He seemed disappointed after all Hob's stories about Anarchadia.

Nenuphar peered into the gloom at Lanson. "It looks like a deserted stage in a theatre," she said.

The only sound was the slow slap, slap, slap of the water against the hull.

"Shall we go ashore?" asked M Cadvare.

"Of course," said Hob who had come up from the engine room now that Heidi had stopped the engines. "What are you waiting for? Shall I go first?"

He shouldered *Nosferatu*'s crate but Julian was the first one ashore. He'd been flying around in excitement at coming home for some time and swooped down to dangle from a lamp post to watch them disembark, obviously hoping that they would enjoy coming home as much as he did.

Hob stepped ashore, put down his crate and turned to face them.

"At last," he said. "Welcome to Anarchadia."

"And to think this whole archipelago has been kept secret for centuries!" breathed Heidi, as she gracefully allowed Hob to help her ashore.

"I can't believe it," breathed M Cadvare.

"Neither can I," whispered Nenuphar, for entirely different reasons. For M Cadvare it seemed his wish had come true. She just felt incredulous.

"Shall we?" M Cadvare asked her.

Without replying she began to clamber over the side of the trawler. There was no swell and, as the tide wasn't far below the high water mark, the *Baggy Point Beauty* was close to the top of the embankment but the stones were slippery as she climbed up. She had to avoid lengths of rope at the top and when she at last stood beside the others it felt as if she had developed sea legs and would have to acclimatise to walking on land again.

"Whaddya think?" asked Hob. He was grinning enough to split his crash helmet.

His companions looked around them.

Nenuphar caught Julian's eye and he wagged his bushy tail.

"It's too dark for my liking," she said.

Hob and Julian looked a little non-plussed.

"Well, obviously, it's not very bright here at the moment," Hob replied, "but even during Dark Time it's a fantastic place!" and he grabbed their hands and forced them to dance on the quayside.

Nenuphar initially had no intention of joining in but Julian began swooping and diving around to encourage her. Despite everything, she found her spirits rising. How could an animal like him be depressed if it really was the end of the world? Perhaps the prospect of certain, inescapable doom made him feel more alive than ever and with this thought a kind of recklessness took her over.

She joined in with the dance and by the time Heidi and M Cadvare wanted to stop to catch their breaths she was grinning from ear to ear almost as much Hob. Her heart pounded and her blood sang in her ears. She could only assume that this was what freedom felt like.

"So," Hob laughed at her, "you do like it here after all!"

"I don't have much to compare it with," she replied.

"Better the devil you don't know, huh?"

"While I'm here I think I'll make the most of it," she replied and M Cadvare, panting with excitement, grinned at her with approval.

"That's the spirit!" said Hob. "Y' know? This human trafficking business is far more rewarding than I ever imagined."

"Are you considering a new career?" Heidi asked him.

"I can think of worse ways of making an afterliving. But I still prefer fosting."

"Where is everyone?" asked Nenuphar.

"It's Dark Time," said Hob. "They're just keeping their heads down."

"You could import loads of people here," said M Cadvare.

"You don't think they've been evacuated, do you?" asked Nenuphar.

"No," answered Heidi. "I've read about this. They're just lying low."

"I still can't believe we're here!" exclaimed M Cadvare.

"Oh ye of little faith," said Hob, indulgently.

"Me neither," said Nenuphar. "I can't believe it was so easy."

"Easy?" said Hob. "Easy? Cadaver sold his soul to get here! You've only come along for the ride. Even then, it was far more difficult than I ever imagined."

"Hob's right," M Cadvare told her, "but it was worth it, even with the prospect of Dark Time!" and he laughed.

"Come on," said Hob. "Let me show you around."

He picked up his crate and they walked along the embankment. Railway lines of many different gauges criss-crossed the cobbles and patches of concrete and tarmac. Some of the narrower gauge lines featured little cast iron turntables in front of the warehouses and rails led from these under wooden double doors or more modern roller shutters. They passed solitary wagons, some with loads of small containers but most of them were empty. Under the legs of a crane they even found a steam railway engine.

"Ah!" said Hob. "Reverend Tregaskis would like this Scottish pug!"

The locomotive, a sturdy four-wheeled shunting engine gave off a welcome warmth although it wasn't really cold. A question mark of smoke curled from its chimney and it ticked and tutted at Hob's remarks as if it understood what he was on about.

A little further on they passed in front of an enormous railway tunnel. Nenuphar had expected two lines of tracks to emerge from this but was a little alarmed to see only one. The rails were noticeably bigger than the others. They were also spaced much wider apart than any other railway tracks that she'd ever seen before. This and the size of the tunnel made her shudder when she came to judge the size of the train that they were meant to take.

She glanced nervously into the tunnel but couldn't see anything. In the other direction the tracks went straight out onto a long quay that must have reached the middle of the River Temmar but there were no other signs of a train.

Although they still hadn't met any people, Nenuphar could feel the bustle that had filled Lanson until recently. Crates waited to be loaded. Here and there were strange road lorries, both ancient and modern, with the names of obscure companies and places painted on their sides and whenever they came across a car or a motorcycle, Hob went into raptures over it, describing its salient points to anyone who would listen and even those who did not. Nenuphar had never seen cars like these before and had no previous experience of motorcycles. Some looked quite ancient while others looked impossibly sleek against the backdrop of this rambling part of the docks. Hob treated anything with an engine as a work of art and, despite herself, Nenuphar began to take an interest in the designs of Edward Turner, Gabriella Morini, Giorgetto Giugiaro and Alec Issigonis.

Hob appeared remarkably nonchalant when faced with the end of the world. With *Nosferatu*'s crate on one shoulder, he wandered arm in arm with Heidi, admiring what he called "road weapons" as if they were exhibits in an art gallery.

"Just who does he think he is?" Nenuphar hissed at M Cadvare. "Isn't he concerned about the end of the world?"

Despite the age of the offices and warehouses, there were few signs of neglect. Very little space was wasted. The dockside had obviously developed over many centuries and evolved all manner of conveniences, both great and small. It retained many of its original features such as wrought iron cranes that swung out from walls and drawbridges that swung over little harbours. In some places the wharves were beautifully curved and Nenuphar realised that they mirrored the graceful lines of sailing vessels that must have fitted snugly against them.

"The sky's gone out!" said M Cadvare, looking back out to sea.

"Exactly," said Hob. "The intense static electricity has knocked out all the electrical appliances."

The sodium harbour lamps gathered around the smaller flickering gas lamps and craned avian necks over them so that their darkened heads could see what light there was.

"That would explain the flaming torches, then," said Nenuphar, looking around at the oily smoke. "Even they burn sulkily.

"There comes a point when a flame makes more smoke than light," Hob told her.

"So it would appear."

"Every sort of combustion is affected, some more than others. If our boat had spark ignition engines instead of diesels, I would have worked myself hoarse whispering up enough power to get us into shore."

"Is Dark Time why the waters are so calm?"

Hob shrugged. "I'm no sailor but I think it probably is. Look at this!"

He ushered Heidi along to admire a particularly noteworthy two seater sports car.

"His enthusiasm is infectious," remarked M Cadvare.

"I hate to admit it but you're right," agreed Nenuphar. "I've never even seen a Triumph GT6 before but now I know the Mk 2 version has the desirable independent rear suspension."

M Cadvare chuckled to himself and then more loudly to Nenuphar. "I feel dangerously over-stimulated."

"That's a shame," she replied with heavy irony. "I'm afraid the further we walk, the more Lanson becomes a two-dimensional backdrop."

"No, it's okay! I feel great. It's clear to me now that all my life I never really felt anything. The sensation of being alive has been growing ever since I met Hob. I never believed it could be this intense! I'm glad that I've set foot in this deserted, darkened and run down dockyard when Dark Time has dampened it down a bit. I can acclimatise to the full on experience of Anarchadia."

"That's if you get the chance."

"Look at this!" Hob called out to them.

"What a lovely Mercedes!" exclaimed Heidi.

"A pagoda roofed 230SL!"

M Cadvare waved at them but turned back to Nenuphar. "Don't you remember when you were young?" he asked her. "Do you remember how intense everything was when you were a teenager? Our initial impressions were formed immediately and yet have been so long-lasting. When you're older you can still remember these things from all those years ago, and what they meant to you, but you can't recall what you were doing last week!"

Nenuphar smiled at him.

"Now I can't remember last week because so much has happened to me since then. Nenny? I feel like I've been re-born. Can't you feel it, too?"

She sighed. "Yes. Yes, I feel it, too, but perhaps not as strongly as you do."

M Cadvare returned her smile with interest. "Well, you are so much younger than me."

"Flatterer."

"Perhaps you've never have lost that feeling of having some control in your life. Maybe your sense of hope and wonder hasn't been knocked out of you."

"No. My feelings are tempered by the thought that this is the end of everything. Dark Time is upon us. It's the end of the world."

"Oh wow!" squealed Heidi, from some way off. "A Morris Minor! Hob? What's a halfshaft?"

"Hob thinks he can fost his way out of this but we both know he can't," Nenuphar told M Cadvare. "He seems to be in complete denial. Ignorance really does seem to be bliss."

She glanced along the quayside and there was Hob taking the Morris Minor to bits to show Heidi a halfshaft.

"But I prefer to do it our way. Suddenly there is no hope at all and in a strange way it's a relief to know that we don't have to struggle anymore. And we struggled for years! How we struggled! Now it's all over."

"If it has to end I'm glad to end it this way." M Cadvare took her hand. "It's a shame it can't go on but this as good an ending as I can imagine."

Nenuphar swallowed hard. Suddenly her mouth was dry. Her heart was fluttering hard as if to escape from her rib cage. For the first time since the end of the world had begun, she felt nervous instead of angry.

"I think the best thing we can do, is count our blessings tonight. If it is tonight. This Dark Time is confusing. But I think we should carry on counting our blessings until the end comes. Don't you?"

An unaccountable joy flooded through Nenuphar at his simple words. She took his other hand and held it tightly, wondering where she could possibly start counting. One moment she had been in fear of her life, now she was in an ecstasy. A few moments ago she saw nothing but the grim futility of their lives. Now she couldn't believe how lucky they both were.

They beamed at each other.

"This is an amazing place, isn't it?" she said

"It's not just the place. It's us."

"We never lost our souls," she told him. "All that time in Mourion we managed to keep them, despite everything."

"So many souls have fallen by the wayside," said M Cadvare, sadly.

"We kept ours till the very end! We should be happy we got this far!"

"I am happy."

"So am I."

CHAPTER 83

M Cadvare took Nenuphar in his arms and kissed her savagely for what would surely be the first and last time. He was pleasantly surprised by his sudden passion and so, it seemed, was Nenuphar. Far from pulling away, she stretched out and offered herself to him like a flower might offer herself to the sun.

Although he had his eyes shut, he could feel her blooming. She moved her limbs gently to increase the surface area of their contact. It felt as if she was exposing herself to him as much as possible, as if her limbs were leaves, photosynthesising with pleasure. He suddenly remembered that she was named after a water lily and had a mad idea that, if she was a plant woman, did her vegetarianism make her some kind of cannibal? But from the way she returned his kiss, it was obvious she was partial to some flesh and this revelation intoxicated him even more.

Although neither of them had the opportunity to breathe, neither of them appeared to be suffocating. Nenuphar felt like pure oxygen to him and his soul, his mind and his heart inhaled deeply. Hob, he felt sure, would have heartily approved of such wanton behaviour.

At last they paused to look at each other and he saw a new and wondrous pleasure in her eyes. But then it faded and he remembered how little time they had.

She glanced away to where Hob was enthusing over a line of parked motorcycles. He'd put *Nosferatu*'s crate down and was talking happily about a "120 degree Laverda" that he'd found.

Heidi was listening politely.

Nenuphar drew a little apart from M Cadvare but only so that she might see him better.

"So," she said, "This is how it ends."

"A kind of happy ending," he ventured.

"But an ending all the same. If I didn't know there was no future I would never have done this."

M Cadvare had to think about that. "No time for regrets," he concluded. "Not much of a future and not much of a past but the present is just right," and despite her slight gloom she laughed.

"Cadaver?"

"Hob?"

"Are you all right?"

"I never felt better!" he replied, squeezing Nenuphar's hand.

Hob grinned at them. "Are any of you hungry?" he asked, effortlessly spinning his crate on its corner on his fore finger.

Julian was swinging on the sign of a tavern, making it squeak. Some bats came flapping out of a warehouse and he swooped to snap some up in his jaws.

"Ju-ju?" Heidi said to him. "Not the endangered species, there's a good boy."

"How can you eat at a time like this?" Nenuphar asked Hob.

He threw *Nosferatu*'s crate into the air and caught it again.

" 'If food be the music of love'," said Hob, " 'pig out! Give me excess of it!' "

"Is that right?" wondered M Cadvare.

"Indubitably," said Hob.

"Do you think we ought to tell him?" Nenuphar whispered to M Cadvare.

"Tell me what?" Hob asked her, his good cheer dipping just a little.

"I mean he seems so happy without knowing."

"Not knowing what?" persisted Hob, a little less happily.

Nenuphar took a big breath. "Hob," she began. "There's something you ought to know."

"Oh yes?"

"You, too, Heidi, although I imagine that you've already worked it out for yourself and are just putting on a brave face for Hob's sake."

"Am I?

"Is she?"

"Aren't you?"

M Cadvare beamed at Nenuphar. She was handling the situation beautifully. "Just listen to her," he told the others. "Believe me, it'll be a blessed relief."

"Blessed relief?"

"Well, maybe not a blessed relief for you Hob, but a relief all the same."

"Okay," said Hob. "We're listening."

"Hob," began Nenuphar. "You know all this Dark Time."

"Yeah?"

"Well, it's not Dark Time."

"What is it, then?"

"Look. I know this may come as a shock to you but it's actually the end of the world."

Hob looked frankly amazed. He stared at Nenuphar incredulously and then looked at M Cadvare as if for confirmation about what she'd said.

Nosferatu's crate wobbled dangerously.

Instinctively, M Cadvare reached out to steady it. He took hold of it and silently indicated that Hob ought to put it down.

Hob seemed to be in a state of sudden shock. Heidi put her arm on his shoulder and he let M Cadvare help him put *Nosferatu*'s crate down, although M Cadvare didn't anticipate how heavy it was and got put down with it.

"End of the world?" Hob said, released from his burden.

"Yes," said Nenuphar, softly, and she and Heidi each took one of his hands and rubbed them gently.

"No it isn't," said Hob.

"Yes it is."

"No it isn't."

"Yes it is."

"No it isn't."

"Yes it is."

"Why do you think it's the end of the world?" Hob asked her, with a little laugh of amazement, as M Cadvare picked himself up again.

"Isn't it obvious?"

"Well, frankly no."

"Weren't you listening to the beautiful young scientist? Haven't you noticed that nothing electrical works? Didn't you just say that nothing will burn properly?"

"Apart from that," said Hob.

"Haven't you noticed how dark the sky is?"

"Nenny, that's Dark Time!"

"No it isn't."

"Yes it is."

"No it isn't."

"Yes it is."

"You're just in denial!"

"No I'm not!"

"Yes you are!"

"No I'm not!"

"Yes you are!"

"Nenny. Please. Don't worry. It'll clear up in a minute!"

CHAPTER 84

"How can you possibly say it will clear up in a minute?" demanded Nenuphar.

"It always does," said Hob.

"Don't give me that crap!"

"Okay I won't. But you did ask so I told you."

"Nenny?" said M Cadvare. "What about counting our blessings?"

"I don't care. He's pissing me off."

By now they were all frowning at her.

"Let me get this straight," said Hob. "You think it's the end of the world because a lot of people have been saying it's about to happen for ages but you've never been to Anarchadia before and don't know what Dark Time is."

"What's that got to do with it?"

"Is that why you think it's the end of the world?"

"Well, what other possible conclusion could you reach?"

Hob shrugged. "That everything's okay?"

"No it's not okay! It's the end of the world!"

"Maybe I didn't explain Dark Time very well," Hob said slowly.

"According to you, I suppose we have plenty of time!"

"As a matter of fact I do. And we have."

"Go on then. Let's hear it – Nick Hob's explanation about Dark Time."

"Right. Here goes. Dark Time is an irregular darkening of the skies over Anarchadia. The ancients called it the *aurora anarchadiensis* but you'll never have heard of that either because they always kept the existence of this occasionally benighted temperate archipelago a secret from the rest of the world. It's noted for dramatic magnetic fluctuations that disrupt all electrical equipment and even make fires burn poorly. Engines can't run during Dark Time, unless you're an accomplished Horsepower Whisperer. Even steam engines are affected although their steam reservoirs allow for limited operation during Dark Time. It affects people, too, often provoking a severe lassitude. Some may nurse headaches or even have nosebleeds. But Dark Time doesn't last long. Nobody knows for certain what causes it but it is accepted as a statement of fact in Anarchadia that eventually, after a matter of hours, Dark Time clears up. And look. It's starting already."

They all looked up.

"Oh yeah," said M Cadvare in wonder.

"You be quiet!" snapped Nenuphar.

"Nenny. If it was the end of the world, do you think I would stick around?"

"You can't fost! That beautiful young scientist stopped you!"

"No she didn't."

"Yes she did!"

"No she didn't."

"Yes she did!"

"Look! I didn't fost because I chose not to."

"You are entitled to your opinion, Hob, no matter how wrong it may be."

"Well, let's agree to differ then," said Hob. "Frankly I've got better things to do than argue with you. We've got places to go and things to do."

"But if you had fosted," put in M Cadvare, "you would have taken us with you. Wouldn't you?"

"I might have," teased Hob, "but maybe not all of you." He turned to Heidi. "You didn't think it was the end of the world, did you?"

"I wasn't absolutely certain," she admitted, "but you didn't seem very worried about it so I was reassured. At least I was until Nenuphar challenged you about it and you looked so surprised you had to put *Nosferatu*'s crate down. If it was the end of the world, I suppose you would just fost."

"Precisely!"

"But he can't fost!" insisted Nenuphar.

"Yes I can."

"No you can't!"

"Yes I can!"

"No you can't!"

"Look, I'm getting fed up with this."

"Go on then! Fost!"

"No," said Hob, with more than a degree of petulance. "There's no need. It's not as if it's the end of the world is it? If it was, I wouldn't have anything to lose by fosting, would I?" He turned to M Cadvare. "I'm an Anarchadian. I'm used to Dark Time."

"I suppose it didn't seem worth mentioning before now," Nenuphar snorted.

"No, I suppose it didn't. Anyway," sighed Hob, "I'm glad that's cleared up our little misunderstanding," and he gave Nenuphar a meaningful look as if Miss Understanding was her new name.

He picked up his crate and looked up and down the dockside.

"I don't actually need to eat," he said, "but a celebratory slap up binge now that Dark Time is coming to an end seems to be in order. Don't you agree?"

Nenuphar was sulking with her arms tight across her chest.

"My treat?" asked Hob.

M Cadvare shuffled his feet.

"I think that's a great idea," said Heidi.

"Good. For the rest of you, I take silence to be acquiescence. I commend to you *The Whistling Tankard*."

Not far away was a tavern, wedged in between two enormous warehouses, and they realised that Julian had been swinging on its pub sign. The sky had brightened just enough for them to make out the image of an overflowing jug of ale with pursed lips. At first sight, *The Whistling Tankard* looked closed, but as they approached they saw the dim light of candles flickering in its windows.

Hob set down *Nosferatu*'s crate by the tavern's porch and pushed aside one of the double doors.

Heidi went through the other door at the same time but instead of finding herself beside Hob she discovered she was at the head of a steep flight of stairs and, unable to stop herself, she descended these rapidly to prevent herself falling. In a clatter of heels she reached the bottom and looked up to see Hob gazing down at her from a banister.

"Mind the step," he said and Nenuphar and M Cadvare peered cautiously through the double doors above her.

She stood on what appeared to be an oversize landing. Many of its oak panels and posts were padded with leather so that a well-aimed drunk could ricochet from one bar to another without any serious harm. Passages led off this landing, and let into wooden panels were vacant booths and stalls where small conspiratorial groups could gather.

But although there must have been other customers in the pub that night, judging from the low hum of conversation that rose from diverse inner sancta, Hob and his companions seemed to have the outer rooms of the tavern all to themselves. Everyone else had burrowed further into *The Whistling Tankard* to escape Dark Time.

"Is Julian allowed in here?" Heidi asked Hob as she climbed back up the stairs.

"Of course he is, provided he behaves himself."

Julian flew in as Nenuphar and M Cadvare joined them, and he alighted on a wagon wheel hanging from the ceiling, festooned with bulbs. Since they were electric and nothing electric seemed to be working, he dangled in a comforting gloom.

The light came from many candles and Hob was right. Nothing seemed to burn very well during Dark Time. Shadows leapt up the walls and then fell back down again.

"This pub looks as if the whole building is drunk," said Nenuphar.

"Well," replied Hob, "its fabric has soaked up vast quantities of spilt ale over the years. You could say that being soaked in alcohol accounts for such a good state of preservation. I believe *The Whistling Tankard* started off as separate drinking dens and these were gradually linked up and eventually given a unified façade."

They stood on a kind of mezzanine floor with a bar running down one side. At one end was another set of steep stairs climbing up the inside wall with a window that might have overlooked the river had it not been for Dark Time. At the other end was a rough granite cliff through which some enterprising soul had tunnelled a passage behind the bar.

The open edge of the platform was balustraded and featured short pews that overlooked some of the conspiratorial corners below. On the far wall, at a slightly higher level, was a balcony big enough for two tables and their chairs, reached by another tunnel cut into the granite.

Nenuphar tested the leather padding covering the rail along the top of the balustrade. It didn't seem to be filled with foam. Horsehair would have been her guess.

Photographs of tramp steamers and extraordinary railway locomotives covered the walls. Others depicted rakish sports cars and disreputable-looking motorcycles. In many pictures, the machines were accompanied by oily, grinning imbeciles.

Hob rang a bell for attention and handed out menus.

"I don't believe it!" cried Nenuphar. "I can eat some of this stuff!"

A pretty young barmaid, dressed in a lumberjack shirt and jeans, came through the passage in the cliff.

"Can I help you?" she asked, pleasantly.

"What would you like to drink?" Hob asked his companions, waving the Engineer of Spades.

"Do you have any fruit juice?" asked Nenuphar.

"Oh yes. Orange, apple, grapefruit, peach, passion fruit, pineapple, rhubarb, blackberry, gooseberry, blueberry, cranberry, elderberry and elderflower champagne. We also have a large range of distoxicants."

"What?" asked M Cadvare.

The barmaid smiled at him. "Distoxicants. They are the opposite of intoxicants and much better for you."

"Intoxicant is another of those words that proves to the wider world that Anarchadia exists," put in Hob.

"Distoxicants act as tonics," the barmaid went on.

"Ah," said the Euphobians.

"They outfect you," she explained.

M Cadvare frowned. "I'm not sure I'm ready for that yet," he said slowly.

"Please yourself."

"I think I would like to see someone else become outfected first."

"But we also have a selection of locally brewed intoxicants – Carrot

Whisky, Speckled Ostrich, Rising Damp, Crank Case, Cam Follower and Valve Lifter. Would they all be from within?" she asked Hob.

"Yep. All three of 'em, from within The Pale."

"I thought so."

"So now you are without," Hob told them, "without control, without any authority but your own, without directives, without conformity, without repression, without centrist propaganda and, best of all, without the Grey Ones."

"No commodity inspectors!" said M Cadvare, gleefully.

"No commodity or comestible inspectors, guaranteed."

"But with Dark Time," added Nenuphar.

"Well, you can't have everything," said Hob, lightly. He turned back to the barmaid. "A litre of orange juice for me, if you would be so kind. Ladies?"

"Half a litre of passion fruit for me, please," said Heidi.

"Half a litre of rhubarb juice for me, please," added Nenuphar.

"Cadaver?"

"I'd like to try some real ale, please."

"If you're from within, you might like some Speckled Ostrich," suggested the barmaid.

"Named after a Wild Hunt MG," said Hob, approvingly. "My treat," and he handed the barmaid a high denomination of pound note. "Keep the change," he told her.

"Why thank you kind sir," she said. "It's a long time since we've had anyone from within The Pale."

"Really?" asked Hob.

"I don't know why. We used to get loads coming through here. It's nice to see some of you again after such a long time. Welcome to Lanson and Anarchadia."

The Euphobians thanked her and she returned behind the bar.

The seafood looked very tempting so they all ordered some, apart from Nenuphar who chose the chamomile and agapanthus surprise.

M Cadvare turned to his companions. "I can't see the Conformorians getting past Davy Jones and his reef, can you?"

"No," said Heidi, with a smile.

"Cause for celebration, wouldn't you say?" suggested Hob. "Journey's end. Your very good health, everybody!"

"*Bonne santé!*"

When the barmaid returned with their cutlery and napkins, Hob ordered three packets of pork scratchings and a packet of cheese and onion crisps.

"I don't like crisps," said Nenuphar, guessing correctly that they were for her.

"You might like these," said the barmaid. She gave her a packet. "The landlord's mother-in-law makes them herself with the finest vegetable oil."

"Really? Are they organic?"

The barmaid nodded. "The potatoes come from my dad's allotment."

Nenuphar wasn't quite convinced.

"Try one," said the barmaid, opening a packet.

"They do look good," said Heidi.

Nenuphar took one. "Is Dark Time going to clear up?" she asked the barmaid.

"Of course it is."

"But how do you know?"

"It always does. Put it this way. It's not quite as predictable as sunrise following sunset but I've never known it not to." The barmaid raised her eyebrows at Hob. "They really aren't from round here, are they?"

"No, they are not," said Hob, "but, y'know, I don't think I have any regrets about bringing them here," and he leaned back and smiled indulgently at them, especially Nenuphar.

Nenuphar felt more at ease with Hob, now, than she did with M Cadvare. It not being the end of the world had changed everything.

M Cadvare gazed her at her a little mawkishly and she folded her arms again and slumped in her chair to appear less attractive and largely succeeded.

"Because of Dark Time, your meals'll take a little while," the barmaid told them.

"No problem," said Hob. "The anticipation enhances the enjoyment."

Nenuphar tried a home made crisp. She ate it slowly, sampling it in different parts of her mouth to confirm the taste. Then she tried another to see if the first one had been a fluke.

"Did you know about Dark Time?" she asked Heidi.

"St Bendix mentions it. Nobody knows what causes it but some people can predict it with a degree of accuracy. It rarely lasts more than six or seven hours, and Anarchadia can go for days or weeks without having one at all."

"Are any of you suffering from headaches at the moment?" Hob asked them.

M Cadvare and Heidi shook their heads, but Nenuphar said, "I am a bit."

"Each Dark Time is different," Hob told them, "and affects people in different ways. The only common feature of each Dark Time is that the darkness doesn't last for ever."

"Except that one day," put in Nenuphar, "you'll fost once too often and then it really will be the end of the world."

"That's right," said Hob, genially, "blame me. Everyone else does."

"Don't you believe what Therese told you?" she asked him.

"Not really," said Hob, "although I will admit that she has aroused my curiosity. You see, Nenny, if I fost all I have to do is not come back."

"You really don't care, do you?"

"I'd be sorry to see the old place go, of course, but you can't put off the inevitable. All things pass as they say. It's just a question of when. Various cults have been gleefully predicting Doomsday ever since this space/time continuum started. Therese Darlmat is entitled to her beliefs, but I do not share them."

"It's not a question of belief but a question of fact," went on Nenuphar.

"Nenny, I can see that you're going to need some time to get used to life in Anarchadia. In the meantime, let's agree to differ again, shall we?"

CHAPTER 85

Kevin Mullins stretched out in front of a smoky fire, deep within *The Whistling Tankard*, supping his pint of Speckled Ostrich, the Soul of All Souls in the snuggest of all snugs. But bumping into Beelzebub had brought on an unwelcome bout of introspection that still wasn't over. He kept to the shadows, a solitary drinker hidden by the wings of his armchair, lost in thought.

"Kevin?"

"Therese! What are you doing here? And where did you get that hat?"

"I made it," she replied.

"But why are you wearing it?"

"Look, Kevin, that's not important right now." She glanced at the watches on her forearms. "Something very weird is going on."

Kevin just stared. "So?"

"Okay, so situation normal but I've just discovered that there are other grauniads associated with this paraverse."

"Other grauniads?"

Therese had to check herself. She had never told Kevin about her part in the demise of his home paraverse and she didn't see any benefit in doing so now.

"Yes. Other grauniads. I believe they have a part to play in the end of this space/time continuum."

"Discontinuum," he corrected her.

"Discontinuum, thanks to you. Describe all the grauniads you've ever seen before."

"Well, there's Thor, Brunhilde, Moon Wolf, Isis, Gaia, Zeus and Gertrude, although we usually call her Gert and leave her rude part out."

Therese smiled thinly. "Have you ever seen a medusa with a stony gaze and snakes for hair, a very small one-eyed giant, a naked old man wearing a flying helmet and socks…"

"If he's wearing socks and a flying helmet then he isn't naked," Kevin pointed out.

"Even with them he is conspicuously naked," insisted Therese.

"But that's like you and me claiming that we're naked right now apart from our clothes!"

Therese rolled her eyes behind her gull wing spectacle frames. "Have you ever seen a small green man?"

"Also naked?"

"No, dressed in foliage."

"No."

"How about a toothsome English Miss dressed in tweed, a pumpkin headed jack o'lantern and a many armed Kali?"

"I've never seen anyone like that."

"I think they will been deliberately interfering with this paraverse. I've just seen them."

"What? Around here?"

"Not around here exactly. Sort of close by."

"Bloody hell!"

"This Dark Time that's happening. It makes fosting difficult. Could it be that we are approaching the end of this paraverse as the grauniads predicted?"

"Well, I suppose it could be. But we often get Dark Time in Anarchadia."

"Do you think the scientists in this paraverse could invent a time machine if faced with certain destruction?"

Kevin shrugged. "It has been known."

"Could anyone have foreseen you going back in time and being reincarnated?"

"Even God was surprised!"

"Just leave God out of this!"

"Therese! What *is* going on?"

"I don't know! Maverick grauniads will been intent on destroying your paraverse. They will been saying Hob and his Wild Hunt de-stabilise not just this paraverse but also the neighbouring ones."

"But you think there's more to it than that."

"Yes. A whole lot more but I'm just guessing. What will been the maverick grauniads up to? What'll been their motive?"

"Does Hob upset the balance among paraverses?"

"I thought he did but…."

"But what?"

"Could they been framing him?"

"Why would they want to do that?"

"Convince me to help them end this paraverse?"

"That doesn't make any sense."

"Maybe they will been de-stabilising the paraverses."

"I'm sure God would've noticed if paraverses were being interfered with."

Therese gave him that special look she reserved for whenever he touched upon religion.

"Ah," said Kevin. "There's something else I should mention. Beelzebub is here in Anarchadia, here in Lanson. Nowadays he's called Malik Tawus, the Peacock Angel. He's nearly in charge of the corporeal world."

"Is he? That might explain a lot if we were to accept his existence."

"He exists," insisted Kevin. "I've met him.

"And God, too, it seems."

"Yes."

"Can you prove their existence?"

"Can anyone prove their existence?"

Therese couldn't answer that.

"Look," began Kevin, "maybe you should keep an open mind. There's an awful lot of funny stuff going on at the moment."

"Yes," agreed Therese.

"And will been going on by the sound of it," added Kevin.

"We're going to have to keep this paraverse going!" Therese told him.

"Hey! What's this us business?"

"Don't you want to live for ever?"

"I have lived for ever!"

"Well don't you want to continue living for ever? It must be better than the alternative."

"An eternity of pleasure in heaven with Eve?"

"You might think you have a choice but I don't. I'm going to need your help, Kevin, if either of us are going to get some answers."

"What I meant was, how can I possibly help?" He smiled ruefully. "I have more experience of finishing things off, not keeping 'em going."

She smiled back at him. "So between us we should have every eventuality covered."

"Okay," he said. "What do I have to do?"

"For the time being, nothing."

"Fine. I can do that."

"I need to find Hob," she said. "If I can't, I might need your soul as bait."

"What!"

"I'll have a good look for him first though."

"What do you need Hob for?"

"Don't you see? He's linked with everything. If the grauniads are against him as they are against us, then maybe we can work with Hob!"

"Let's do it then."

"I must be off" said Therese.

"I need the lavatory," said Kevin.

"I'm alright," said Therese. "I went before I came."

They stood up.

Behind the bar, the landlord of *The Whistling Tankard* had assumed the pose of all barmen when business is slow. He was wiping a glass. He seemed surprised to see Kevin emerge from the comfortable embrace of the winged armchair and grimaced when he saw his hat.

"Aren't you hot in that?" he asked him.

"What? Oh, this thing? No. No, I hardly know it's there."

The landlord gazed at it critically.

Kevin thought that he looked like a bespectacled dandelion gone to seed.

"You may not be aware of it," said the landlord, "but the rest of us are."

Then he caught sight of Therese in hers. "Bloody hell! Another one!"

"Another one?" demanded Therese. "What do you mean another one?"

"Well, two of you together like this," he replied.

"Have you seen anyone else looking like me?"

"I should think not!"

"Hmm," said Therese. "That's okay then. Farewell Kevin."

"Goodbye Therese. And good luck."

He smiled at the perplexed landlord and entered the Gents. He caught sight of himself in the mirror as he entered and saw why his hat might make the other patrons feel uncomfortable. As he washed his hands he checked his appearance again. The coloured stripes of the woollen Discretion of the Soul Hat clashed awfully.

In the safety of the lavatories, he adjusted his hat. He even took it off but had a strange feeling that if the Horsepower Whisperer was close by, maybe even in *The Whistling Tankard* itself, he would somehow be able to detect his soul through the fabric of the building.

He could even see Hob in his mind's eye, sitting at a table in the pub, quietly drinking his orange juice and then drifting off into a perplexed brown study as Kevin exposed his soul even slightly.

Cautiously, he replaced his hat, checked his reflection one more time and emerged from the lavatory.

The landlord caught his eye again as he emerged

"You quite sure you don't want to take that thing off?"

"Never!" exclaimed Kevin. "I feel naked without it."

"Please yourself," said the landlord.

"I intend to," replied Kevin.

"I just don't want you upsetting my regulars."

"I am one of your regulars. It's just that you don't recognise me with this hat on."

"Oh yeah? Well I certainly can't see straight. I think I'll just throw some sand in my eyes to calm them down a bit."

With as much dignity as he could muster, Kevin wandered out of the snug towards the exit. *The Whistling Tankard* was quiet tonight, but in one of the outermost bars he noticed four people finishing their meals on a balcony. They were accompanied by a genial flitterfox who dangled from the wagon wheel hanging from the rafters. Occasionally they threw him scraps of food, and the flitterfox would swoop and snap them up.

One was a pretty dark-haired girl in a white dress. Next to her was a nondescript young man within whom something burned. Kevin was fairly sure they were recent refugees from Euphobia.

Beside them was a very beautiful woman, elegantly dressed and with film-star good looks. Kevin thought he'd seen her before somewhere.

The women gasped as soon as they saw his hat, and even the man between them, whose colour sense was nowhere near as highly developed, winced.

The fourth member of this quartet was obviously a skirrow. He wore the classic visored helmet of a Horsepower Whisperer, but there was something else again about him and with a thrill Kevin realised that this man was a Soul Trader.

He was the first Soul Trader he'd met for a long time and the first one to find him while wearing his Discretion of the Soul Hat. It appeared to be working, too, for the Soul Trader was not regarding him with glee at the chance of adding his soul to his collection. Like the others, he seemed appalled at Kevin's colour sense.

Just before Kevin ducked thankfully out of sight, the Soul Trader pulled out a spirit level. Kevin had seen them do this before. He'd broken so many of these instruments, but this one didn't break. The Soul Trader just looked at it and tapped its gauge as if there was no reading at all.

CHAPTER 86

Hob burst out of *The Whistling Tankard* and fell over a smart traffic cone waiting for him on the steps outside. He picked himself up, grabbed the cone and kicked it so hard it flew over the *Baggy Point Beauty* and landed in the River Temmar.

His gaze fell upon *Nosferatu*'s crate and, as he stood there, the others burst through the doors.

"What is it?" asked Heidi.

"They're here," he whispered.

"Who are?"

"The soulless ones."

"In Anarchadia?"

"Are you sure?" asked M Cadvare.

Hob showed him his spirit level. "You know what they say."

M Cadvare nodded. "Fish fart never lies."

"He didn't look like a Grey One," said Heidi.

"You mean that guy in the awful hat?" asked Nenuphar.

Hob nodded.

M Cadvare glared at him. "You said, 'No commodity inspectors, guaranteed.' "

"That's right, Cadaver. This is Anarchadia and they have no place here!"

"If they *are* here, our souls are no safer than they were in Euphobia!"

"I know," said Hob.

"Maybe it was just the one," Nenuphar suggested.

Hob gazed up at the sky.

It was dark, but it was a normal darkness.

"Something's changed," said Hob.

He threw *Nosferatu*'s crate onto his shoulders.

"Come on! From the top of this hill, we'll be able to see nearly the whole of Lanson, and if the Grey Ones really are here, then we'll be able to tell. I can get some fuel for *Nosferatu* and then I can rid Anarchadia of the Conformorians! There can't be many of them!"

Hob almost ran up the hill behind *The Whistling Tankard* and the others had difficulty keeping up with him. Only Julian stayed ahead of him as he flitted from lamp post to lamp post, and he regarded Hob's agitation with evident concern.

Hob led them past rows of warehouses and workshops and fine old houses and terraces. Just before the top of the hill was a high wall that barred their way.

"The Necropolis!" said Hob, turning his head this way and that.

"What's The Necropolis?" asked M Cadvare.

"It's the city of the dead," Heidi said softly as Hob turned left along a cobbled alleyway that ran beside the wall.

They saw now that Hob was making for a gate at the end of another street that ran parallel to theirs.

Hob rattled the wrought-iron gates but found they were chained and padlocked. The top of the wall was tiled and it dipped on either side of the gateway before arching up over the gates but it was too high for his companions to climb.

"Yield to me, small engine of secrets," they heard him say, and the padlock burst apart and he was through.

At the gates his companions paused.

"What is this place?" asked Nenuphar as she peered through the gateway.

"The Necropolis is Lanson's great burial ground," Heidi told them in a low voice. "We're still on the edge of the city. Centuries ago, the graveyards inside the old city walls became inundated as the population grew. To reduce the chance of disease, a new place of rest was consecrated far beyond the overcrowded city walls. It even had its own railway. But Lanson subsequently grew to engulf it and The Necropolis spread until it reached the docks. Come on!"

She went through the gates and, although they lingered at the entrance for a moment, M Cadvare and Nenuphar followed her.

Between overgrown graves and tombs they ran up a broad path that made for the crest of the hill. It was made out of pebbles and heavily cambered with a sizeable gutter on each side. Similar paths branched off it at random but these were choked with grass. Gradually, the horizon beyond became visible and, in the false dawn that followed Dark Time, they saw the lights of a huge city beneath them.

On the summit of the hill they took in the sweep of the river they'd left behind them. It curved around from the west and headed north into the centre of Olde Lanson Towne. And right in the middle of the old town was a startling new development. Glass tower-blocks rose over the old buildings. They were grouped in a circle, like the wagons of unwelcome settlers in the Wild West, and seemed to be part of a defensive enclave.

"Look!" said M Cadvare. "There's Hob."

Hob stood some way off, further down the hill, next to *Nosferatu*'s crate, taking in the scene.

They hurried down to join him, stumbling over rusty rails half-hidden by weeds. Hob didn't turn to greet them.

"I suppose it was too much to expect," said Nenuphar, looking at the glass towers. "Nowhere is completely free of the Grey Ones any more."

"So it would seem," murmured Hob. "Behold the grey flag of inconvenience!"

There were several Euphobian flags, all flying from flagpoles on the corners of the new towers, just like they had in Mourion.

A breeze blew through the ancient yew trees, and Heidi embraced Hob as M Cadvare and Nenuphar took each other's hands.

"But the Anarchadians will fight!" insisted Heidi. "They've spurned the Conformorians for centuries. Now will be no different."

"That's right," said Hob. "Now that I'm home, things are gonna change around here."

Hob's rucksack squeaked in agreement.

He stood up and reached inside his jacket to pull out The Glove.

"I need to get hold of some more brimstone. Then we can begin!"

The wind blew more strongly, rattling the branches of the old trees nearby, and a voice spoke out from the darkness.

"So, Monsieur Pilchard, we meet at last."

Rank upon rank of Grey Ones emerged from the gloom and with them were many members of the clergy.

"But this time, the advantage is ours, I feel."

"Archcommissioner Taube," Heidi managed to say.

"Surprised to see us here?" he asked them.

Hob looked around and saw pump-action Holy Water cannon, short-fuse incense bombs and value-sized packets of communion wafers.

"The luck of a Thousand Stars won't get us out of this," he whispered to Heidi.

"********** ** *******!(Resistance is useless!)" agreed someone.

"Commissioner Gris is here as well," said Archcommissioner Taube, and the raspberry-blowing commissioner stepped out from behind a wonky marble angel so that they could all see him better.

Despite everything, Hob laughed.

"Let it not be said that we lack the spirit to see the funny side of everything," said an equally amused M Cadvare.

"Spare me the homespun homilies," advised Archcommissioner Taube, "and let Madame Bland go. Your situation is hopeless."

"Let my friends here go first," said Hob, indicating M Cadvare and Nenuphar.

"No!" they said, but Hob held up his hand. "When faced with complete disaster the only recourse is total defiance. This way, Cadaver, you and Nenny and Heidi can continue the fight again."

"The fight hasn't even started," said Archcommissioner Taube. "None of you are going anywhere. You have no form of sanctuary. We've travelled a long, long way to get Madame Bland back."

Hob frowned. "Are you saying you're after her, not me?"

"Precisely. And Madame Bland has led us to you."

A smart traffic cone by Hob's boots suddenly looked very indignant.

"You, Monsieur Pilchard, are a bonus. Or should I say, Mister Nicholas Eldritch Hob?"

"You have named me," replied Hob. "I am indeed that man."

Behind his back he made some hand signals to M Cadvare and Nenuphar to move away.

"I am Old Weird Wheels himself, the Metal Guru, the Repossession Man, the Crypto-Engineer, His Malign Weirdness, the Grand Whizz-Herd and Master of the Engine Henge, the Lord High Prince of Rock'n'Roll, Dr Bravado, the Horsepower Whisperer and Soul Trader, none other than that infamous libertine and free radical from Anarchadia, that trafficker of traffic of no accepted fashionality, Nicholas Eldritch Hob!"

"Of course, that counts for very little now that we have *The Red Book of St Bendix*. It was Madame Bland who obtained a copy for us. By the way, Madame, your husband is here."

"*Bonsoir, cherie*," said a nondescript figure by a mausoleum.

"Don't you *cherie* me!" growled Heidi.

"If it was not for Madame Bland's help in its translation, we might still not be able to control you."

"Control? Me? Impossible!"

"Fortunately for us, she presented her evidence and warned us of your arrival in Euphobia."

"That's not true!" Heidi declared, but then she realised that it might look that way.

"We have the transcripts and the video footage if you're interested, Hob."

Heidi bit her bottom lip.

Some Conformorians surrounded her, but it seemed as if they were escorting her to safety.

"It was your apparent partner in crime that showed us the key to your downfall, Hob," said Archcommissioner Taube.

Hob looked hard at Heidi. "Is this true?" he asked her.

"It's not how it seems!" she cried.

"I'd step away from Hob if I were you, Madame Bland," said Archcommissioner Taube. "I would just like to thank you for your help in apprehending Euphobia's most wanted man."

"I only got so far with the translation and then they stole it from me!"

"What?" yelled Hob.

"Since then we've been tracking you," Archcommissioner Taube went on. "Of course, we realised that, sooner or later, you would inevitably arrive in Anarchadia. So, here we all are. I would move a little further away from him if I were you, Madame Bland."

"This can't be right," muttered M Cadvare as Nenuphar clung to him. "But Hob ..."

"Go on!" Hob yelled at her. "Get away from me! Leave me be!"

Heidi was crying too much to answer.

"Do as he says, Madame Bland," said Archcommissioner Taube, almost gently.

Reluctantly, Heidi bowed her head and made her way to the edge of the circle of Grey Ones as far away as possible from Commissioner Bland.

A very confused Julian swooped down to her and she buried her face in his fur.

"So now you know," said Archcommissioner Taube.

But instead of looking defeated, a strange gurgle was coming from Hob's throat. The reflections in his visor swirled rapidly.

"When faced with complete disaster the only recourse is total defiance! Glove? Protect them!" and he jerked a thumb over his shoulder before charging the Conformorians.

The Glove flew behind M Cadvare and Nenuphar and felled a swathe of Grey Ones between them and the gate into The Necropolis.

M Cadvare was so surprised he stayed rooted to the spot, but Nenuphar shouted, "Run!" and only then was he able to move.

Hob had no other weapons ready, but his defiance made the Grey Ones before him fall back and he brandished a pair of two-fingered salutes at them.

Heidi was screaming and scratching and punching and kicking at her false escort, but there were too many of them and she was too far away to help Hob.

The Glove took down some monks wielding incense bombs to Hob's right and to his left was Julian, scattering an order of the Sisters of the Blessed Alohas.

"Fire!" shouted Archcommissioner Taube as Hob grabbed him.

If they had been firing machine guns Hob would have been all right but they weren't. They drenched him with Holy Water.

The Glove swooped to defend Hob and burst through Archcommissioner Taube's chest, but he was already dead or what passed for dead among Conformorians, for Hob had broken his neck as he'd grabbed him.

The Conformorians then let Hob have everything they had, and he was thrown to the ground as he released his fatal grip on Archcommissioner Taube.

Holy Water splashed onto The Glove who fell helplessly to the ground.

Heidi screamed as Hob was swept across the graveyard and pinned against *Nosferatu*'s packing case.

Julian swooped down and tore off the ear of one of the Grey Ones squirting Hob with a Holy Water cannon. He rose into the air and pulled a face, spat out the ear and retched from the vile tang of the Conformorian's blood. There was a short burst of gunfire, and Heidi screamed again as Julian fell, his wings perforated into useless tatters.

A pack of Sisters of the Blessed Alohas jammed their longboards into the earth around Hob, fencing him in with his crate. Monks and clerics of all denominations ran up to lob incense bombs into the enclosure while others directed their Holy Water cannons between the gaps and emptied them over Hob. Nuns broke communion wafers into stainless steel mixing bowls and vigorously mixed them with Holy Water to produce a frothing mixture that expanded rapidly.

The monks, nuns, clerics and laity poured their mixture over Hob and stood back as the mixture expanded to the tops of their longboards and oozed out between them.

"I'm cured! I'm cured!" rejoiced Commissioner Gris, as cheerfully as a Conformorian could manage.

He nodded to the Sisters of the Blessed Alohas and they removed their longboards and smoothed the surface within to produce an austere tomb. On each side, as well as the lid, they engraved the following legend.

Here lies Ernest Pilchard

"Right!" said Commissioner Gris. "That'll be the last we'll see of him!"

Hob will rise again in *The Grey Ones*, part two of *The Soul Trader* Trilogy.

Coming soon from Bob Blackman

THE WORMTON LAMB

MAD MAX CROSSED WITH ALL CREATURES GREAT AND SMALL

Forget the stars, tealeaves or bathwater. The future for telling the future is the motorscope.

If you're in a traffic jam – you're gonna be late.

Obviously.

If only Slake hadn't souped up Mrs Osmotherly's 2CV. She might then have been able to read the road signs properly and save Mr Heckmondwike a whole lot of trouble.

What she has spotted, though, is Nick Hob, the Horsepower Whisperer. If Hob is abroad in the Wold, whose soul can he be after?

But everyone's problems are exhibiting accelerated growth.

It's big. It's woolly. It's already got cloven hooves and soon it'll have horns.

It is the terrible Lamb of Wormton.

www.anarchadia.co.uk

In preparation by Bob Blackman

THE GREY ONES

GEORGE ORWELL'S 1984 MEETS THE HITCH–HIKER'S GUIDE TO THE GALAXY

Monsieur Cadvare and Nenuphar find themselves in Anarchadia, without the dubious protection of Nick Hob, the Horsepower Whisperer, only to discover that the Grey Ones have got there first.

The Soul of All Souls, Kevin Mullins, is hiding from the soul traders. They don't know what he would sell his soul for. Come to that, neither does he.

Therese Darlmat is frantically trying to stabilise the paraverses but the Peacock Angel is in Lanson and the Grey Ones have a proposal for him they know he can't resist.

Then there is the farewell gig to end all farewell gigs. They've re-formed although they'll never reform. They've been away for 65 million years but now they're back – The Monsters, the greatest rock band the world has ever seen.

With Hob entombed in a giant communion wafer, hope is fading fast as the forces of bland are set to stop the Wild Hunt for ever.

PART TWO OF THE SOUL TRADER TRILOGY

www.anarchadia.co.uk

In preparation by Bob Blackman

THE SINGING SANDS

LIKE THE DA VINCI CODE BUT WITH MORE BEACHES AND HORSEPOWER

Roy Shaddocks goes to Wheal Ramoth as a favour to Carbines, an engine sorcerer who might even rival Nick Hob.

He soon settles into the newly formed design team and adapts to life in Bendisporth, racing in the Wild Hunt on his Suzuki X7 and getting to know the posh girls from the nice enclave.

But gradually his curiosity about the fate of earlier engineers in the area grows, especially as the first one of all was the Great Smith himself, the legendary St Bendix.

St Bendix lived some 1,500 years before and established a radical theological college until it was swallowed by the sands for its "quickedness" and now nobody really knows where it was.

But Roy discovers there's still a link between going fast and the teachings of St Bendix.

And when that's the case, Nick Hob – the Horsepower Whisperer and Soul Trader – can never be far away.

www.anarchadia.co.uk

In preparation by Bob Blackman

THE WILD HUNT

SPINAL TAP AND THE GUMBALL RALLY ROLLED INTO ONE

The Forces of Bland have double-crossed the Forces of Evil. They've been artfully manipulating the oldest struggle for thousands of years and now there's nothing to stop them destroying our very souls for ever.

With the Forces of Good driven underground and the Forces of Evil undergoing the worst sort of purgatory and muzak imaginable, hope seems an impossible luxury.

But isn't that Monsieur Cadvare driving one of Hob's souped up automobiles? And isn't that Nenuphar with him – the animal charming vegetarian?

If they can spring Hob and the other Soul Traders from purgatory, enlist the help of The Monsters (the ultimate rock band), rev up the Horsepower Wars again, stop Kevin Mullins losing his soul and get good and evil to co-operate with each other for a change, then a solution might present itself.

Pretty big if.

PART THREE OF THE SOUL TRADER TRILOGY

www.anarchadia.co.uk

Printed in the United Kingdom
by Lightning Source UK Ltd.
135726UK00001B/31-42/P